Unicorn vs. Goblins

Another Phoebe and Her Unicorn Adventure

Complete Your Phoebe and Her Unicorn Collection

Phoebe and Her Unicorn
Dana Simpson

Unicorn on a Roll
Another Phoebe and Her Unicorn Adventure
Dana Simpson

Razzle Dazzle Unicorn
Another Phoebe and Her Unicorn Adventure
Dana Simpson

Unicorn Crossing
Another Phoebe and Her Unicorn Adventure
Dana Simpson

Phoebe and Her Unicorn in
The Magic Storm
Dana Simpson

Unicorn of Many Hats
Another Phoebe and Her Unicorn Adventure
Dana Simpson

Phoebe and Her Unicorn in
Unicorn Theater
Dana Simpson

Unicorn Bowling
Another Phoebe and Her Unicorn Adventure
Dana Simpson

The Unicorn Whisperer
Another Phoebe and Her Unicorn Adventure
Dana Simpson

Camping with Unicorns
Another Phoebe and Her Unicorn Adventure
Dana Simpson

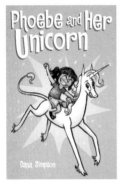

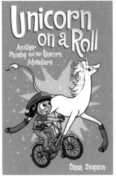

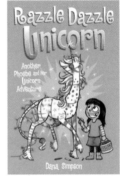

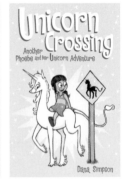

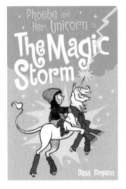

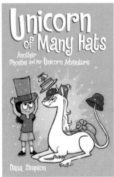

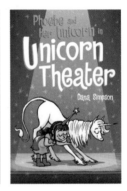

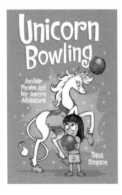

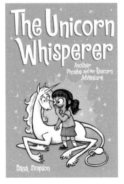

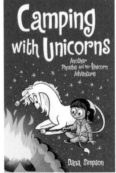

Unicorn vs. Goblins

Another Phoebe and Her Unicorn Adventure

Dana Simpson

Andrews McMeel
PUBLISHING®

INTRODUCTION

CORY: You know what I think? We should write about how we found out about Phoebe and why we love her.

POESY: Wait, how DID we find out about Phoebe?

CORY: Don't you remember? I brought the first book home, but I didn't like the cover, so I stuck it on your shelf and forgot about it and then—

POESY: —One day I took it off the shelf. We read it, and we liked it.

CORY: That's what I remember, too, more or less. I came into your room to shout at you to brush your hair for school, and you were reading this great comic book and laughing. I told you to put it down and brush your hair and came back five minutes later, and you were still reading it and laughing.

POESY: There's too many "and"s in that sentence.

CORY: Then I took it away from you. I read it, and I started laughing, too.

POESY: Nah, my description is totally better.

[Let the record show that here, Poesy asked to re-read some of the strips in this volume and took the laptop away from me. I couldn't get it back until Alice distracted her with guacamole, and I took the computer back.]

POESY: I like the part where Phoebe goes to music camp and Marigold makes a friend.

[At this point, Cory asked Poesy to draw a Phoebe and Marigold, on a rocket-skateboard, playing music.]

POESY: You mean a hoverboard.

pheobe + Marigold = pheobe gold

CORY: It's easy to compare Phoebe to Calvin and Marigold to Hobbes—I did it when I reviewed that first collection ("If Hobbes was a snarky unicorn and Calvin was an awesome little girl"), but Calvin was kind of a creep, especially to little girls. By contrast, Phoebe has a very well-adjusted relationship with the young dudes in her life—and still manages to be funny as heck when they come around.

I love—LOVE—how Dana finesses the way that Phoebe's parents relate to Marigold, too. Calvin's mom and dad rolled their eyes every time Calvin talked with spittle-flecked excitement about his imaginary friend. But Phoebe's parents are cooled out by Marigold's SHIELD OF BORINGNESS, which means that they can react to her as if she were just one of Phoebe's little pals, albeit a pal with a horn, hooves, and magic powers.

But best of all is Marigold. I mean, her last name is HEAVENLY NOSTRILS. Say that aloud with me. HEAVENLY. NOSTRILS. How much fun is that to say?

All the mischief, the pure id and self-centered, delightful sociopathy of youth is evenly divided between Phoebe and Marigold. They're each other's best friends and worst influences.

When *Sesame Street* launched, the show was all kids' jokes. Think of Barney the $#@@{!#* Dinosaur. About as much fun for adults as a fiberglass smoothie. But Jim Henson and the Children's Television Workshop pulled the show and went back to the drawing board, redesigning it so that it had as many adult jokes as kid ones—and so that adults and kids would have a reason to sit and watch together. Whatever value the show had, they reasoned, it would be multiplied if parents and kids shared an experience together, if they had something to talk about after.

The same principle guided the design of Disneyland. Walt Disney was sick of sitting on the sidelines, watching his daughters go around and around the Griffith Park carousel, so he built a theme park full of stuff that kids could bring their grown-ups on. The rest is history.

[Poesy is now singing a Spice Girls song. Where did she learn that?]

There's just enough humor here that sails over kids' heads and lands squarely on their grown-ups to make this an indispensable read for adults, but there's also an infinitude of kid stuff that we both laughed at. I love so many things about this book, but most of all, I love that we read it together.

— Poesy Taylor Doctorow (age 7)
— Cory Doctorow (age 44)
Burbank, California
August 2015

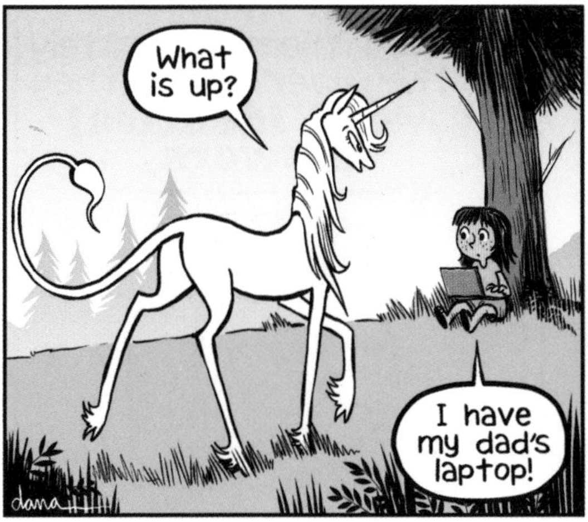
What is up?
I have my dad's laptop!
dana

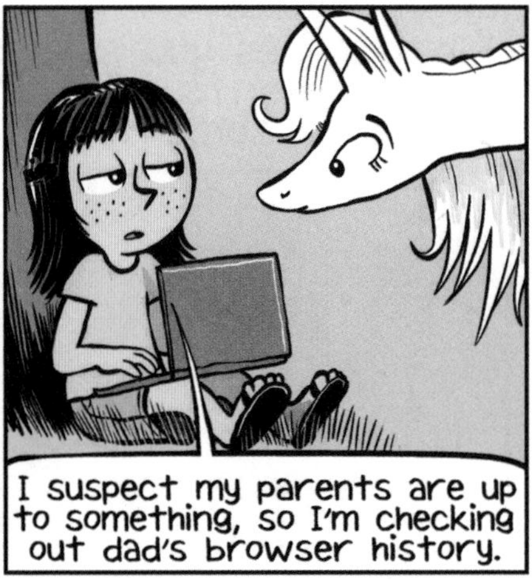
I suspect my parents are up to something, so I'm checking out dad's browser history.

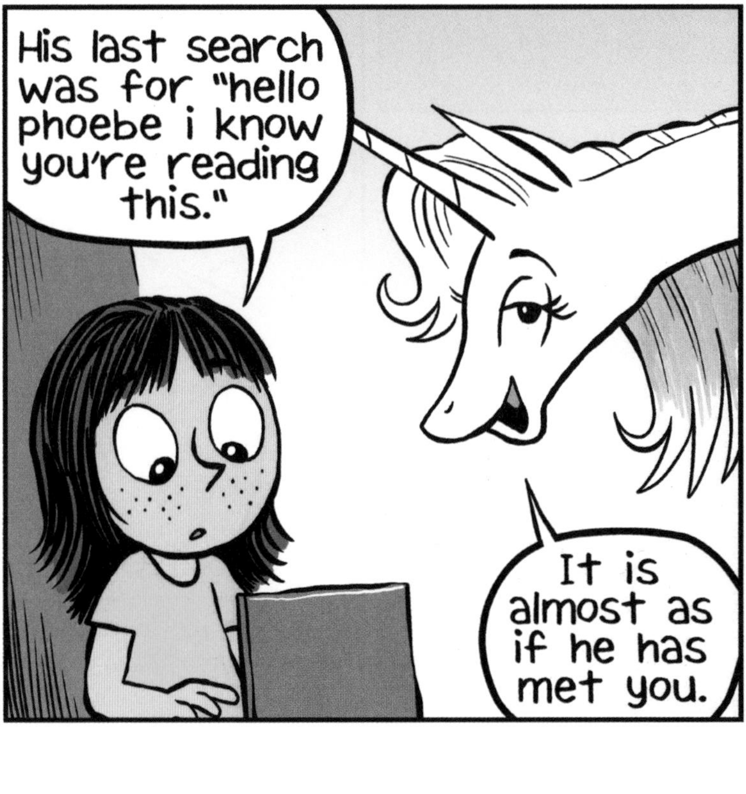
His last search was for "hello phoebe i know you're reading this."
It is almost as if he has met you.

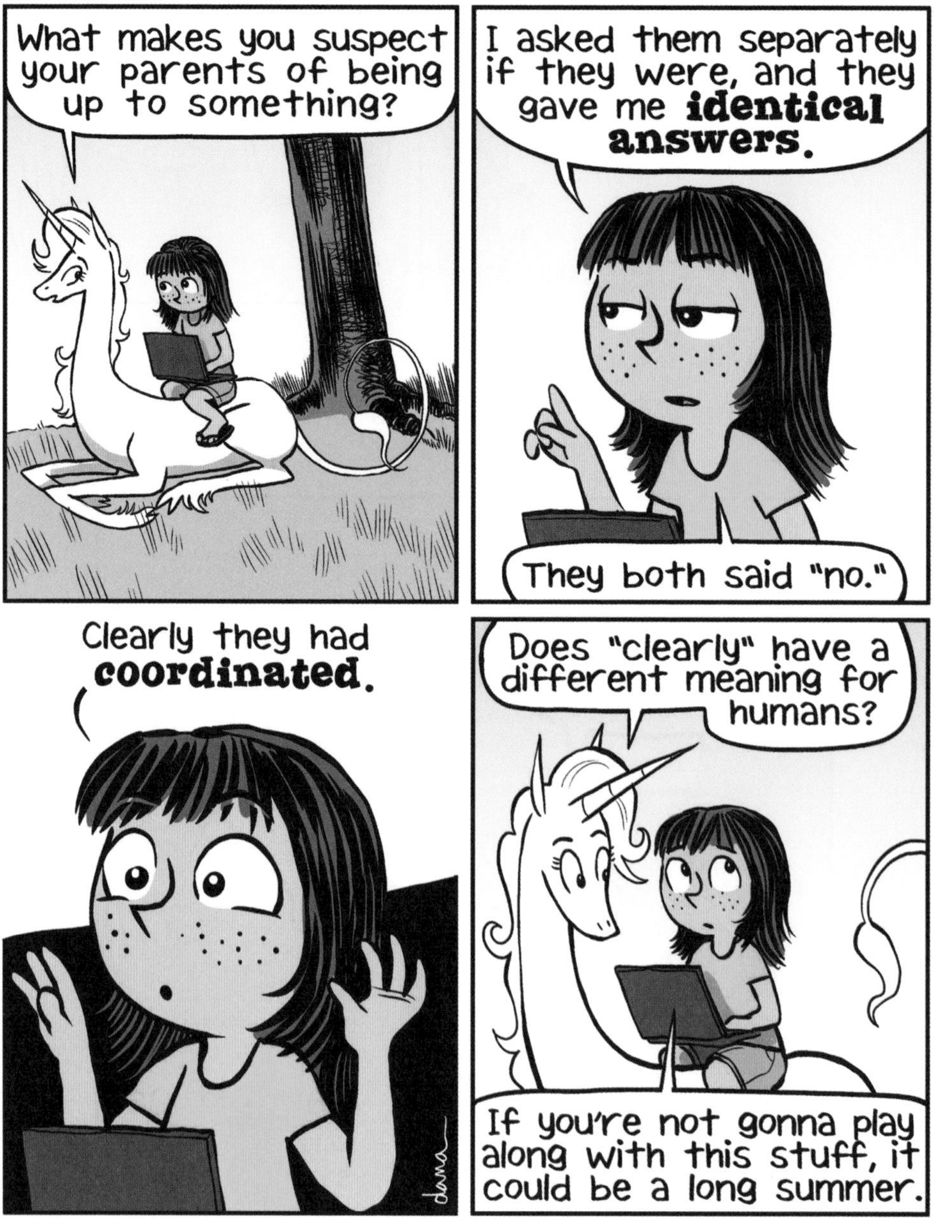
What makes you suspect your parents of being up to something?
I asked them separately if they were, and they gave me **identical answers**.
They both said "no."
Clearly they had **coordinated**.
Does "clearly" have a different meaning for humans?
If you're not gonna play along with this stuff, it could be a long summer.

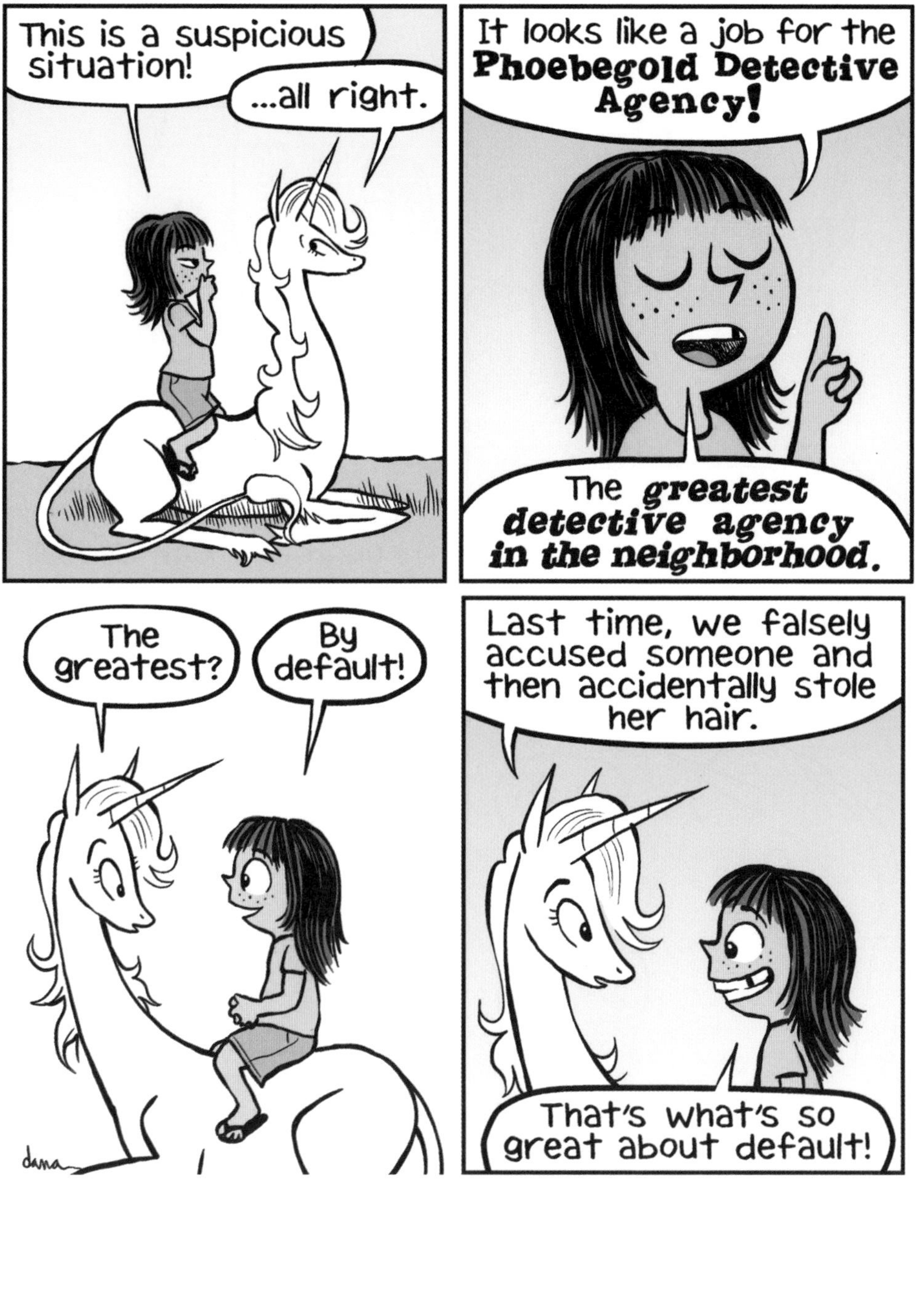
This is a suspicious situation!
...all right.
It looks like a job for the **Phoebegold Detective Agency!**
The ***greatest detective agency in the neighborhood.***
The greatest?
By default!
Last time, we falsely accused someone and then accidentally stole her hair.
That's what's so great about default!
dana

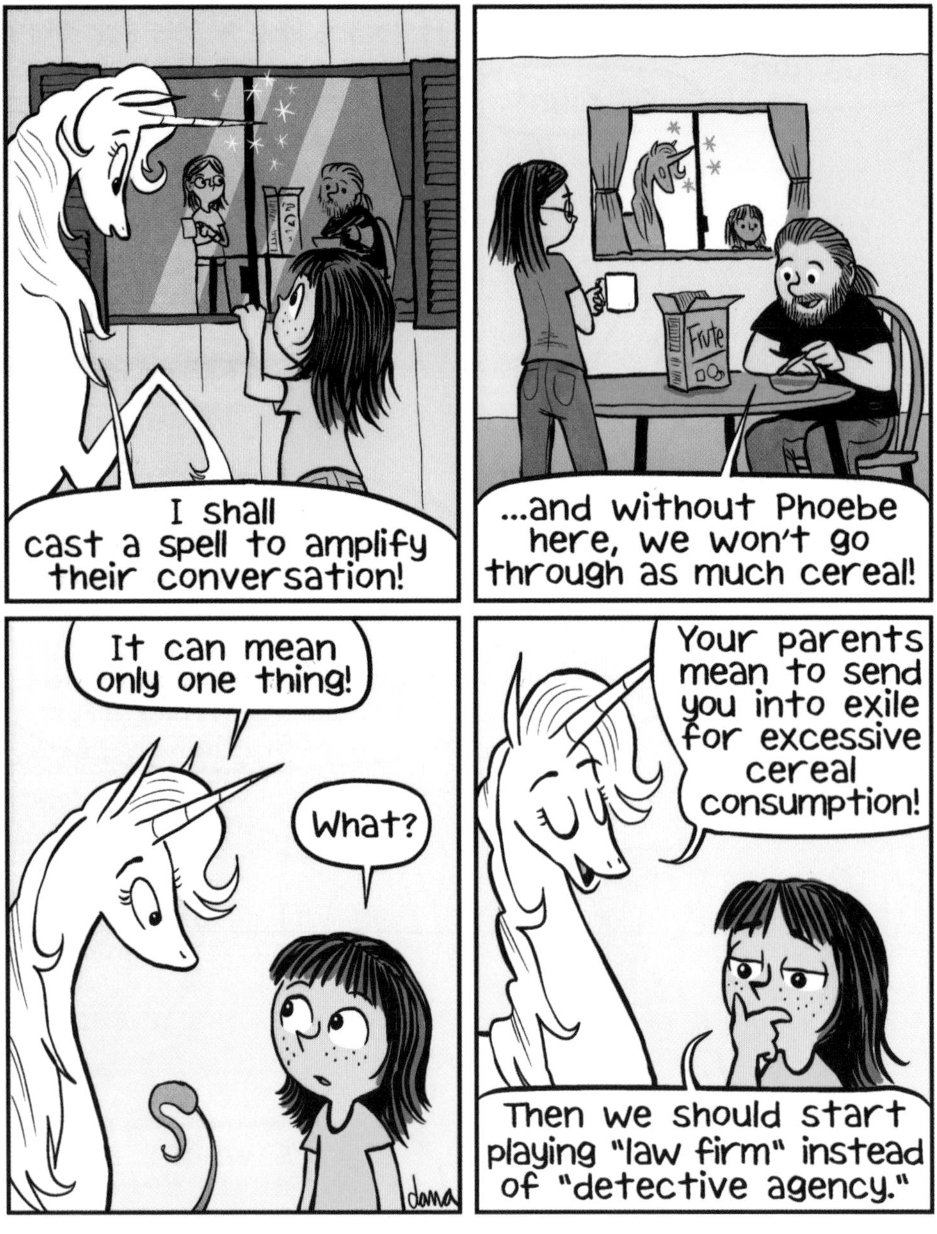
I shall cast a spell to amplify their conversation!
...and without Phoebe here, we won't go through as much cereal!
Frute
It can mean only one thing!
What?
Your parents mean to send you into exile for excessive cereal consumption!
Then we should start playing "law firm" instead of "detective agency."
dana

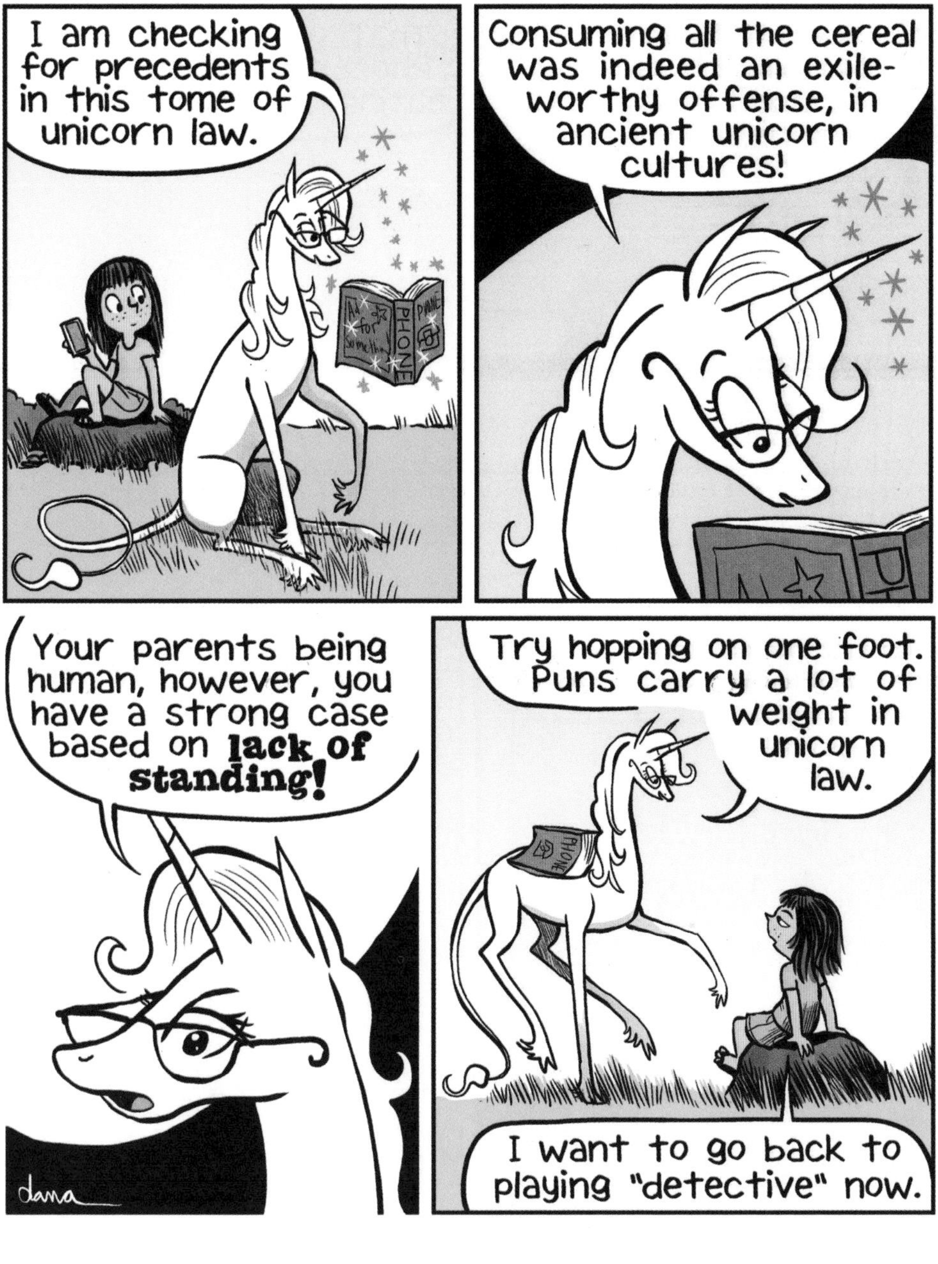
I am checking for precedents in this tome of unicorn law.
PHONE
Consuming all the cereal was indeed an exile-worthy offense, in ancient unicorn cultures!
Your parents being human, however, you have a strong case based on **lack of standing!**
dana
Try hopping on one foot. Puns carry a lot of weight in unicorn law.
PHONE
I want to go back to playing "detective" now.

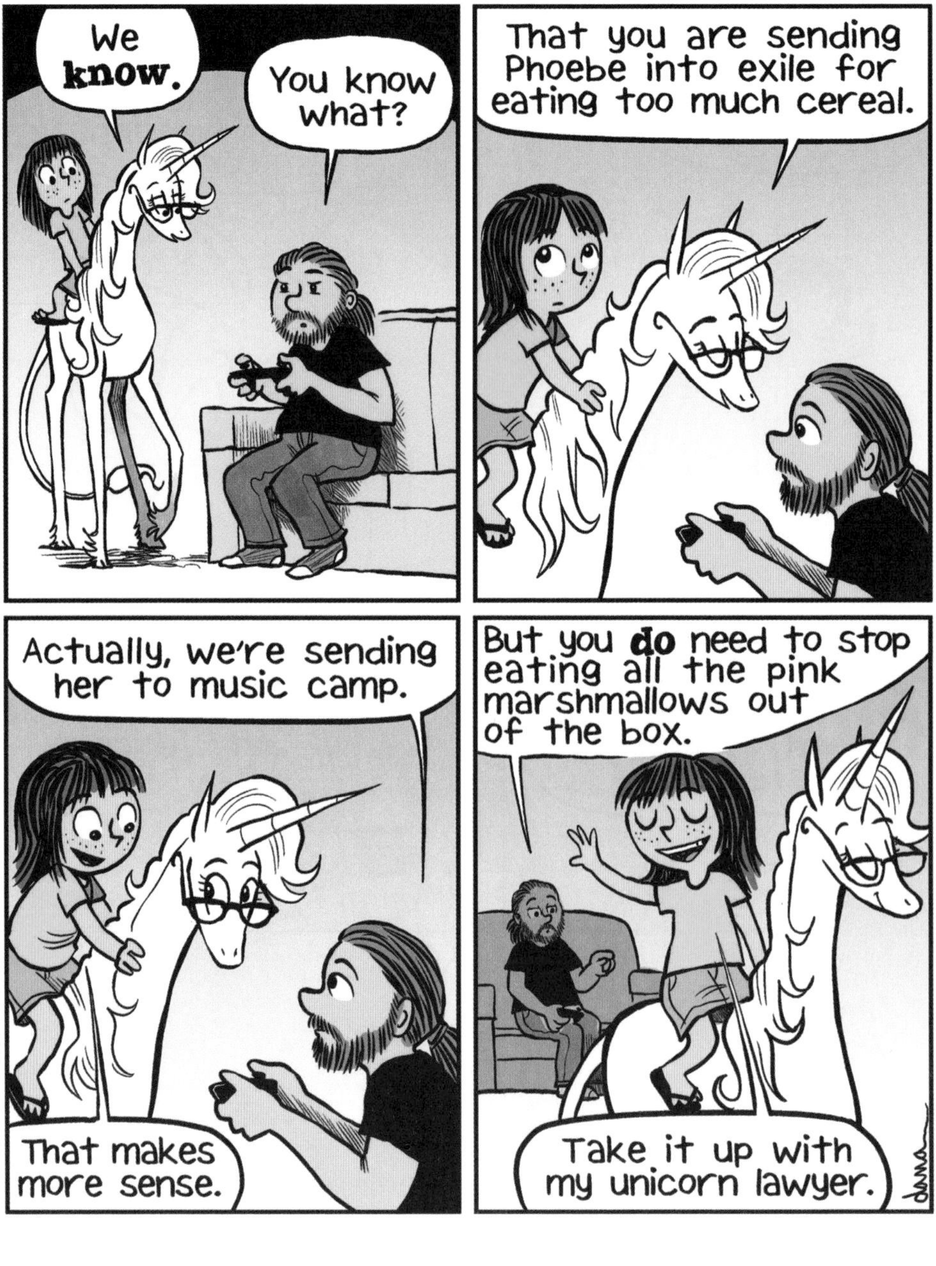
We **know.**
You know what?
That you are sending Phoebe into exile for eating too much cereal.
Actually, we're sending her to music camp.
That makes more sense.
But you **do** need to stop eating all the pink marshmallows out of the box.
Take it up with my unicorn lawyer.
dana

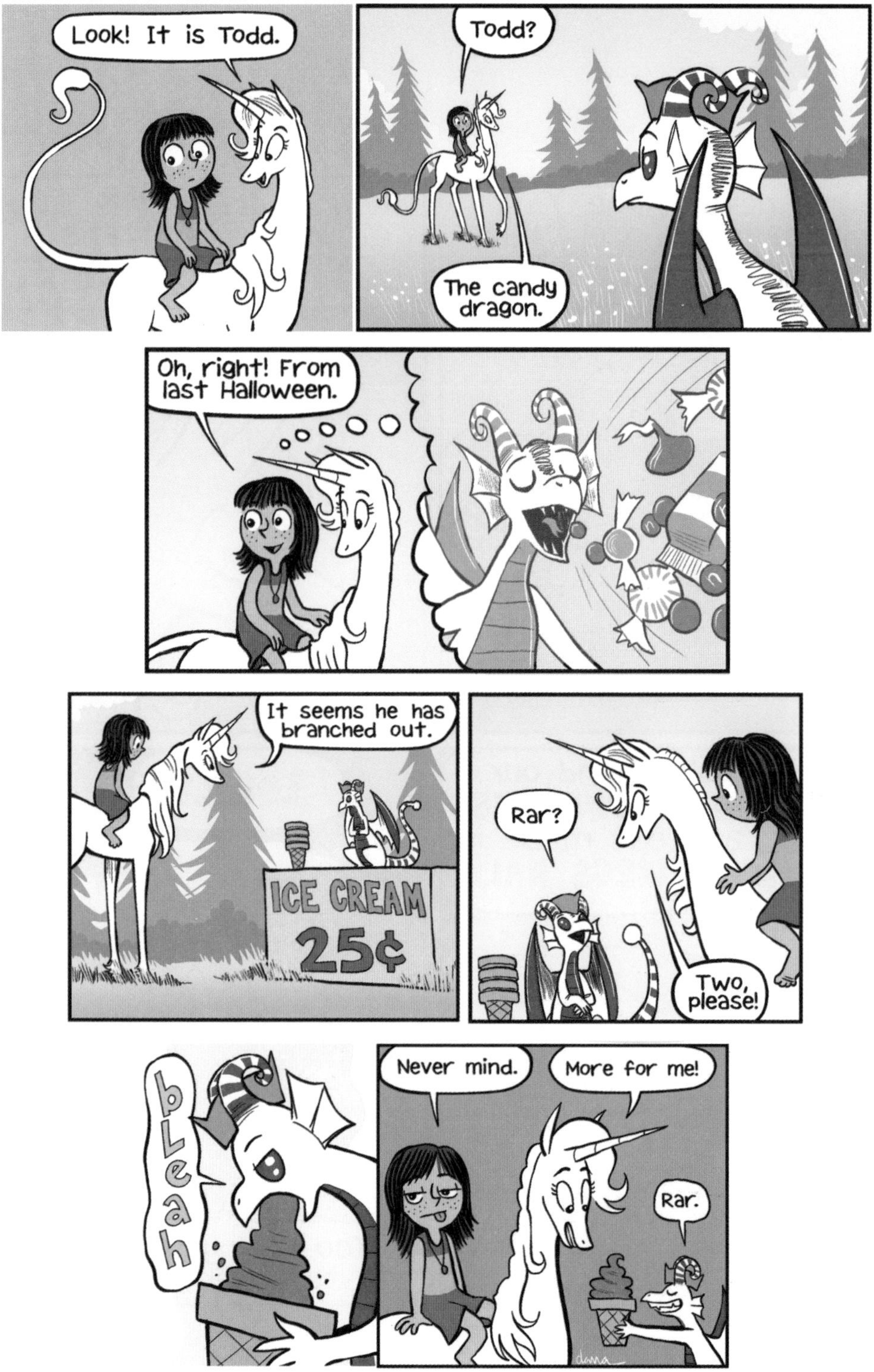
Look! It is Todd.
Todd?
The candy dragon.
Oh, right! From last Halloween.
It seems he has branched out.
ICE CREAM
25¢
Rar?
Two, please!
bleah
Never mind.
More for me!
Rar.
dana

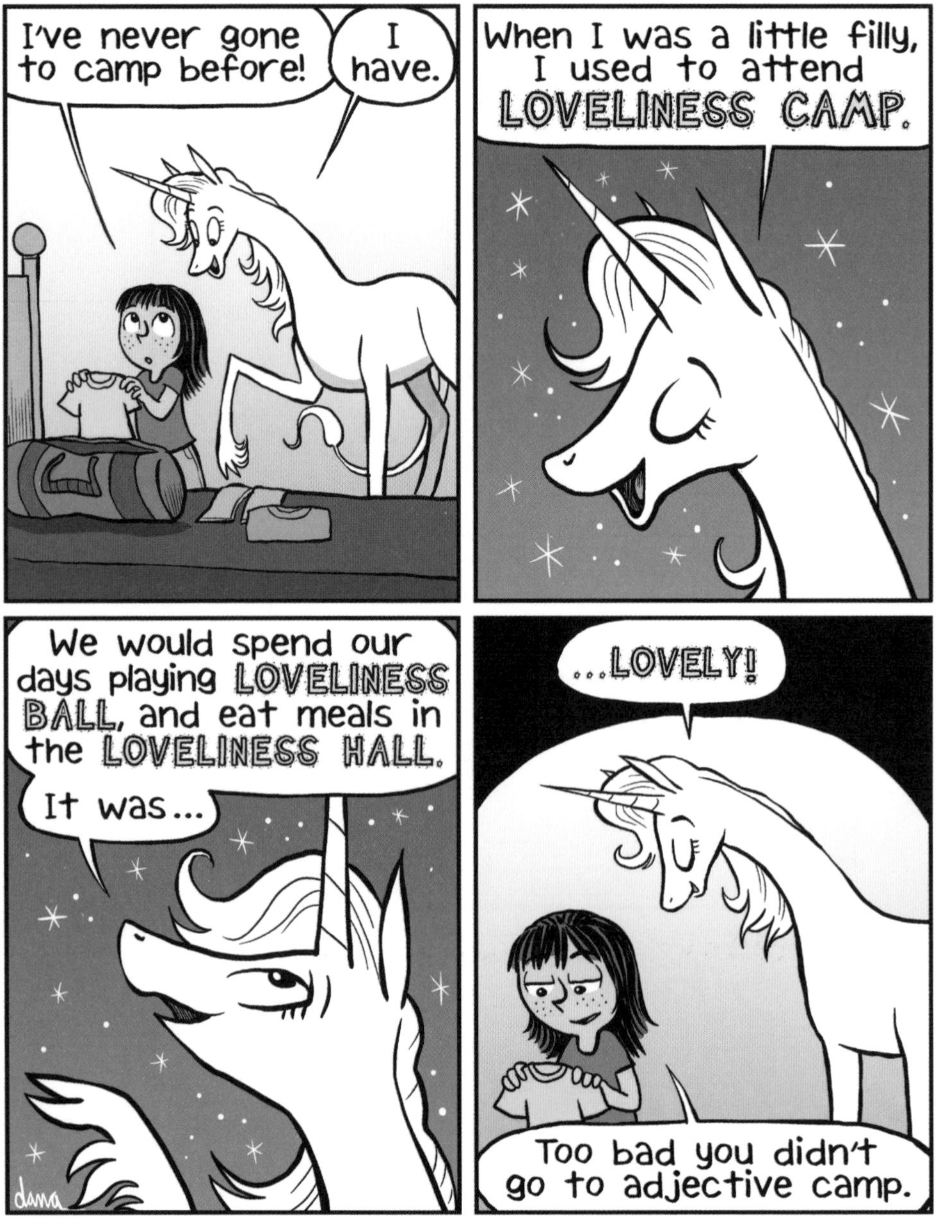
I've never gone to camp before!
I have.
When I was a little filly, I used to attend LOVELINESS CAMP.
We would spend our days playing LOVELINESS BALL, and eat meals in the LOVELINESS HALL.
It was...
...LOVELY!
Too bad you didn't go to adjective camp.
dana

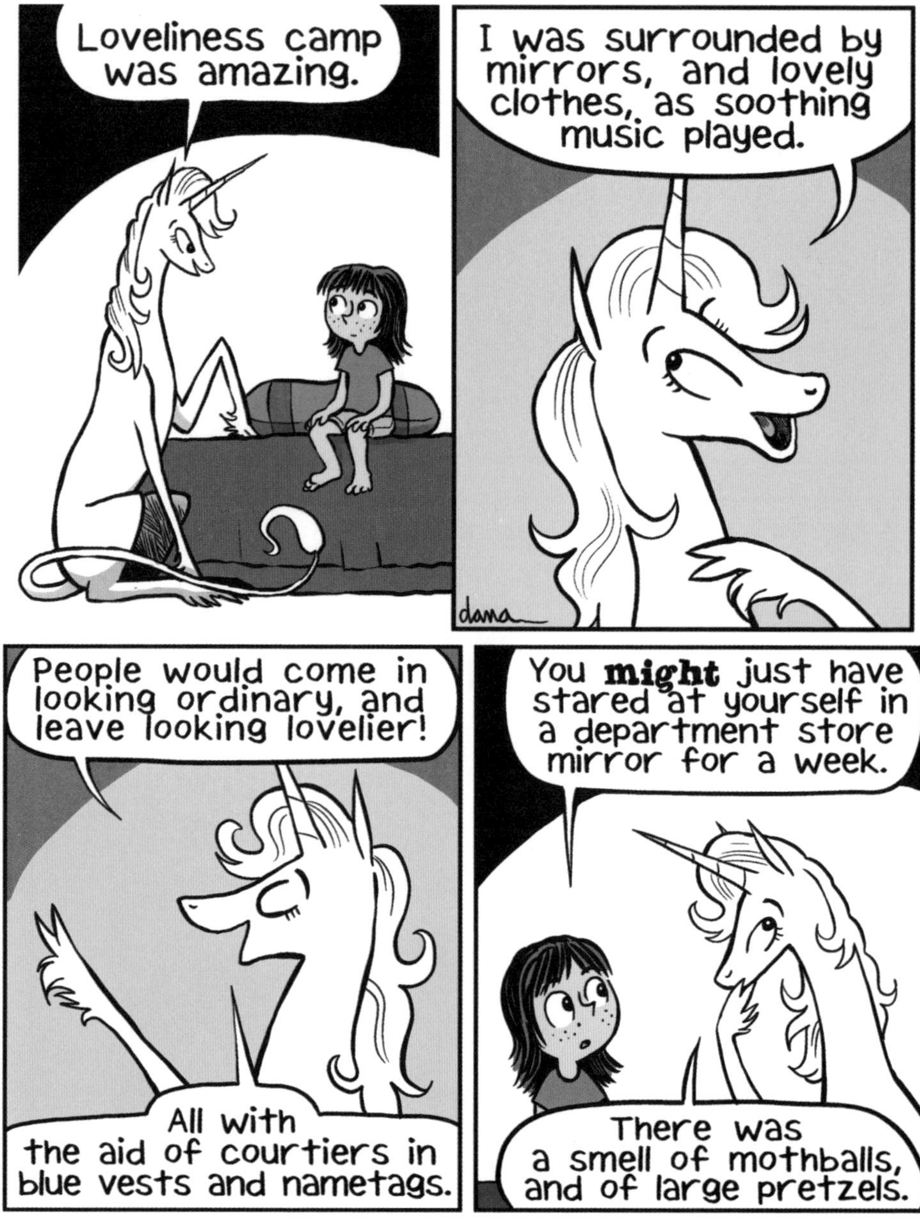
Loveliness camp was amazing.
I was surrounded by mirrors, and lovely clothes, as soothing music played.
dana
People would come in looking ordinary, and leave looking lovelier!
All with the aid of courtiers in blue vests and nametags.
You **might** just have stared at yourself in a department store mirror for a week.
There was a smell of mothballs, and of large pretzels.

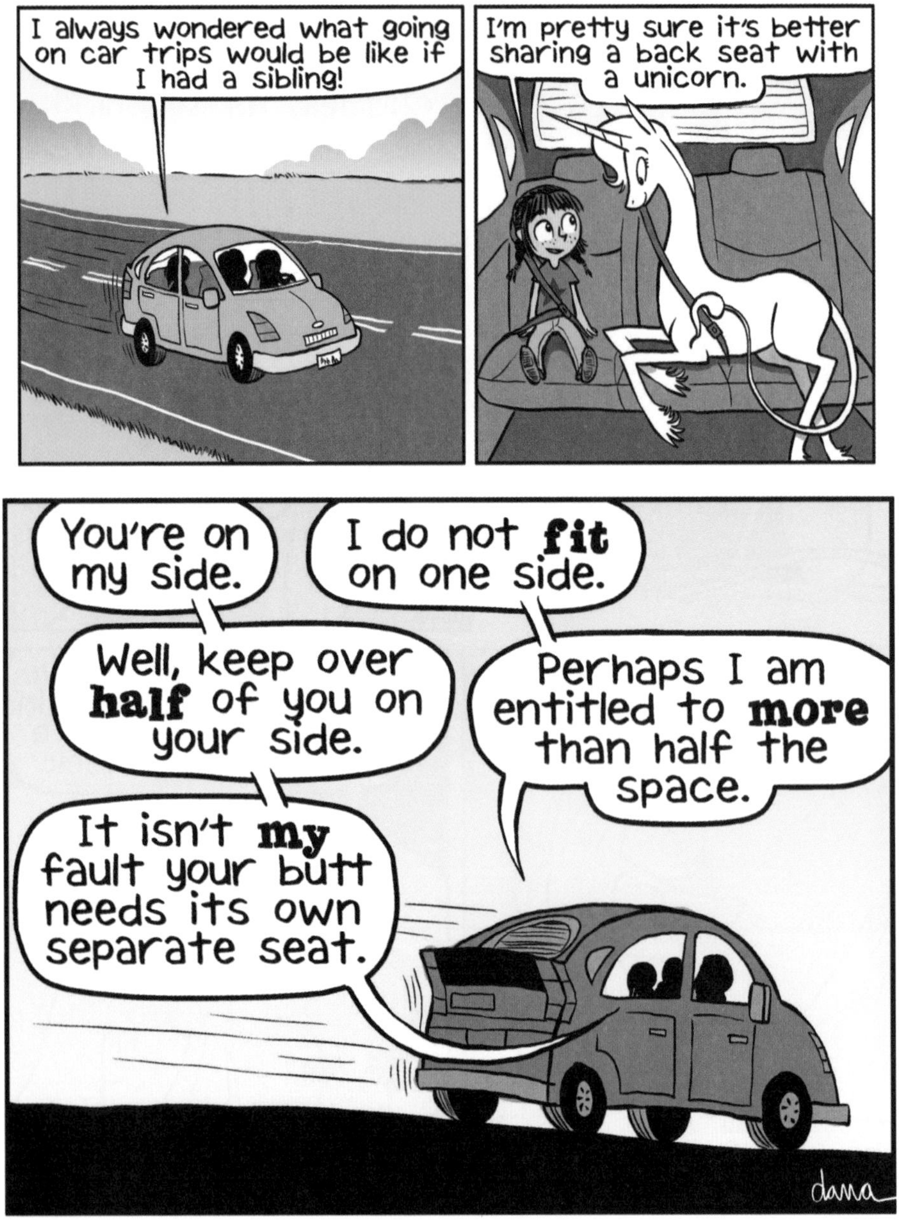
I always wondered what going on car trips would be like if I had a sibling!
I'm pretty sure it's better sharing a back seat with a unicorn.
You're on my side.
I do not **fit** on one side.
Well, keep over **half** of you on your side.
Perhaps I am entitled to **more** than half the space.
It isn't **my** fault your butt needs its own separate seat.
dana

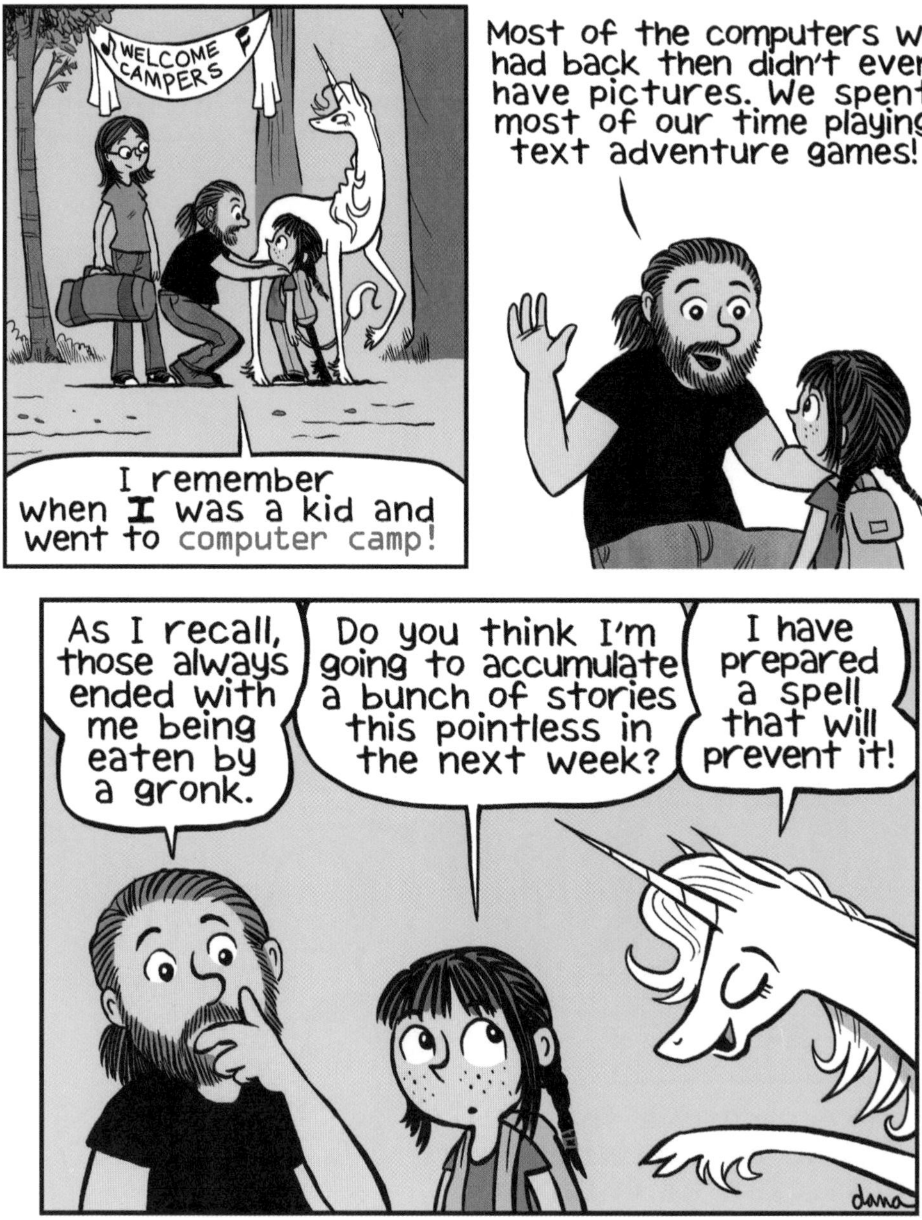
WELCOME CAMPERS
I remember when I was a kid and went to computer camp!
Most of the computers we had back then didn't even have pictures. We spent most of our time playing text adventure games!
As I recall, those always ended with me being eaten by a gronk.
Do you think I'm going to accumulate a bunch of stories this pointless in the next week?
I have prepared a spell that will prevent it!
dana

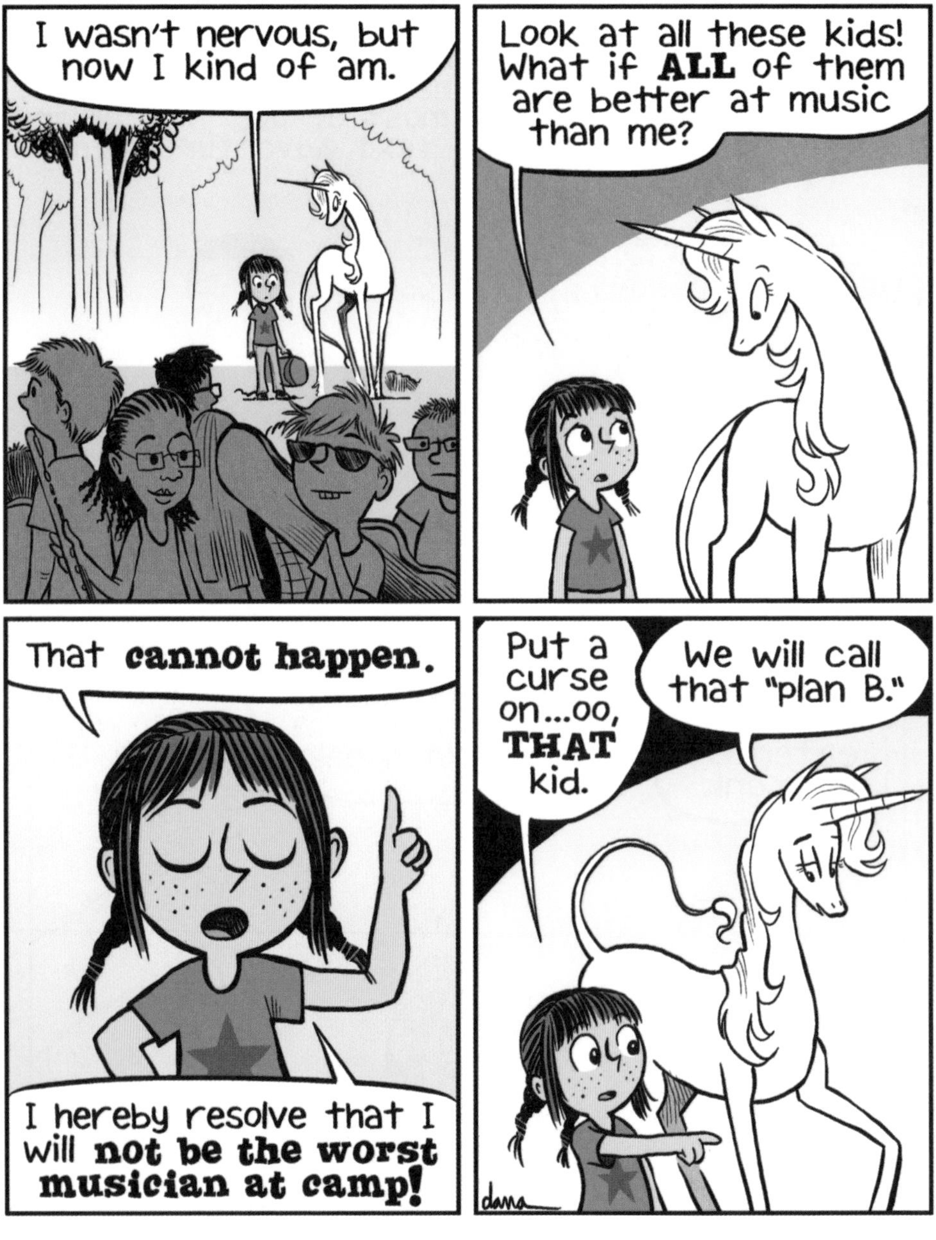
I wasn't nervous, but now I kind of am.
Look at all these kids! What if **ALL** of them are better at music than me?
That **cannot happen**.
I hereby resolve that I will **not be the worst musician at camp!**
Put a curse on...oo, **THAT** kid.
We will call that "plan B."
dana

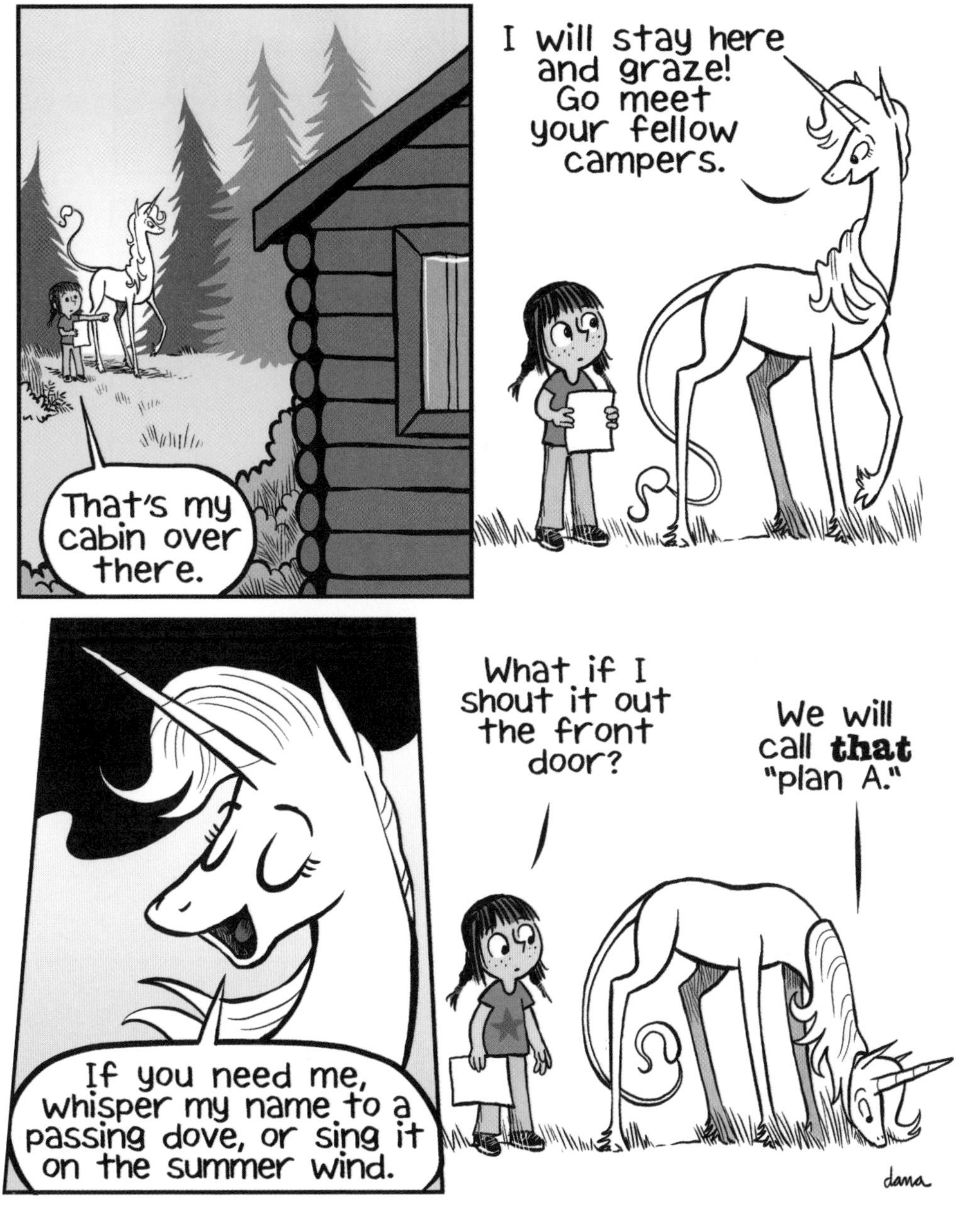
That's my cabin over there.
I will stay here and graze! Go meet your fellow campers.
If you need me, whisper my name to a passing dove, or sing it on the summer wind.
What if I shout it out the front door?
We will call **that** "plan A."
dana

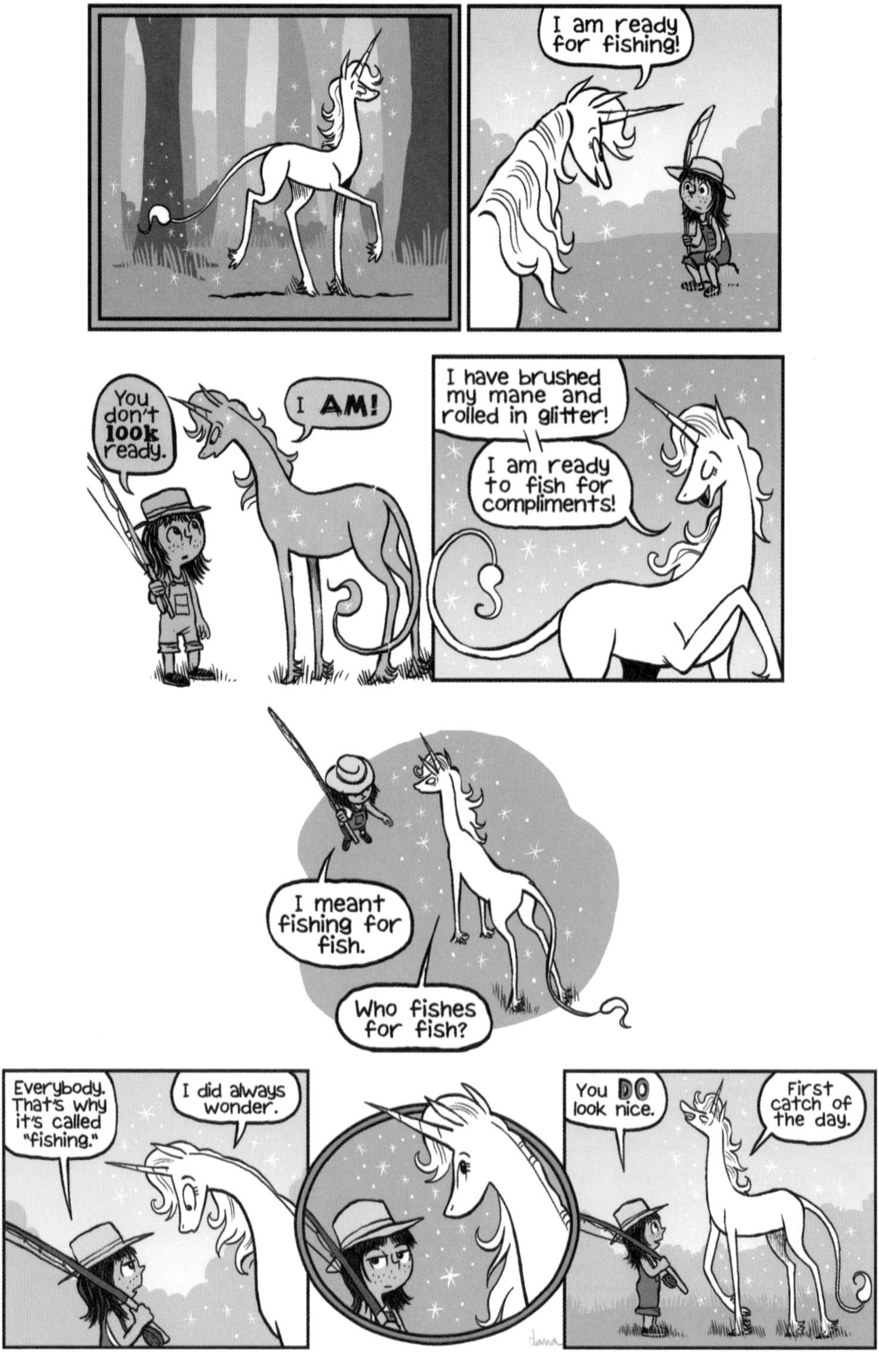
I am ready for fishing!
You don't **look** ready.
I **AM!**
I have brushed my mane and rolled in glitter!
I am ready to fish for compliments!
I meant fishing for fish.
Who fishes for fish?
Everybody. That's why it's called "fishing."
I did always wonder.
You **DO** look nice.
First catch of the day.
dana

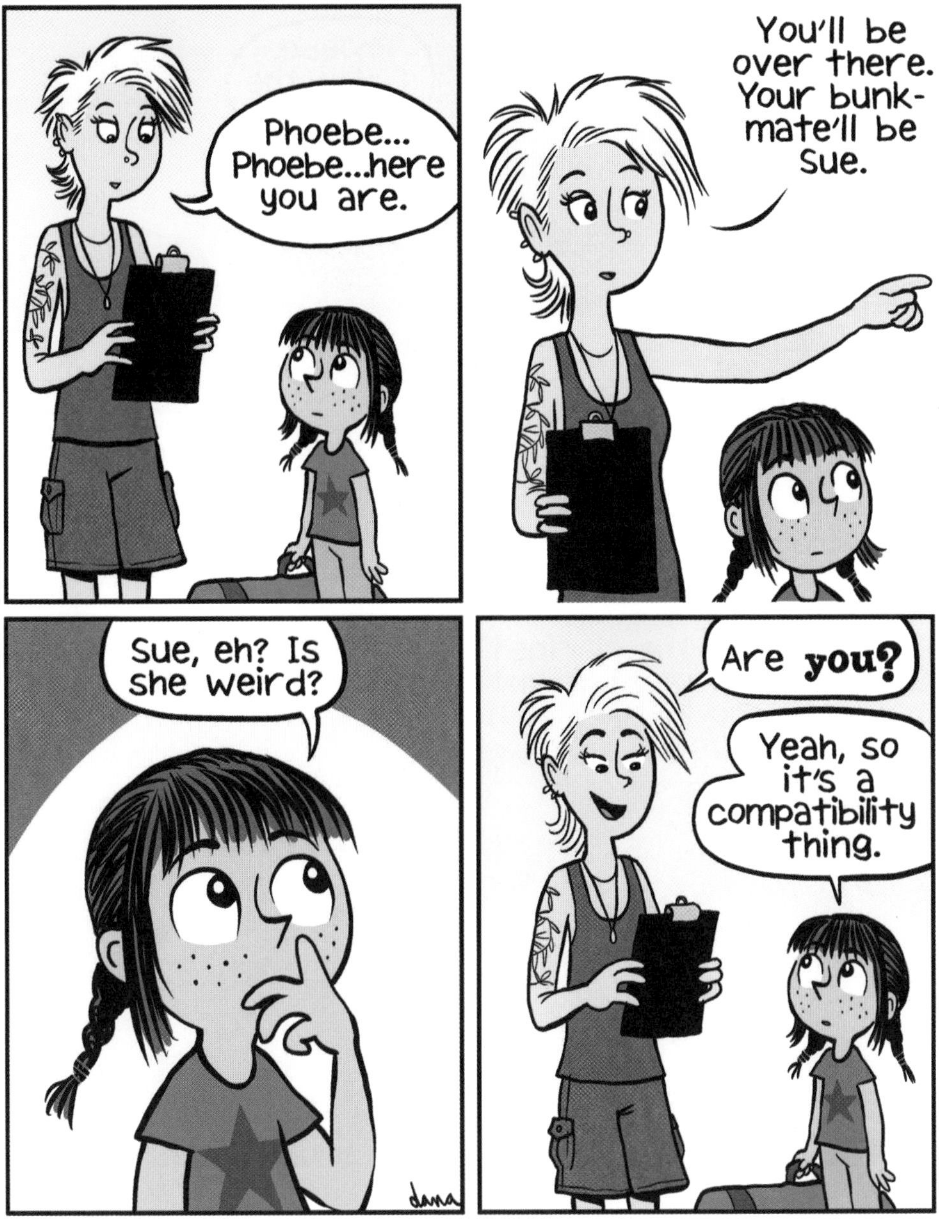
Phoebe... Phoebe...here you are.
You'll be over there. Your bunk-mate'll be Sue.
Sue, eh? Is she weird?
Are **you?**
Yeah, so it's a compatibility thing.
dana

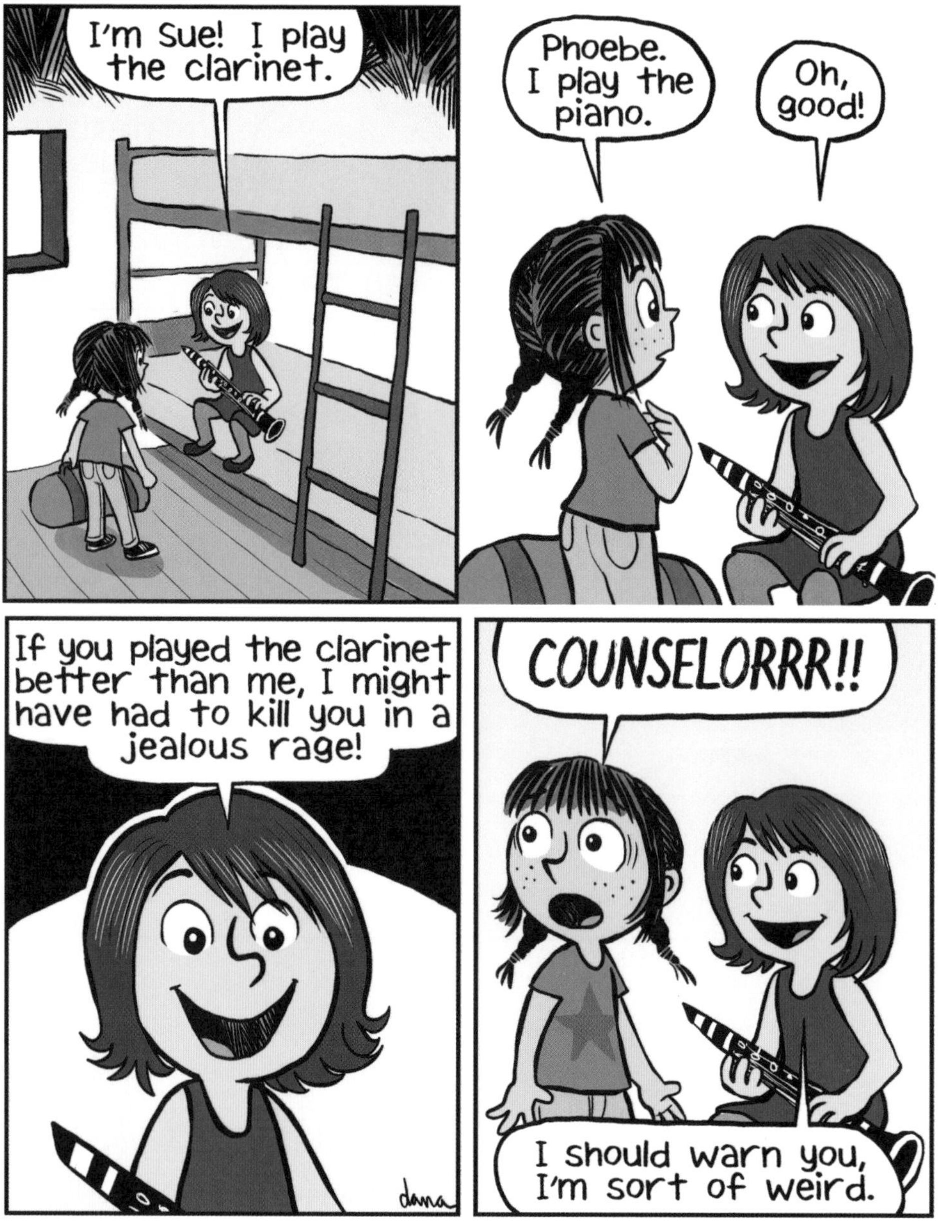
I'm Sue! I play the clarinet.
Phoebe. I play the piano.
Oh, good!
If you played the clarinet better than me, I might have had to kill you in a jealous rage!
COUNSELORRR!!
I should warn you, I'm sort of weird.
dana

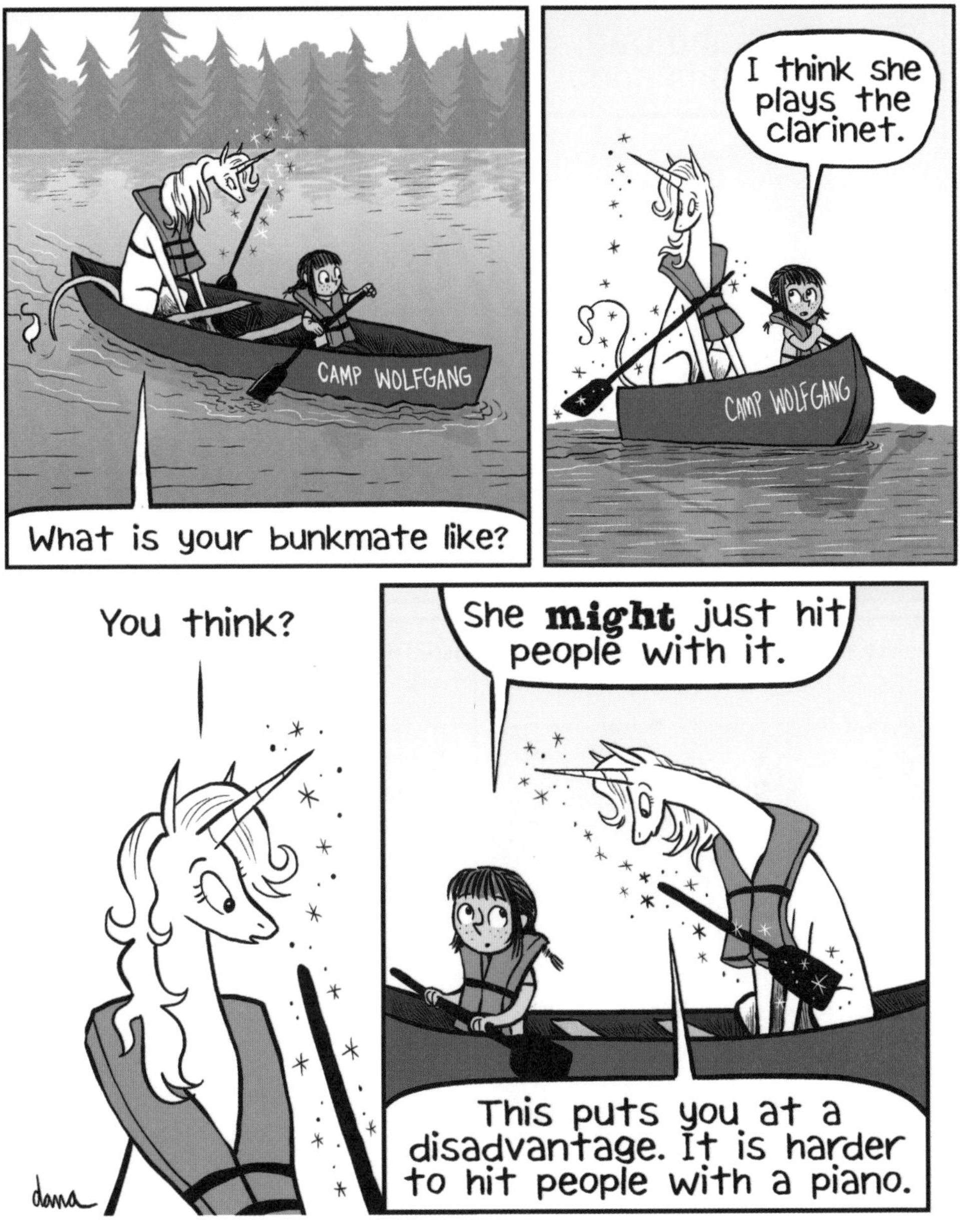

CAMP WOLFGANG
What is your bunkmate like?
I think she plays the clarinet.
CAMP WOLFGANG
You think?
She **might** just hit people with it.
This puts you at a disadvantage. It is harder to hit people with a piano.
dana

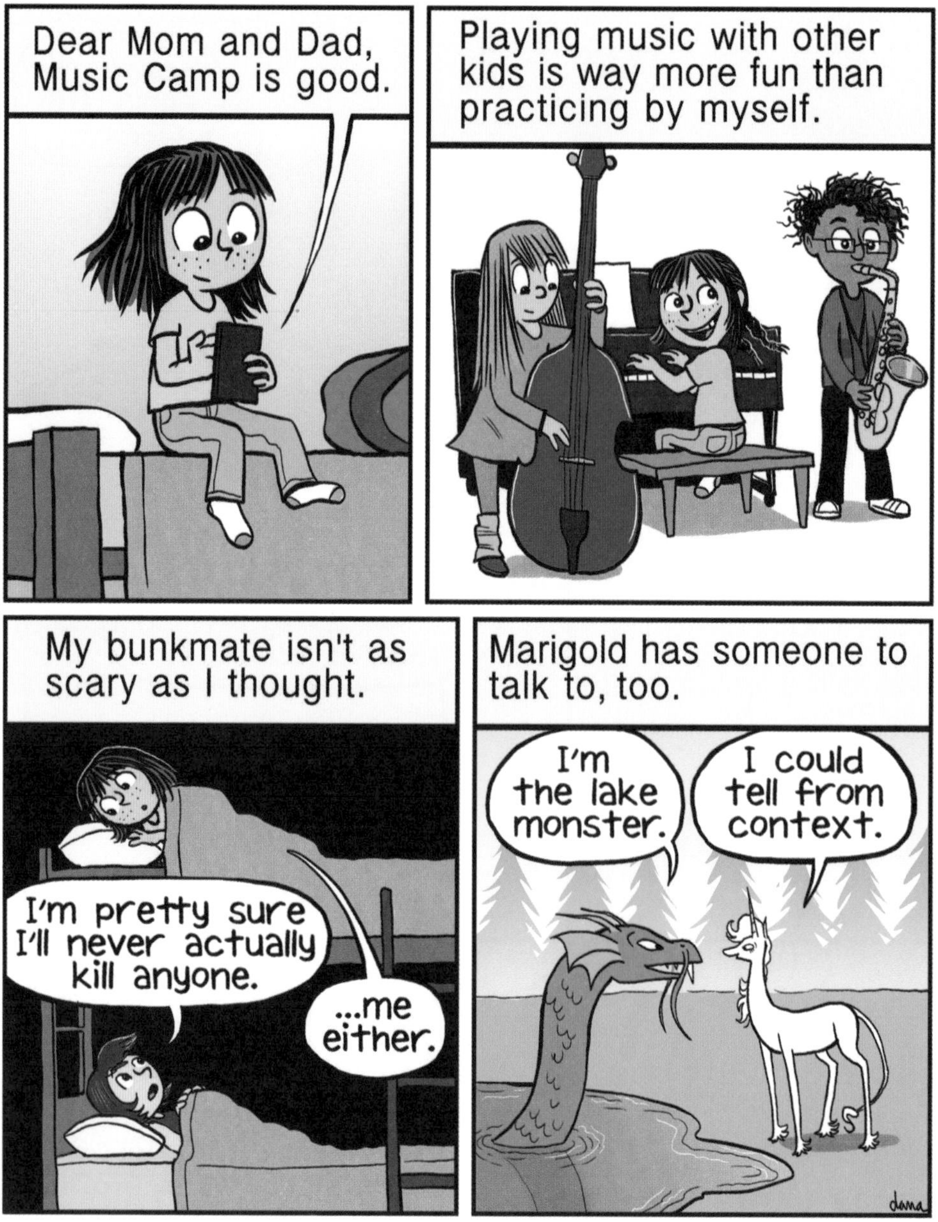
Dear Mom and Dad,
Music Camp is good.
Playing music with other kids is way more fun than practicing by myself.
My bunkmate isn't as scary as I thought.
I'm pretty sure I'll never actually kill anyone.
...me either.
Marigold has someone to talk to, too.
I'm the lake monster.
I could tell from context.
dana

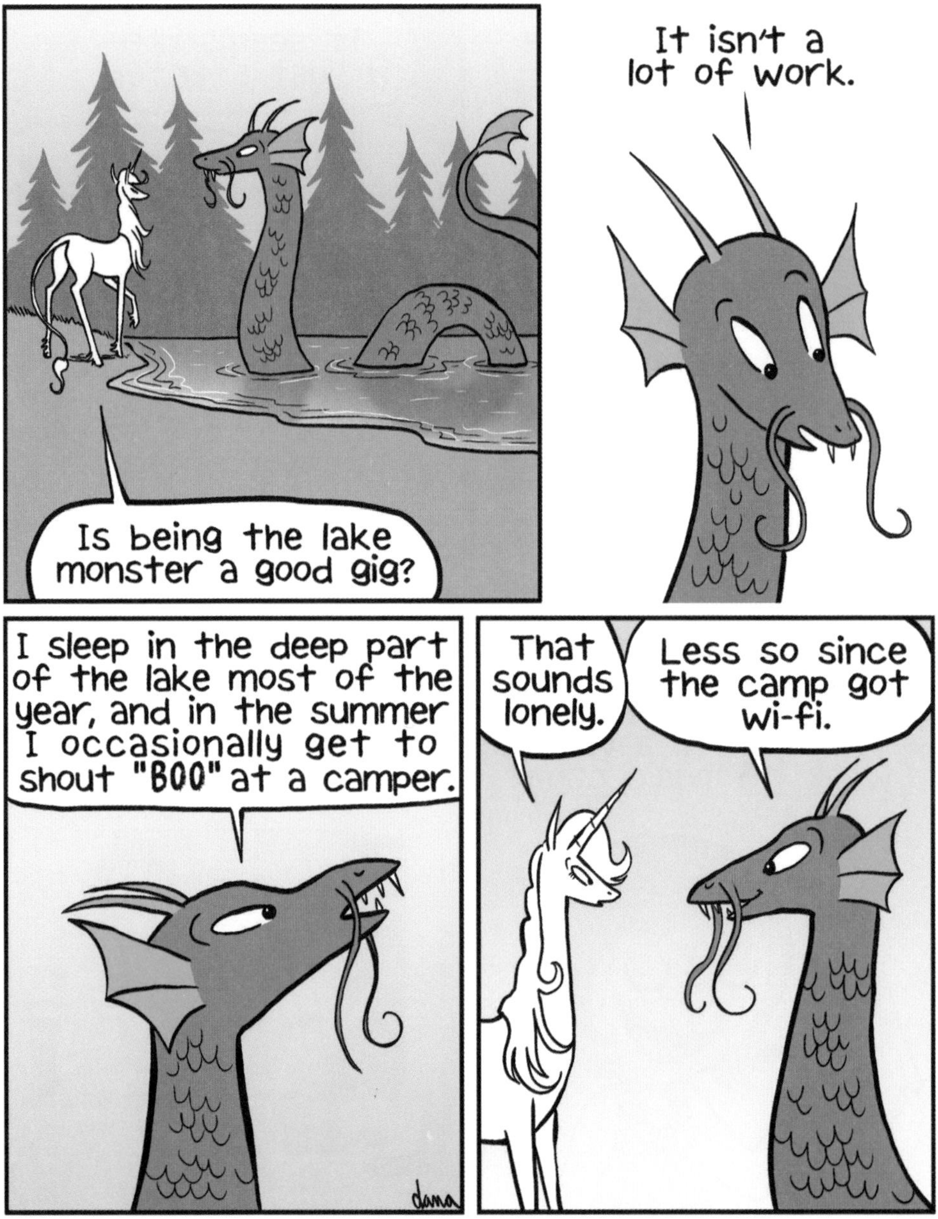
Is being the lake monster a good gig?
It isn't a lot of work.
I sleep in the deep part of the lake most of the year, and in the summer I occasionally get to shout "BOO" at a camper.
That sounds lonely.
Less so since the camp got wi-fi.
dana

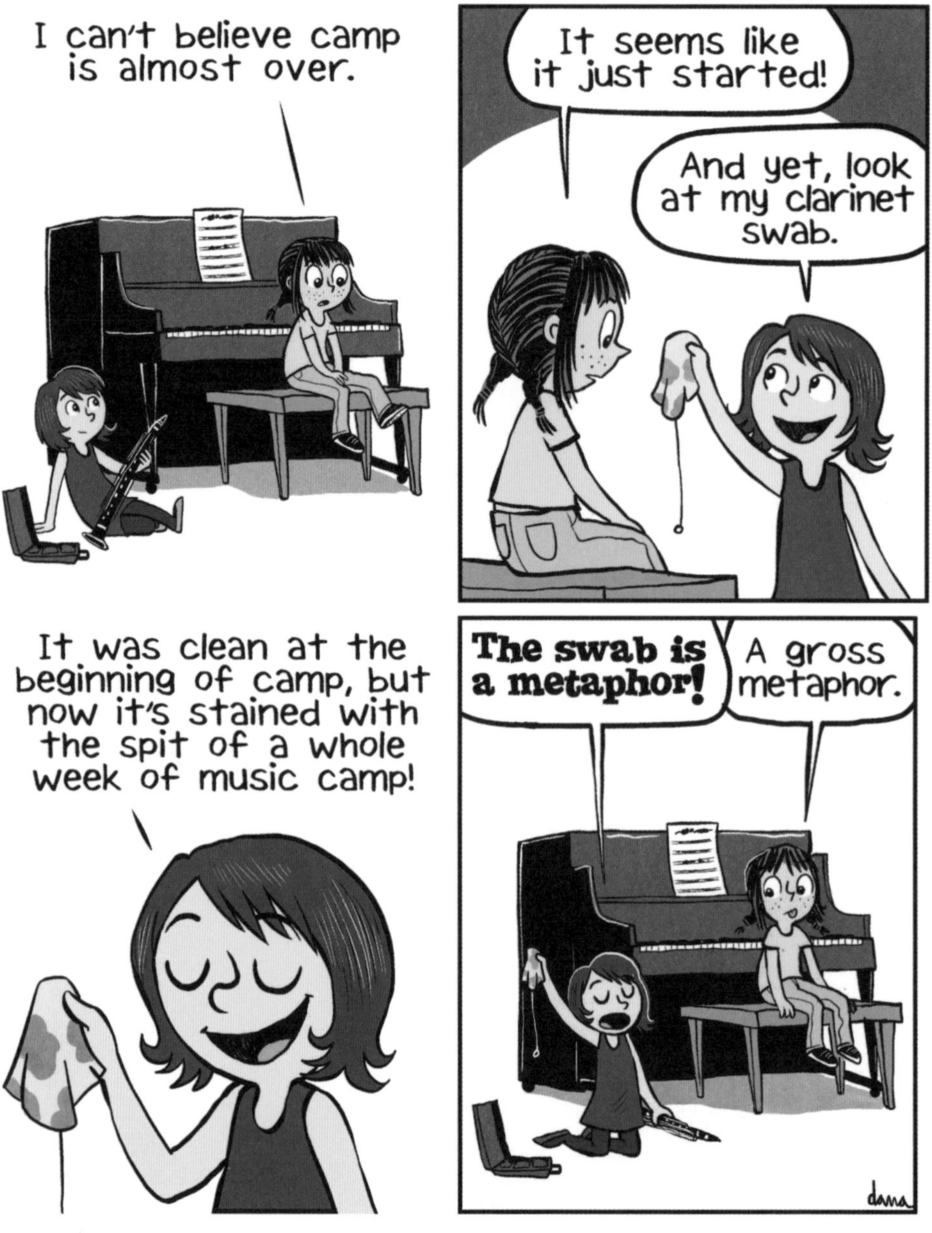
I can't believe camp is almost over.
It seems like it just started!
And yet, look at my clarinet swab.
It was clean at the beginning of camp, but now it's stained with the spit of a whole week of music camp!
The swab is a metaphor!
A gross metaphor.
dana

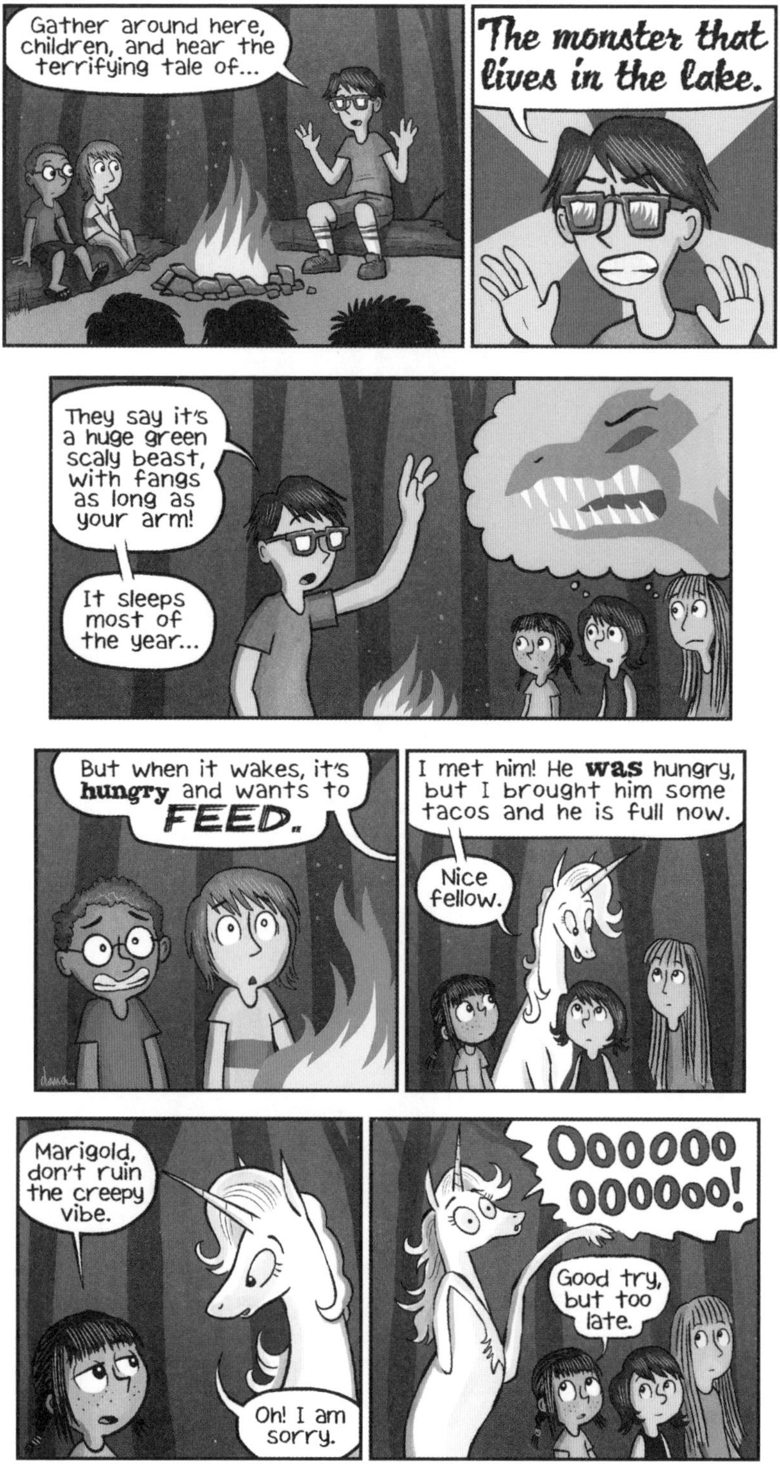

Gather around here, children, and hear the terrifying tale of...
The monster that lives in the lake.
They say it's a huge green scaly beast, with fangs as long as your arm!
It sleeps most of the year...
But when it wakes, it's **hungry** and wants to **FEED.**
I met him! He **was** hungry, but I brought him some tacos and he is full now.
Nice fellow.
Marigold, don't ruin the creepy vibe.
Oh! I am sorry.
OOOOOO OOOOoo!
Good try, but too late.

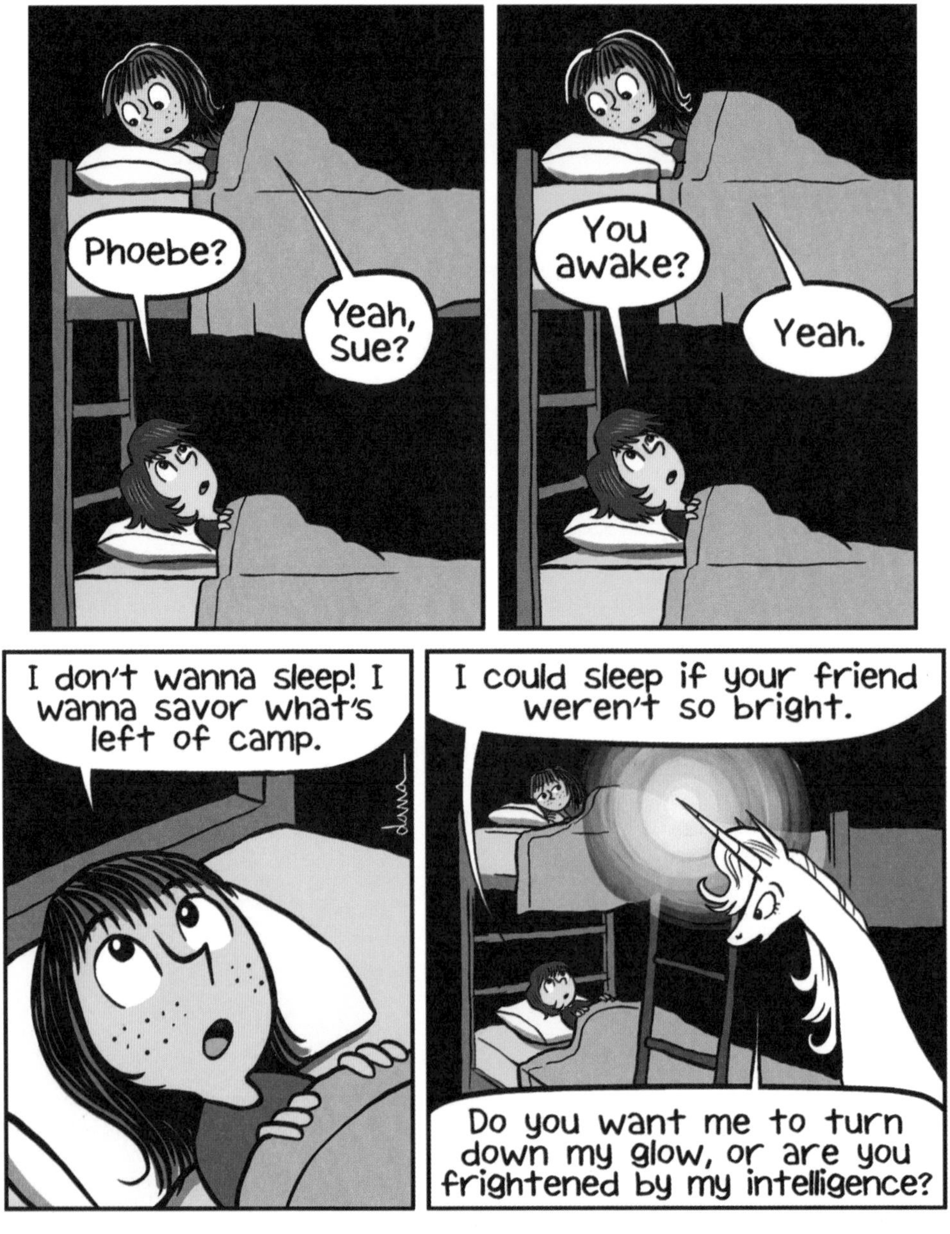
Phoebe?
Yeah, Sue?
You awake?
Yeah.
I don't wanna sleep! I wanna savor what's left of camp.
I could sleep if your friend weren't so bright.
Do you want me to turn down my glow, or are you frightened by my intelligence?

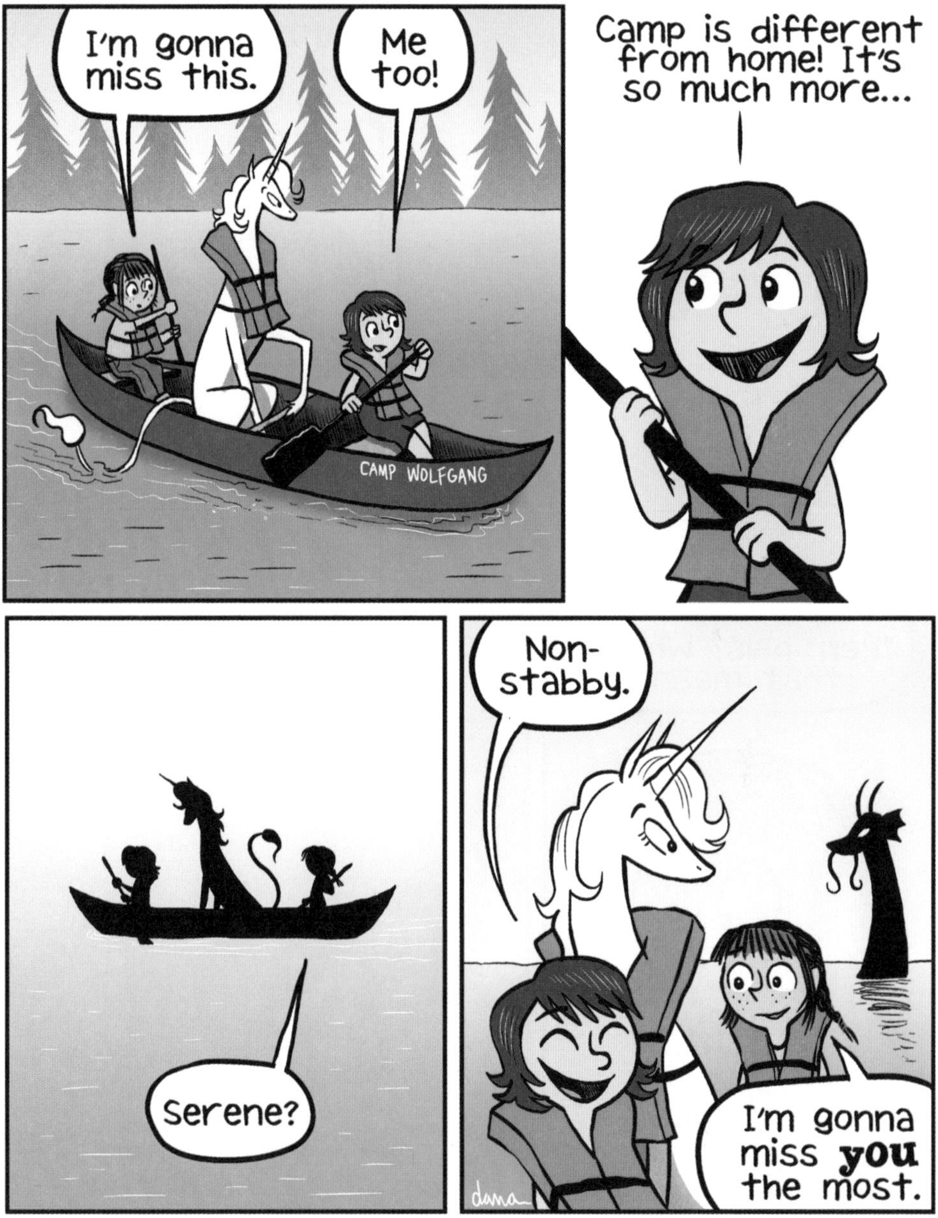
I'm gonna miss this.
Me too!
CAMP WOLFGANG
Camp is different from home! It's so much more...
Serene?
Non-stabby.
I'm gonna miss **you** the most.
dana

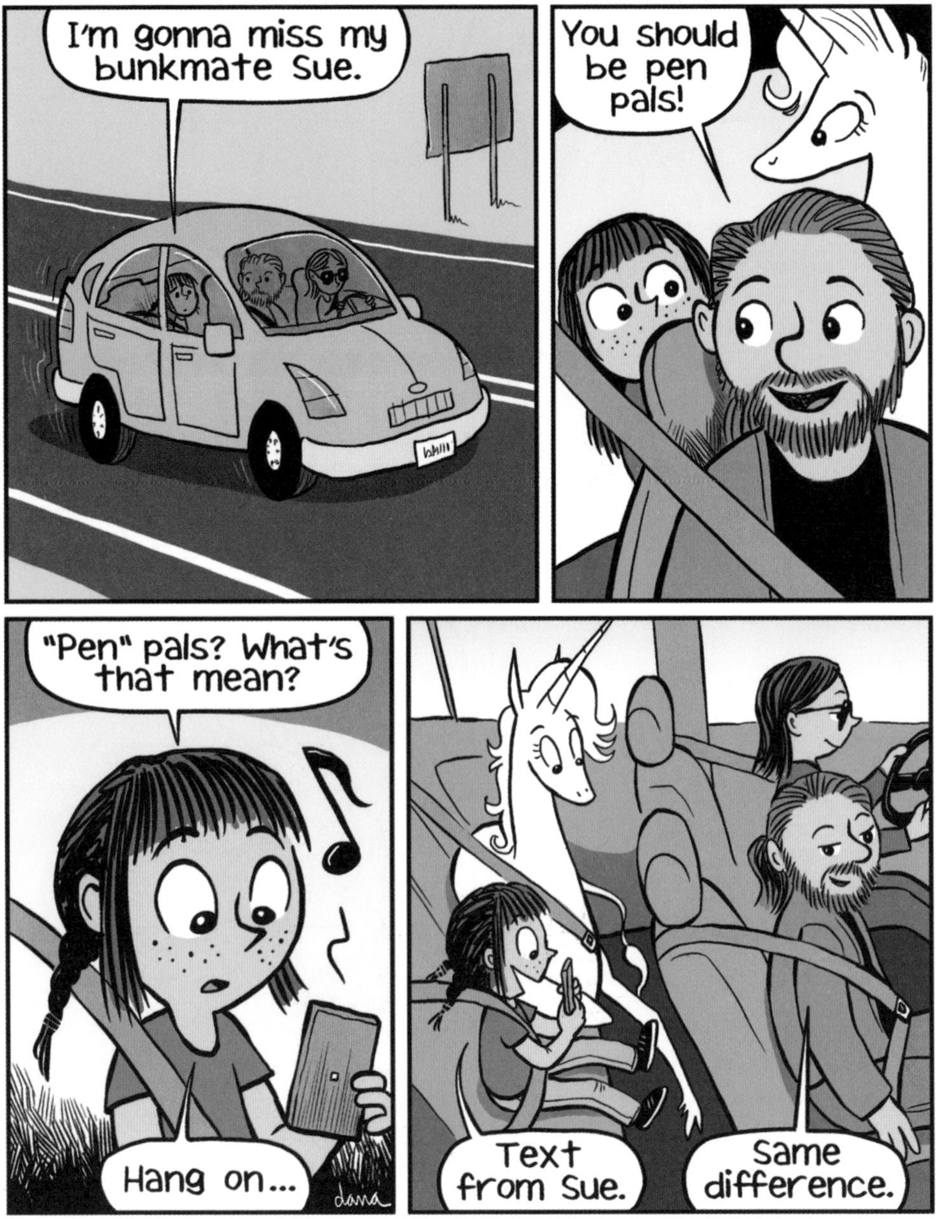
I'm gonna miss my bunkmate Sue.
You should be pen pals!
"Pen" pals? What's that mean?
Hang on...
dana
Text from Sue.
Same difference.

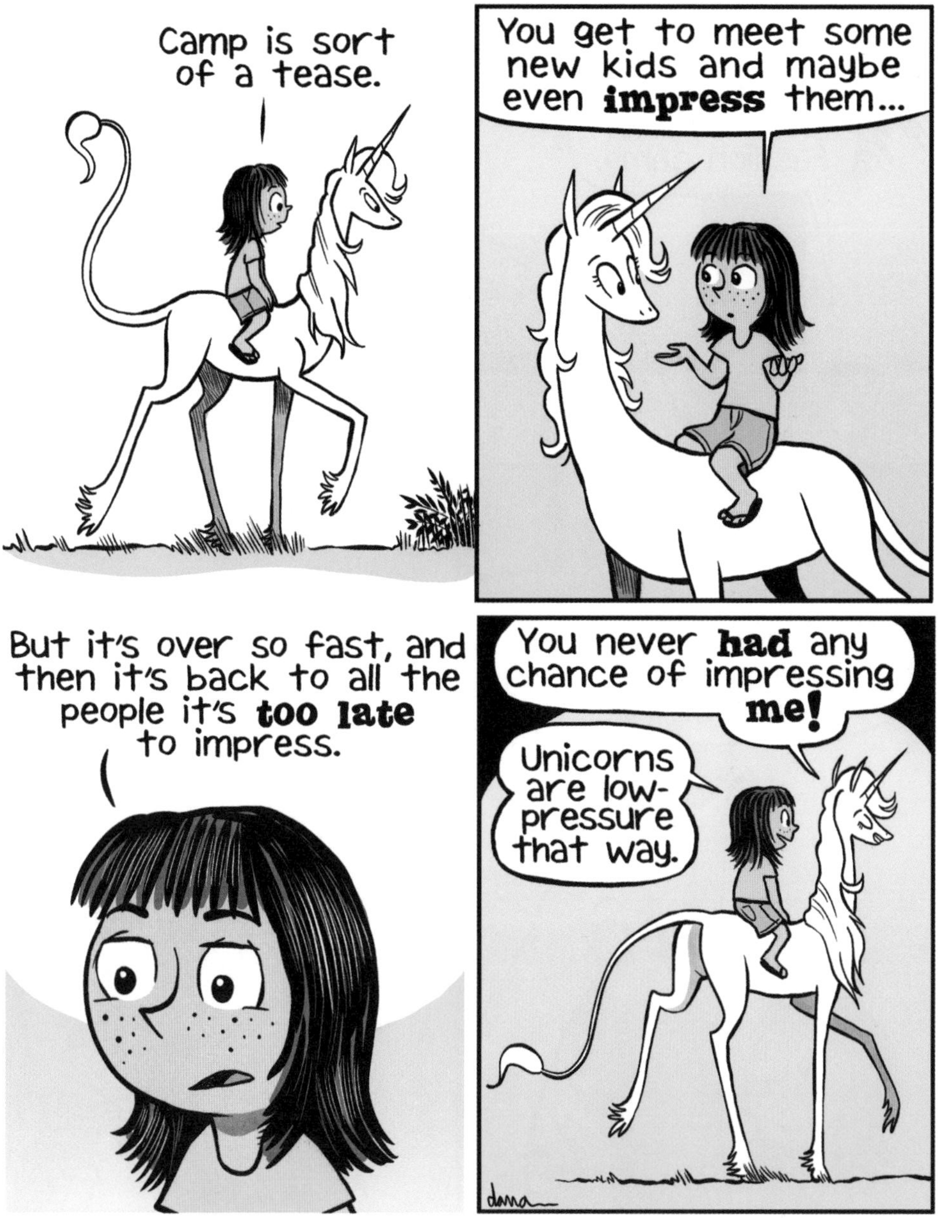
Camp is sort of a tease.
You get to meet some new kids and maybe even **impress** them...
But it's over so fast, and then it's back to all the people it's **too late** to impress.
You never **had** any chance of impressing **me!**
Unicorns are low-pressure that way.
dana

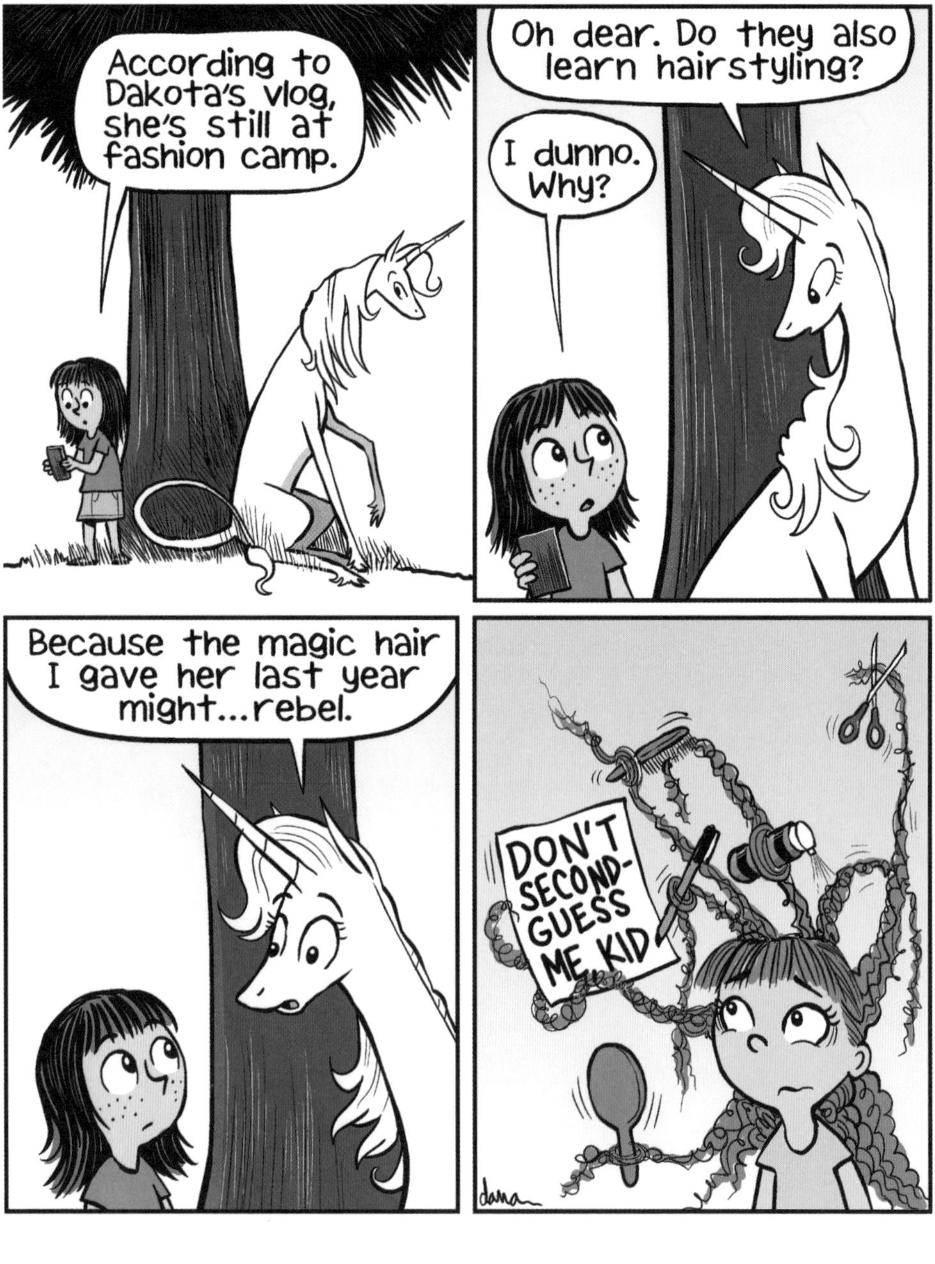
According to Dakota's vlog, she's still at fashion camp.
Oh dear. Do they also learn hairstyling?
I dunno. Why?
Because the magic hair I gave her last year might...rebel.
DON'T SECOND-GUESS ME KID
dana

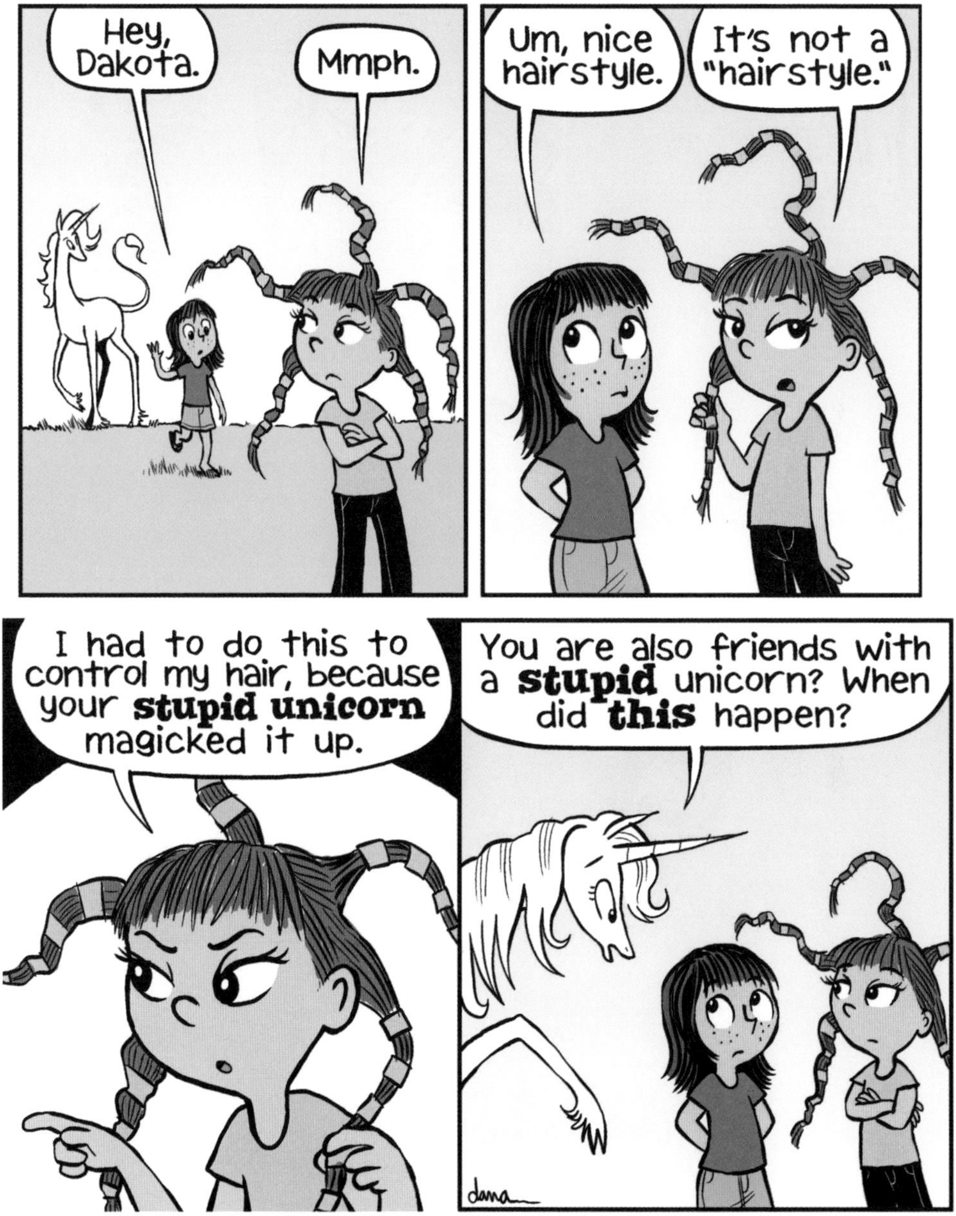
Hey, Dakota.
Mmph.
Um, nice hairstyle.
It's not a "hairstyle."
I had to do this to control my hair, because your **stupid unicorn** magicked it up.
You are also friends with a **stupid** unicorn? When did **this** happen?
dana

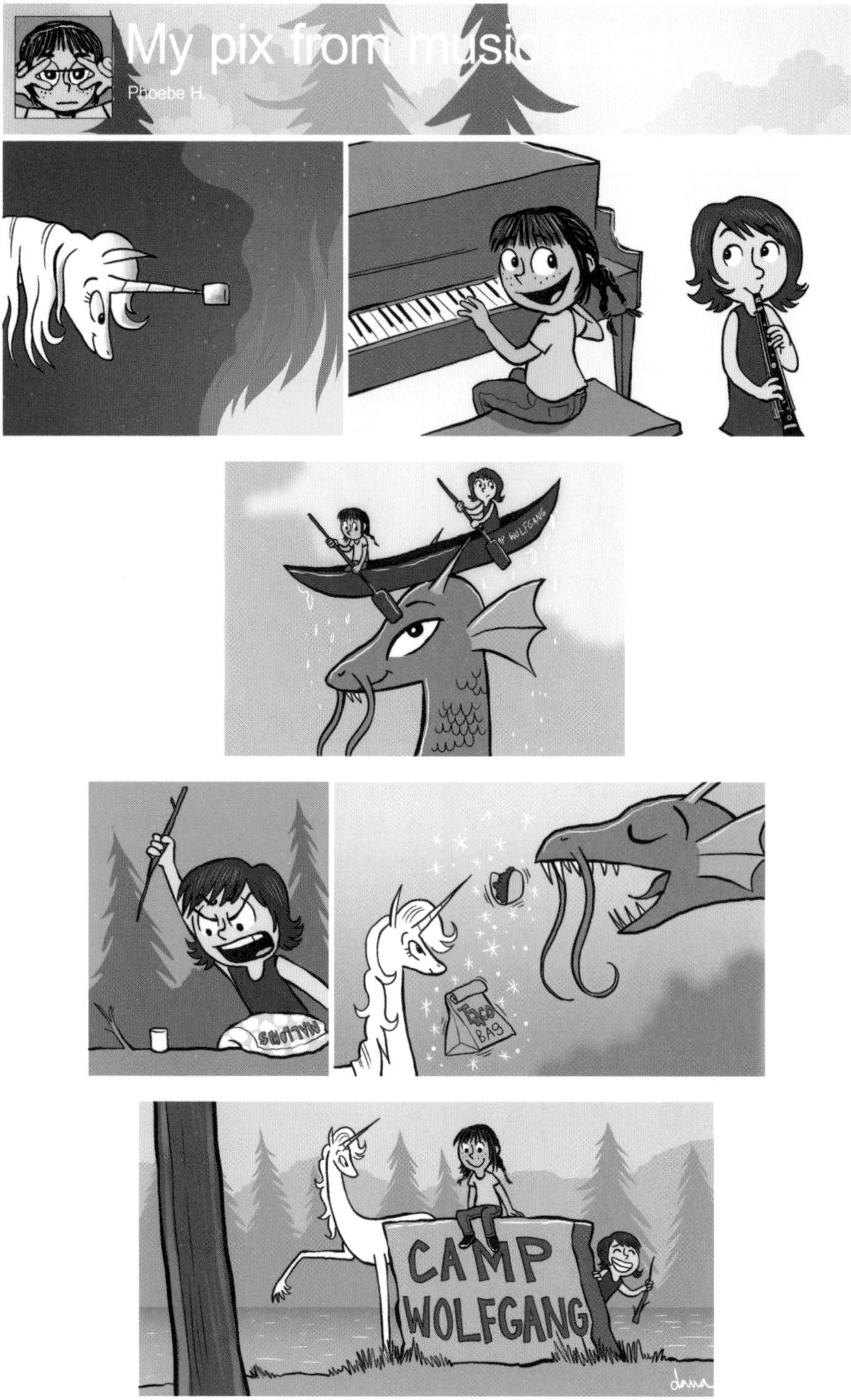

My pix from music
Phoebe H.
WOLFGANG
MALLOWS
TACO BAG
CAMP WOLFGANG
dana

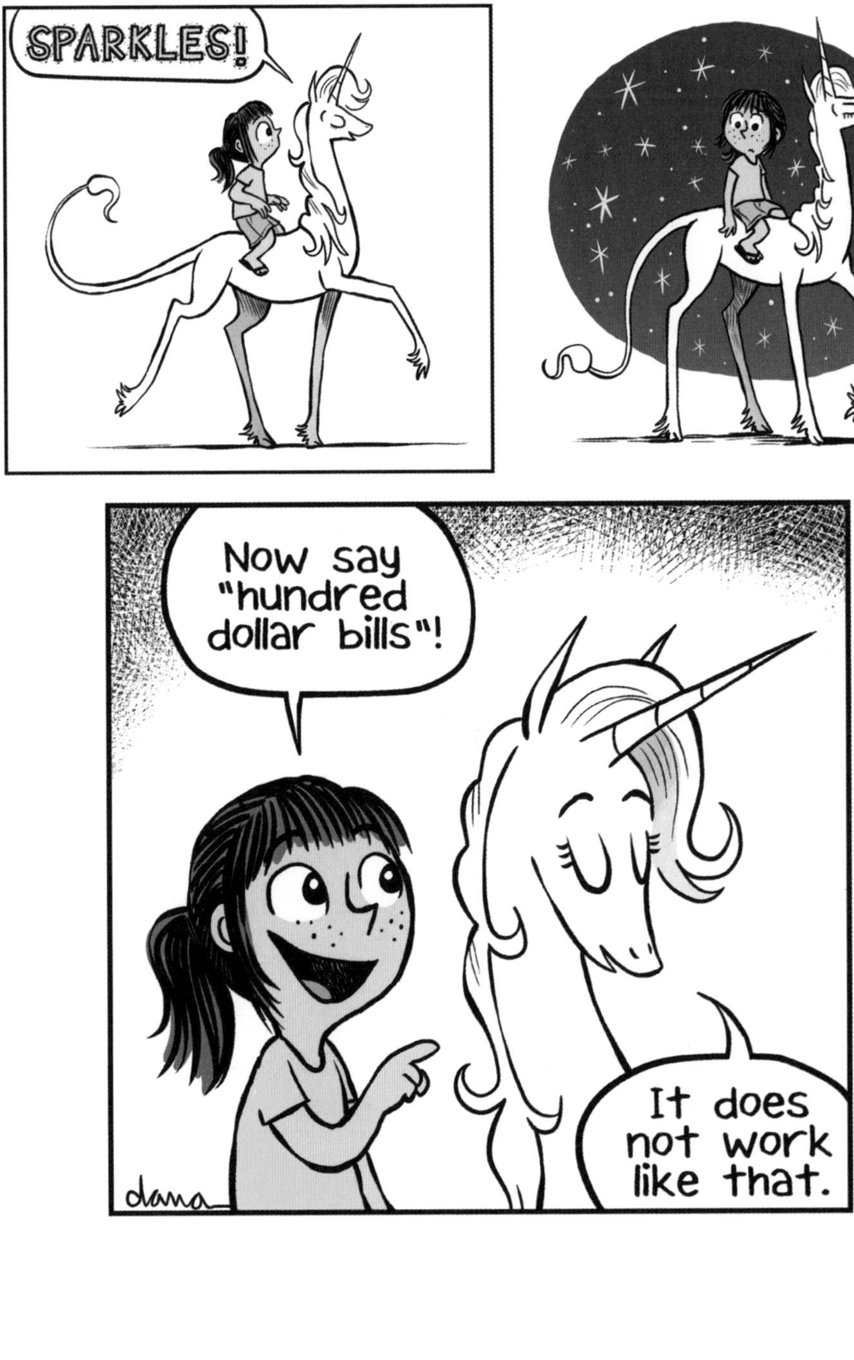
SPARKLES!
Now say "hundred dollar bills"!
It does not work like that.
dana

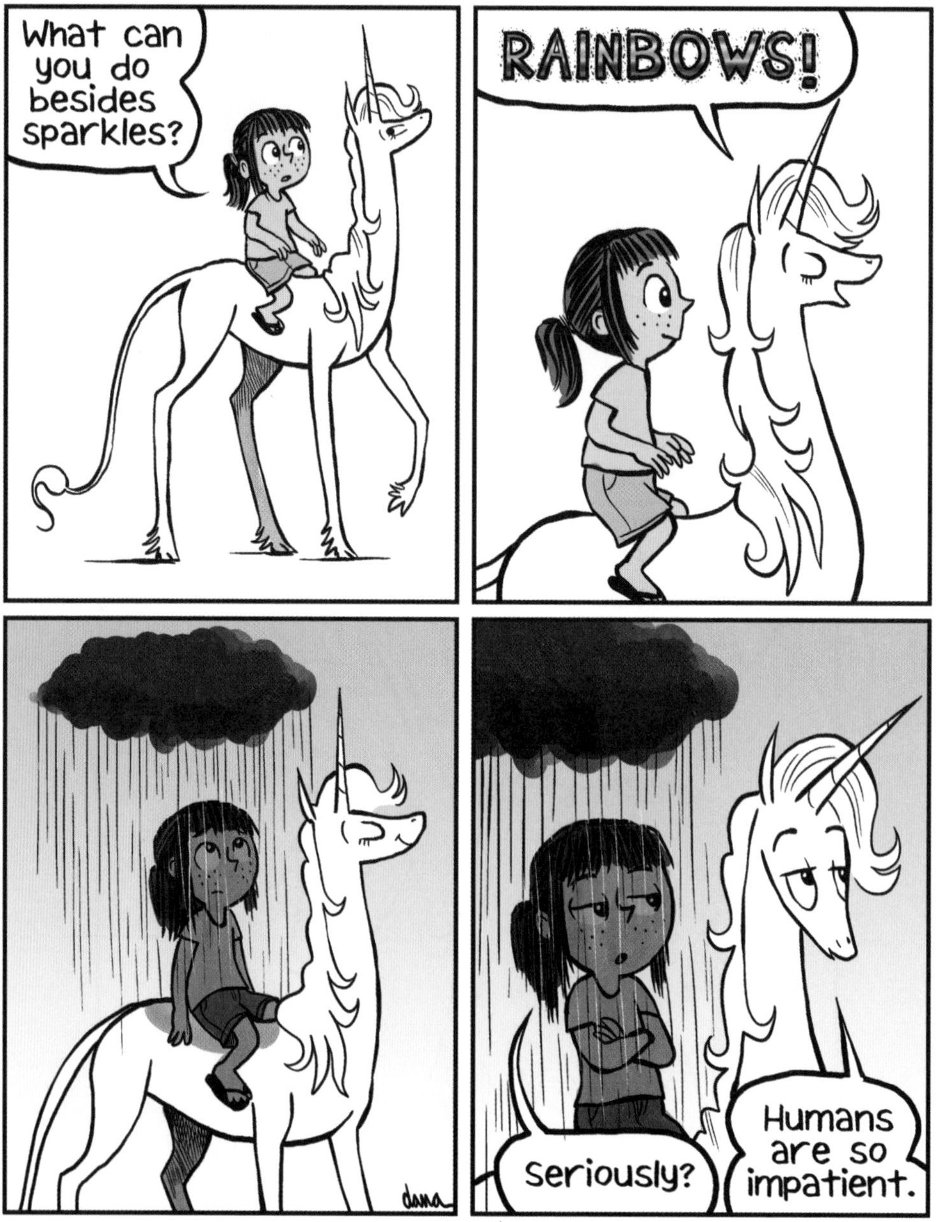
What can you do besides sparkles?
RAINBOWS!
Seriously?
Humans are so impatient.
dana

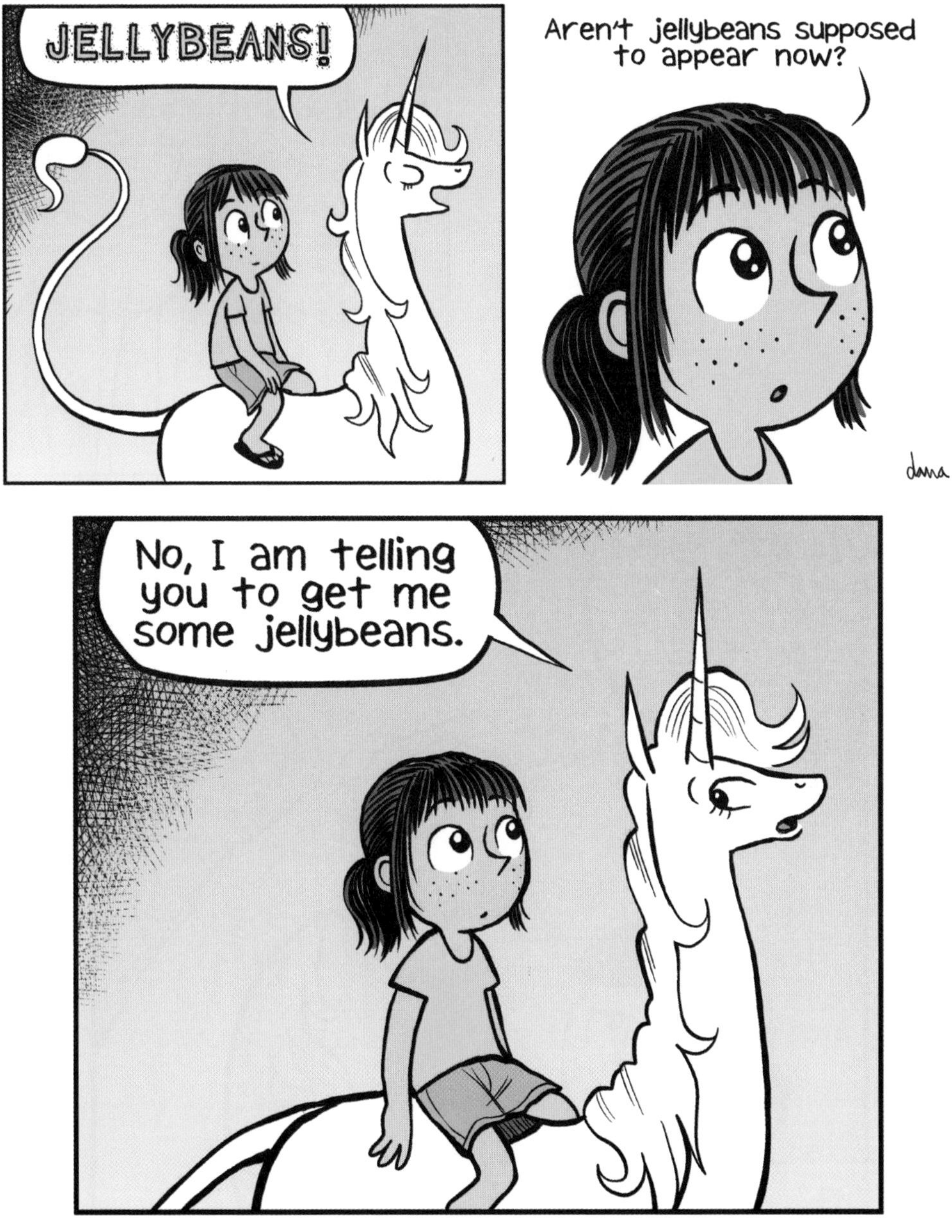
JELLYBEANS!
Aren't jellybeans supposed to appear now?
dana
No, I am telling you to get me some jellybeans.

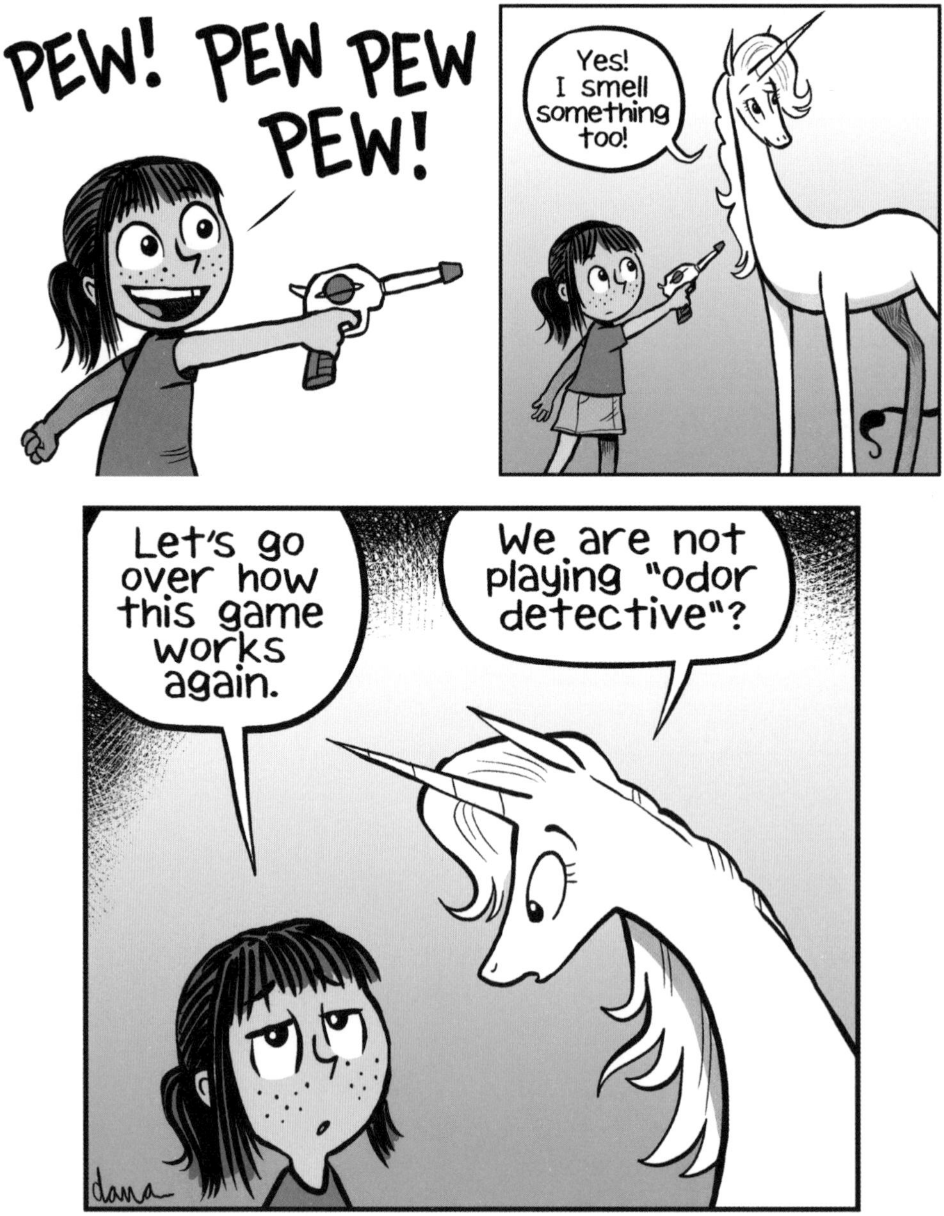
PEW! PEW PEW PEW!
Yes! I smell something too!
Let's go over how this game works again.
We are not playing "odor detective"?
dana

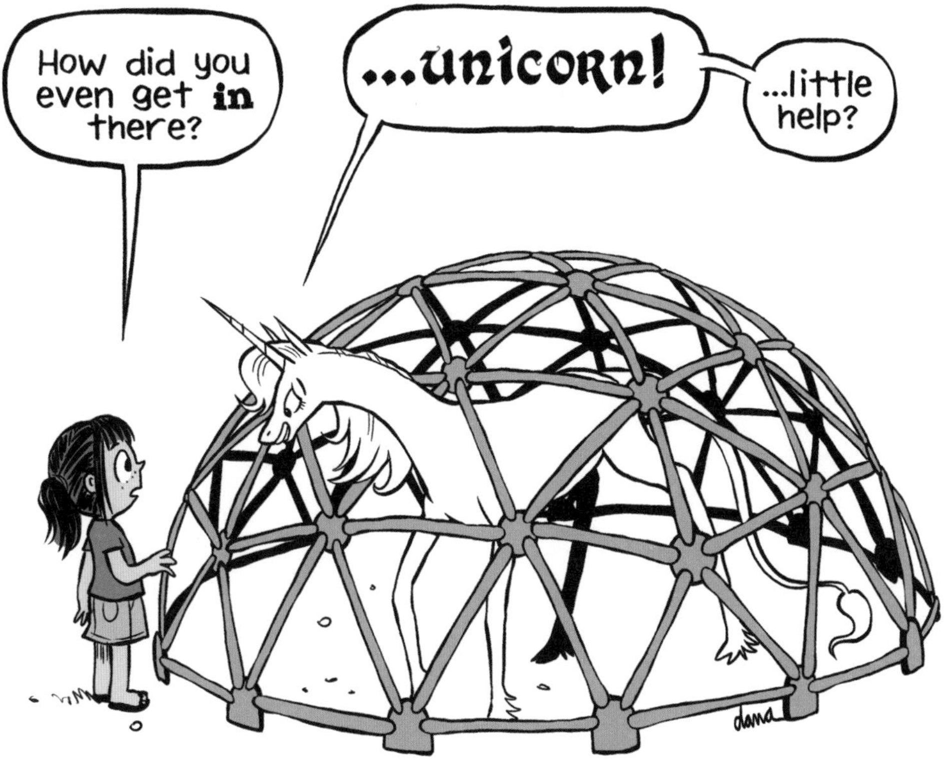
How did you even get **in** there?
...UNICORN!
...little help?
dana

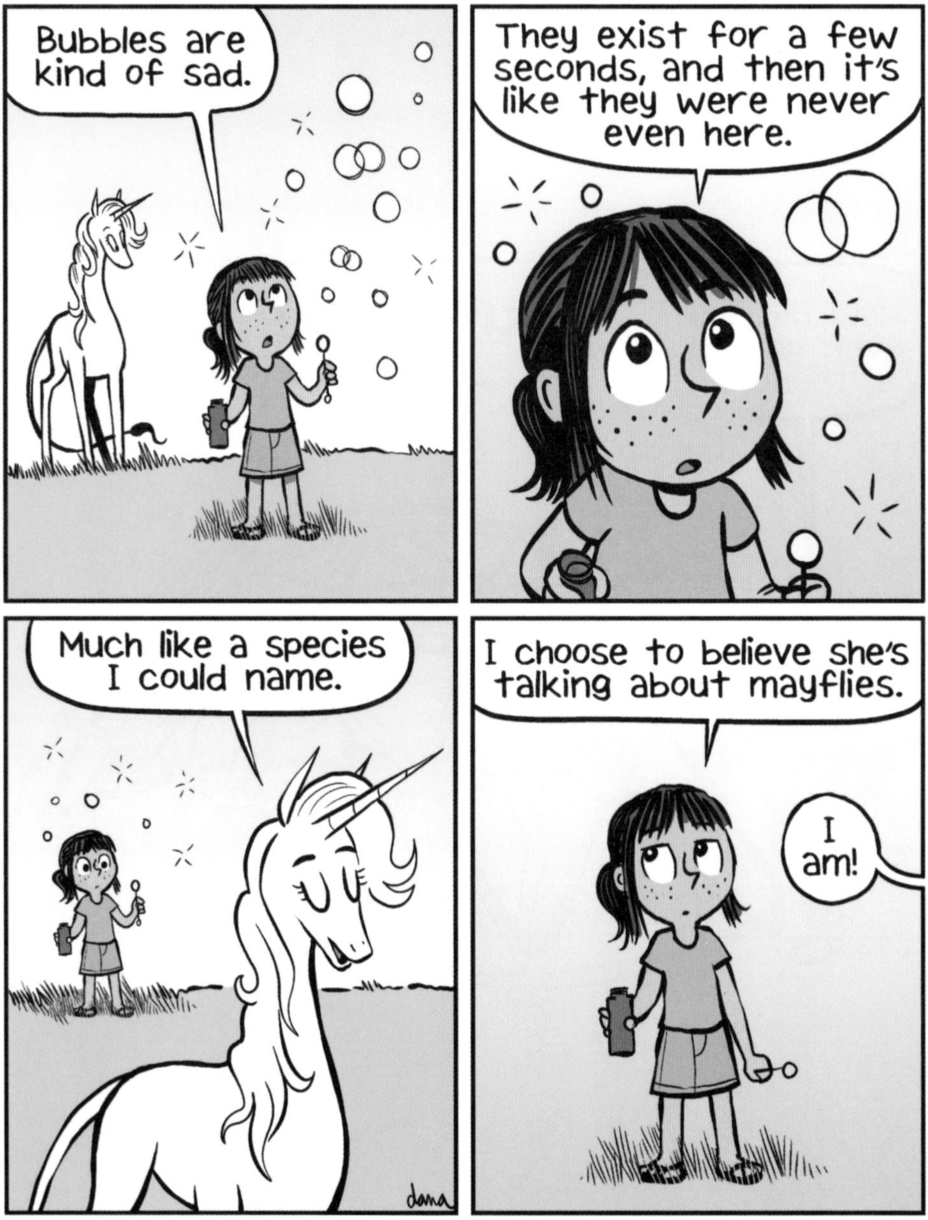
Bubbles are kind of sad.
They exist for a few seconds, and then it's like they were never even here.
Much like a species I could name.
I choose to believe she's talking about mayflies.
I am!

I'd never even seen a firefly until last year when we were on vacation.
Little dancing lights. I begged my parents to move someplace that had them.
But here, there is a UNICORN.
Finding that out did change the equation.

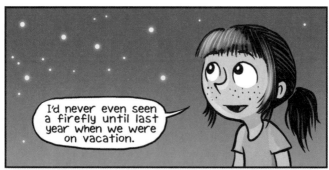

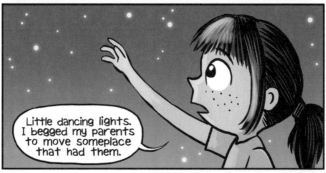

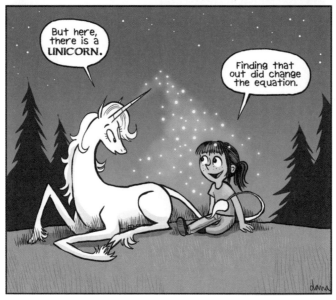

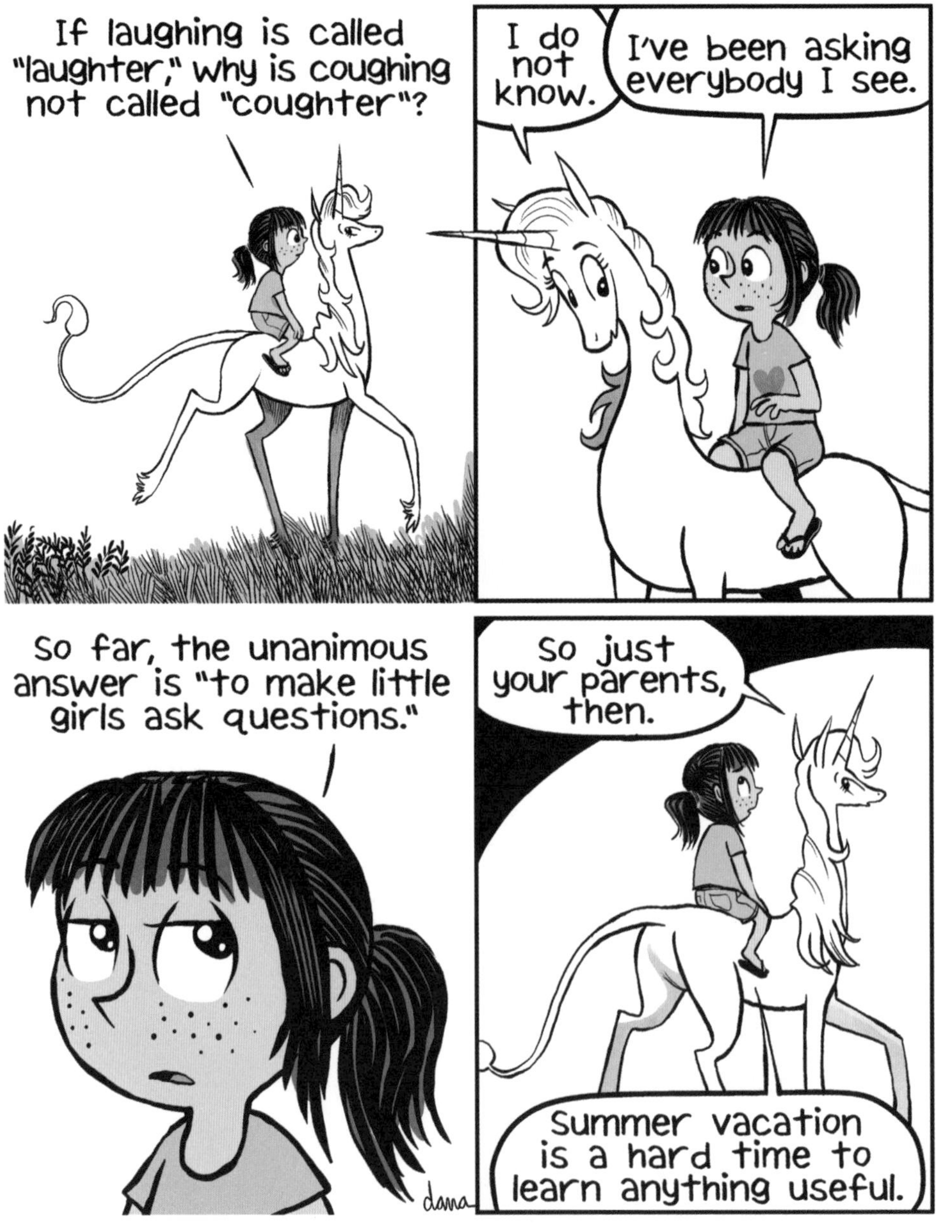
If laughing is called "laughter," why is coughing not called "coughter"?
I do not know.
I've been asking everybody I see.
So far, the unanimous answer is "to make little girls ask questions."
So just your parents, then.
Summer vacation is a hard time to learn anything useful.
dana

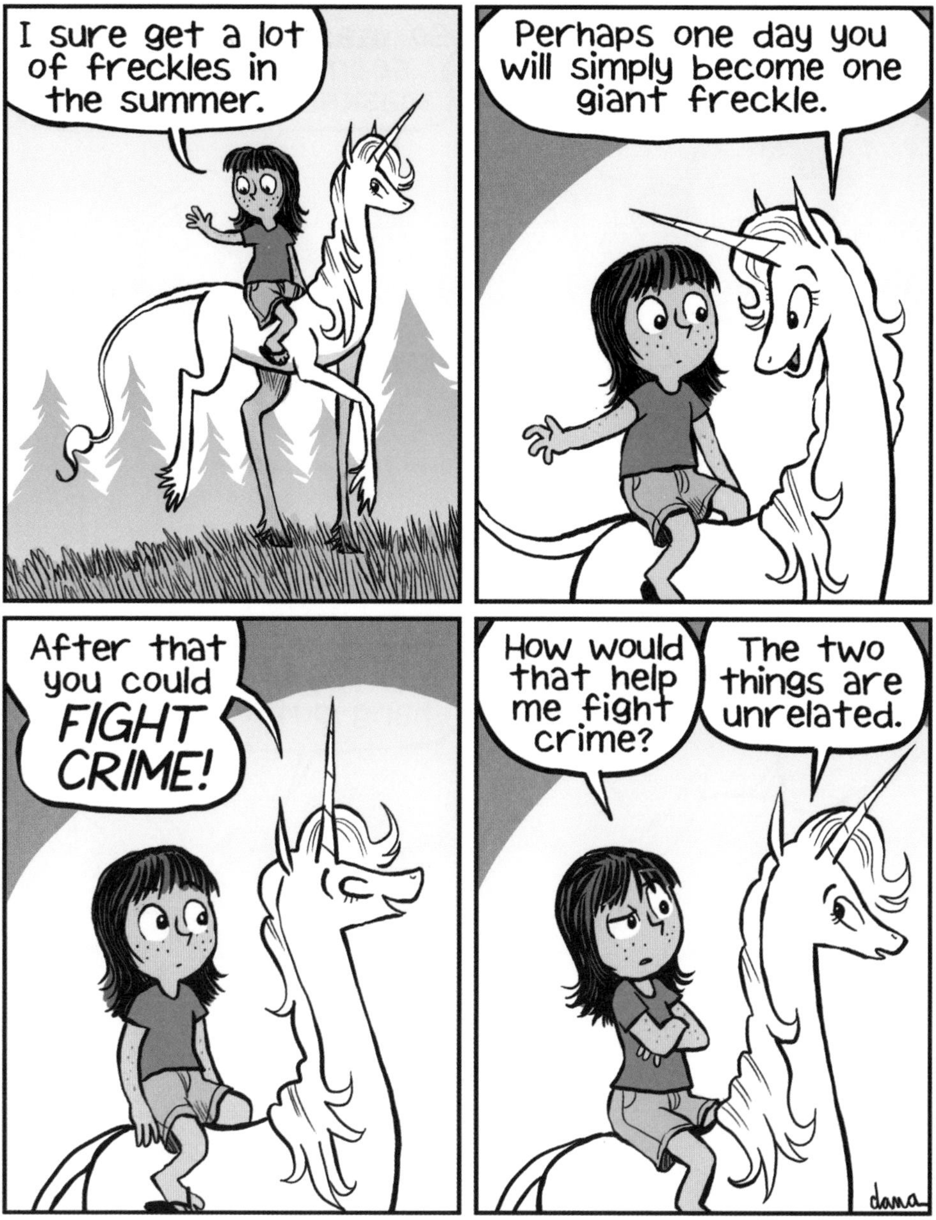
I sure get a lot of freckles in the summer.
Perhaps one day you will simply become one giant freckle.
After that you could FIGHT CRIME!
How would that help me fight crime?
The two things are unrelated.
dana

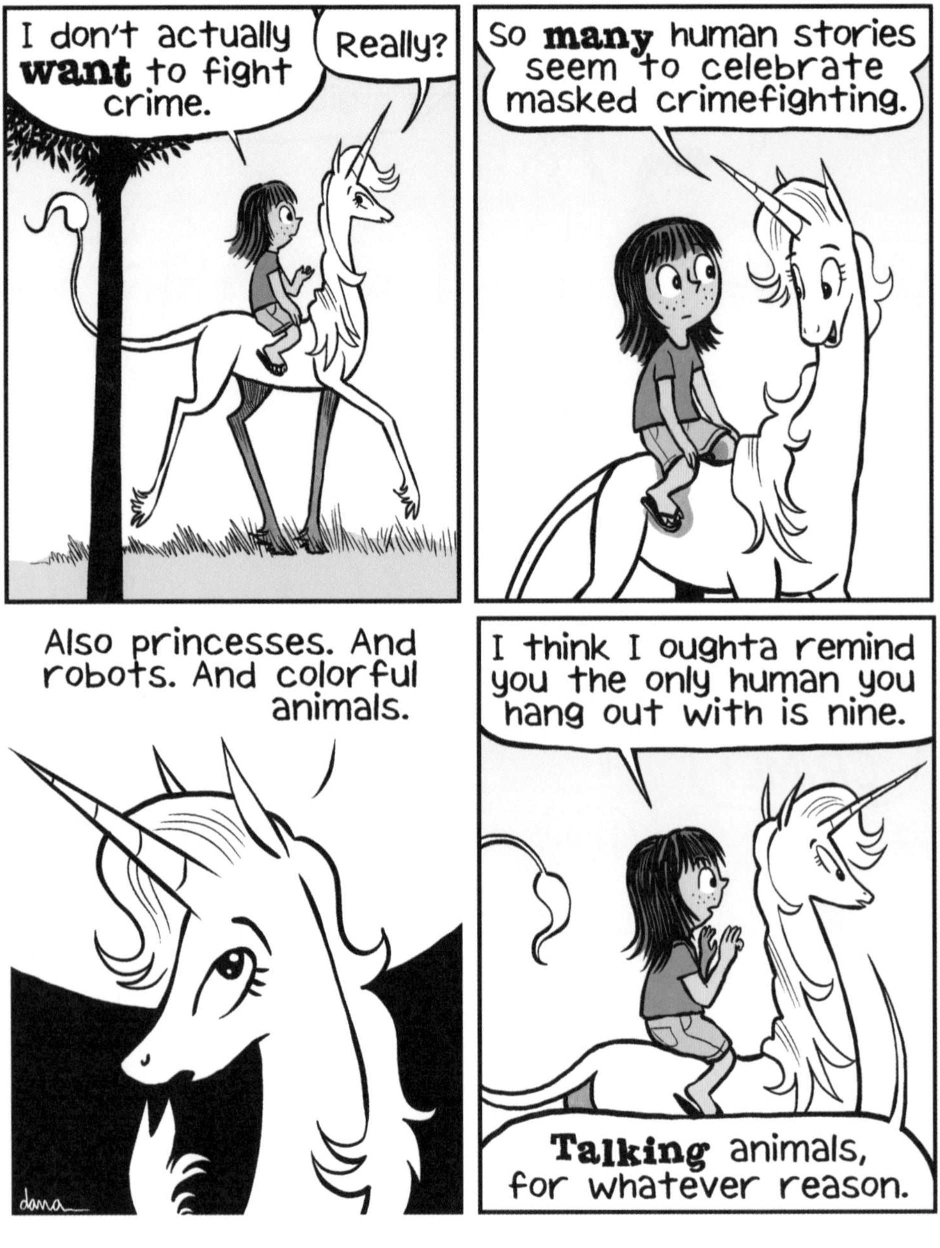
I don't actually **want** to fight crime.
Really?
So **many** human stories seem to celebrate masked crimefighting.
Also princesses. And robots. And colorful animals.
I think I oughta remind you the only human you hang out with is nine.
Talking animals, for whatever reason.
dana

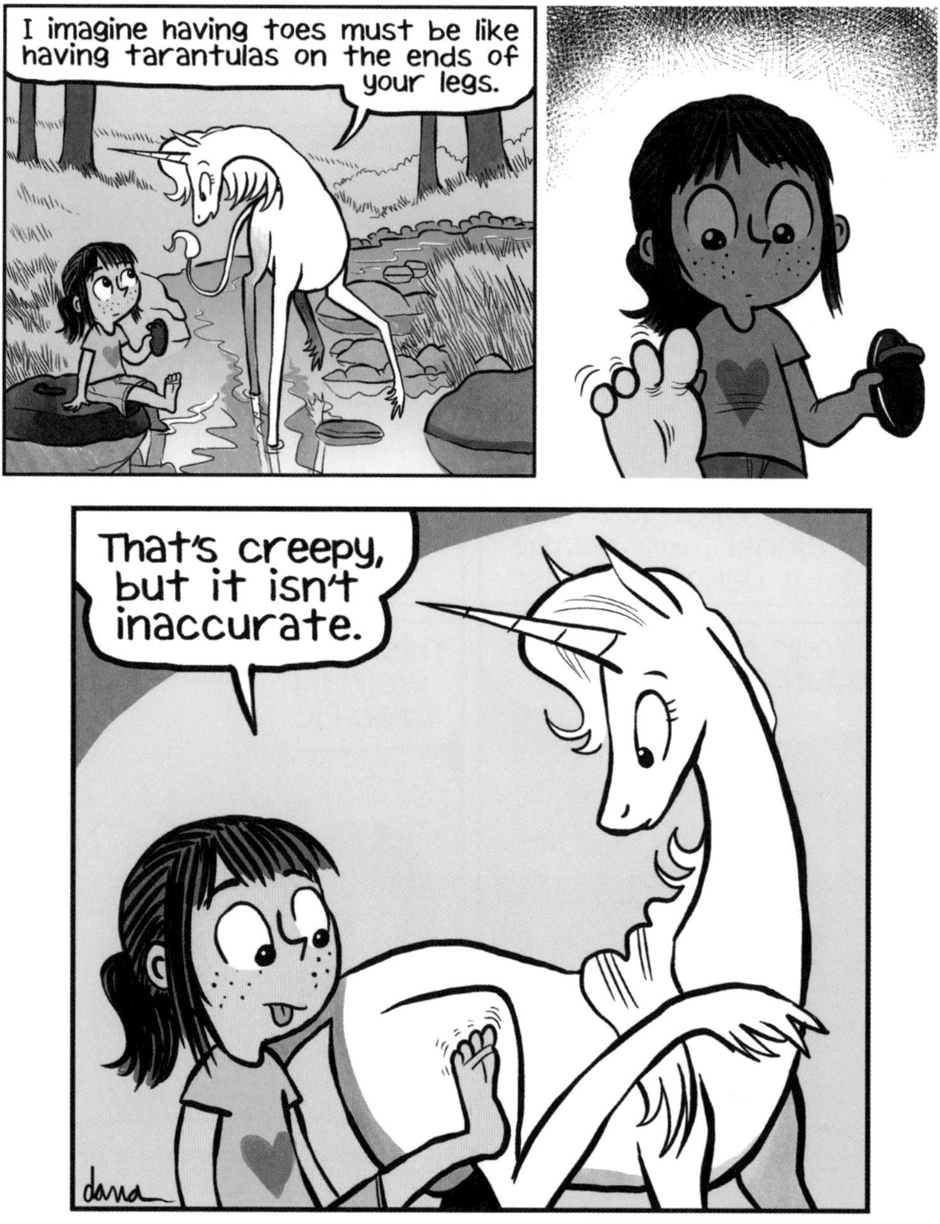
I imagine having toes must be like having tarantulas on the ends of your legs.
That's creepy, but it isn't inaccurate.
dana

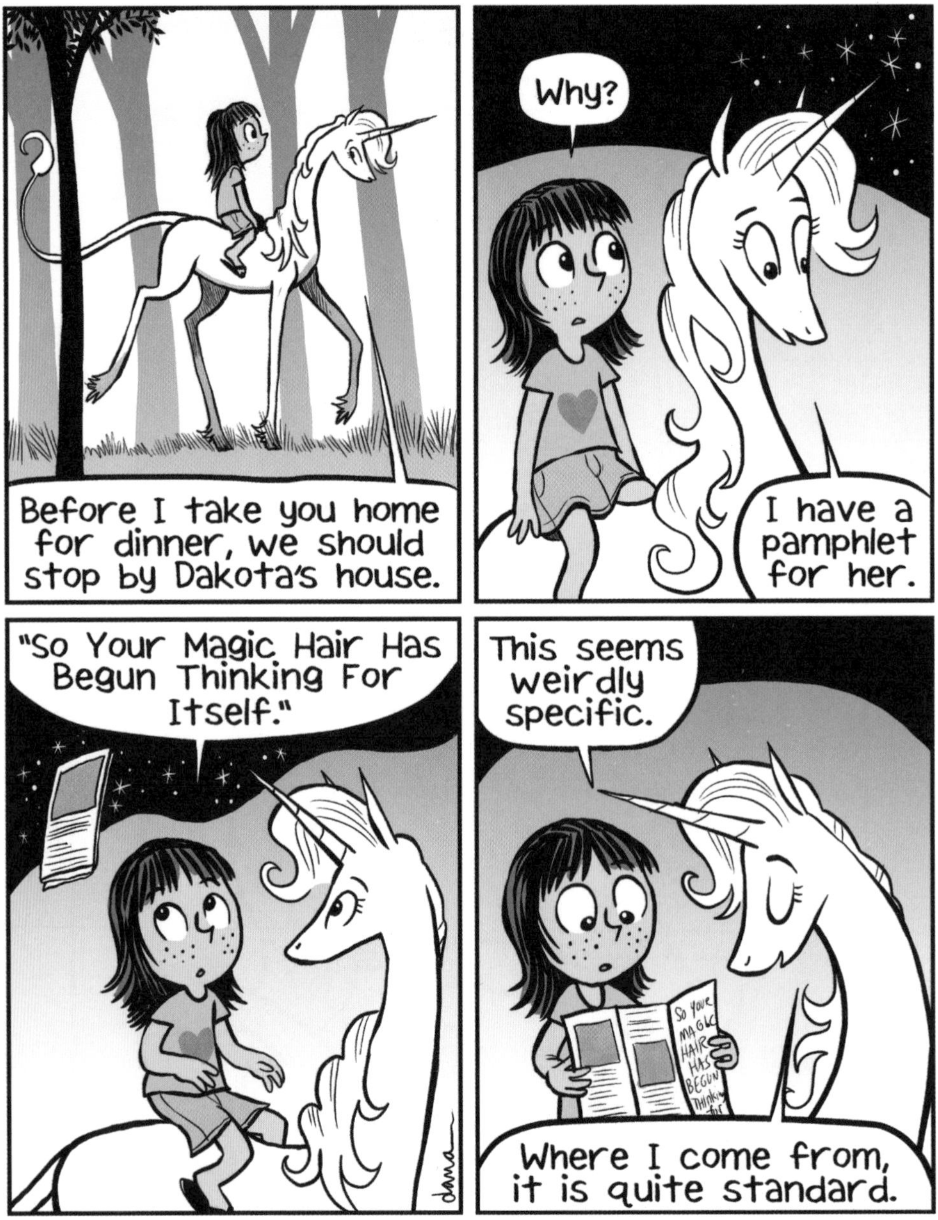
Before I take you home for dinner, we should stop by Dakota's house.
Why?
I have a pamphlet for her.
"So Your Magic Hair Has Begun Thinking For Itself."
This seems weirdly specific.
Where I come from, it is quite standard.

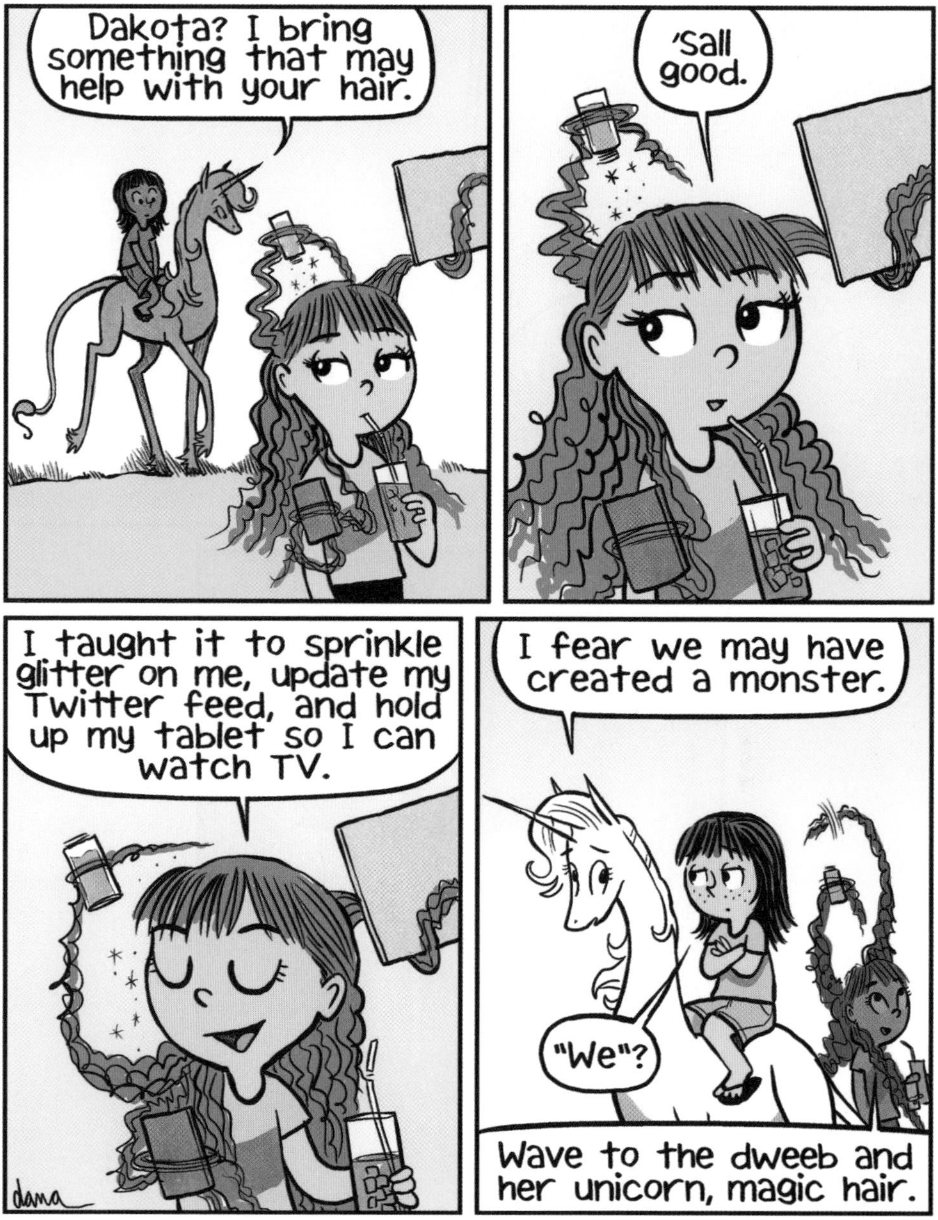
Dakota? I bring something that may help with your hair.
'Sall good.
I taught it to sprinkle glitter on me, update my Twitter feed, and hold up my tablet so I can watch TV.
dana
I fear we may have created a monster.
"We"?
Wave to the dweeb and her unicorn, magic hair.

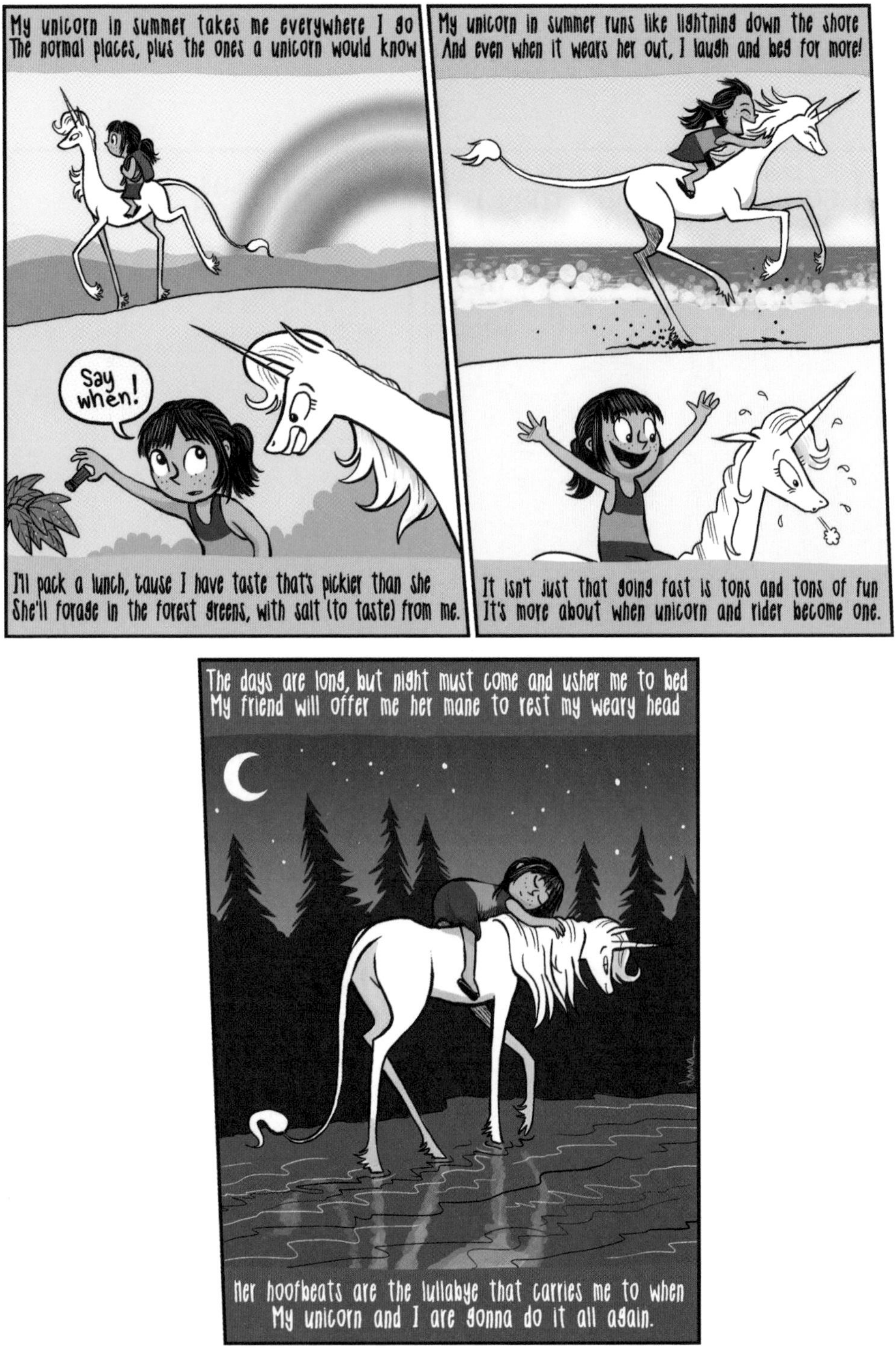
My unicorn in summer takes me everywhere I go
The normal places, plus the ones a unicorn would know
Say when!
I'll pack a lunch, cause I have taste that's pickier than she
She'll forage in the forest greens, with salt (to taste) from me.
My unicorn in summer runs like lightning down the shore
And even when it wears her out, I laugh and beg for more!
It isn't just that going fast is tons and tons of fun
It's more about when unicorn and rider become one.
The days are long, but night must come and usher me to bed
My friend will offer me her mane to rest my weary head
Her hoofbeats are the lullabye that carries me to when
My unicorn and I are gonna do it all again.

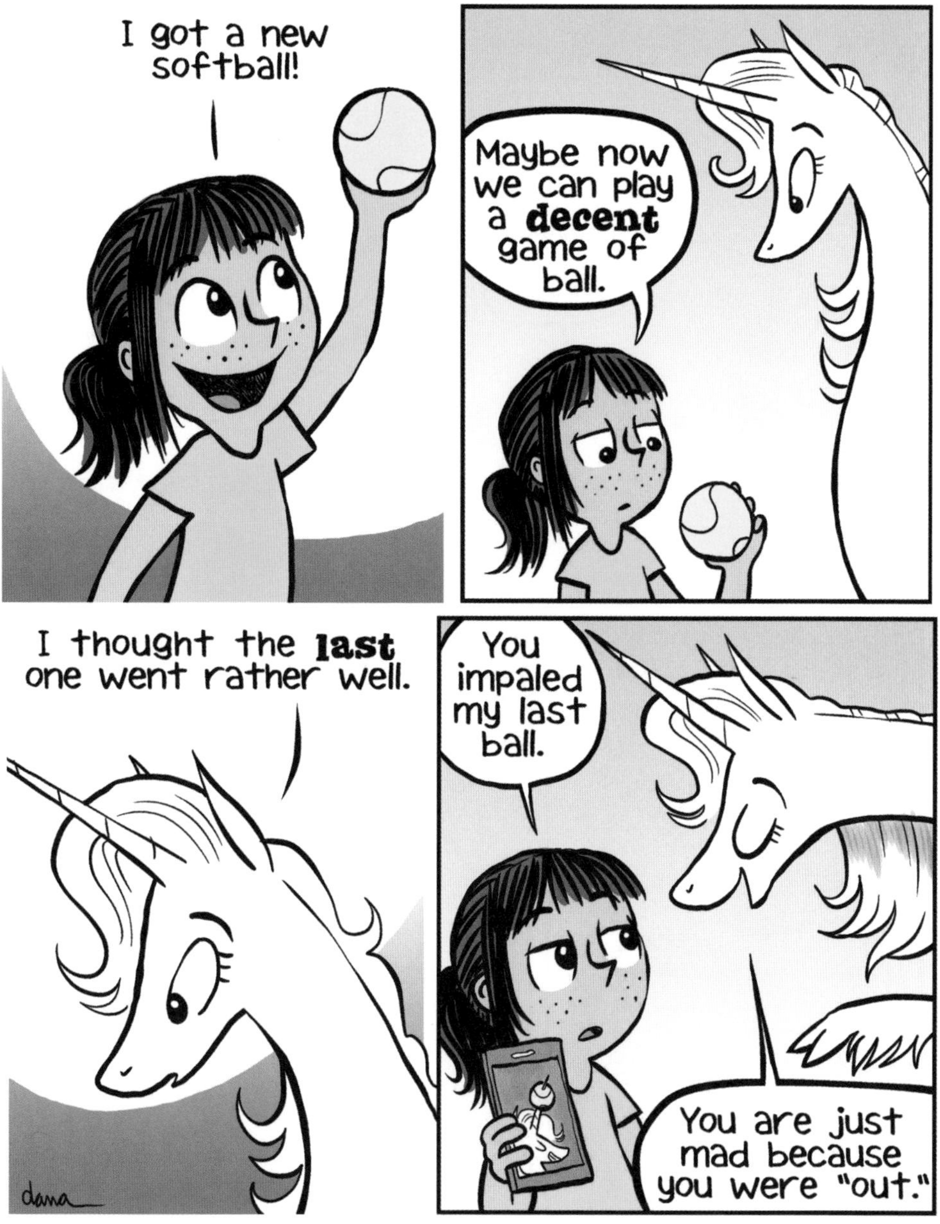
I got a new softball!
Maybe now we can play a **decent** game of ball.
I thought the **last** one went rather well.
You impaled my last ball.
You are just mad because you were "out."
dana

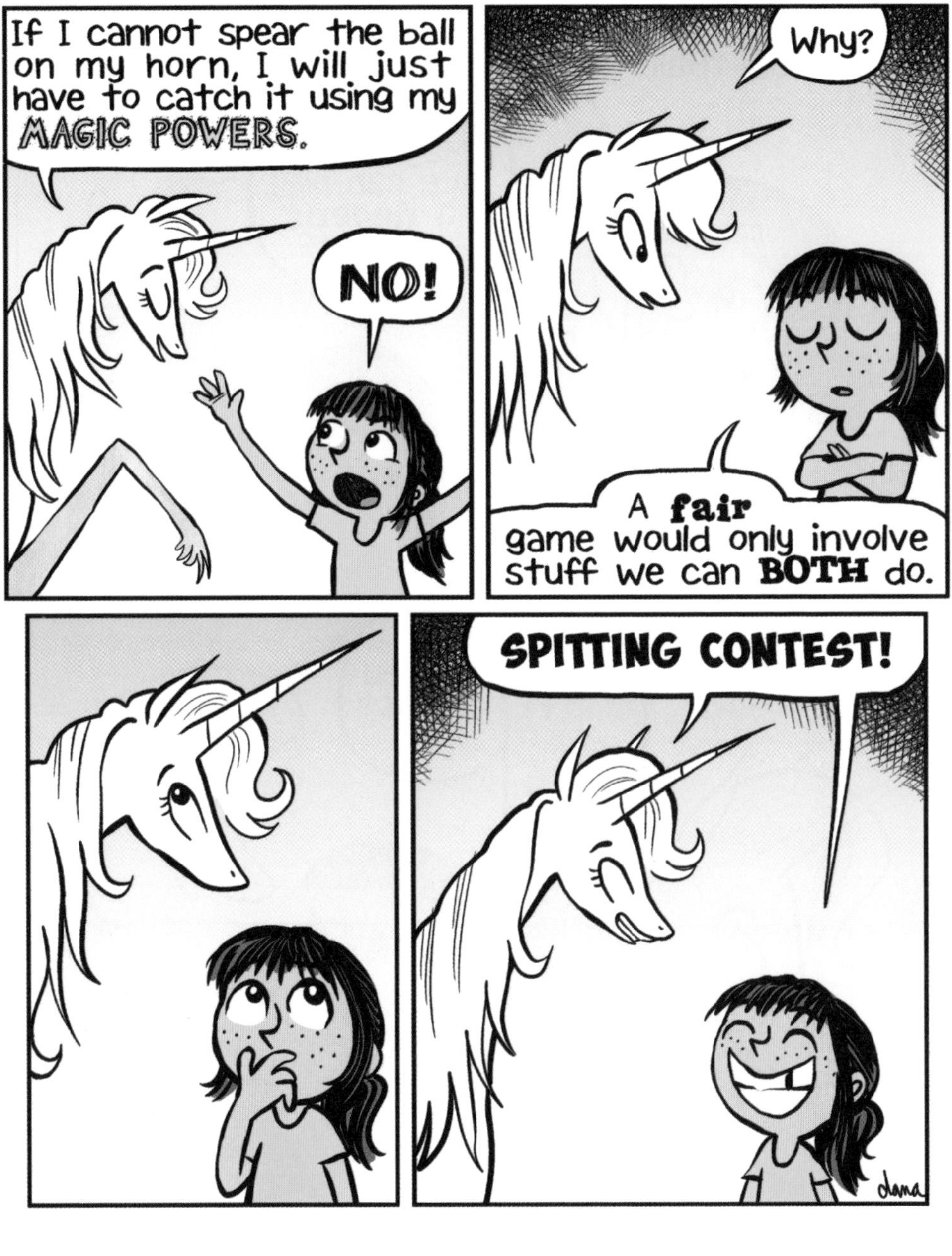

If I cannot spear the ball on my horn, I will just have to catch it using my MAGIC POWERS.
NO!
Why?
A fair game would only involve stuff we can BOTH do.
SPITTING CONTEST!
dana

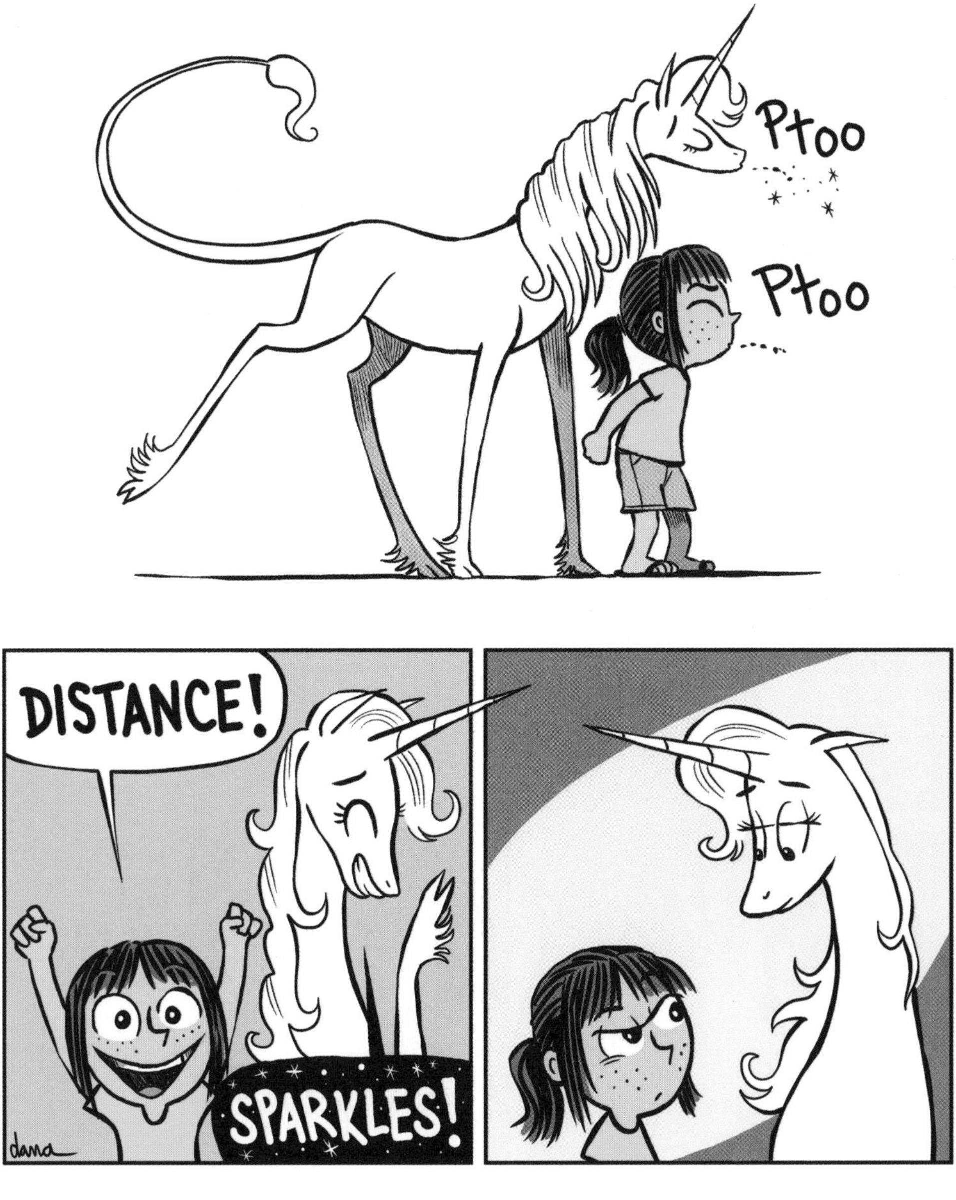
Ptoo
Ptoo
DISTANCE!
SPARKLES!
dana

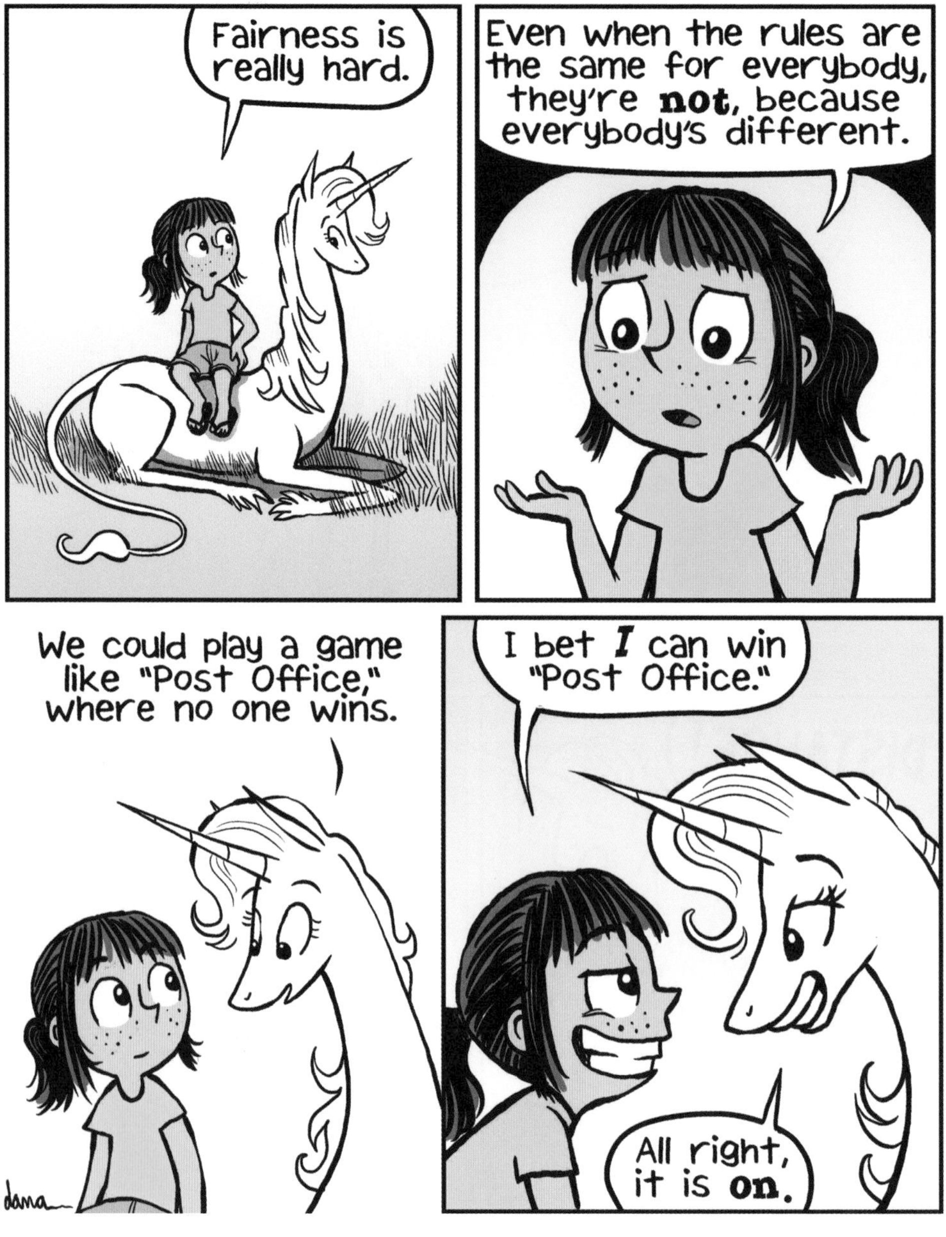

Fairness is really hard.
Even when the rules are the same for everybody, they're **not**, because everybody's different.
We could play a game like "Post Office," where no one wins.
I bet ***I*** can win "Post Office."
All right, it is **on**.
dana

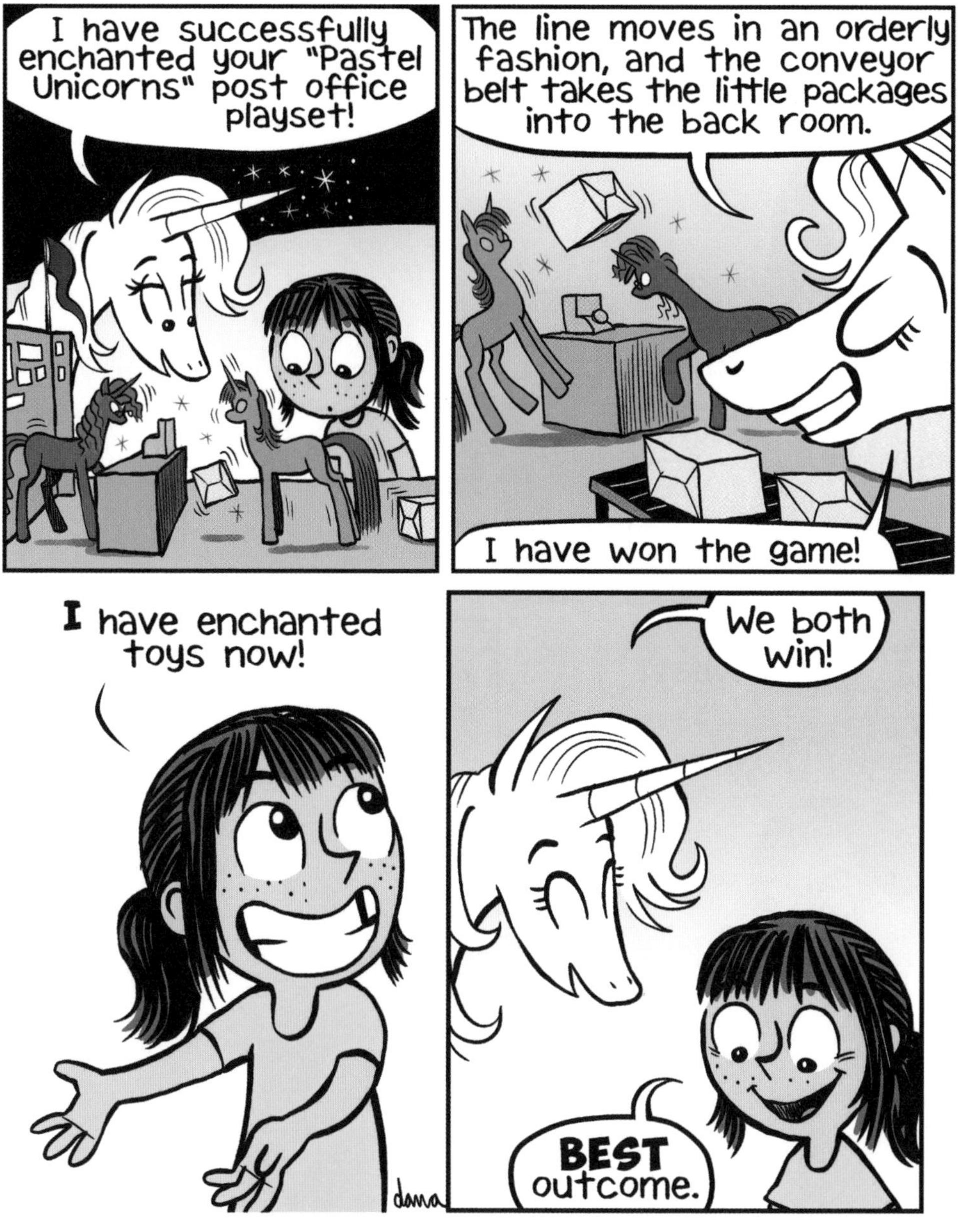
I have successfully enchanted your "Pastel Unicorns" post office playset!
The line moves in an orderly fashion, and the conveyor belt takes the little packages into the back room.
I have won the game!
I have enchanted toys now!
We both win!
BEST outcome.
dana

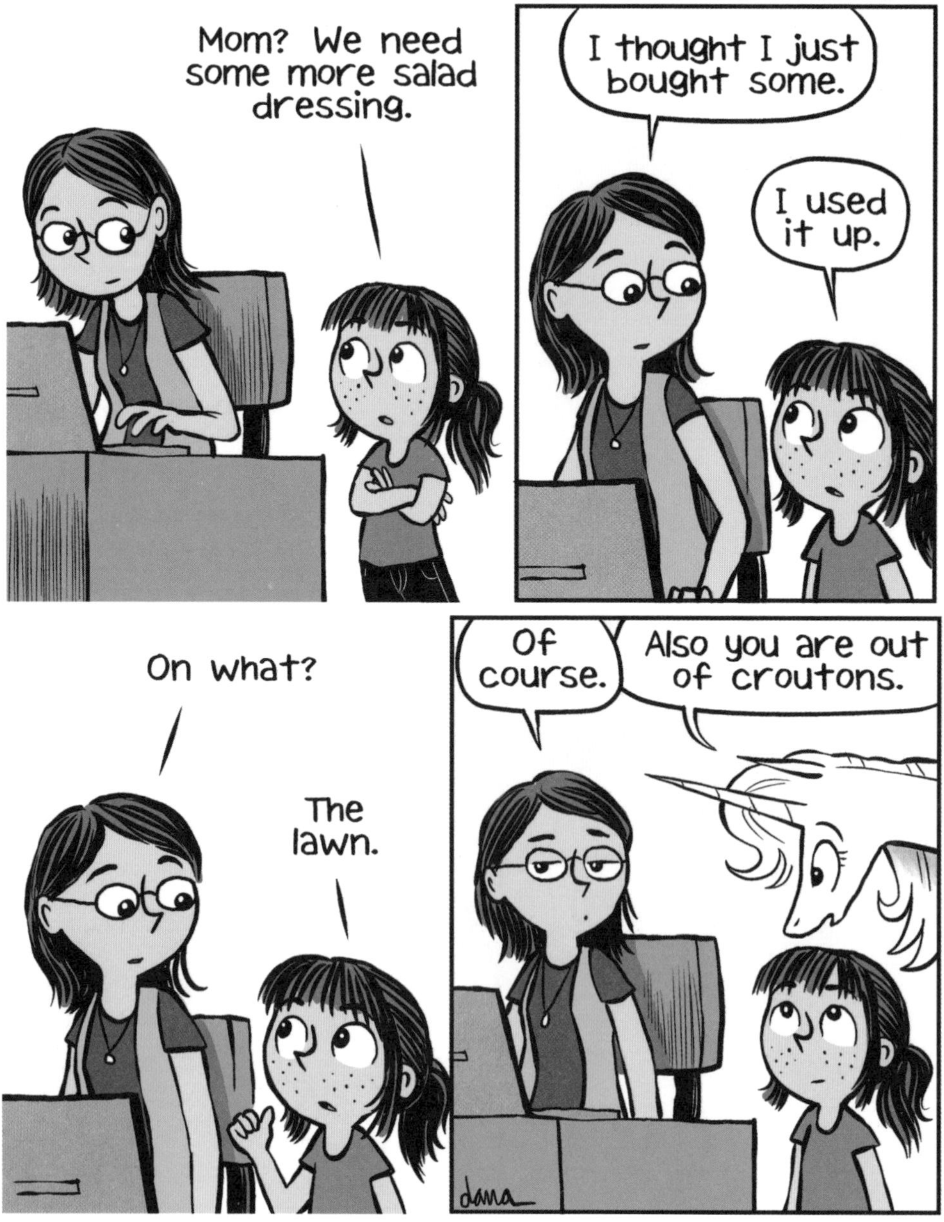
Mom? We need some more salad dressing.
I thought I just bought some.
I used it up.
On what?
The lawn.
Of course.
Also you are out of croutons.
dana

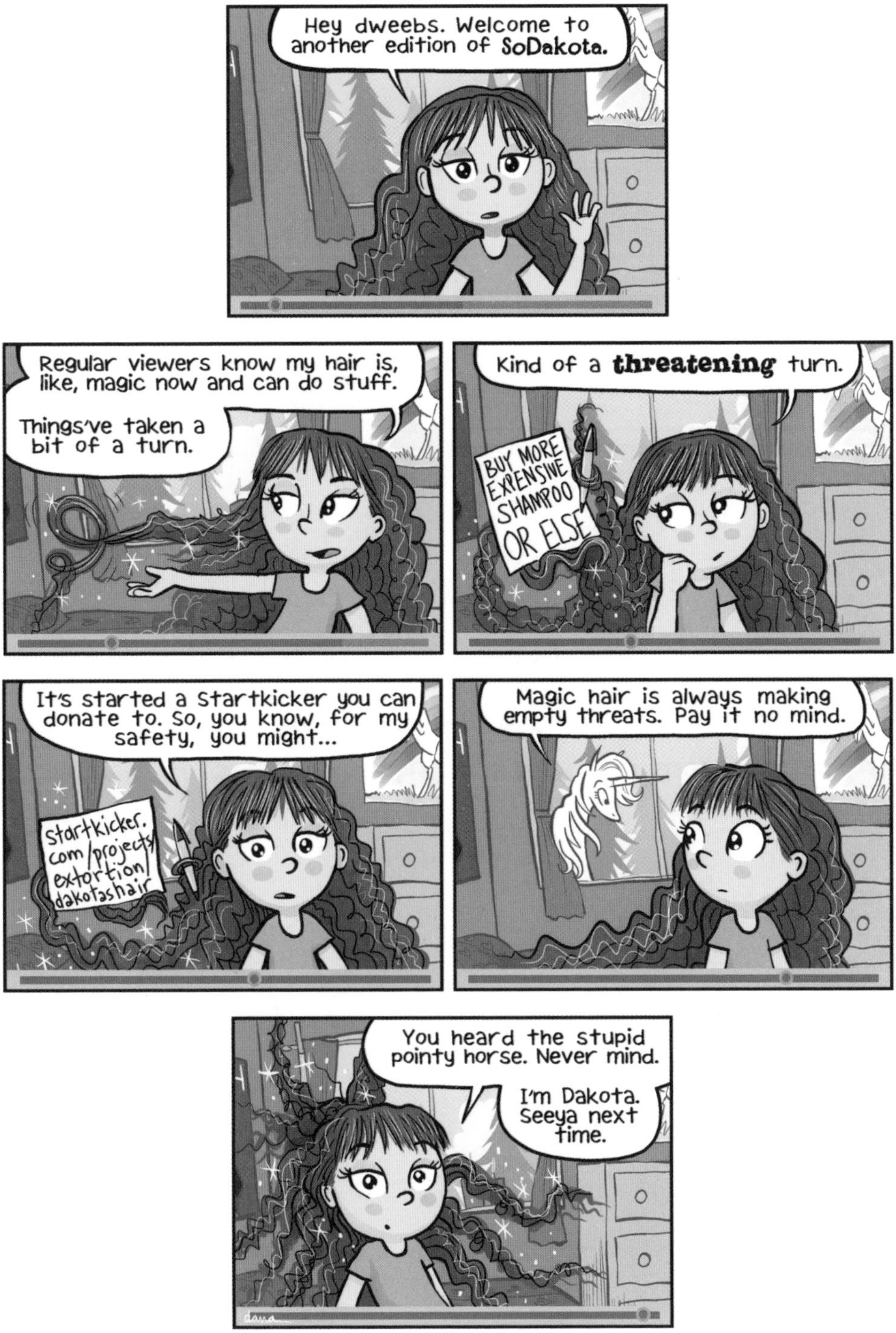
Hey dweebs. Welcome to another edition of SoDakota.
Regular viewers know my hair is, like, magic now and can do stuff.
Things've taken a bit of a turn.
Kind of a threatening turn.
BUY MORE EXPENSIVE SHAMPOO OR ELSE
It's started a Startkicker you can donate to. So, you know, for my safety, you might...
startkicker.com/projects/extortion/dakotashair
Magic hair is always making empty threats. Pay it no mind.
You heard the stupid pointy horse. Never mind.
I'm Dakota. Seeya next time.
dana

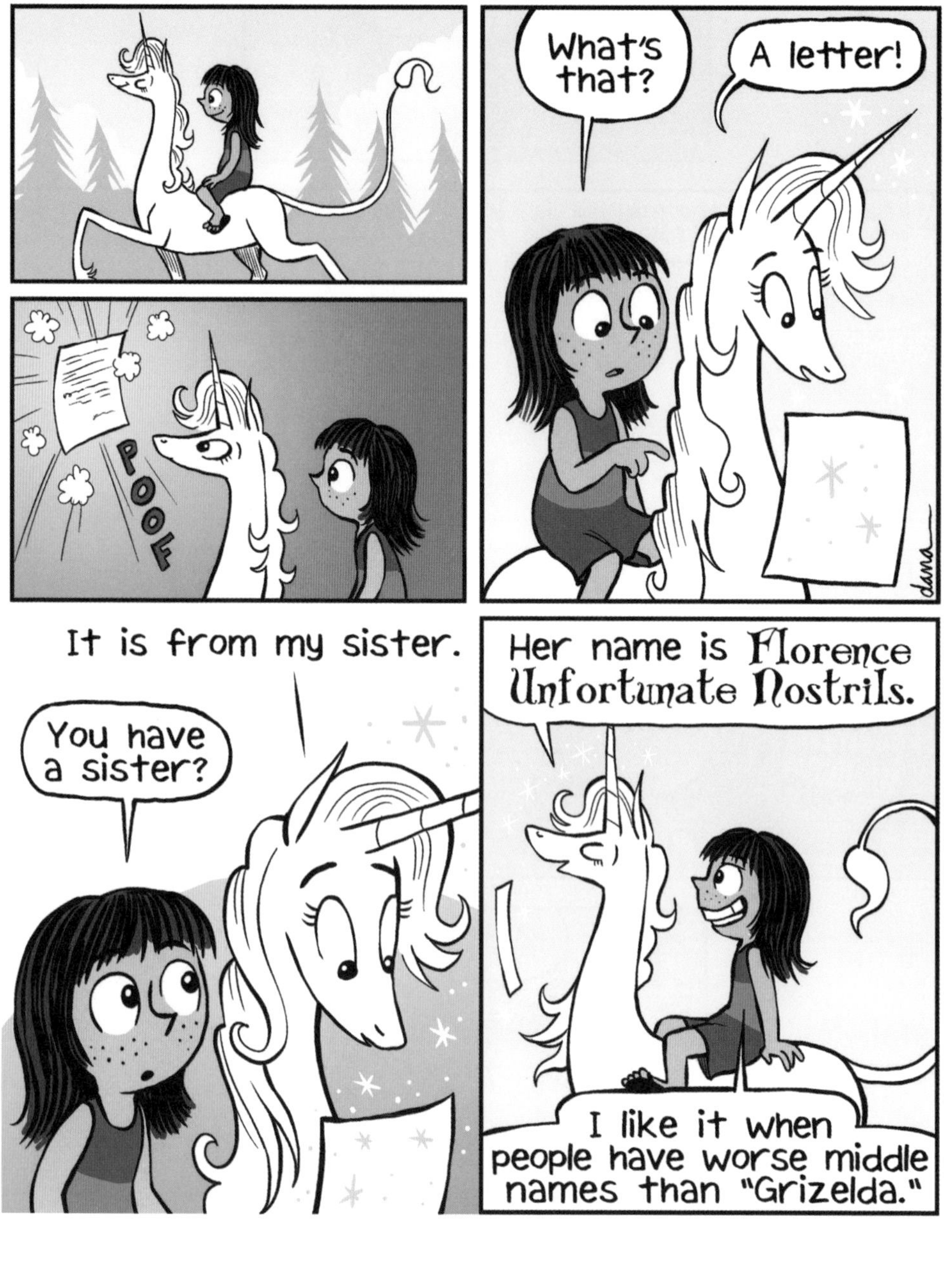
POOF
What's that?
A letter!
It is from my sister.
You have a sister?
Her name is Florence Unfortunate Nostrils.
I like it when people have worse middle names than "Grizelda."
dana

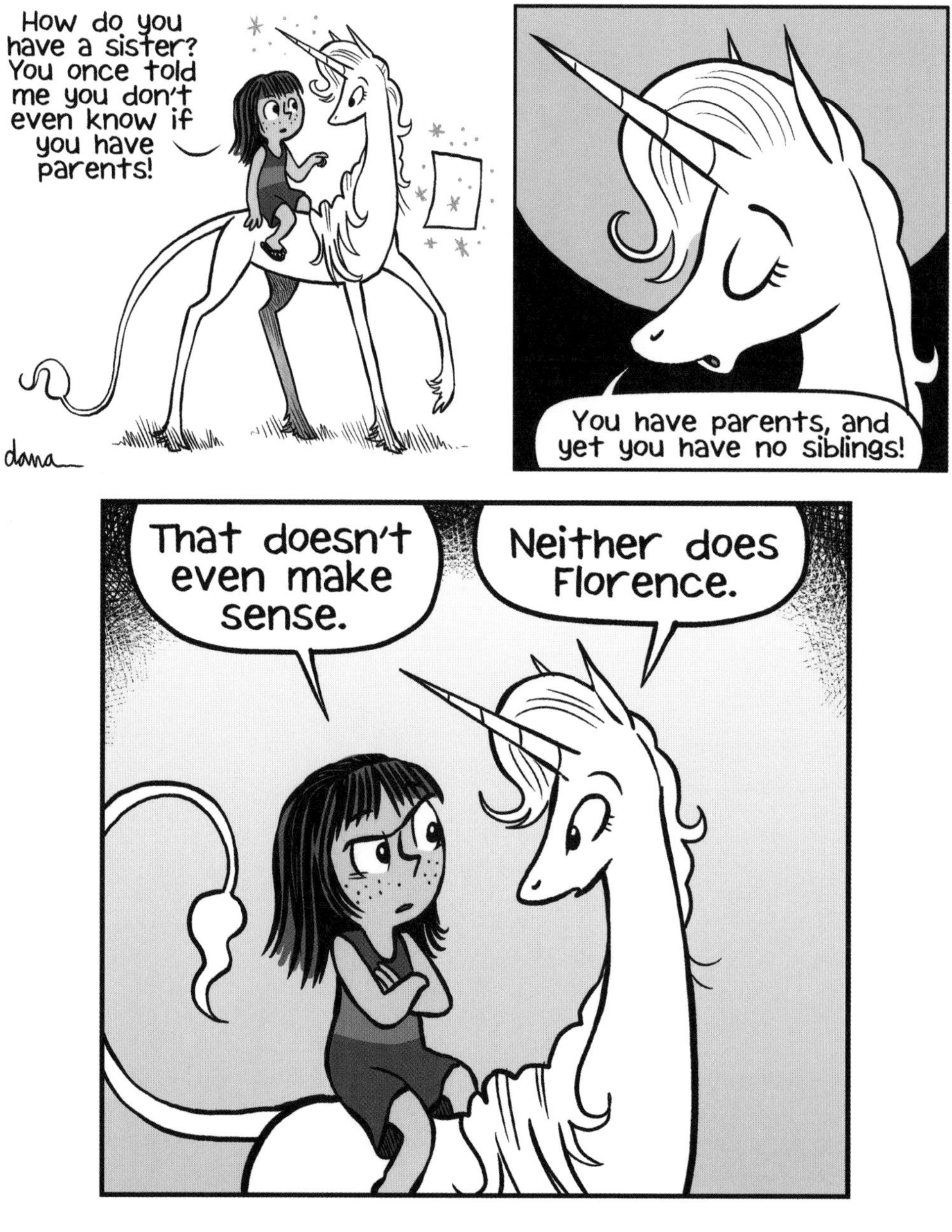
How do you have a sister? You once told me you don't even know if you have parents!
dana
You have parents, and yet you have no siblings!
That doesn't even make sense.
Neither does Florence.

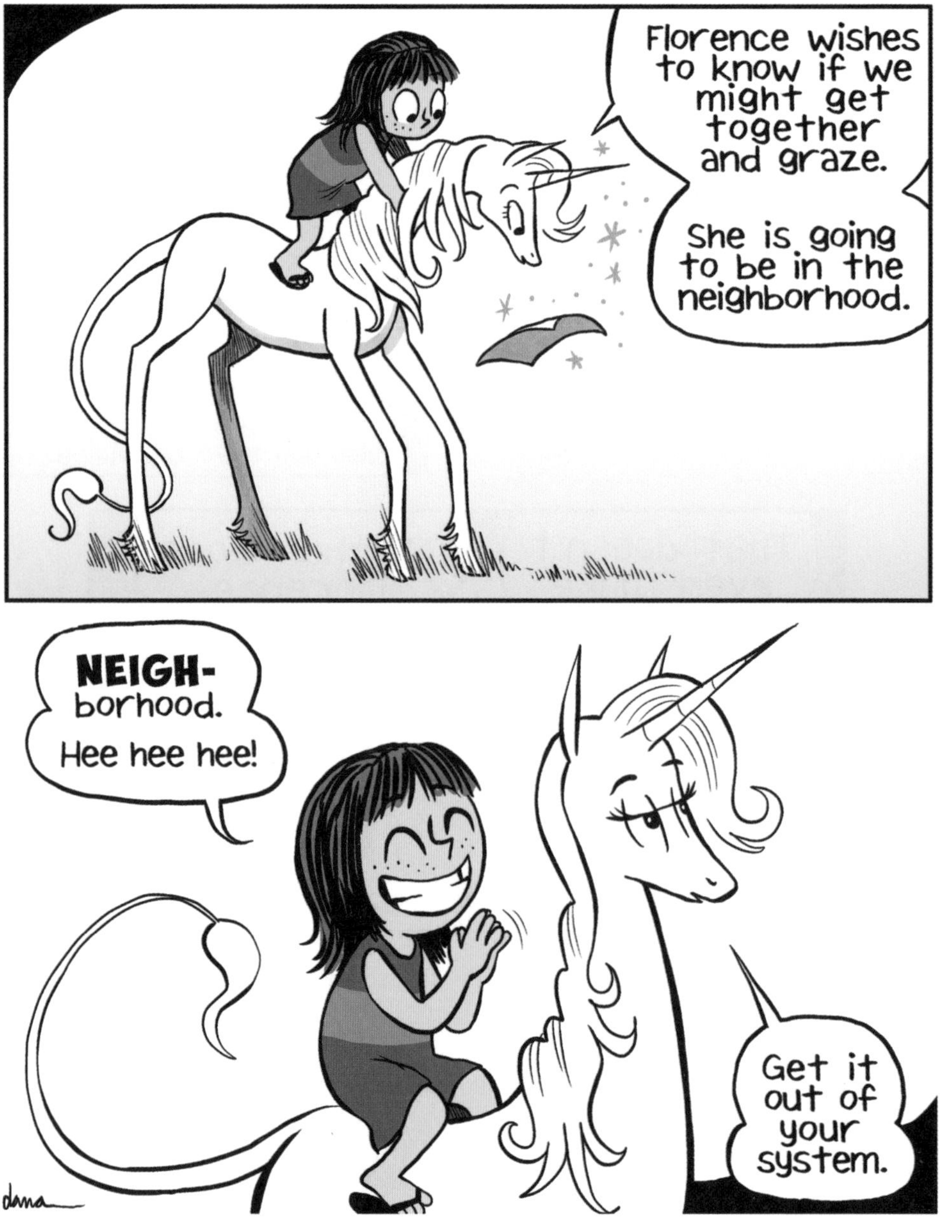
Florence wishes to know if we might get together and graze.
She is going to be in the neighborhood.
NEIGH-borhood.
Hee hee hee!
Get it out of your system.
dana

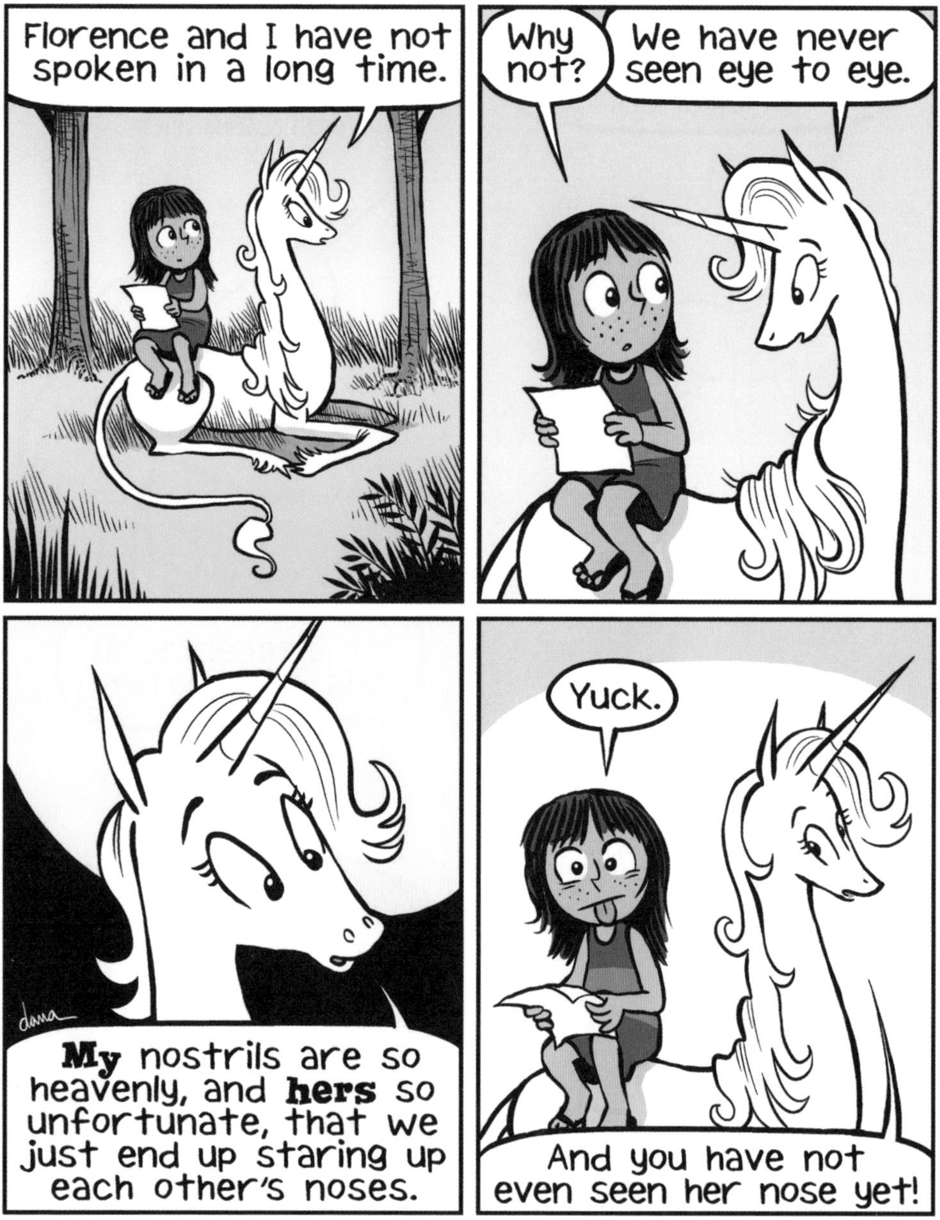
Florence and I have not spoken in a long time.
Why not?
We have never seen eye to eye.
My nostrils are so heavenly, and **hers** so unfortunate, that we just end up staring up each other's noses.
dana
Yuck.
And you have not even seen her nose yet!

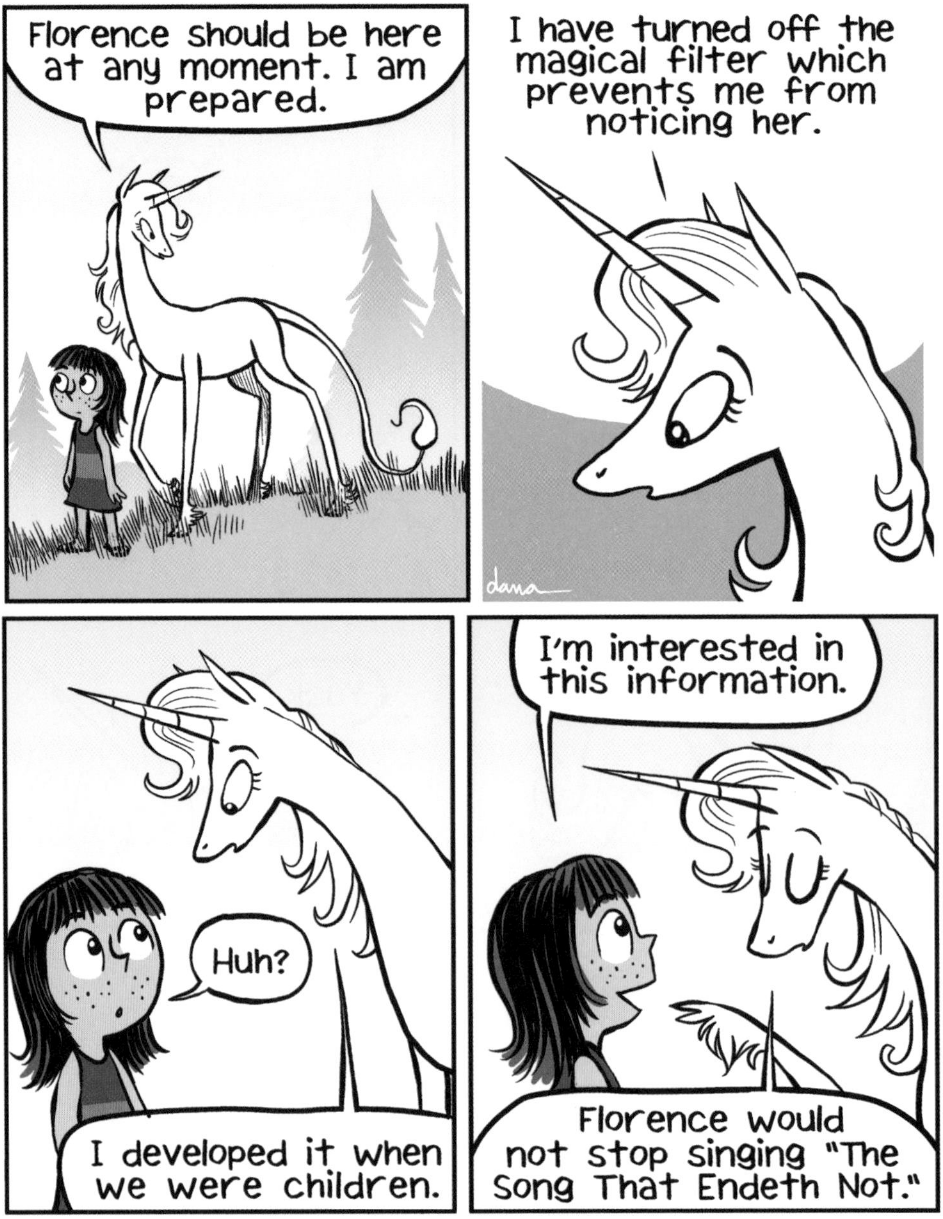
Florence should be here at any moment. I am prepared.
I have turned off the magical filter which prevents me from noticing her.
dana
Huh?
I developed it when we were children.
I'm interested in this information.
Florence would not stop singing "The Song That Endeth Not."

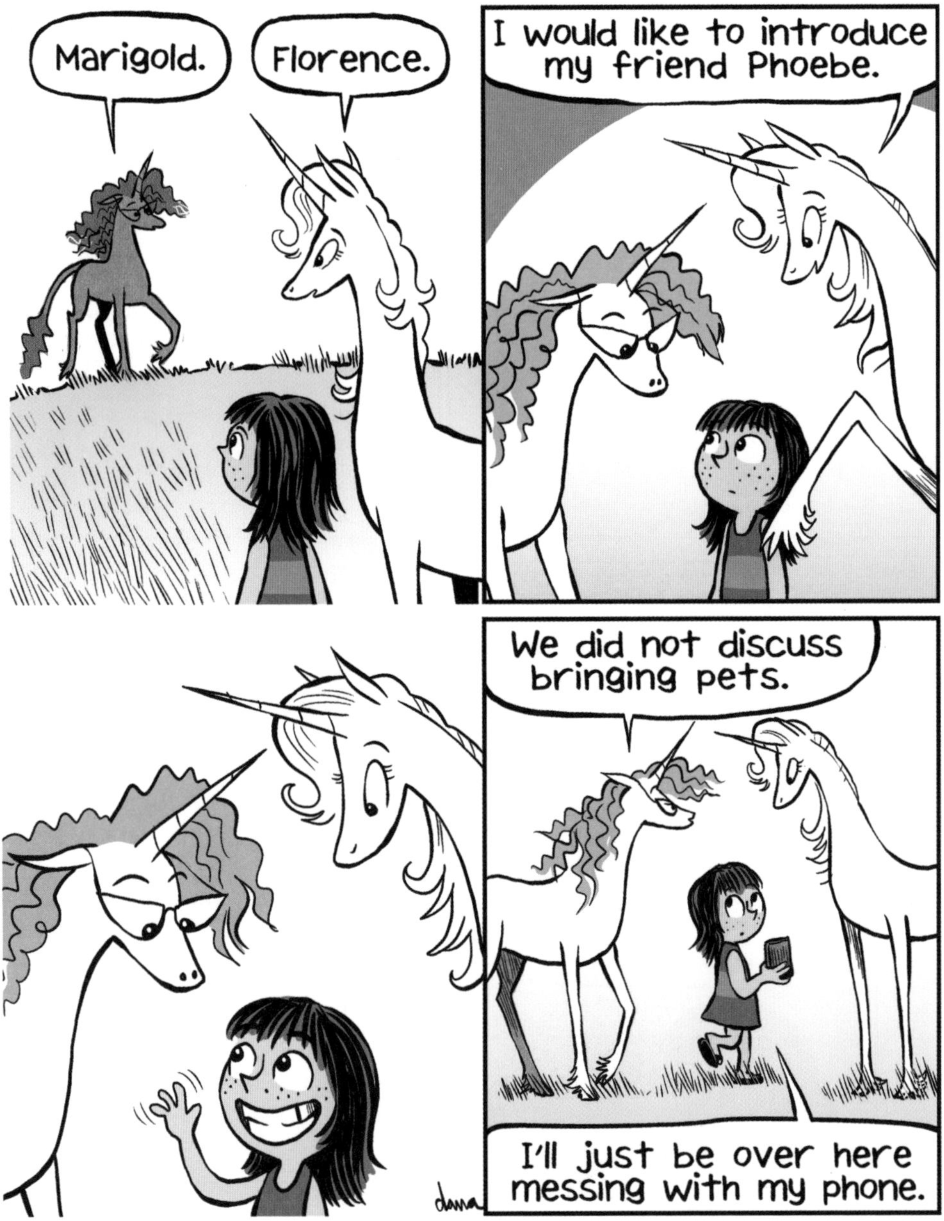
Marigold.
Florence.
I would like to introduce my friend Phoebe.
We did not discuss bringing pets.
I'll just be over here messing with my phone.
dana

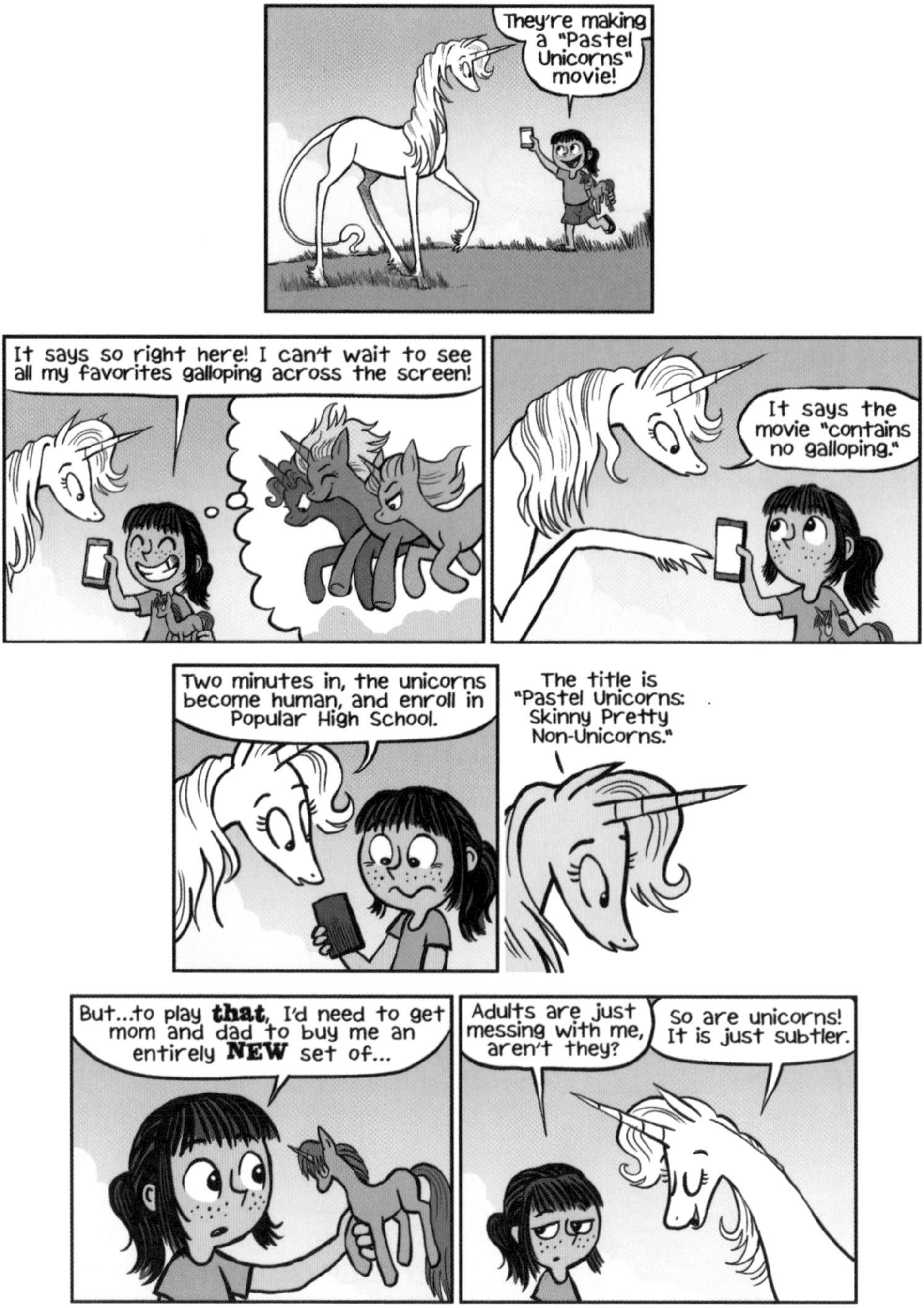
They're making a "Pastel Unicorns" movie!
It says so right here! I can't wait to see all my favorites galloping across the screen!
It says the movie "contains no galloping."
Two minutes in, the unicorns become human, and enroll in Popular High School.
The title is "Pastel Unicorns: Skinny Pretty Non-Unicorns."
But...to play **that**, I'd need to get mom and dad to buy me an entirely **NEW** set of...
Adults are just messing with me, aren't they?
So are unicorns! It is just subtler.

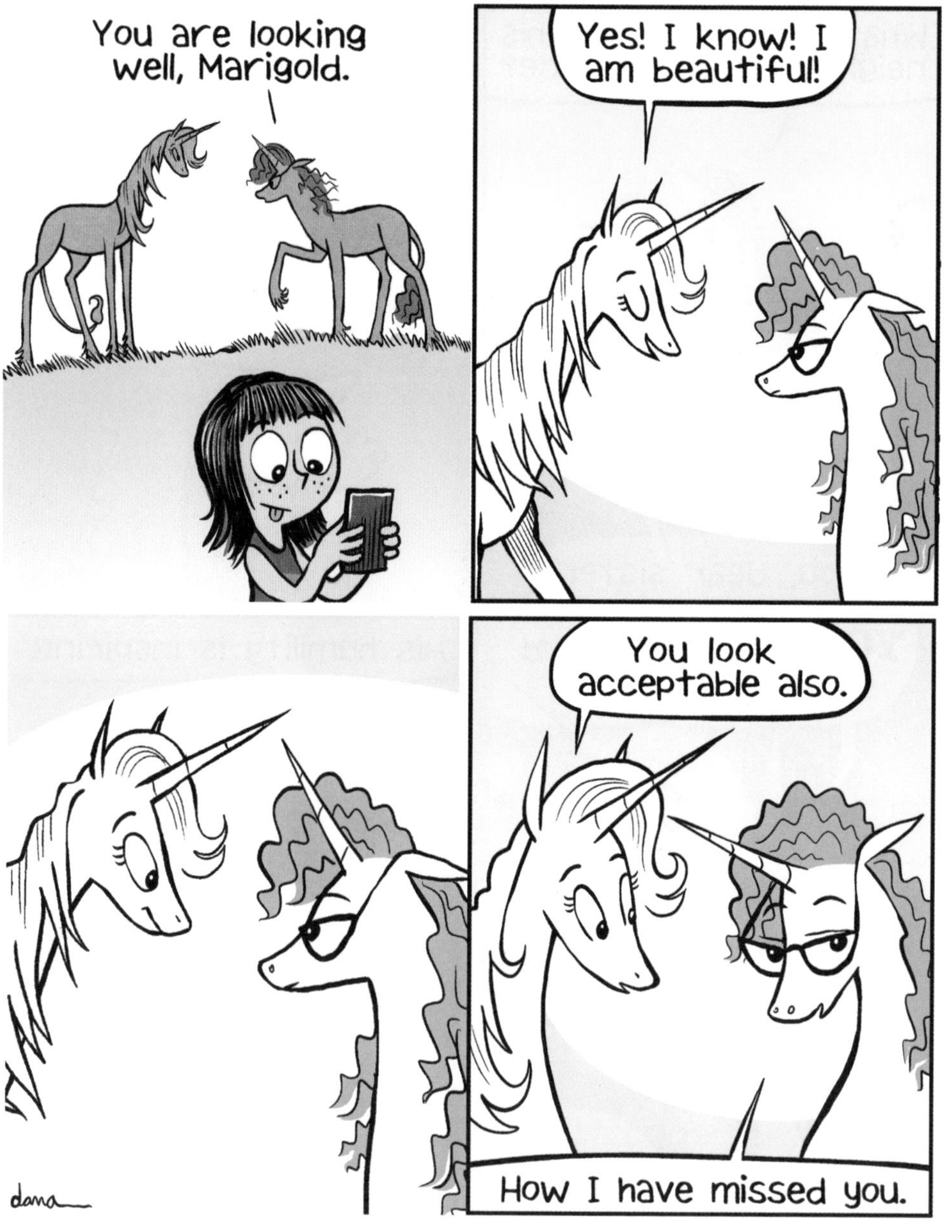
You are looking well, Marigold.
Yes! I know! I am beautiful!
You look acceptable also.
How I have missed you.
dana

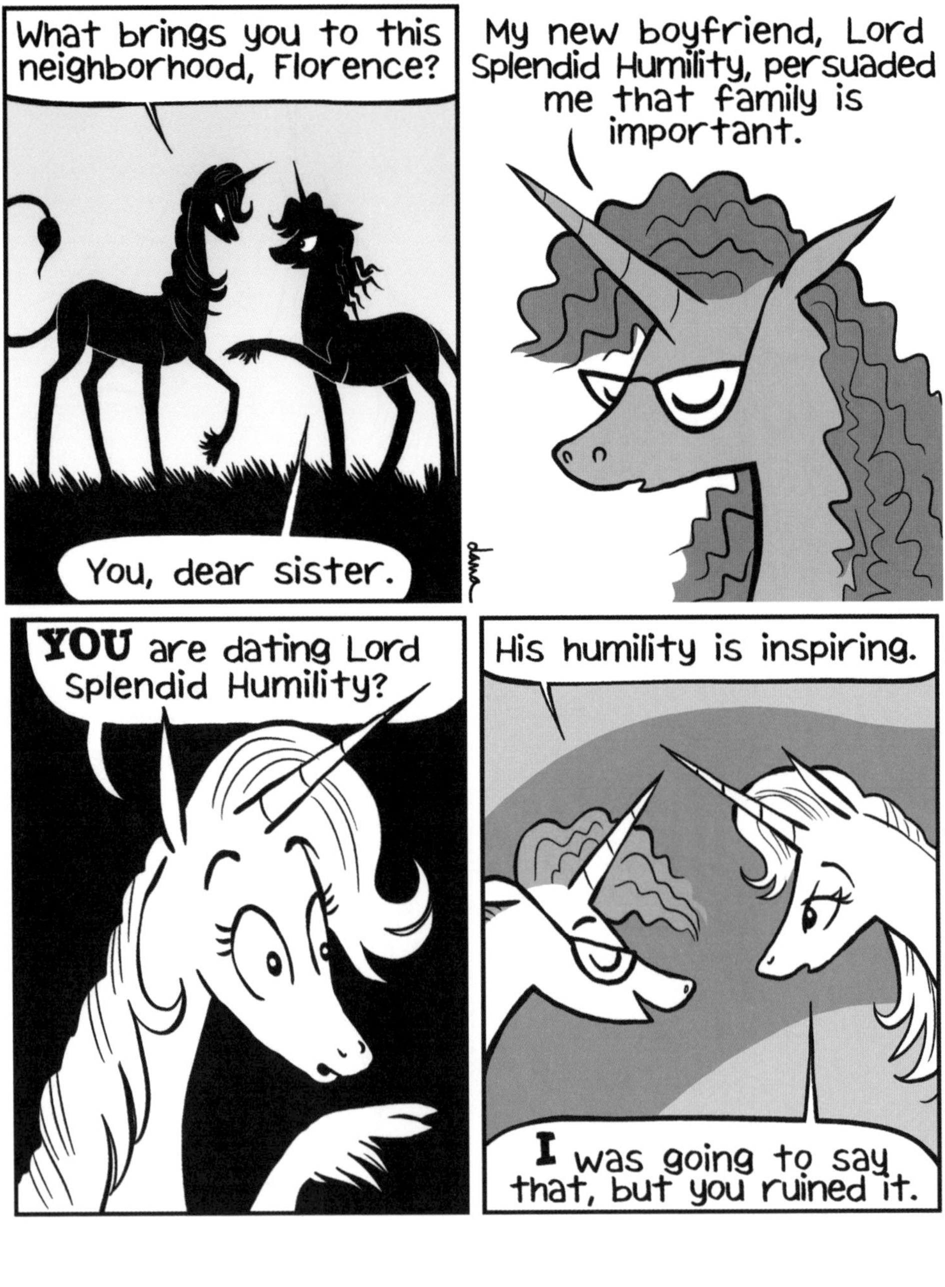
What brings you to this neighborhood, Florence?
You, dear sister.
My new boyfriend, Lord Splendid Humility, persuaded me that family is important.
YOU are dating Lord Splendid Humility?
His humility is inspiring.
I was going to say that, but you ruined it.

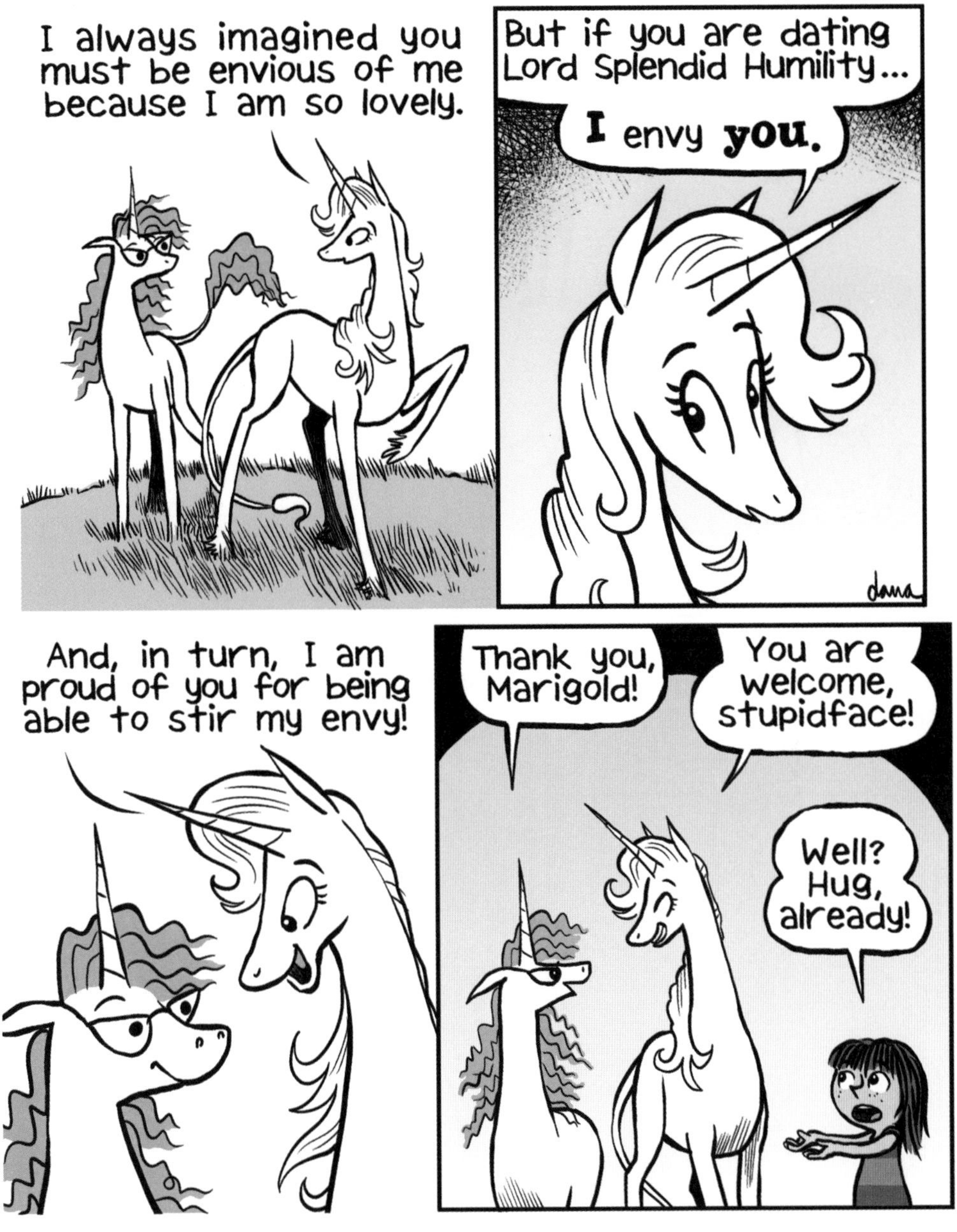
I always imagined you must be envious of me because I am so lovely.
But if you are dating Lord Splendid Humility...
I envy **you**.
dana
And, in turn, I am proud of you for being able to stir my envy!
Thank you, Marigold!
You are welcome, stupidface!
Well? Hug, already!

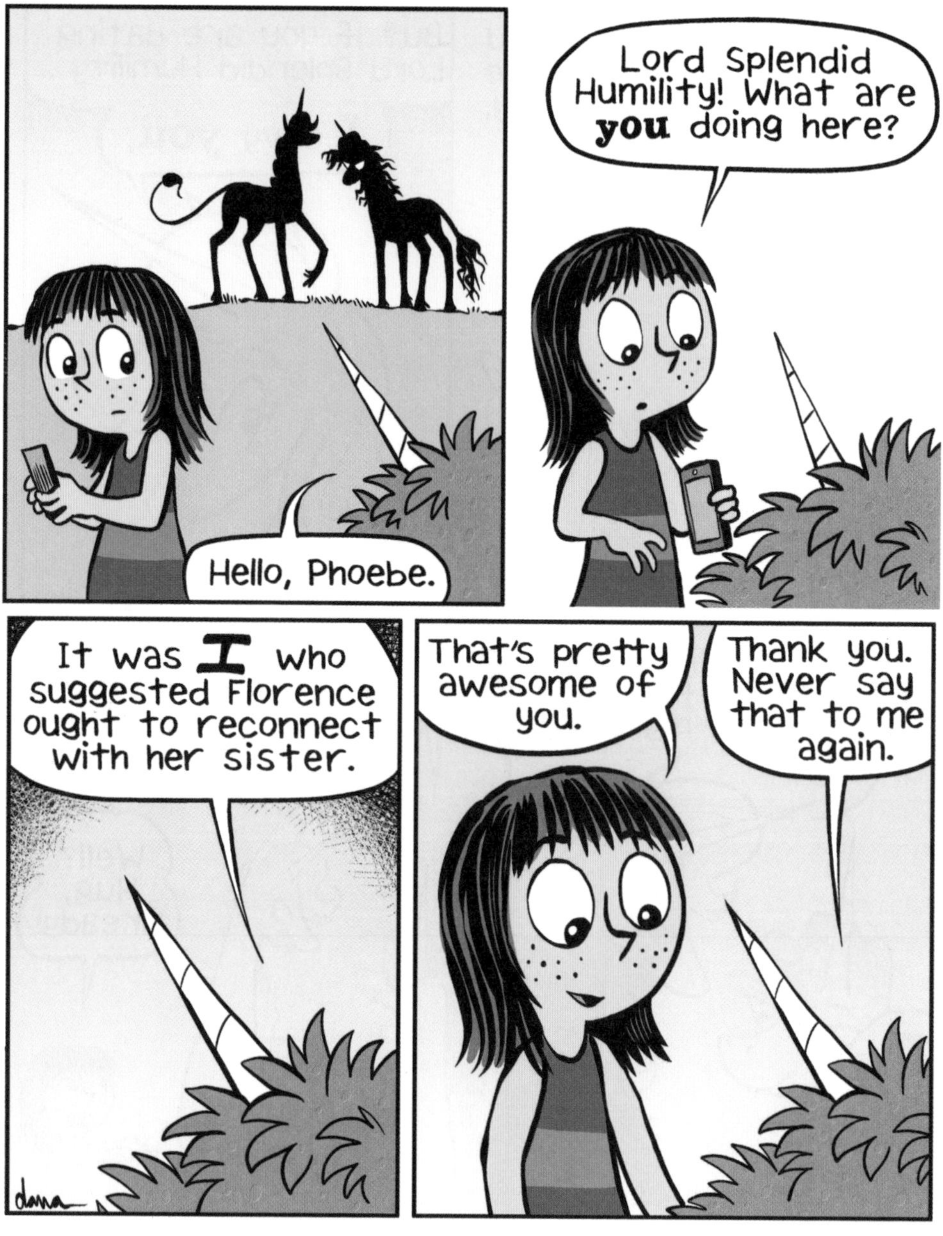
Hello, Phoebe.
Lord Splendid Humility! What are **you** doing here?
It was **I** who suggested Florence ought to reconnect with her sister.
That's pretty awesome of you.
Thank you. Never say that to me again.

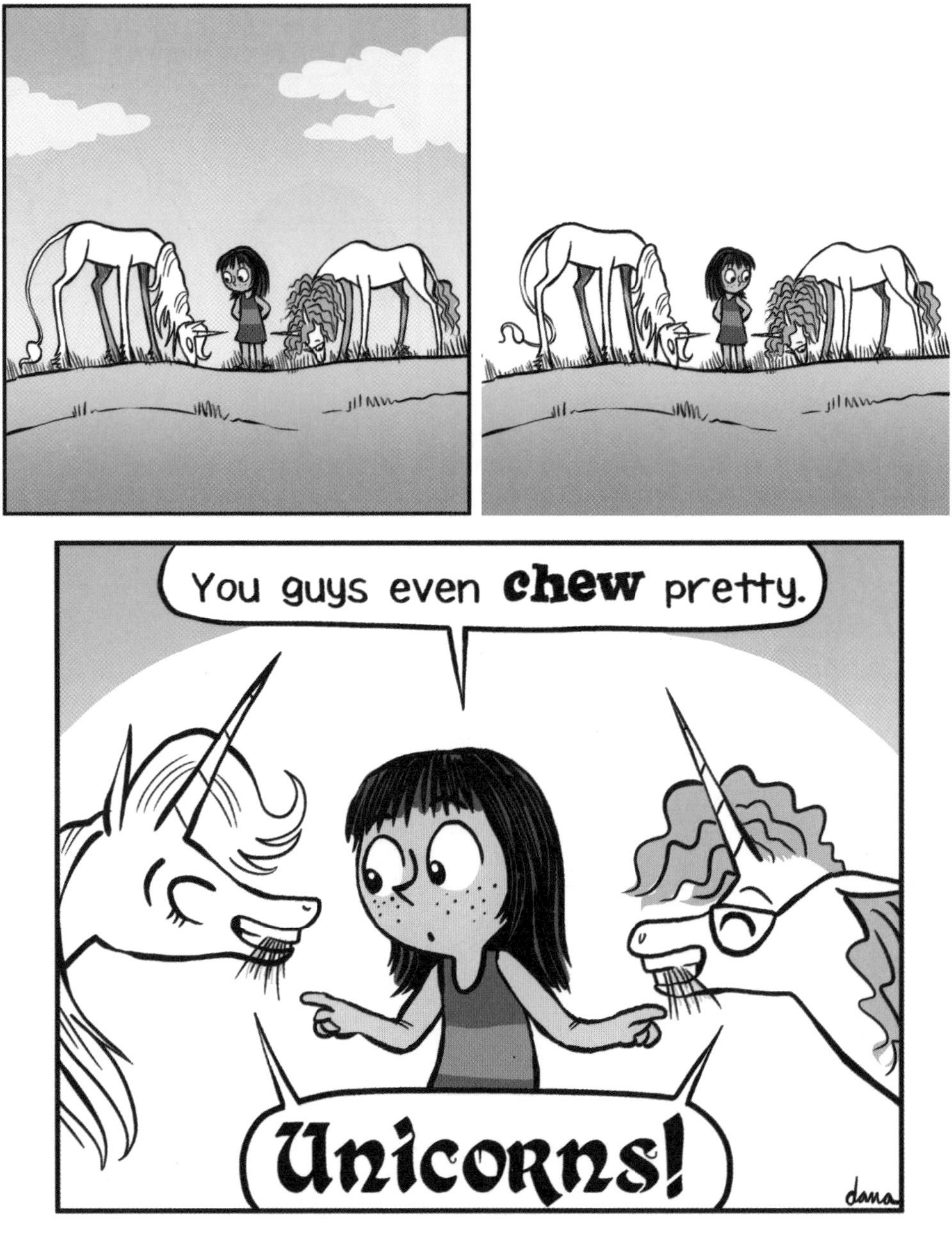
You guys even **chew** pretty.
Unicorns!
dana

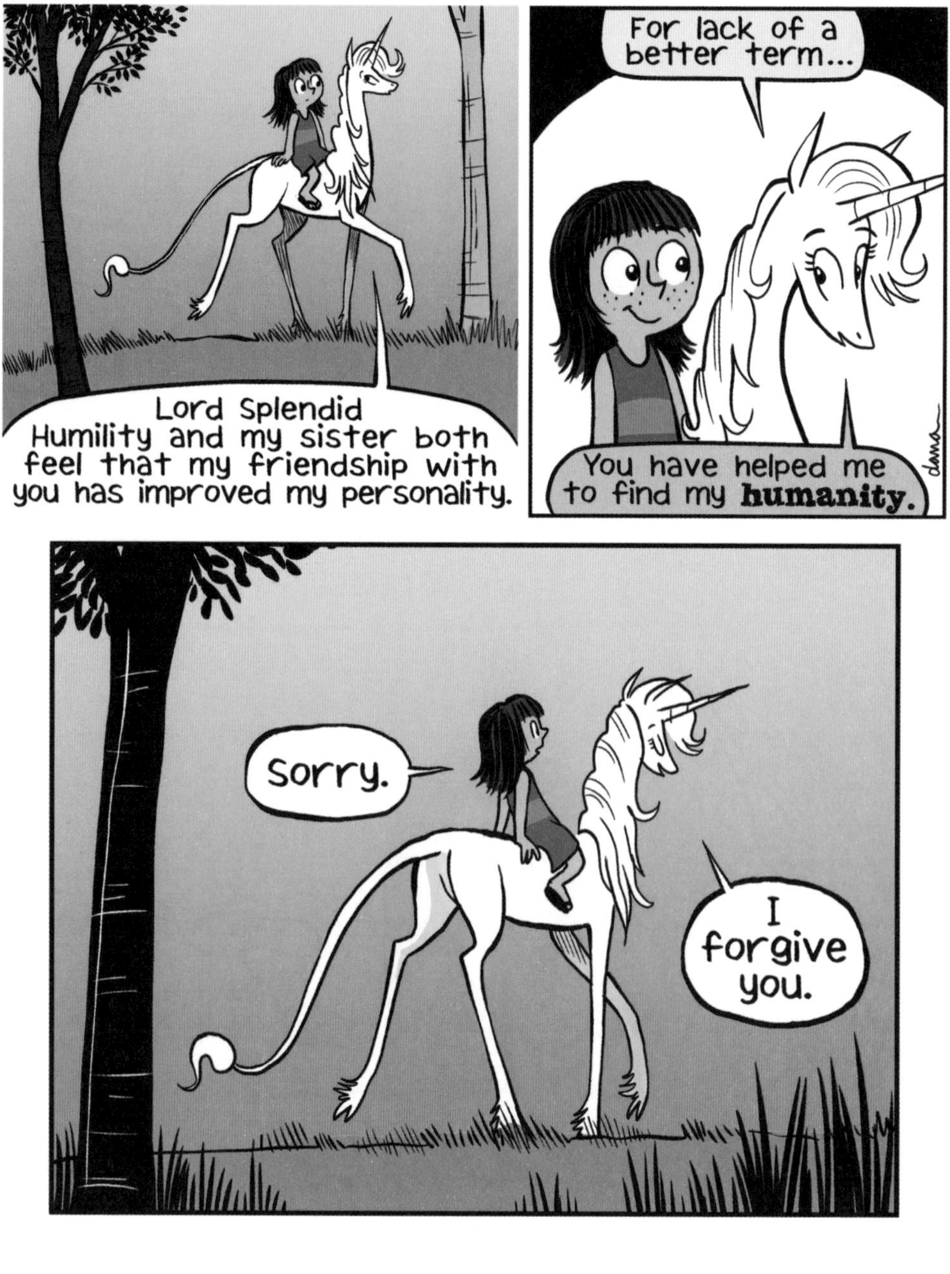
Lord Splendid Humility and my sister both feel that my friendship with you has improved my personality.
For lack of a better term...
You have helped me to find my **humanity.**
dana
Sorry.
I forgive you.

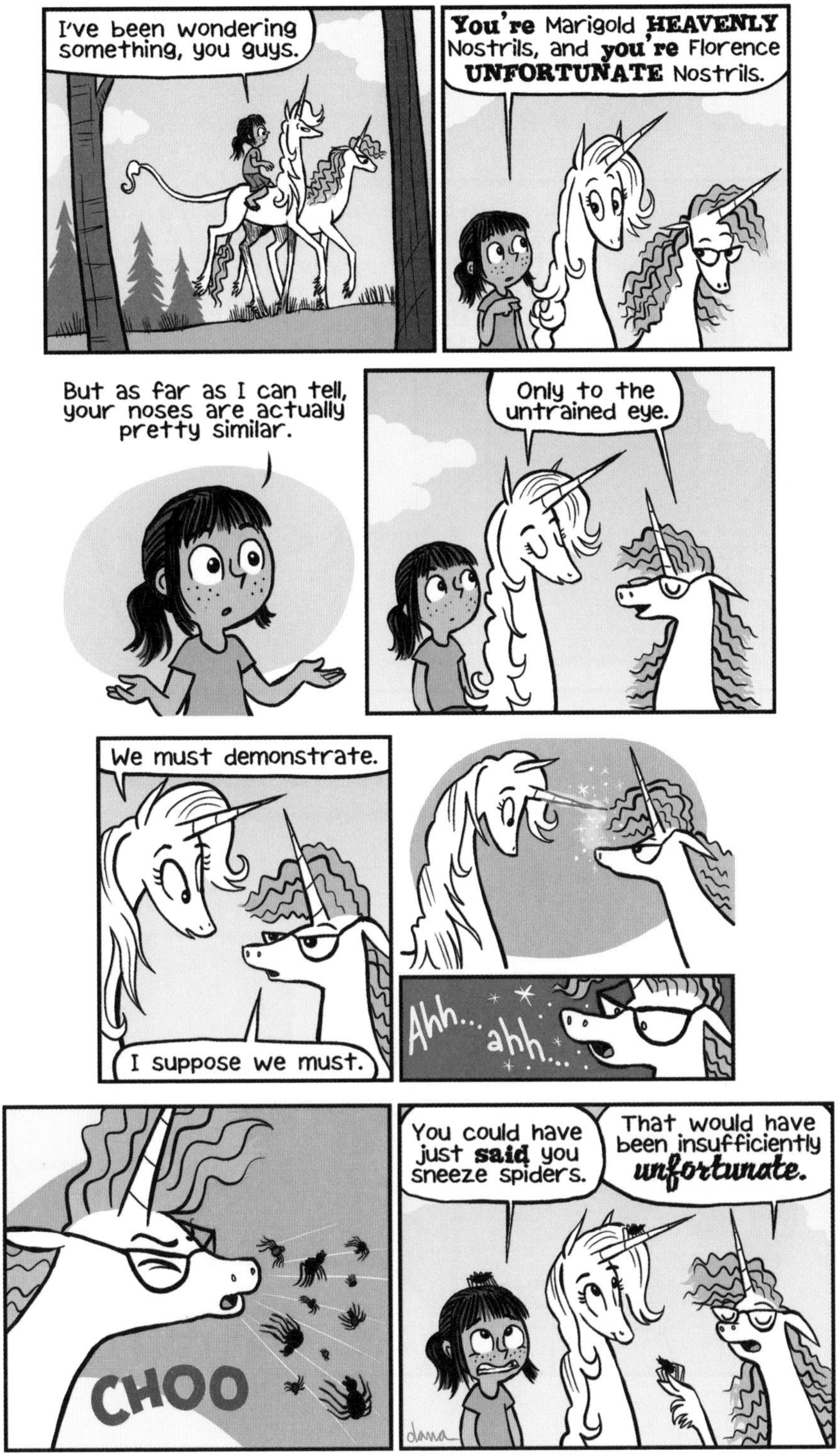
I've been wondering something, you guys.
You're Marigold HEAVENLY Nostrils, and you're Florence UNFORTUNATE Nostrils.
But as far as I can tell, your noses are actually pretty similar.
Only to the untrained eye.
We must demonstrate.
I suppose we must.
Ahh... ahh...
CHOO
You could have just said you sneeze spiders.
That would have been insufficiently unfortunate.
dana

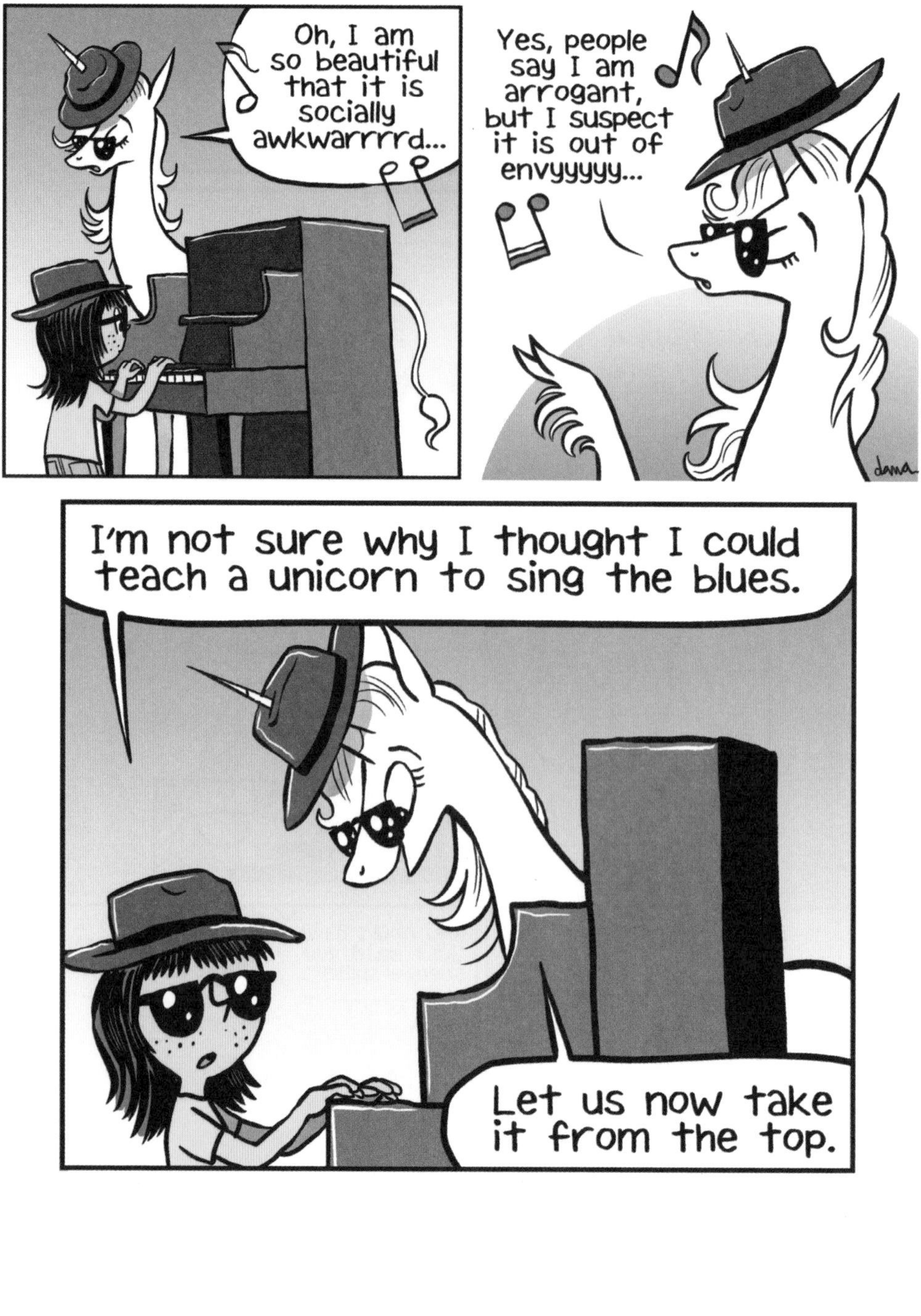
Oh, I am so beautiful that it is socially awkwarrrrd...
Yes, people say I am arrogant, but I suspect it is out of envyyyyy...
dana
I'm not sure why I thought I could teach a unicorn to sing the blues.
Let us now take it from the top.

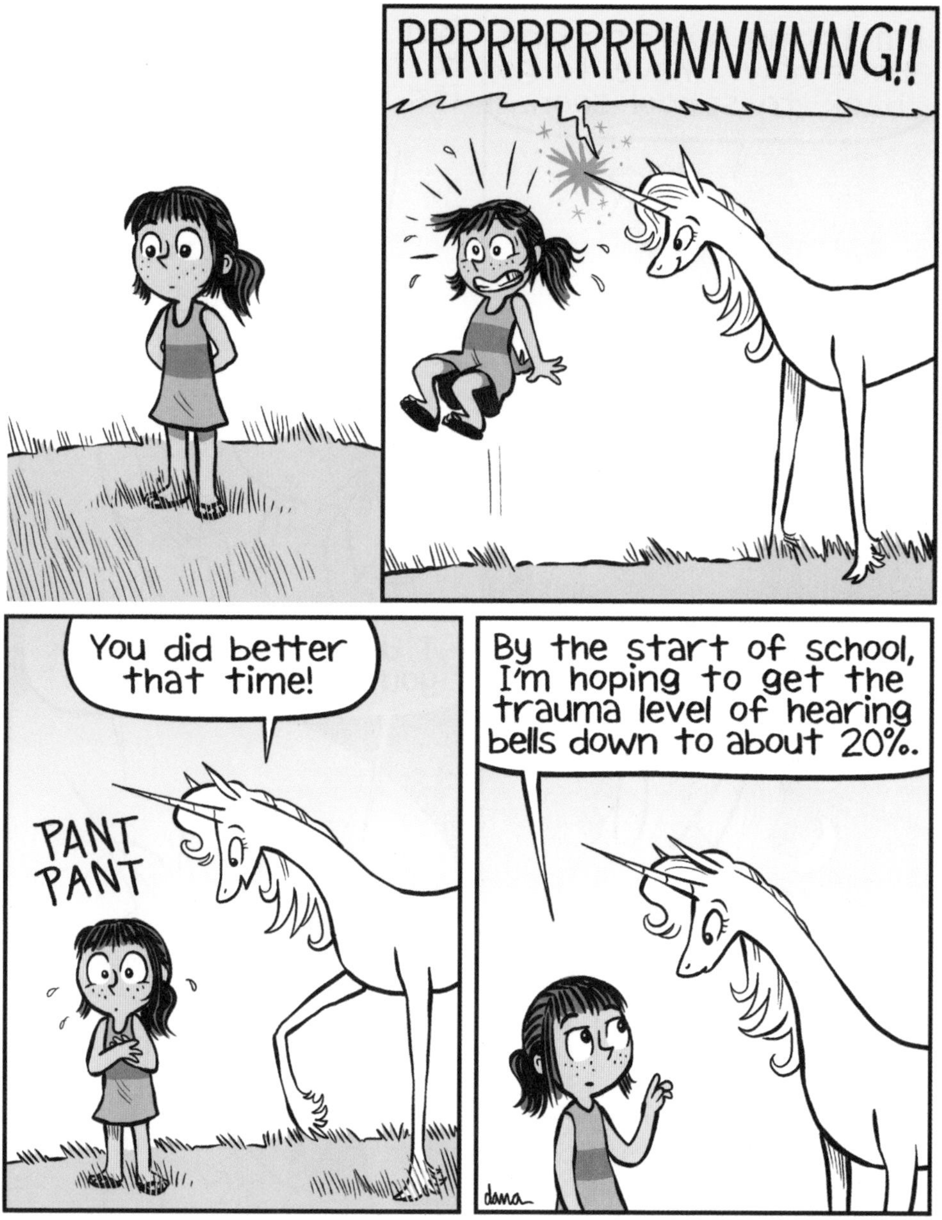
RRRRRRRRRINNNNNG!!
You did better that time!
PANT PANT
By the start of school, I'm hoping to get the trauma level of hearing bells down to about 20%.
dana

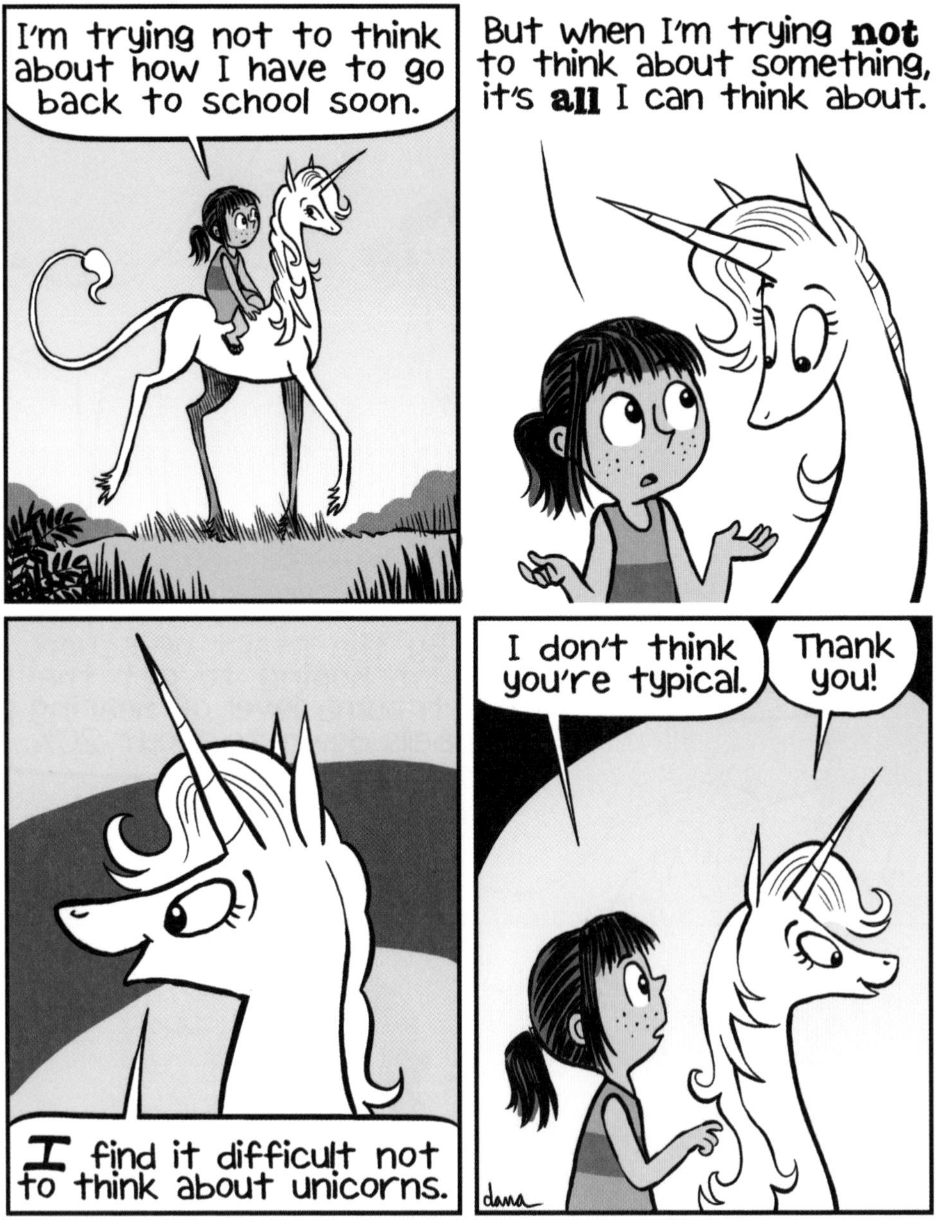
I'm trying not to think about how I have to go back to school soon.
But when I'm trying **not** to think about something, it's **all** I can think about.
I find it difficult not to think about unicorns.
I don't think you're typical.
Thank you!
dana

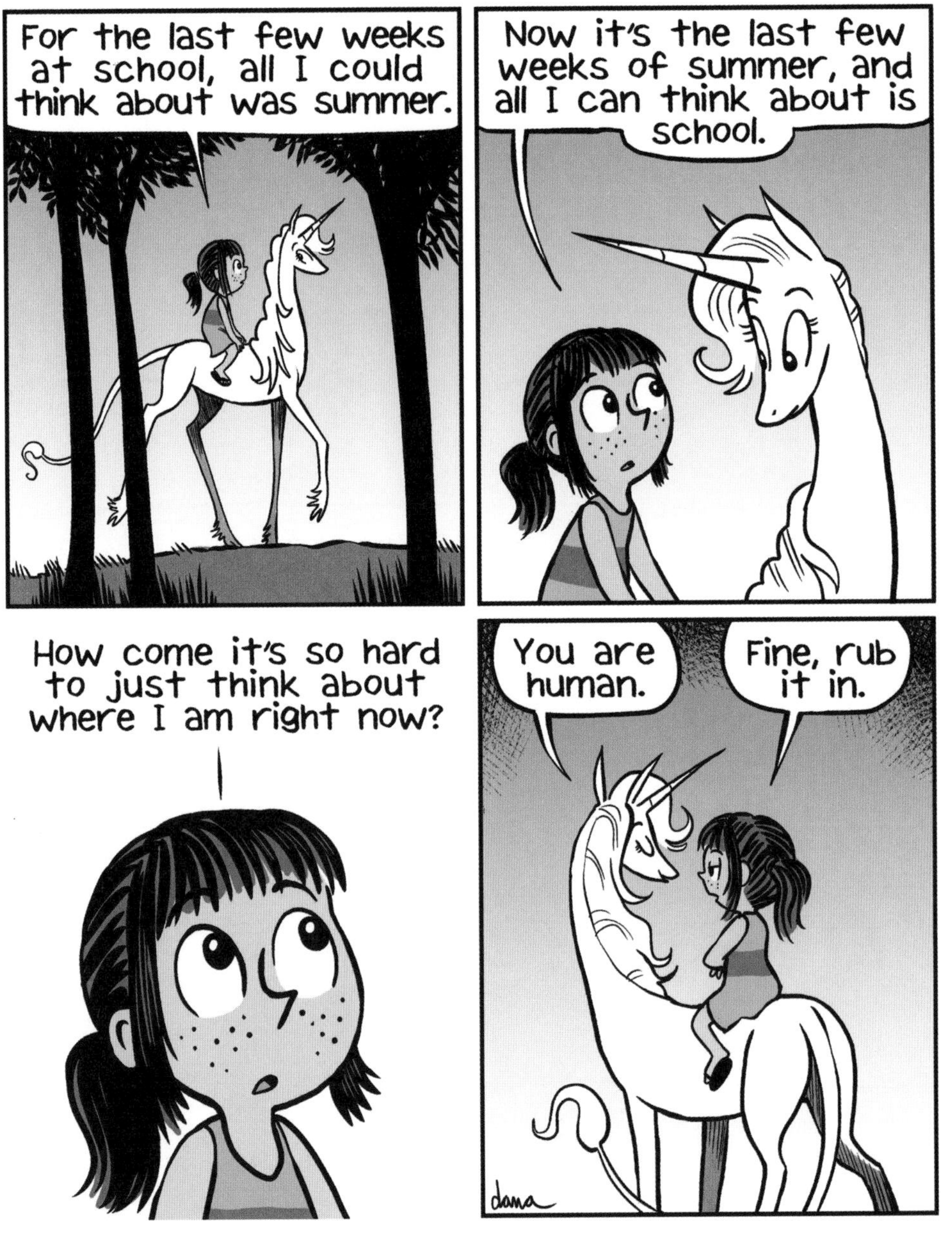
For the last few weeks at school, all I could think about was summer.
Now it's the last few weeks of summer, and all I can think about is school.
How come it's so hard to just think about where I am right now?
You are human.
Fine, rub it in.
dana

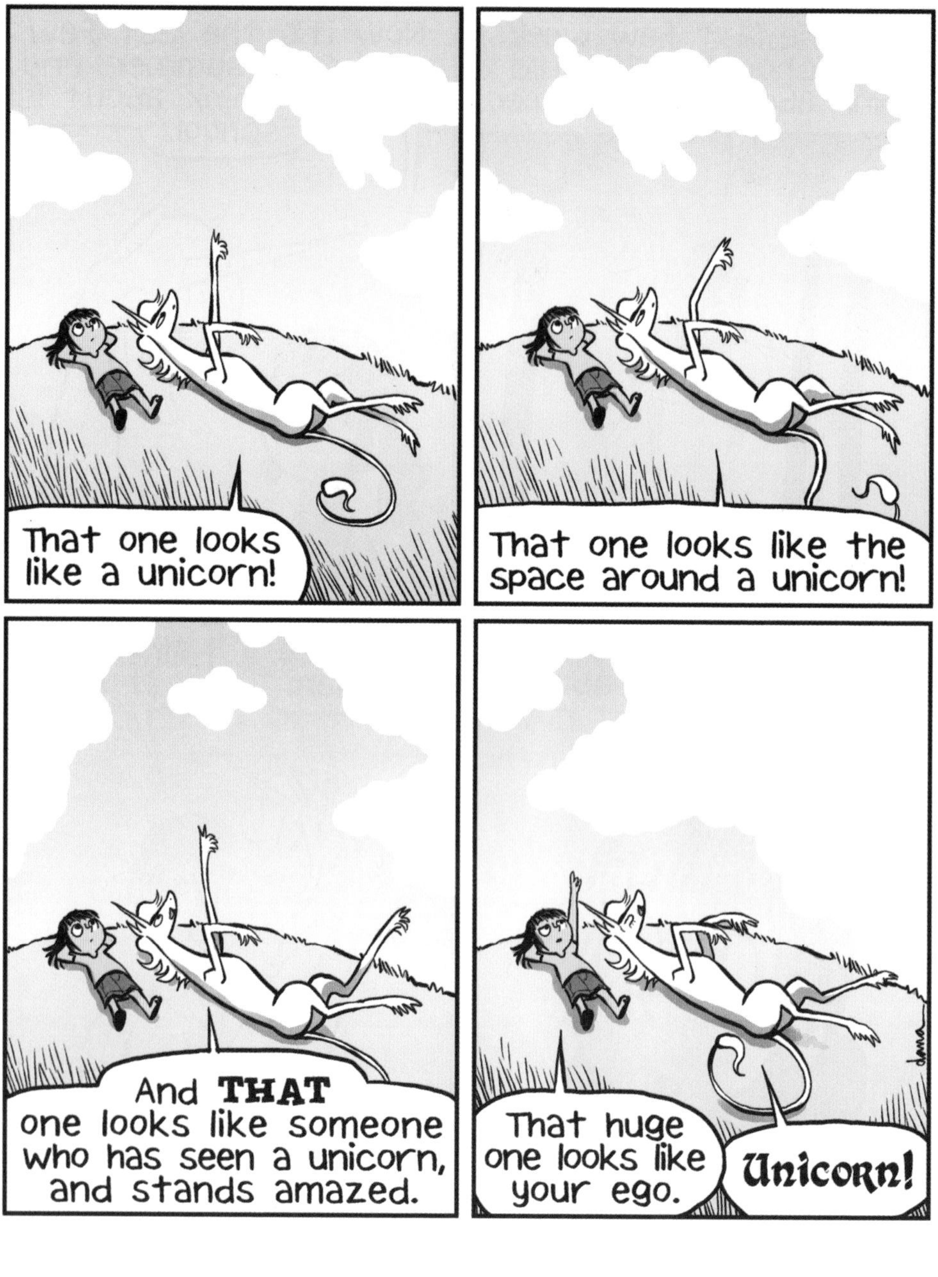
That one looks like a unicorn!
That one looks like the space around a unicorn!
And THAT one looks like someone who has seen a unicorn, and stands amazed.
That huge one looks like your ego.
Unicorn!

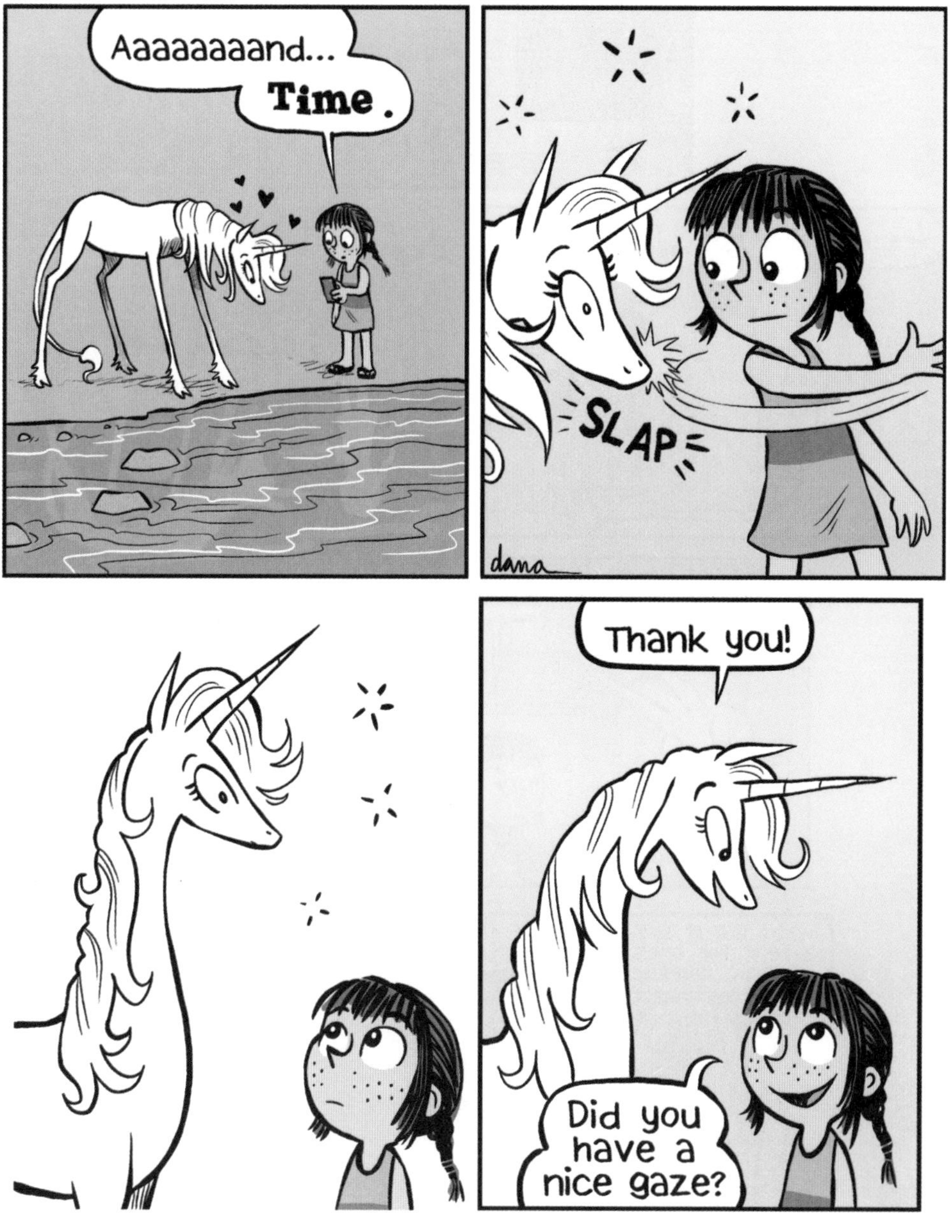
Aaaaaaaand...
Time.
SLAP
dana
Thank you!
Did you have a nice gaze?

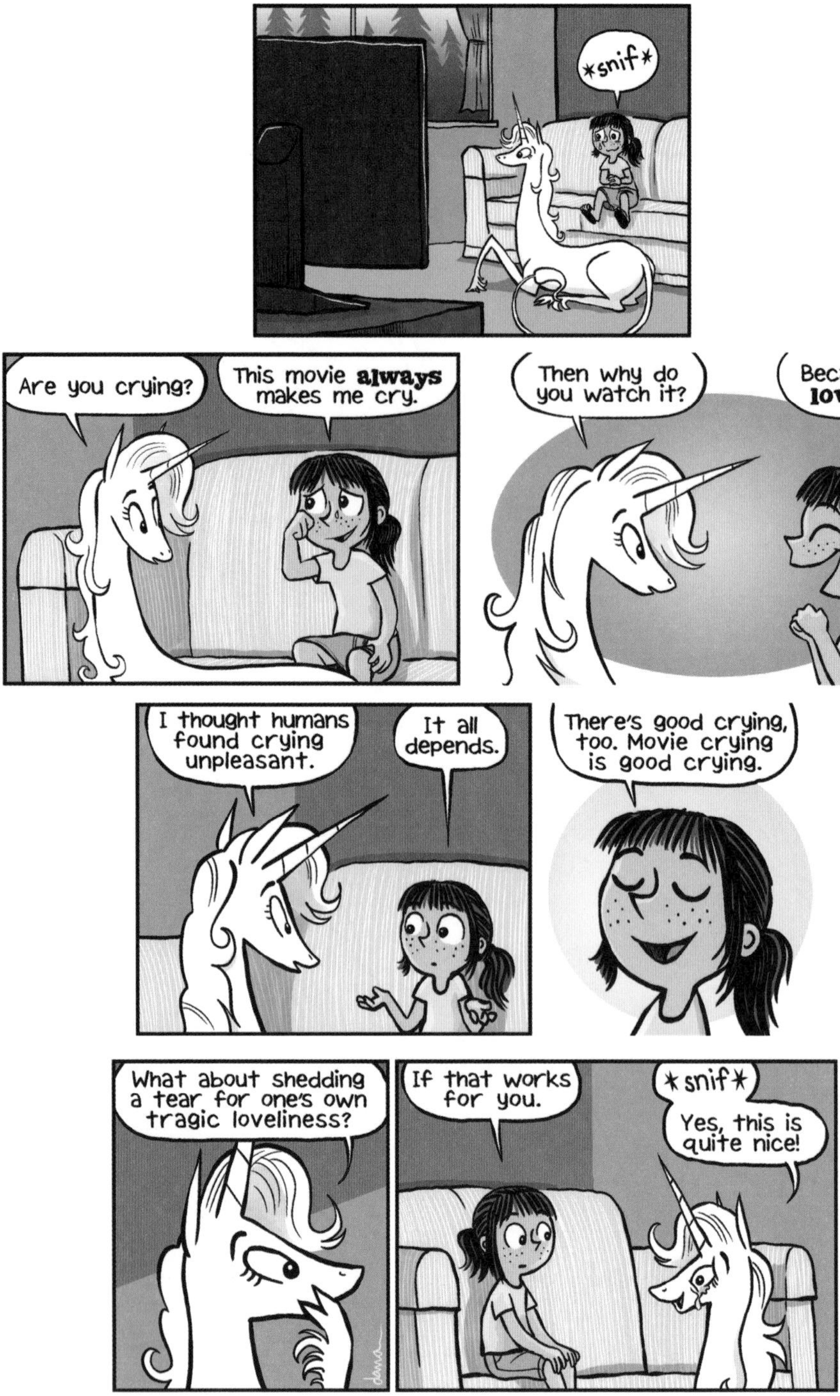
snif
Are you crying?
This movie **always** makes me cry.
Then why do you watch it?
Because I **love** it!
I thought humans found crying unpleasant.
It all depends.
There's good crying, too. Movie crying is good crying.
What about shedding a tear for one's own tragic loveliness?
If that works for you.
snif
Yes, this is quite nice!

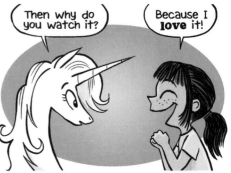

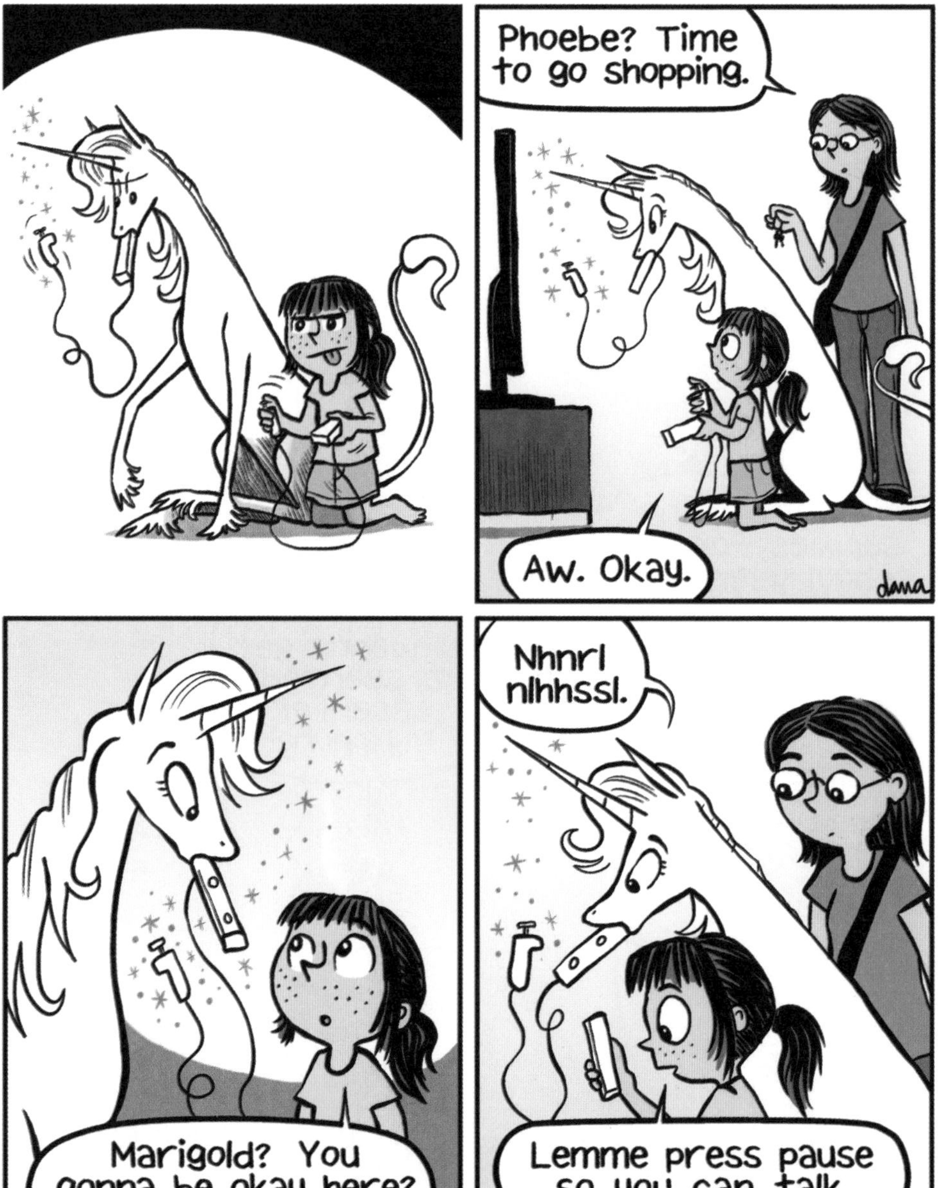
Phoebe? Time to go shopping.
Aw. Okay.
dana
Marigold? You gonna be okay here?
Nhnrl nlhhssl.
Lemme press pause so you can talk.

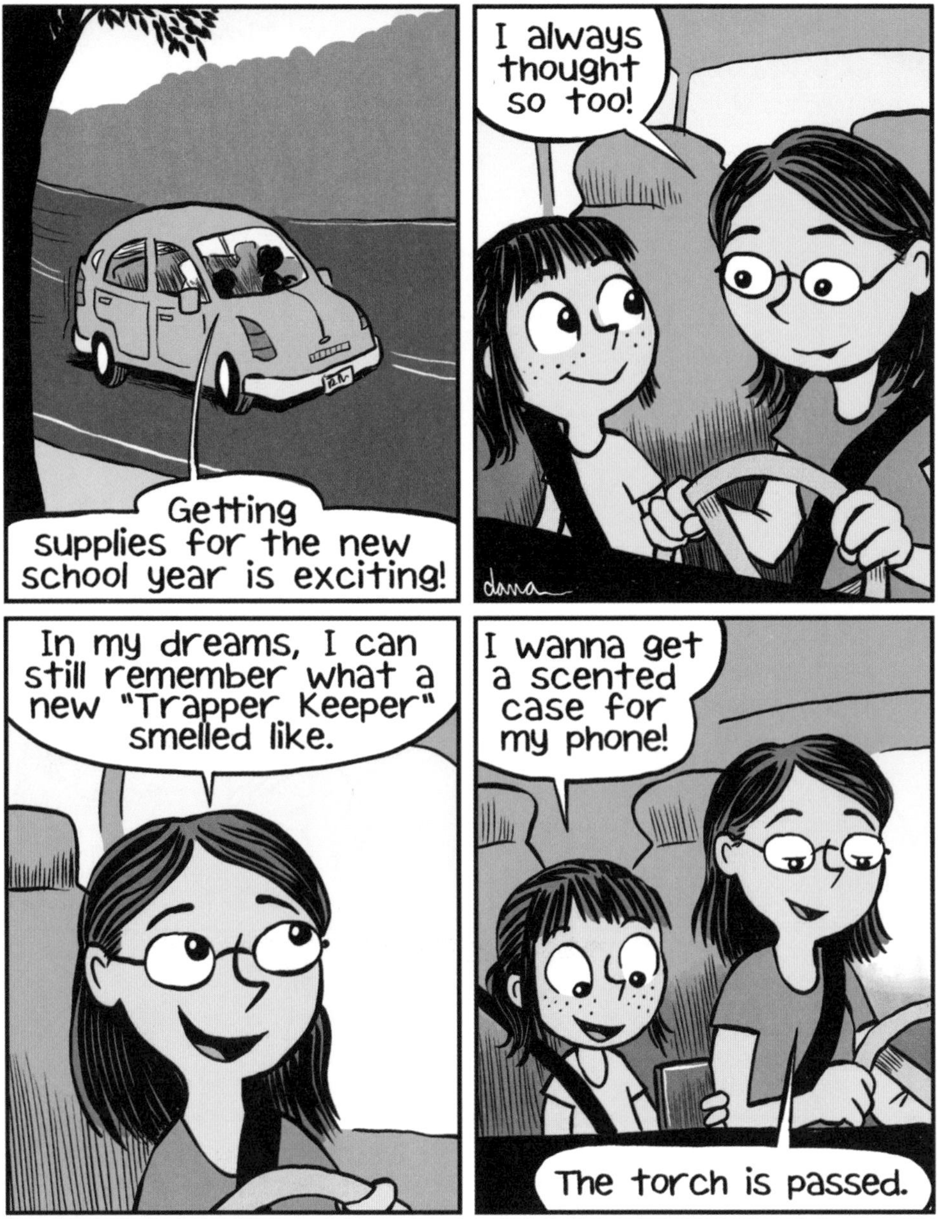

Getting supplies for the new school year is exciting!
I always thought so too!
dana
In my dreams, I can still remember what a new "Trapper Keeper" smelled like.
I wanna get a scented case for my phone!
The torch is passed.

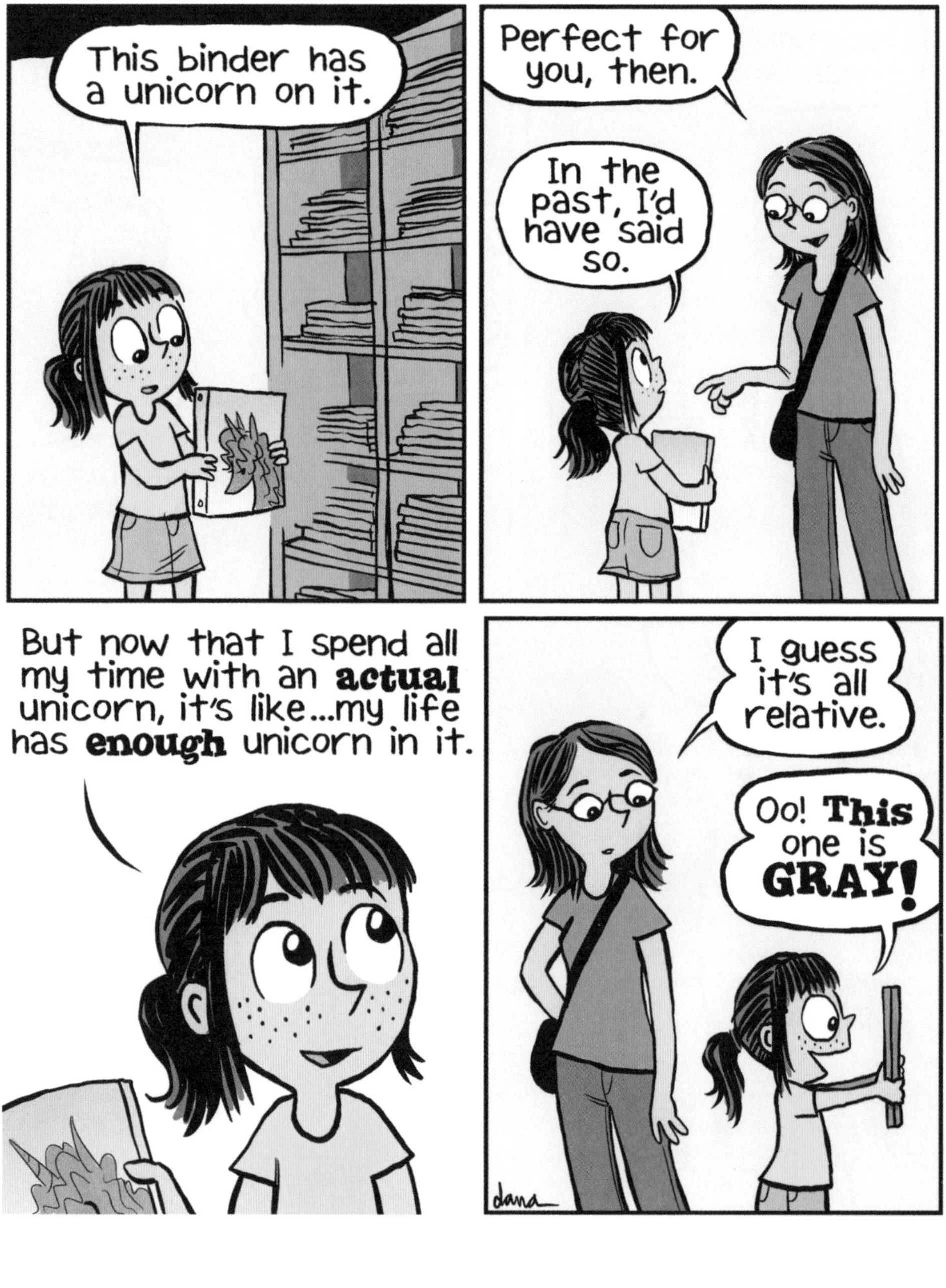
This binder has a unicorn on it.
Perfect for you, then.
In the past, I'd have said so.
But now that I spend all my time with an actual unicorn, it's like...my life has enough unicorn in it.
I guess it's all relative.
Oo! This one is GRAY!
dana

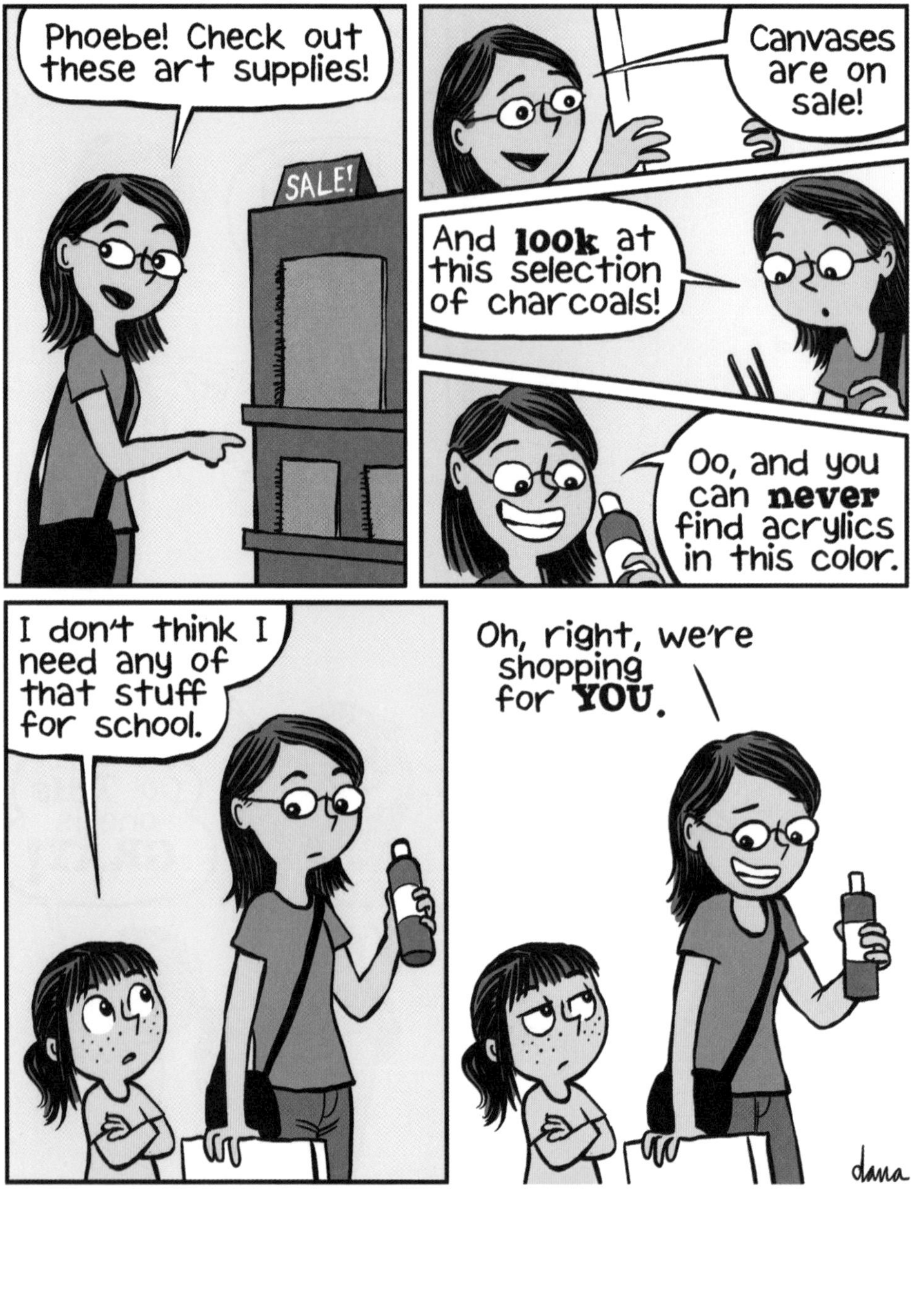
Phoebe! Check out these art supplies!
SALE!
Canvases are on sale!
And look at this selection of charcoals!
Oo, and you can never find acrylics in this color.
I don't think I need any of that stuff for school.
Oh, right, we're shopping for YOU.
dana

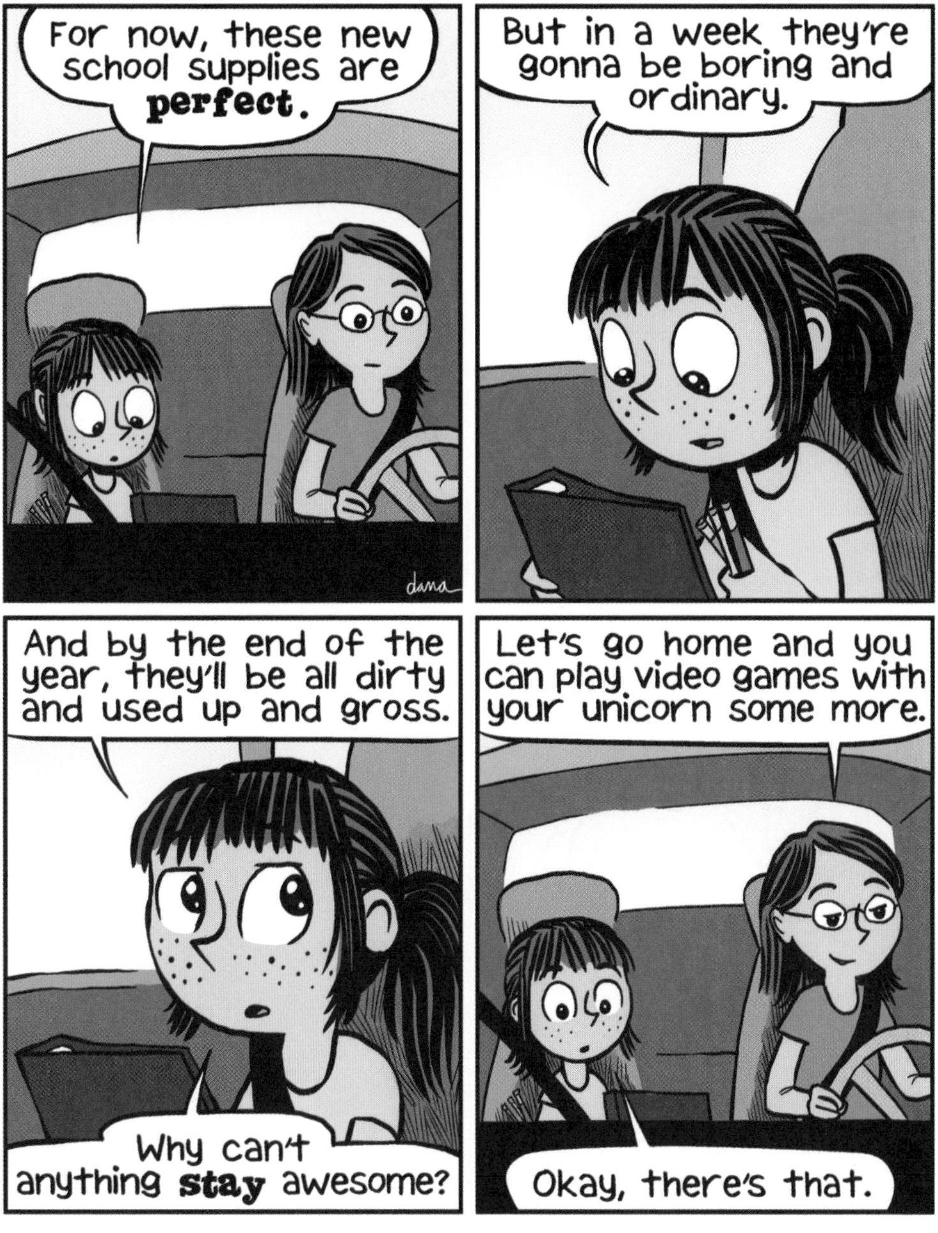
For now, these new school supplies are **perfect**.
But in a week they're gonna be boring and ordinary.
And by the end of the year, they'll be all dirty and used up and gross.
Why can't anything **stay** awesome?
Let's go home and you can play video games with your unicorn some more.
Okay, there's that.
dana

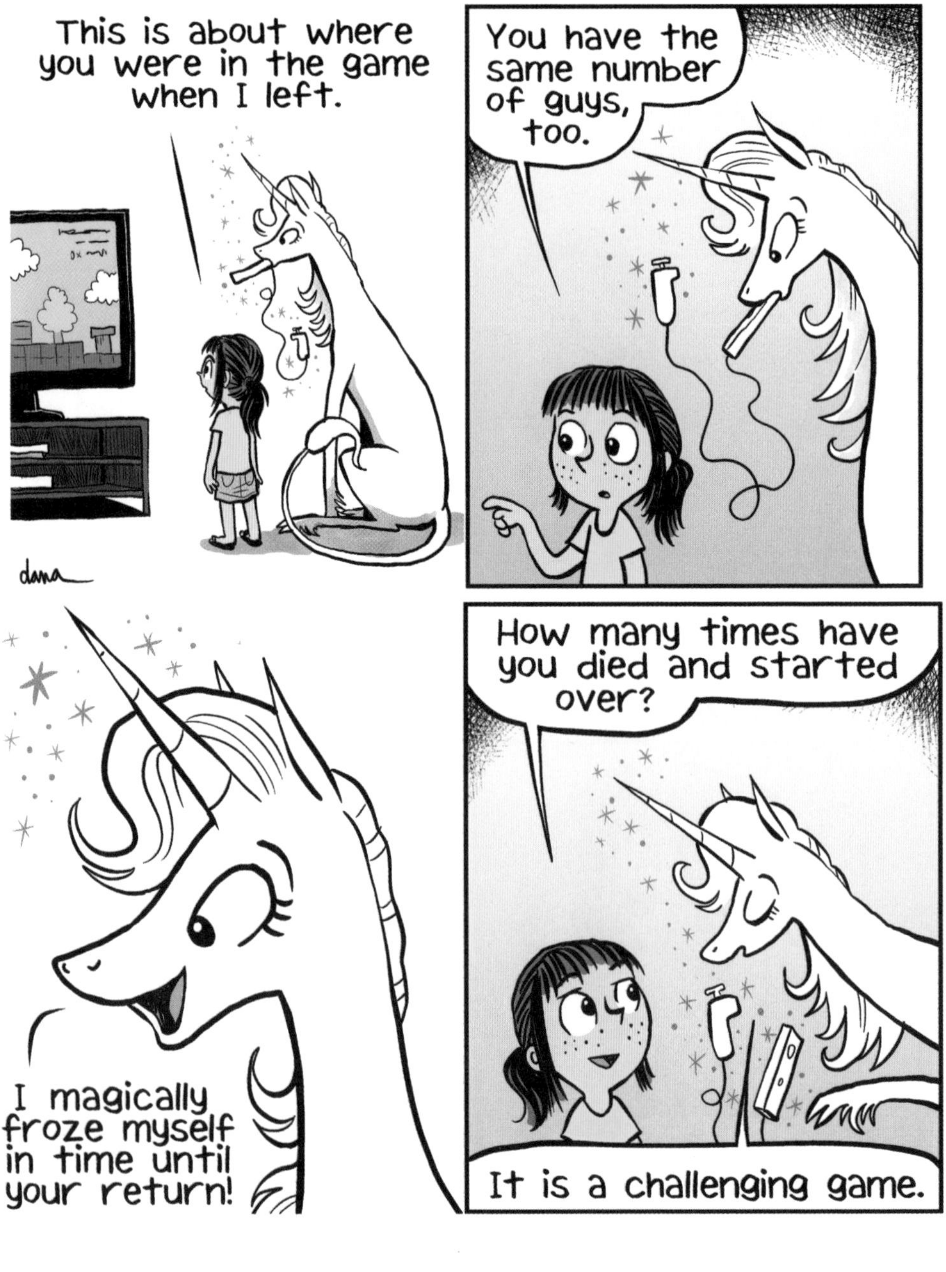
This is about where you were in the game when I left.
dana
You have the same number of guys, too.
I magically froze myself in time until your return!
How many times have you died and started over?
It is a challenging game.

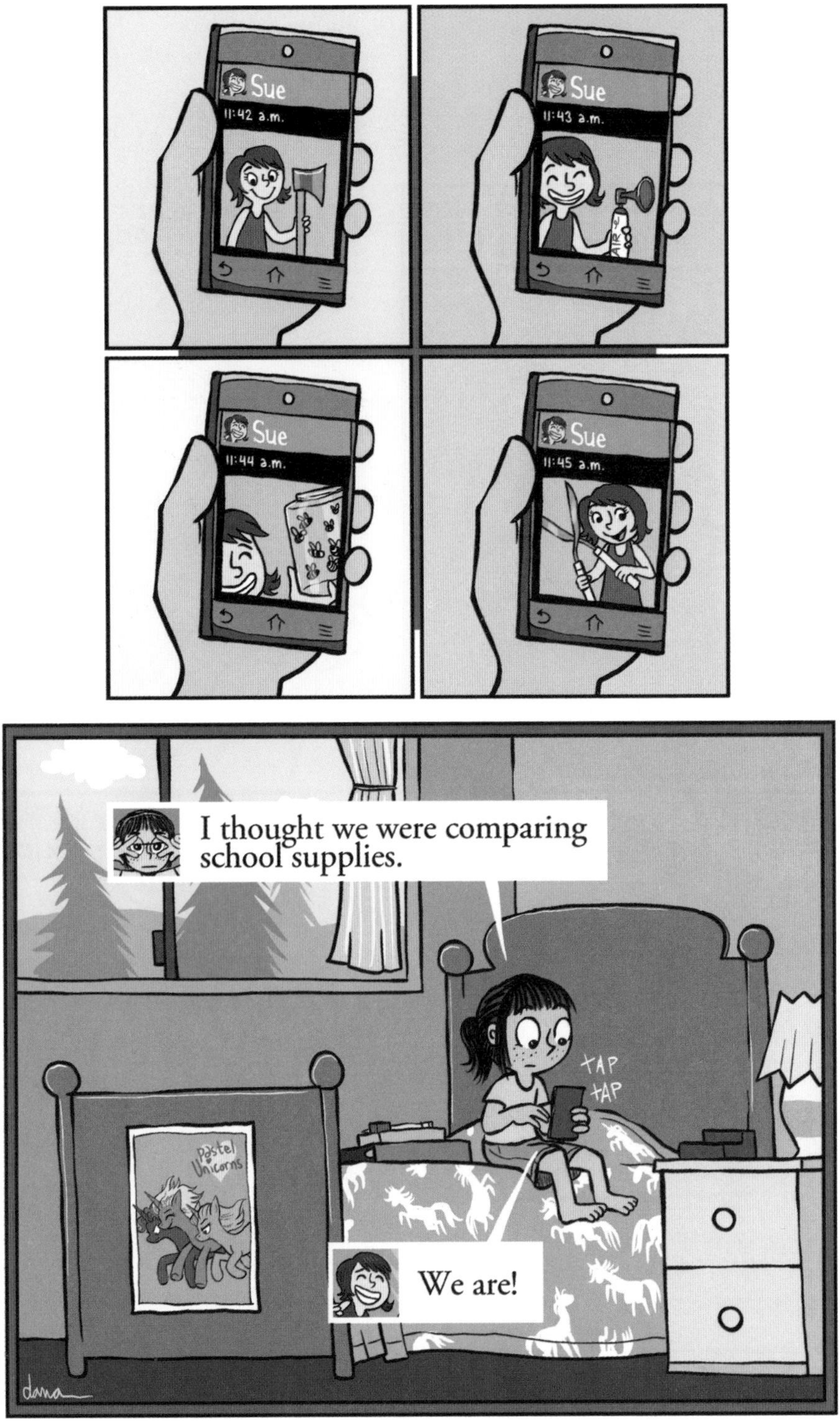
Sue
11:42 a.m.
Sue
11:43 a.m.
AIR
Sue
11:44 a.m.
Sue
11:45 a.m.
I thought we were comparing school supplies.
pastel Unicorns
TAP TAP
We are!
dana

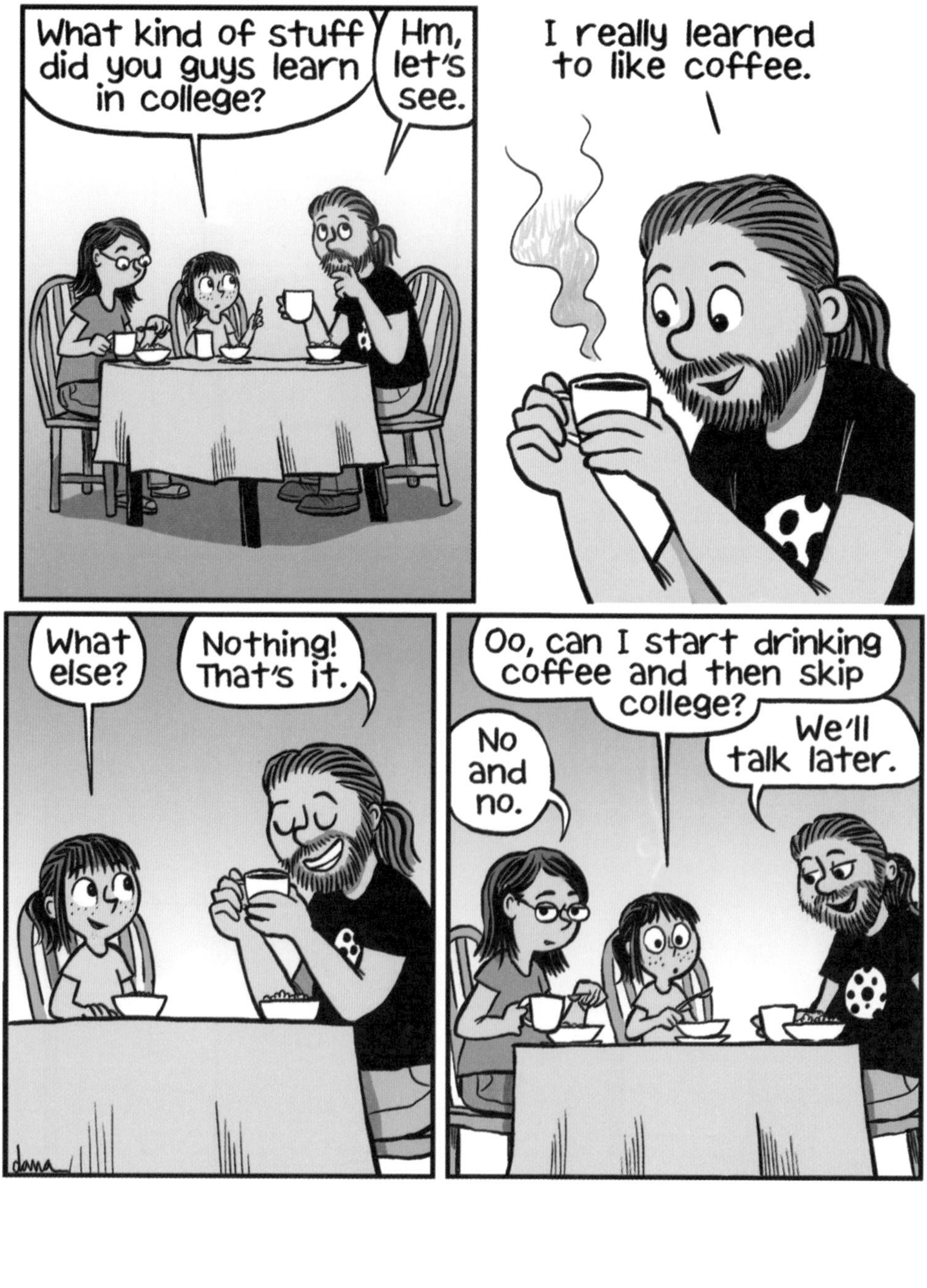
What kind of stuff did you guys learn in college?
Hm, let's see.
I really learned to like coffee.
What else?
Nothing! That's it.
Oo, can I start drinking coffee and then skip college?
No and no.
We'll talk later.
dana

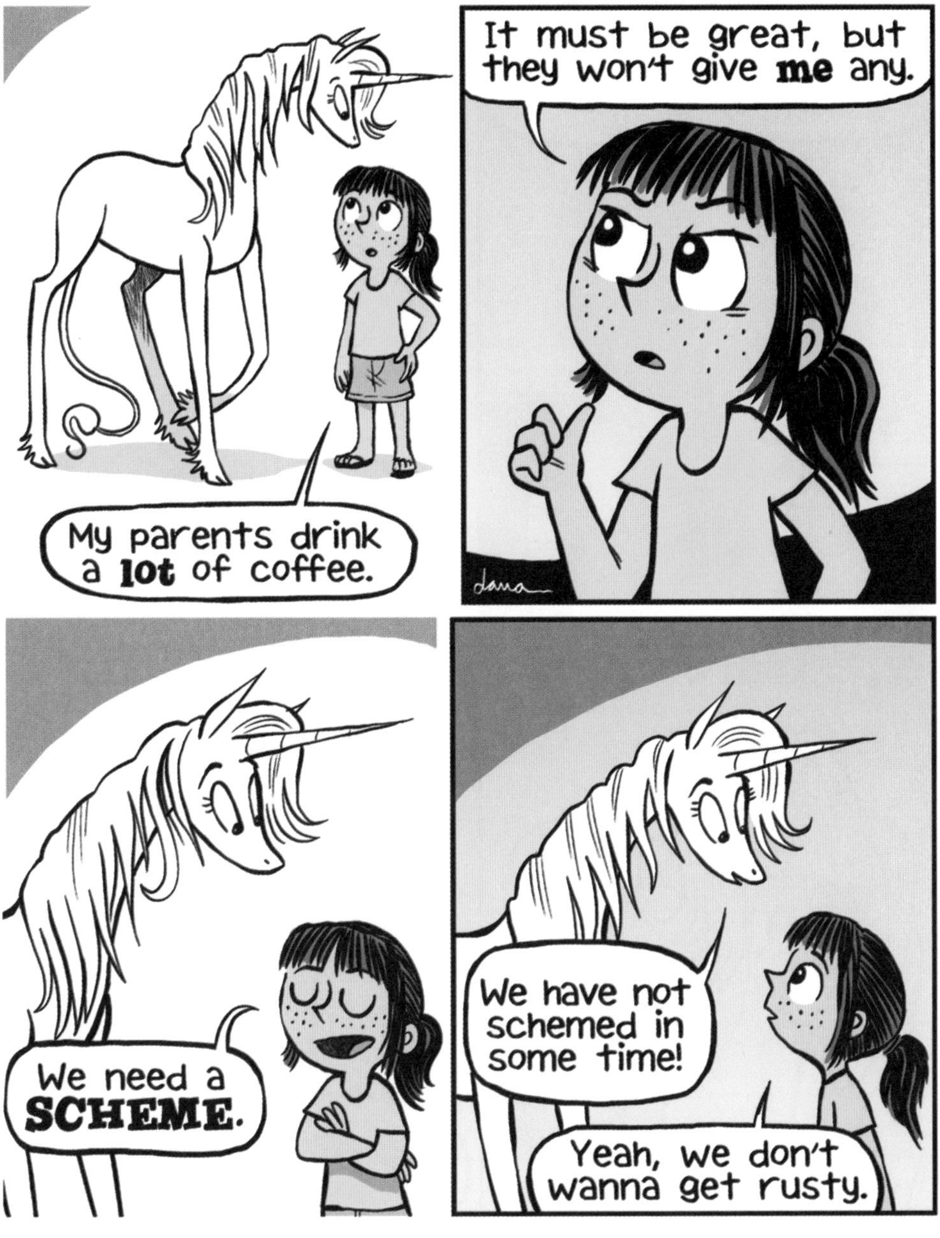
My parents drink a **lot** of coffee.
It must be great, but they won't give **me** any.
We need a **SCHEME**.
We have not schemed in some time!
Yeah, we don't wanna get rusty.

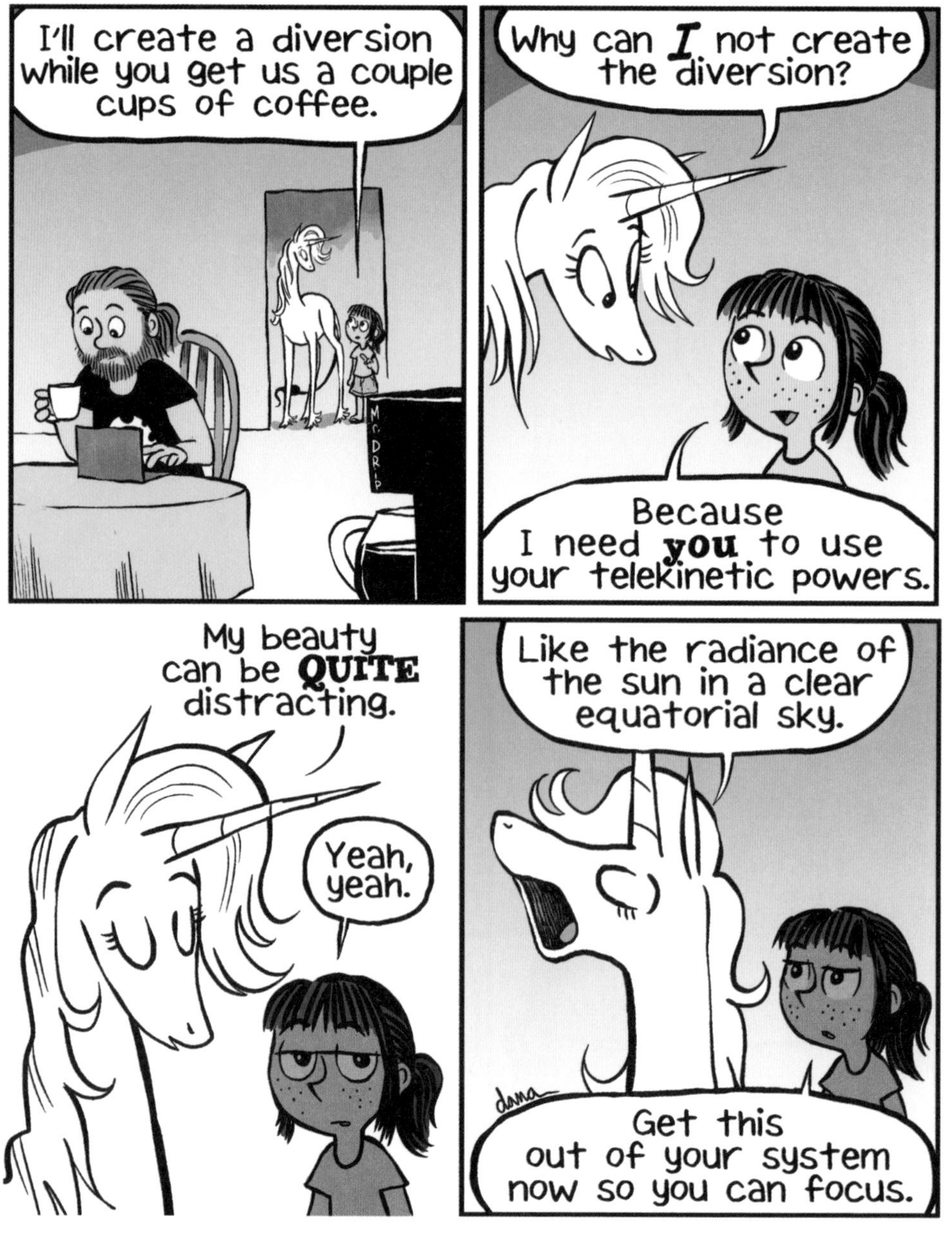
I'll create a diversion while you get us a couple cups of coffee.
Mr. DRIP
Why can I not create the diversion?
Because I need you to use your telekinetic powers.
My beauty can be QUITE distracting.
Yeah, yeah.
Like the radiance of the sun in a clear equatorial sky.
Get this out of your system now so you can focus.

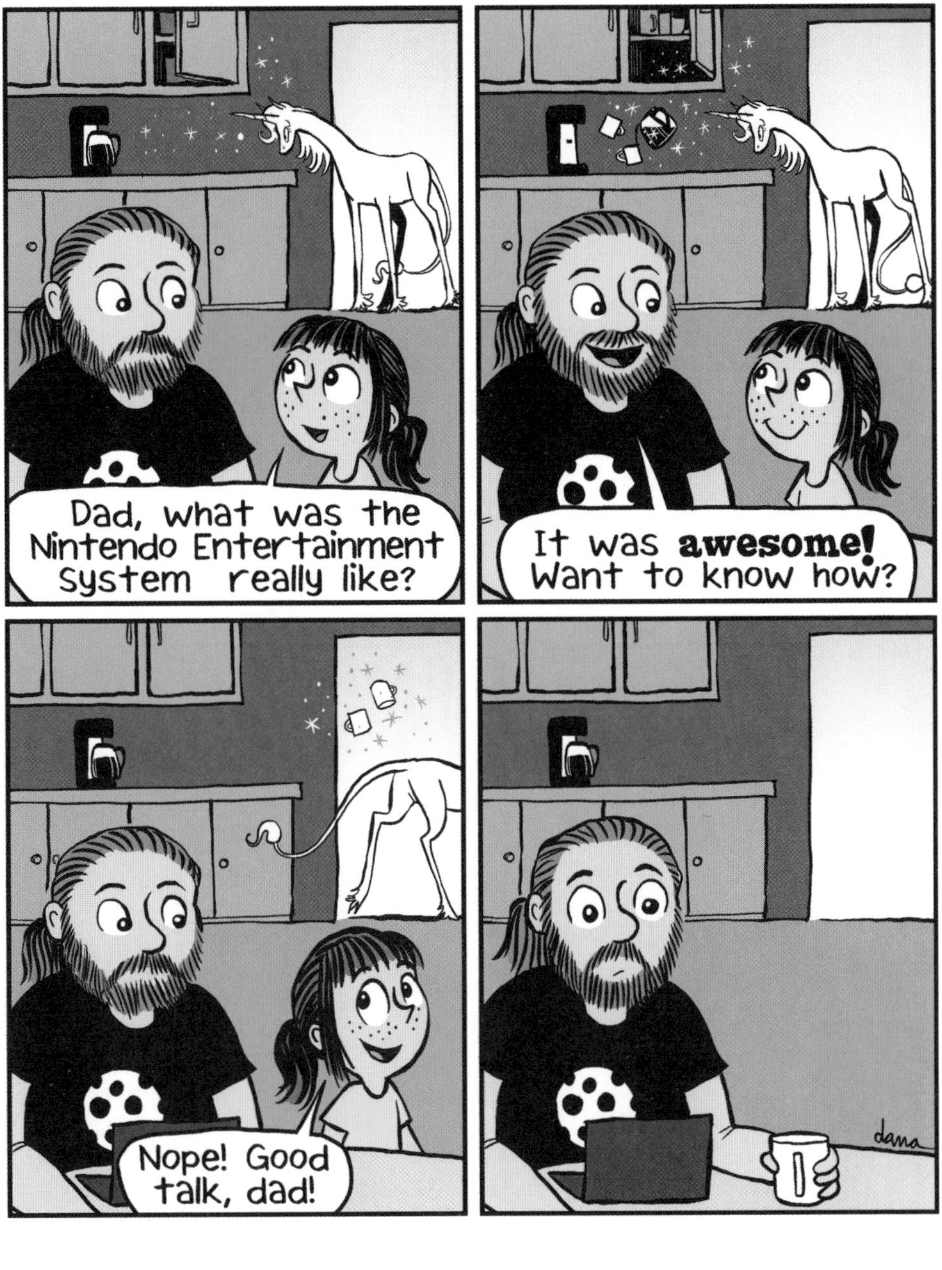
Dad, what was the Nintendo Entertainment System really like?
It was **awesome!** Want to know how?
Nope! Good talk, dad!
dana

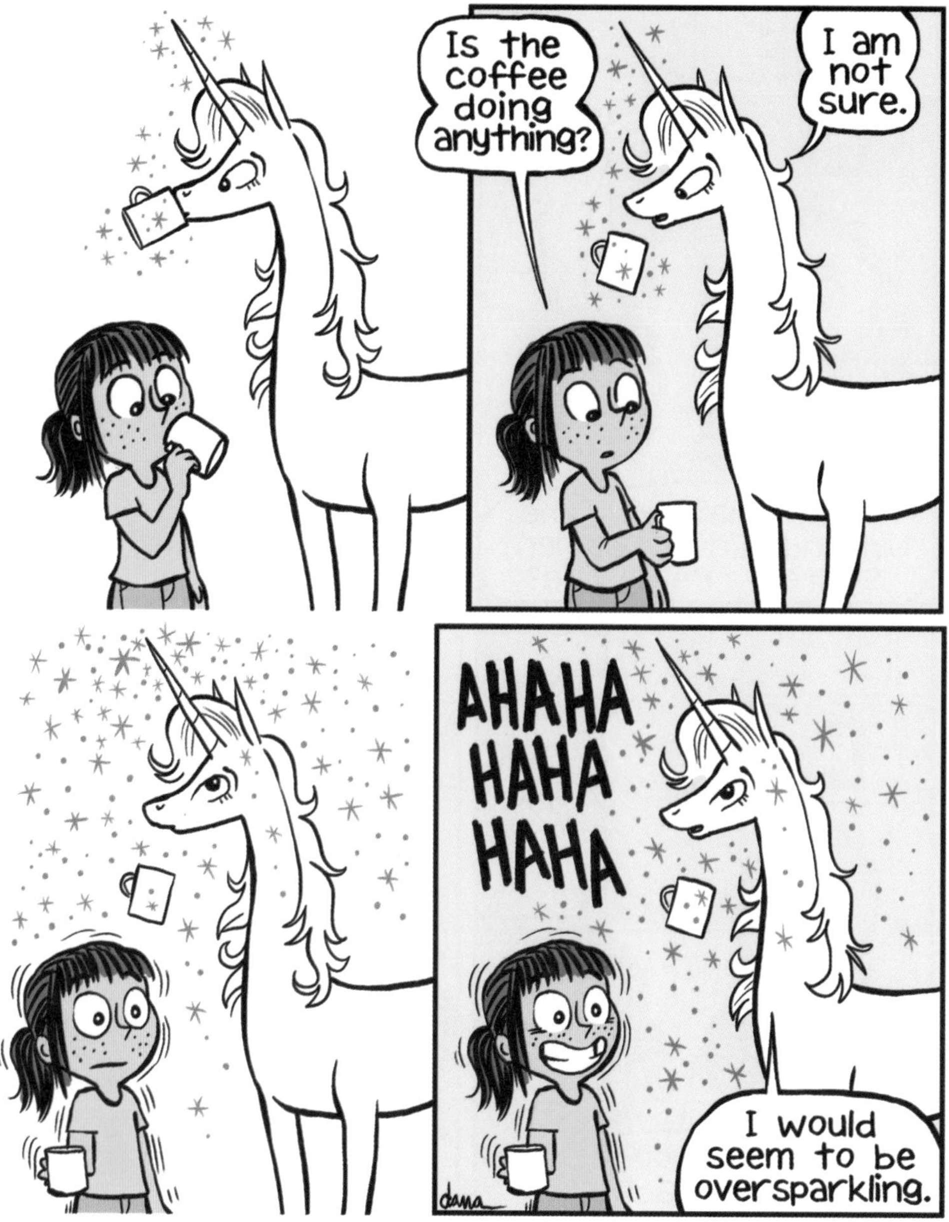
Is the coffee doing anything?
I am not sure.
AHAHA HAHA HAHA
I would seem to be oversparkling.

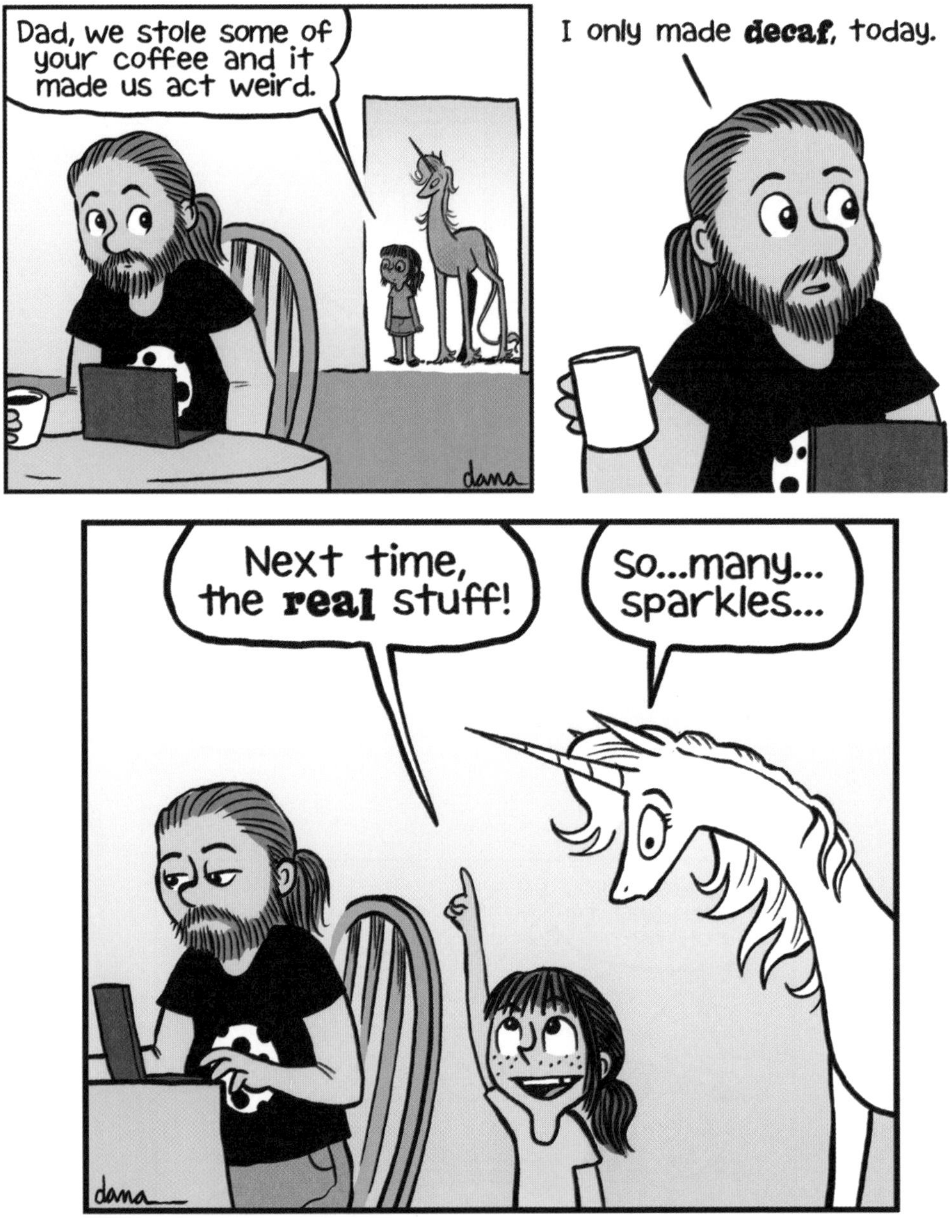
Dad, we stole some of your coffee and it made us act weird.
I only made **decaf**, today.
Next time, the **real** stuff!
So...many... sparkles...
dana

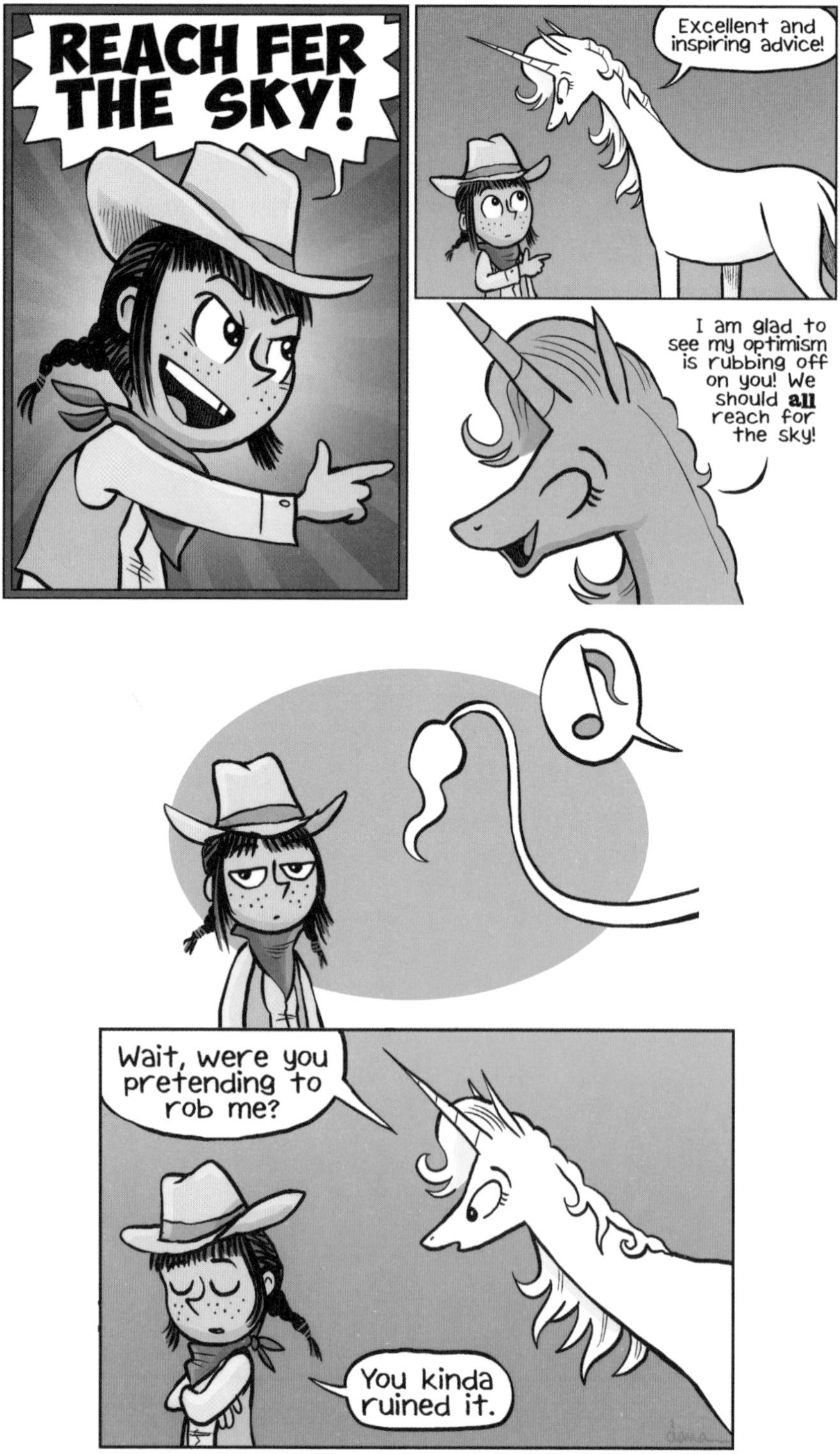
REACH FER THE SKY!
Excellent and inspiring advice!
I am glad to see my optimism is rubbing off on you! We should **all** reach for the sky!
Wait, were you pretending to rob me?
You kinda ruined it.

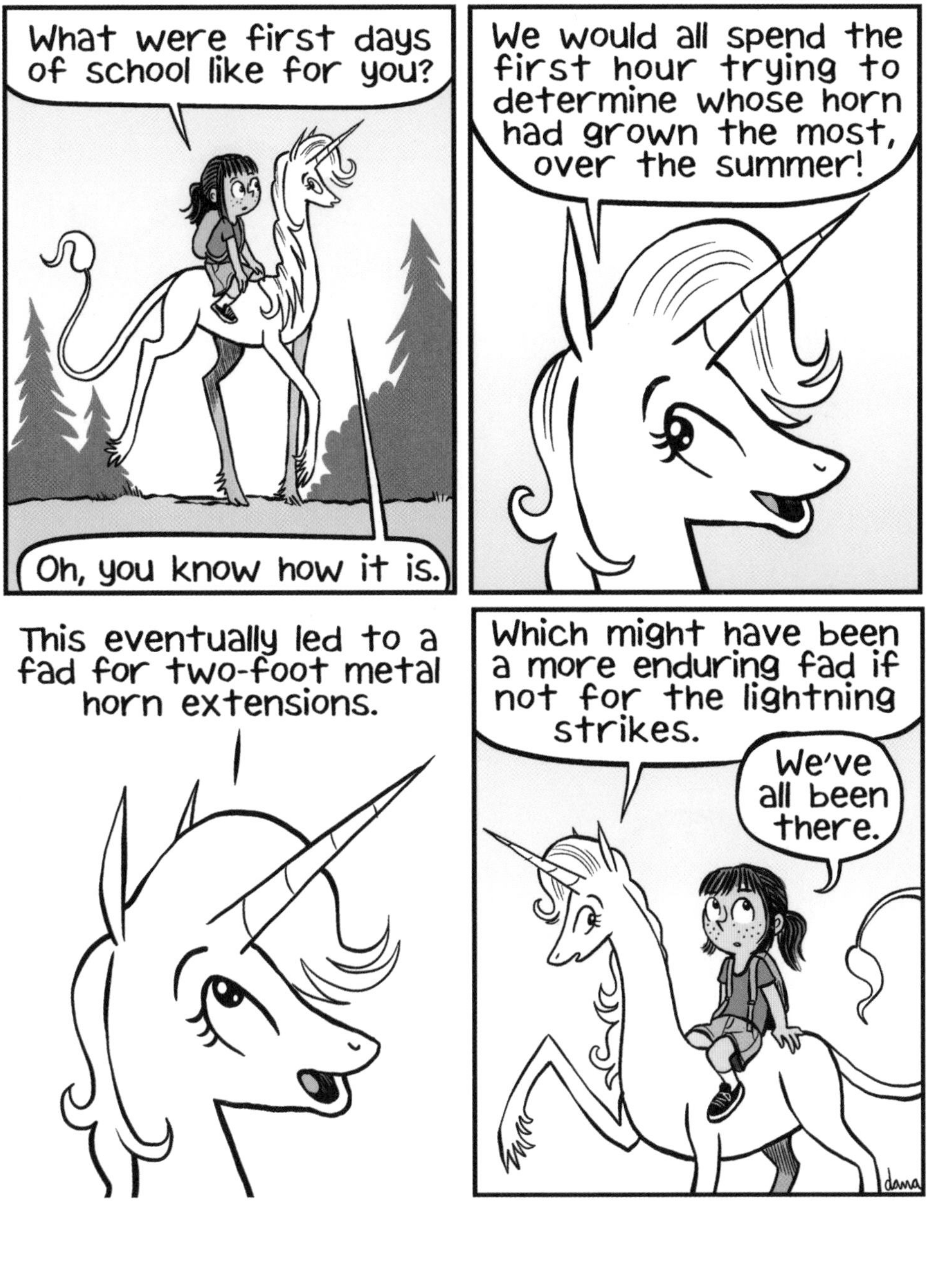
What were first days of school like for you?
Oh, you know how it is.
We would all spend the first hour trying to determine whose horn had grown the most, over the summer!
This eventually led to a fad for two-foot metal horn extensions.
Which might have been a more enduring fad if not for the lightning strikes.
We've all been there.
dana

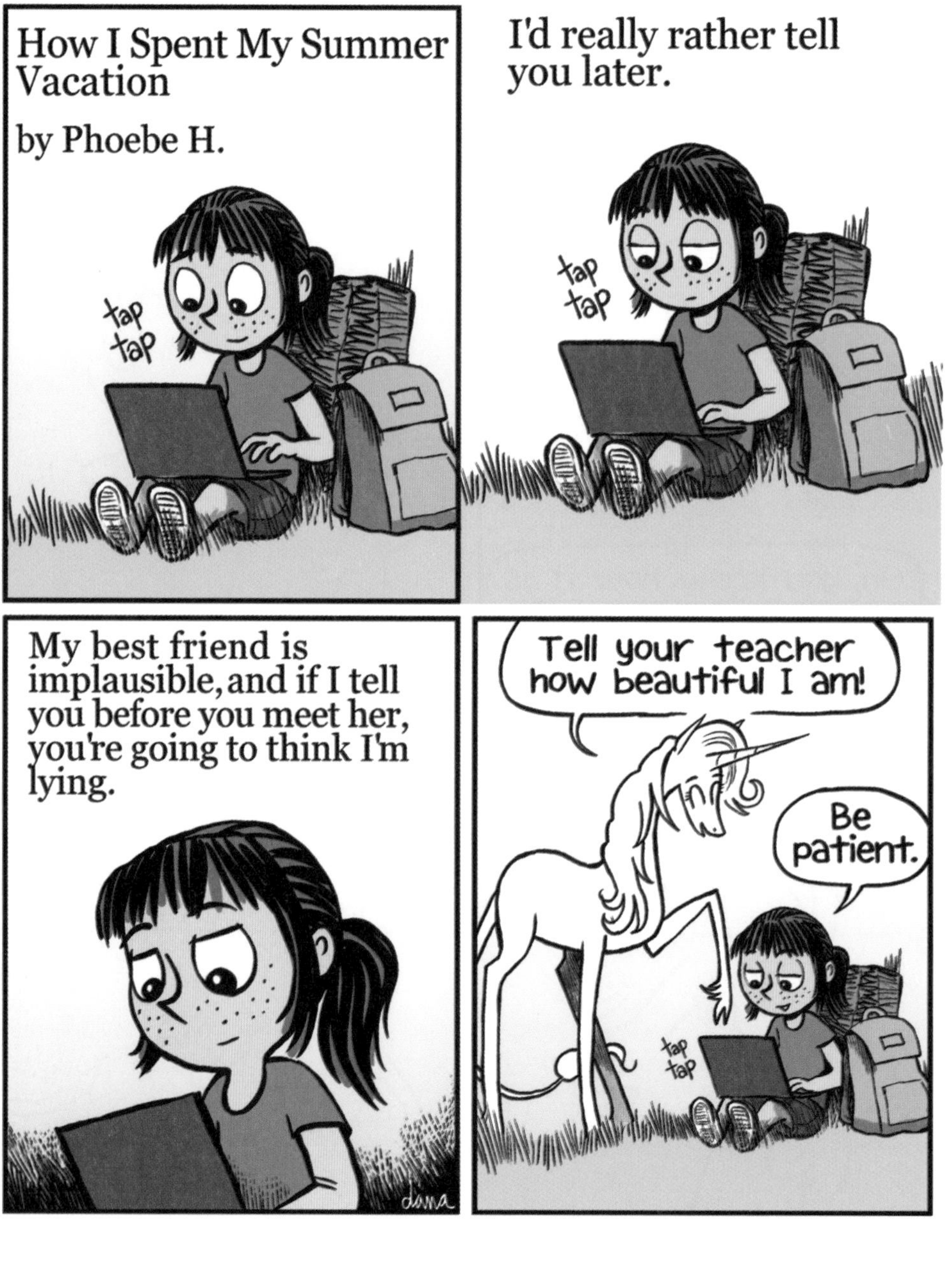
How I Spent My Summer Vacation
by Phoebe H.
tap tap
I'd really rather tell you later.
tap tap
My best friend is implausible, and if I tell you before you meet her, you're going to think I'm lying.
Tell your teacher how beautiful I am!
Be patient.
tap tap

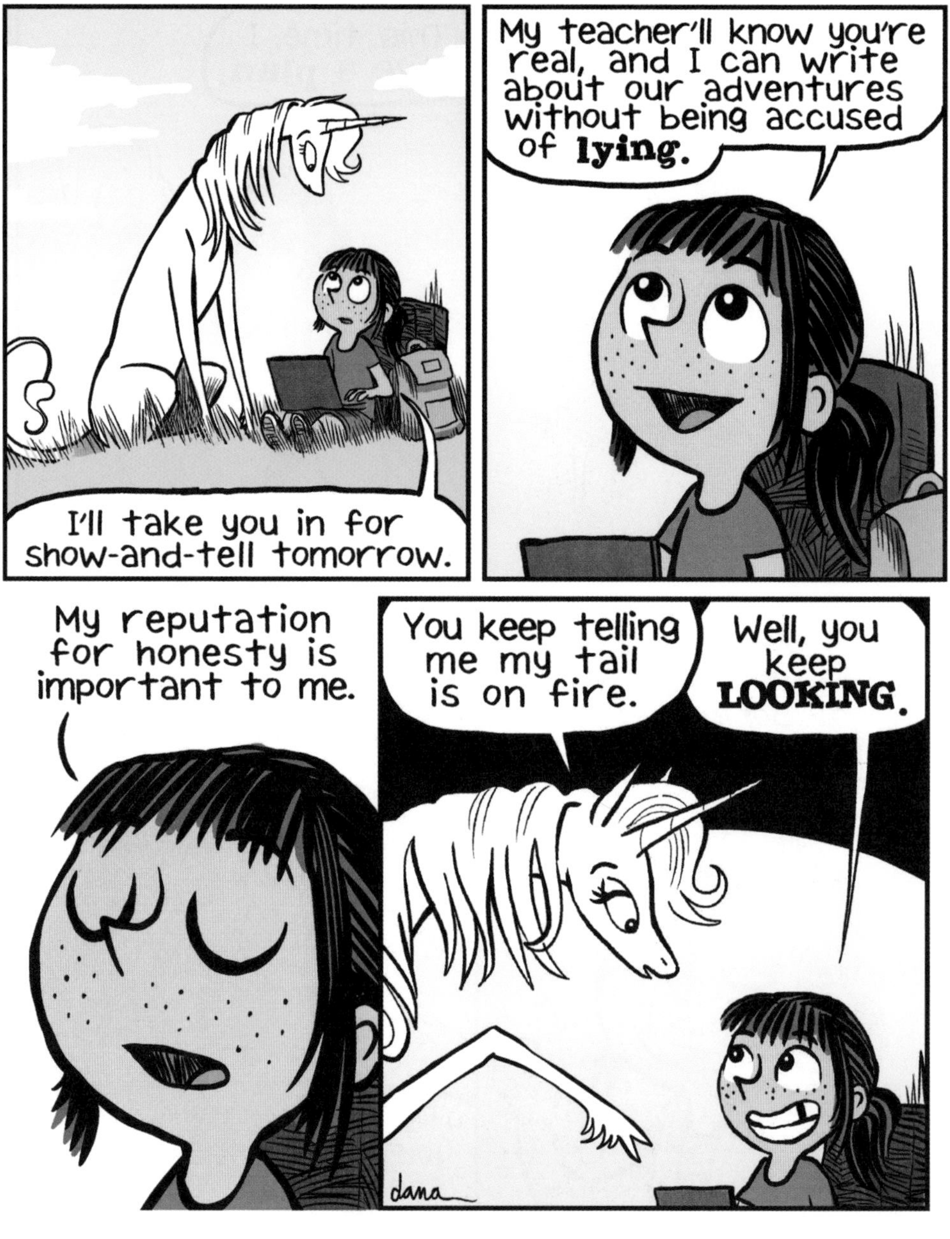
I'll take you in for show-and-tell tomorrow.
My teacher'll know you're real, and I can write about our adventures without being accused of **lying**.
My reputation for honesty is important to me.
You keep telling me my tail is on fire.
Well, you keep **LOOKING**.
dana

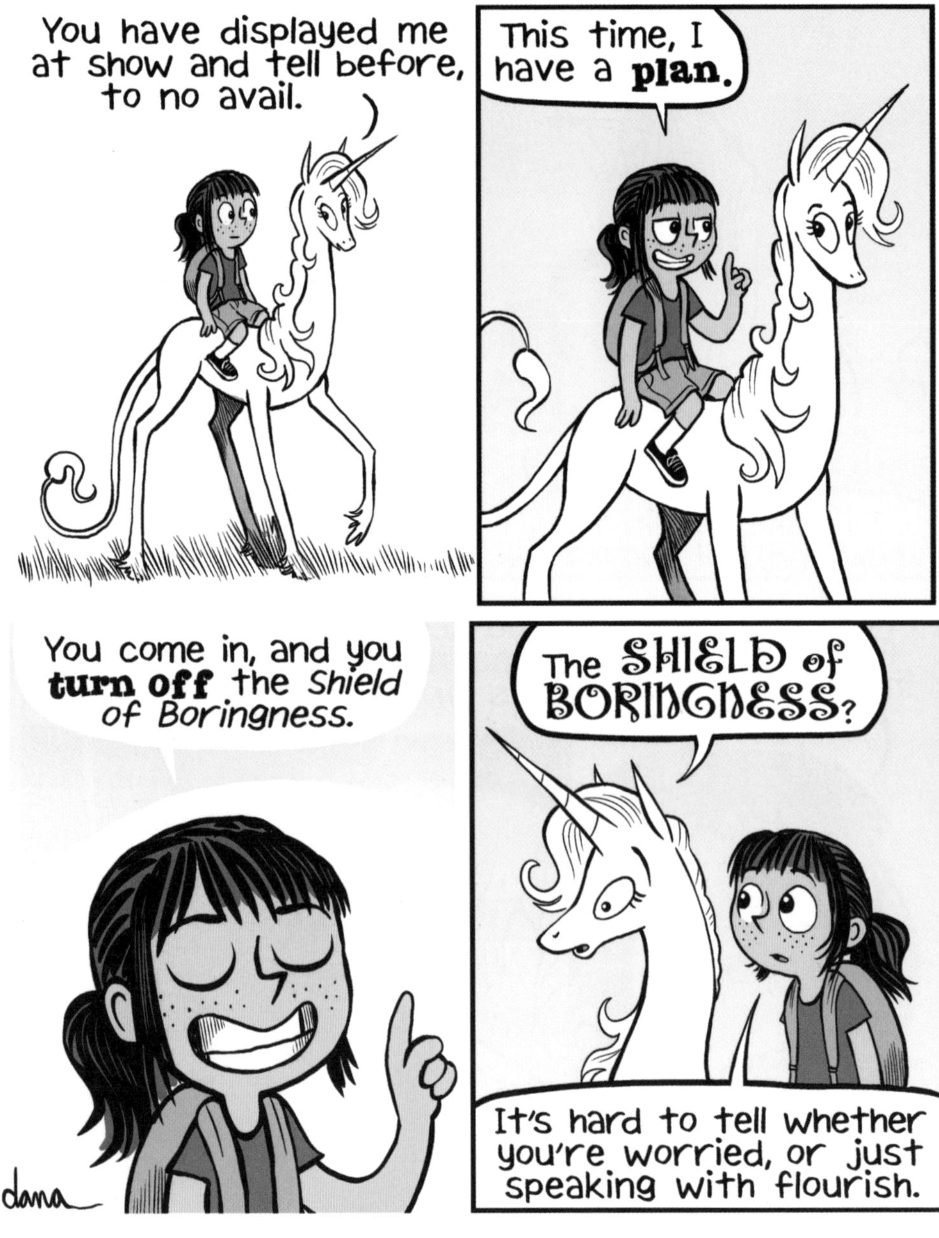
You have displayed me at show and tell before, to no avail.
This time, I have a **plan.**
You come in, and you **turn off** the *Shield of Boringness.*
The SHIELD of BORINGNESS?
It's hard to tell whether you're worried, or just speaking with flourish.
dana

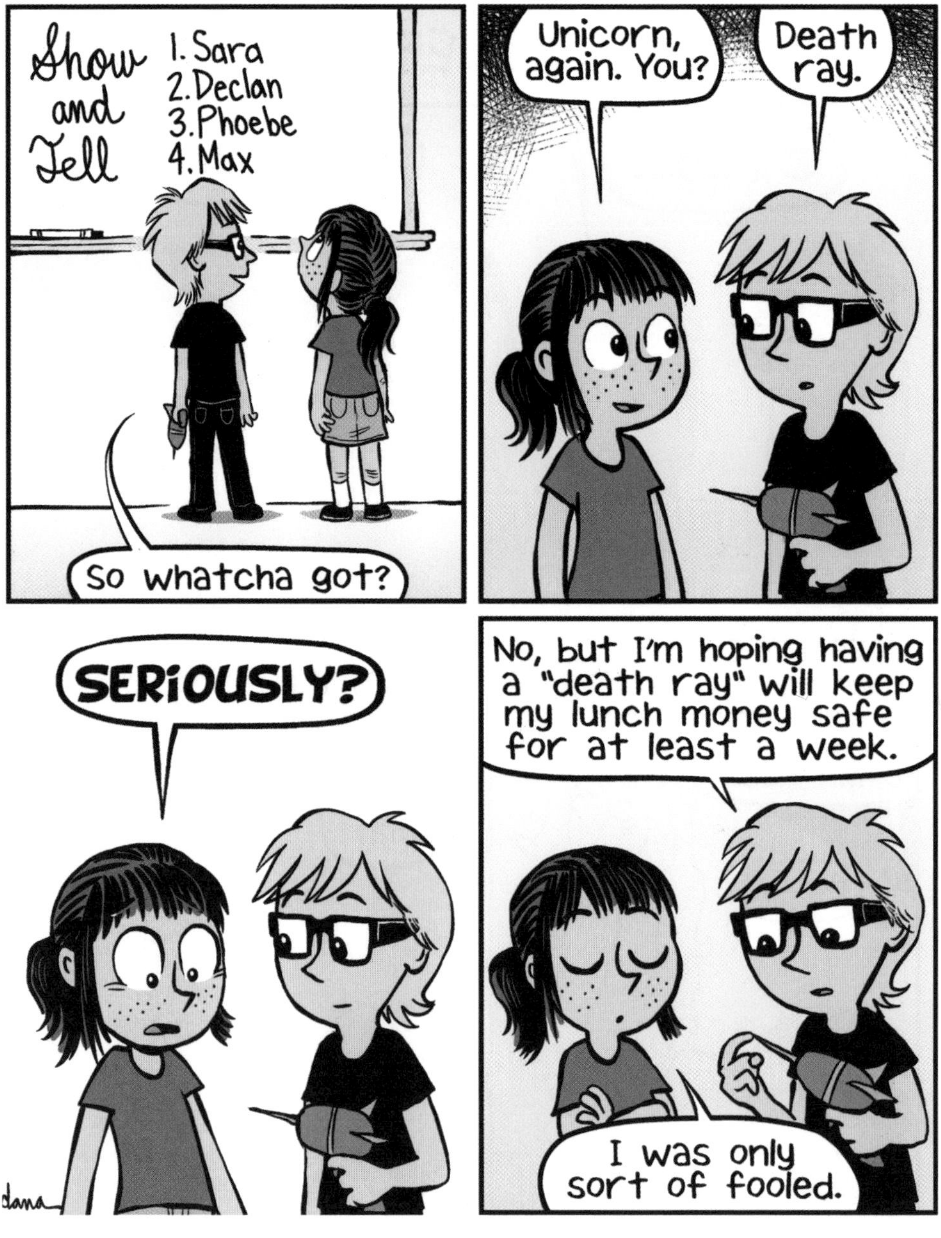
Show and Tell
1. Sara
2. Declan
3. Phoebe
4. Max
So whatcha got?
Unicorn, again. You?
Death ray.
SERIOUSLY?
No, but I'm hoping having a "death ray" will keep my lunch money safe for at least a week.
I was only sort of fooled.
dana

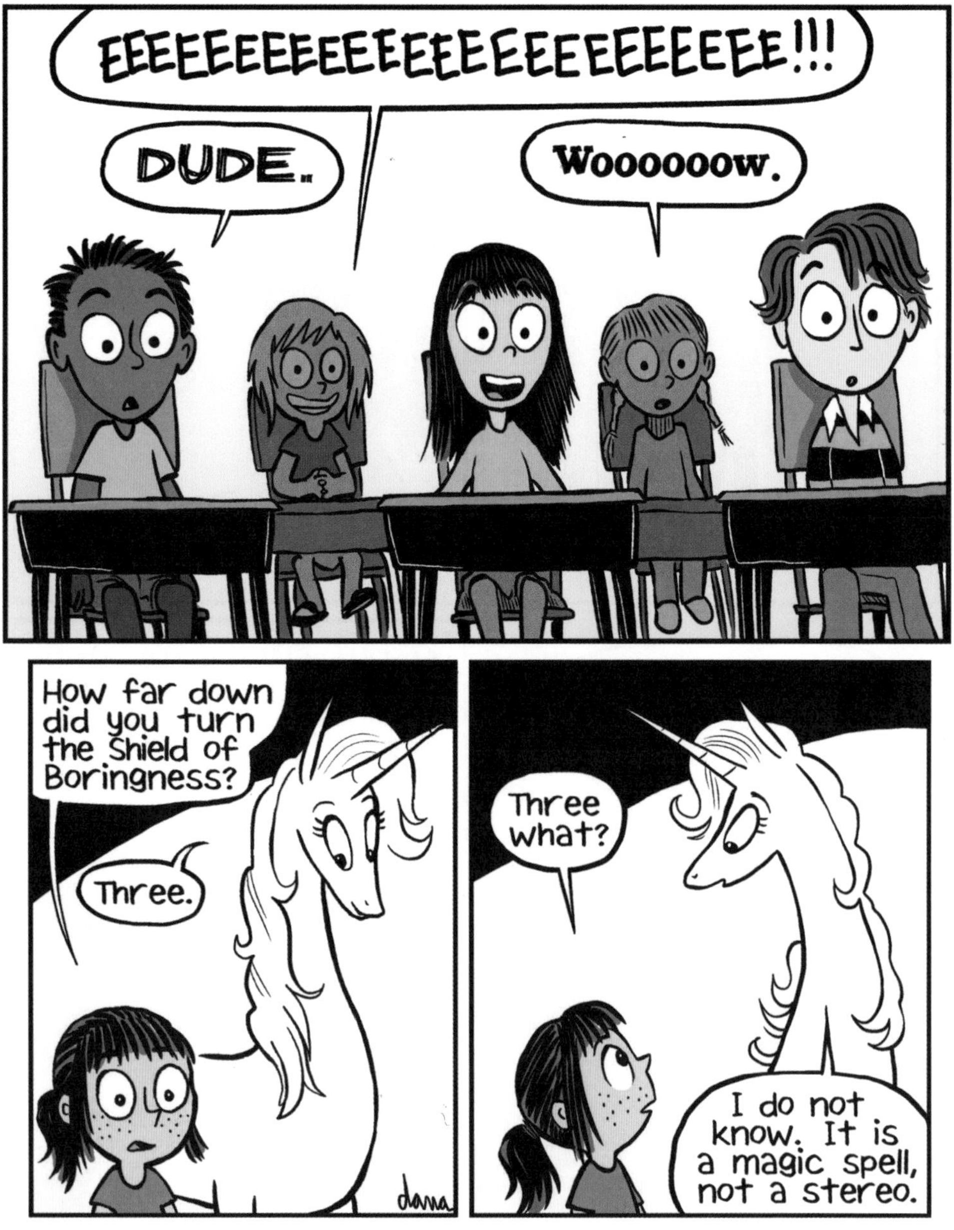

EEEEEEEEEEEEEEEEEEEEEEEE!!!
DUDE.
Wooooooow.
How far down did you turn the Shield of Boringness?
Three.
Three what?
I do not know. It is a magic spell, not a stereo.

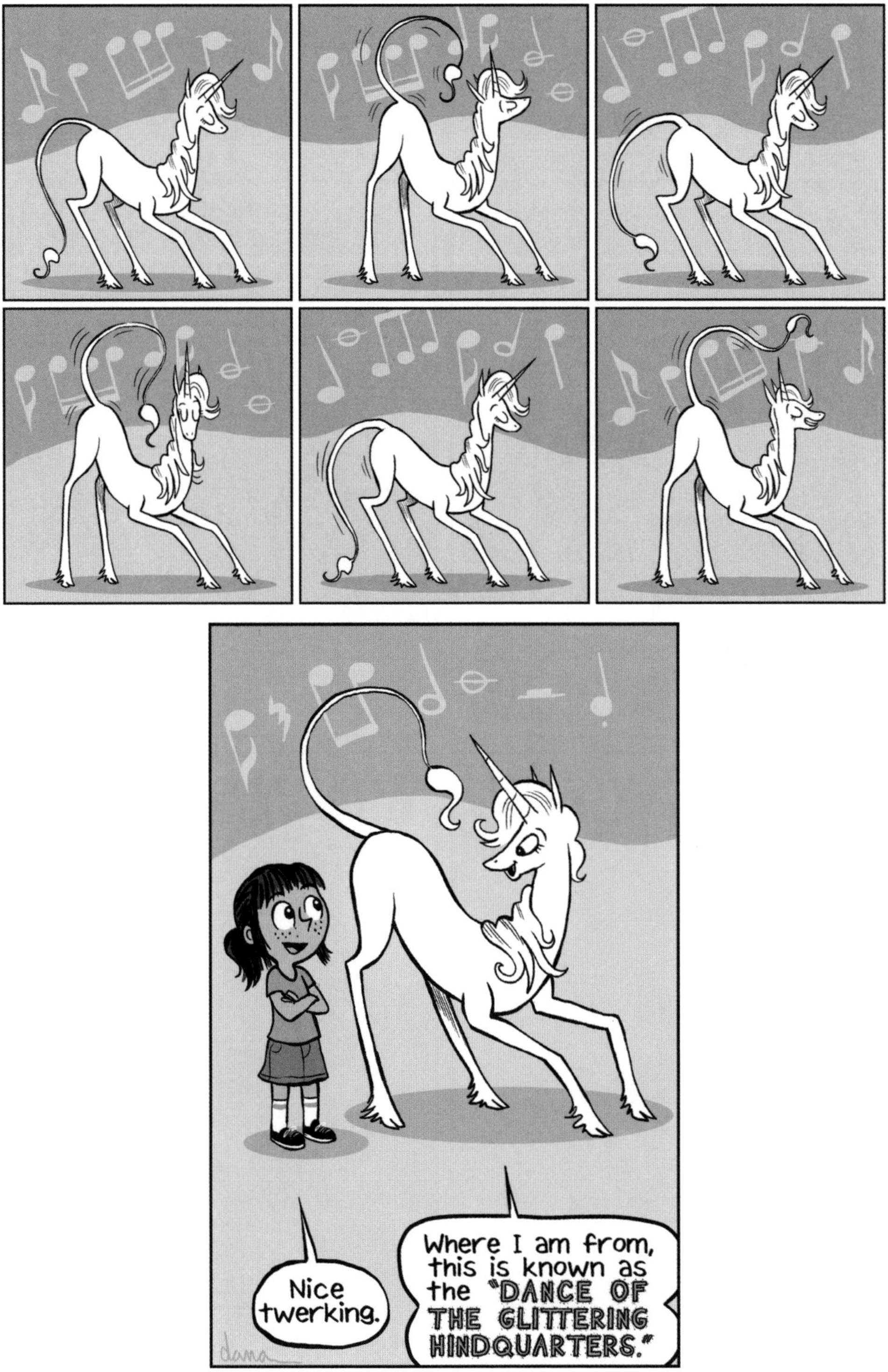
Nice twerking.
Where I am from, this is known as the "DANCE OF THE GLITTERING HINDQUARTERS."
dana

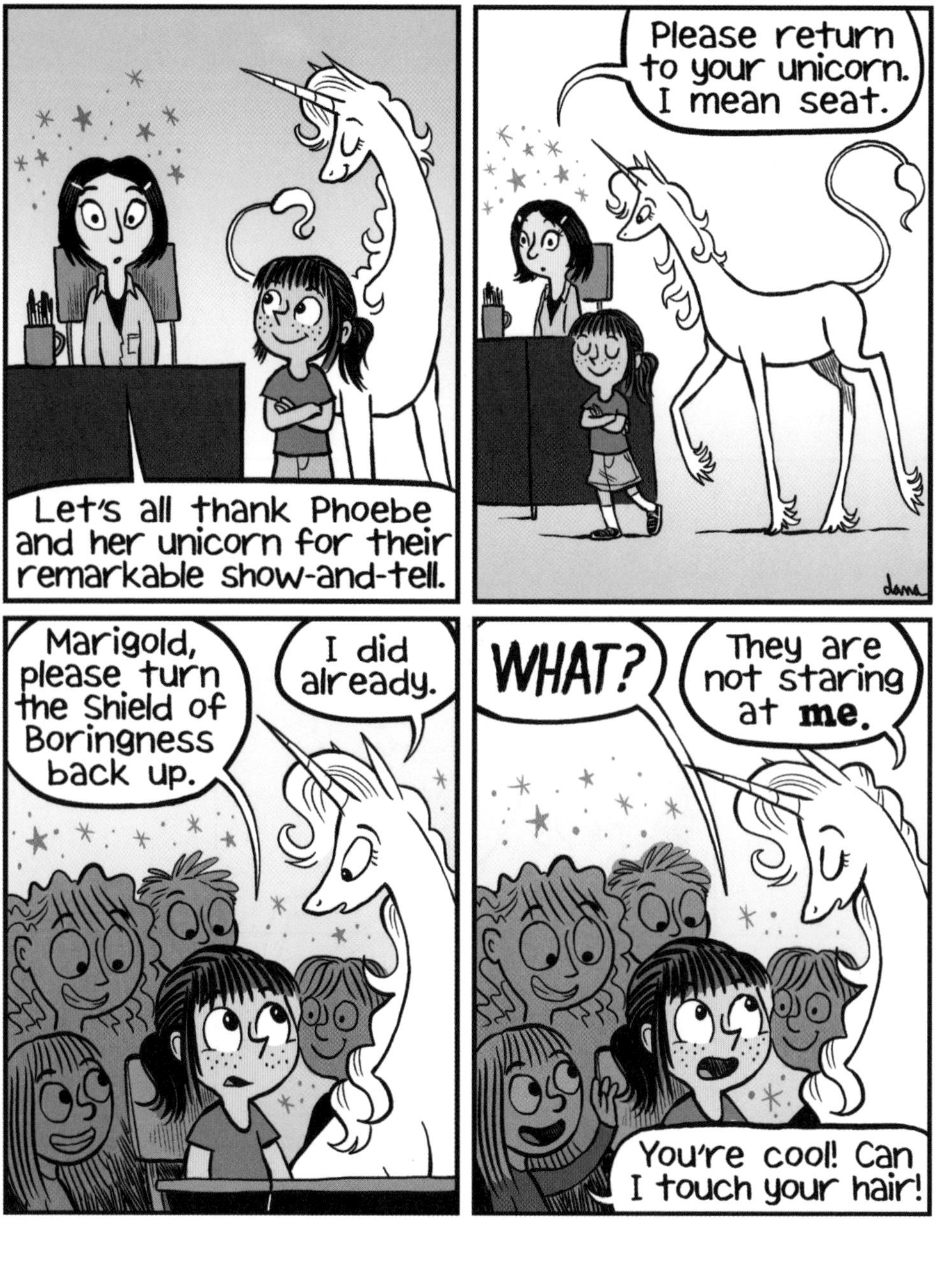
Let's all thank Phoebe and her unicorn for their remarkable show-and-tell.
Please return to your unicorn. I mean seat.
dana
Marigold, please turn the Shield of Boringness back up.
I did already.
WHAT?
They are not staring at **me**.
You're cool! Can I touch your hair!

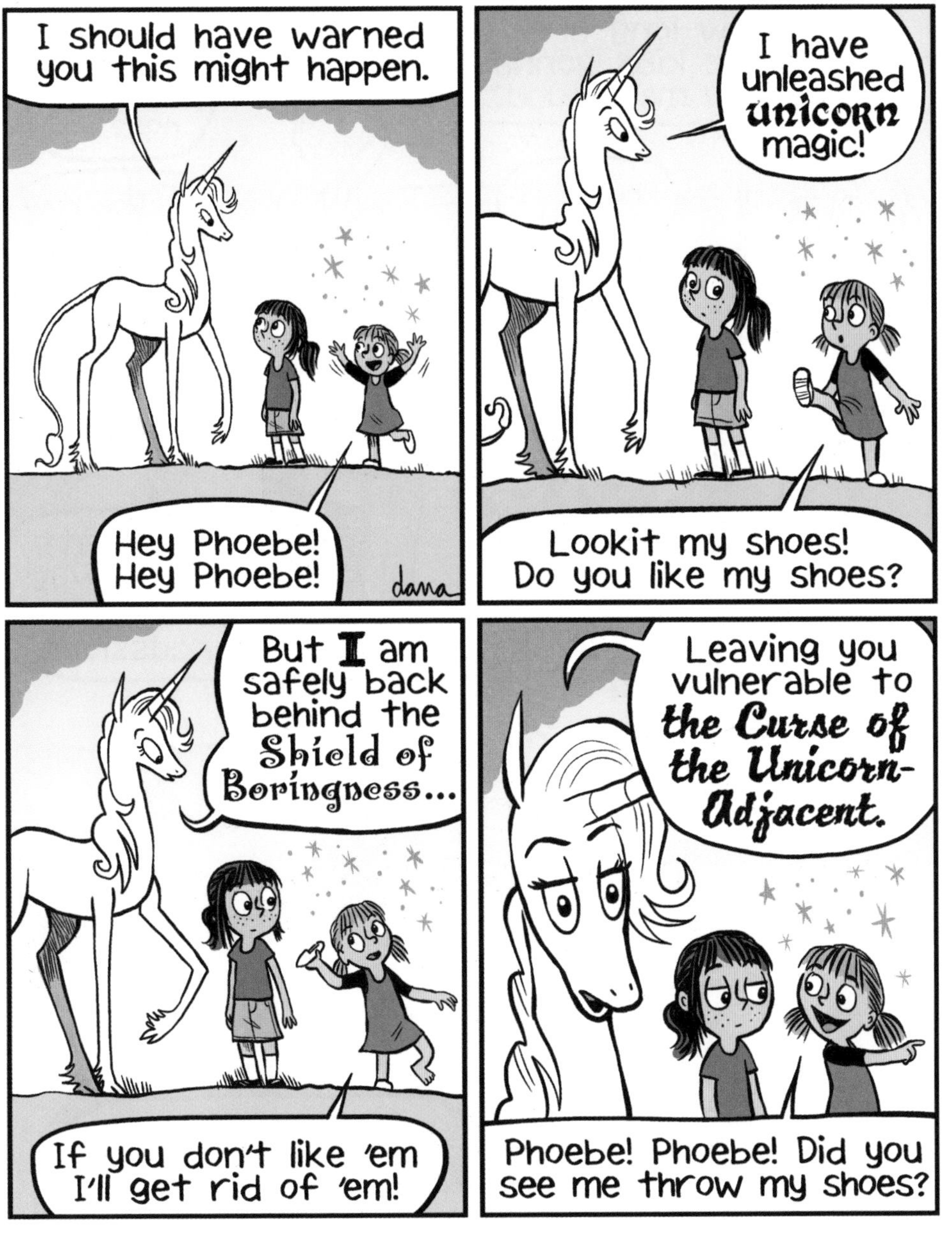
I should have warned you this might happen.
Hey Phoebe! Hey Phoebe!
dana
I have unleashed UNICORN magic!
Lookit my shoes! Do you like my shoes?
But I am safely back behind the Shield of Boringness...
If you don't like 'em I'll get rid of 'em!
Leaving you vulnerable to the Curse of the Unicorn-Adjacent.
Phoebe! Phoebe! Did you see me throw my shoes?

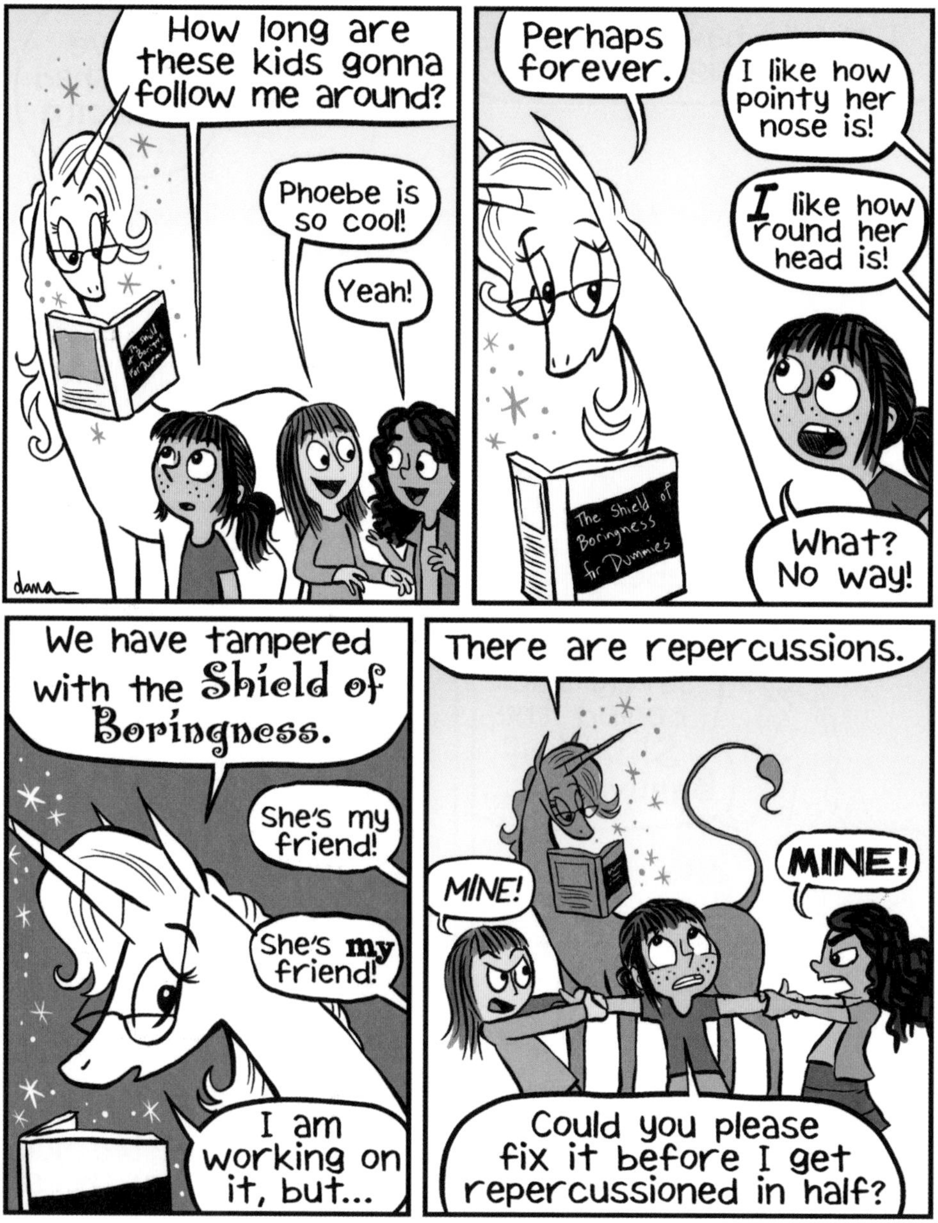
How long are these kids gonna follow me around?
Phoebe is so cool!
Yeah!
dana
Perhaps forever.
I like how pointy her nose is!
I like how round her head is!
The Shield of Boringness for Dummies
What? No way!
We have tampered with the Shield of Boringness.
She's my friend!
She's **my** friend!
I am working on it, but...
There are repercussions.
MINE!
MINE!
Could you please fix it before I get repercussioned in half?

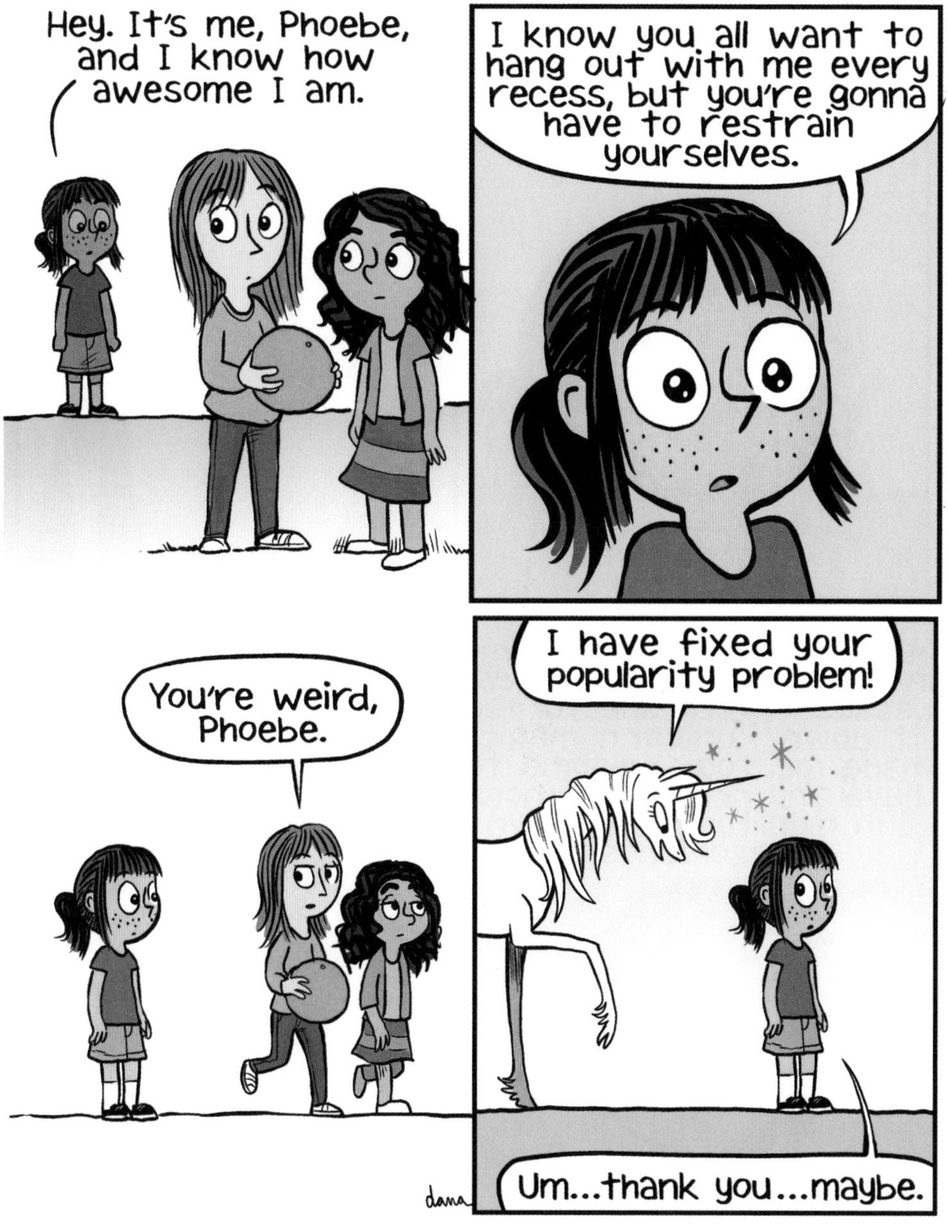

Hey. It's me, Phoebe, and I know how awesome I am.
I know you all want to hang out with me every recess, but you're gonna have to restrain yourselves.
You're weird, Phoebe.
I have fixed your popularity problem!
Um...thank you...maybe.
dana

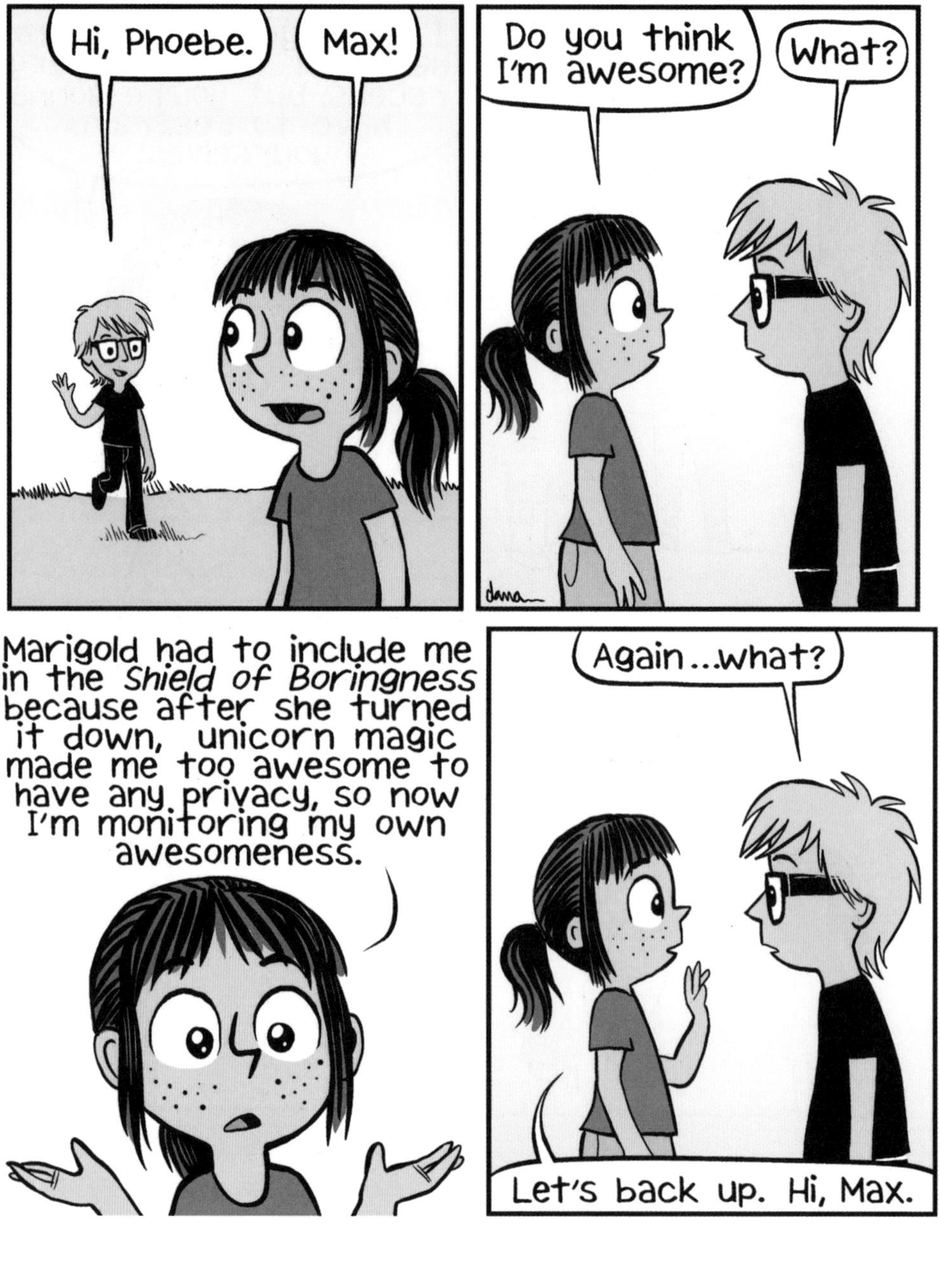
Hi, Phoebe.
Max!
Do you think I'm awesome?
What?
Marigold had to include me in the *Shield of Boringness* because after she turned it down, unicorn magic made me too awesome to have any privacy, so now I'm monitoring my own awesomeness.
Again...what?
Let's back up. Hi, Max.

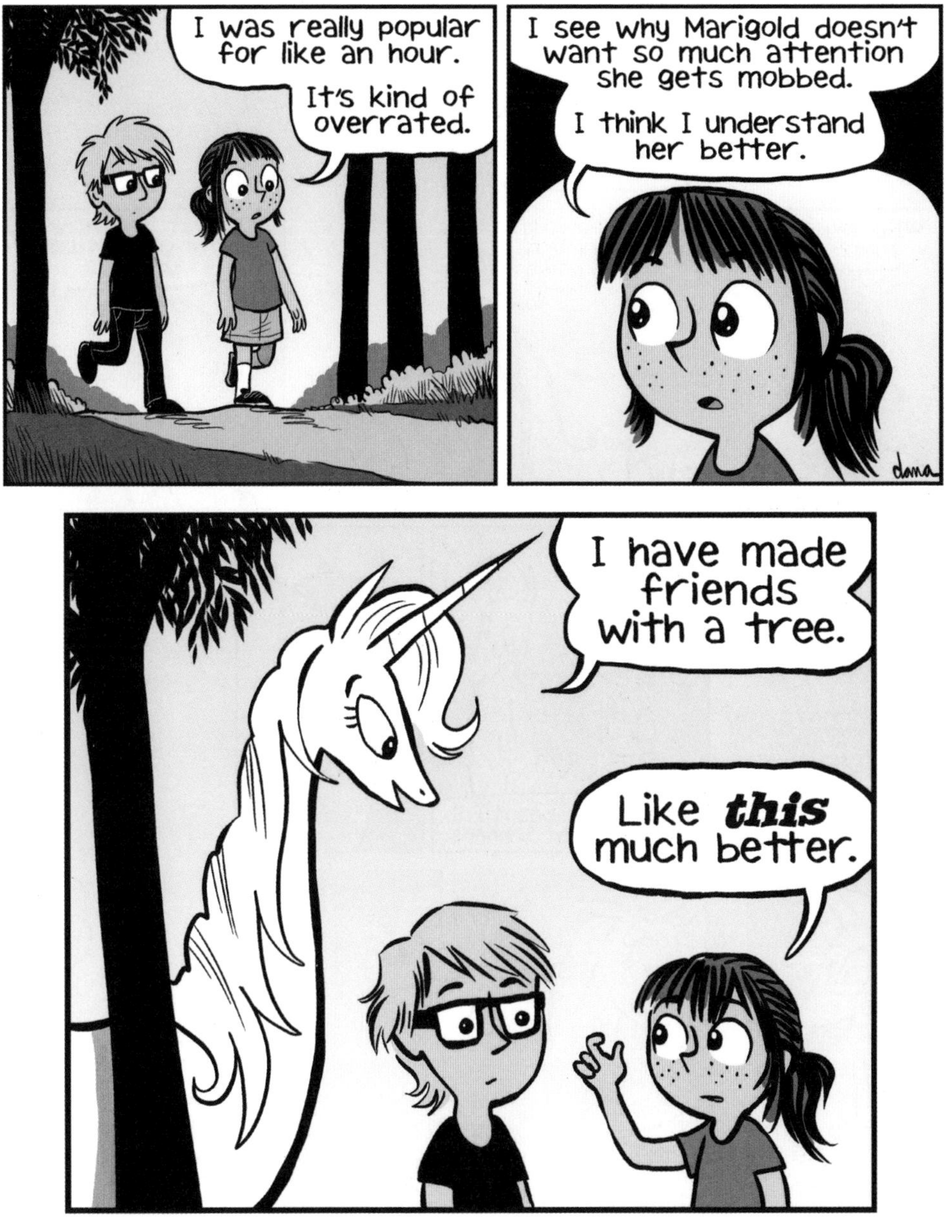
I was really popular for like an hour.
It's kind of overrated.
I see why Marigold doesn't want so much attention she gets mobbed.
I think I understand her better.
dana
I have made friends with a tree.
Like ***this*** much better.

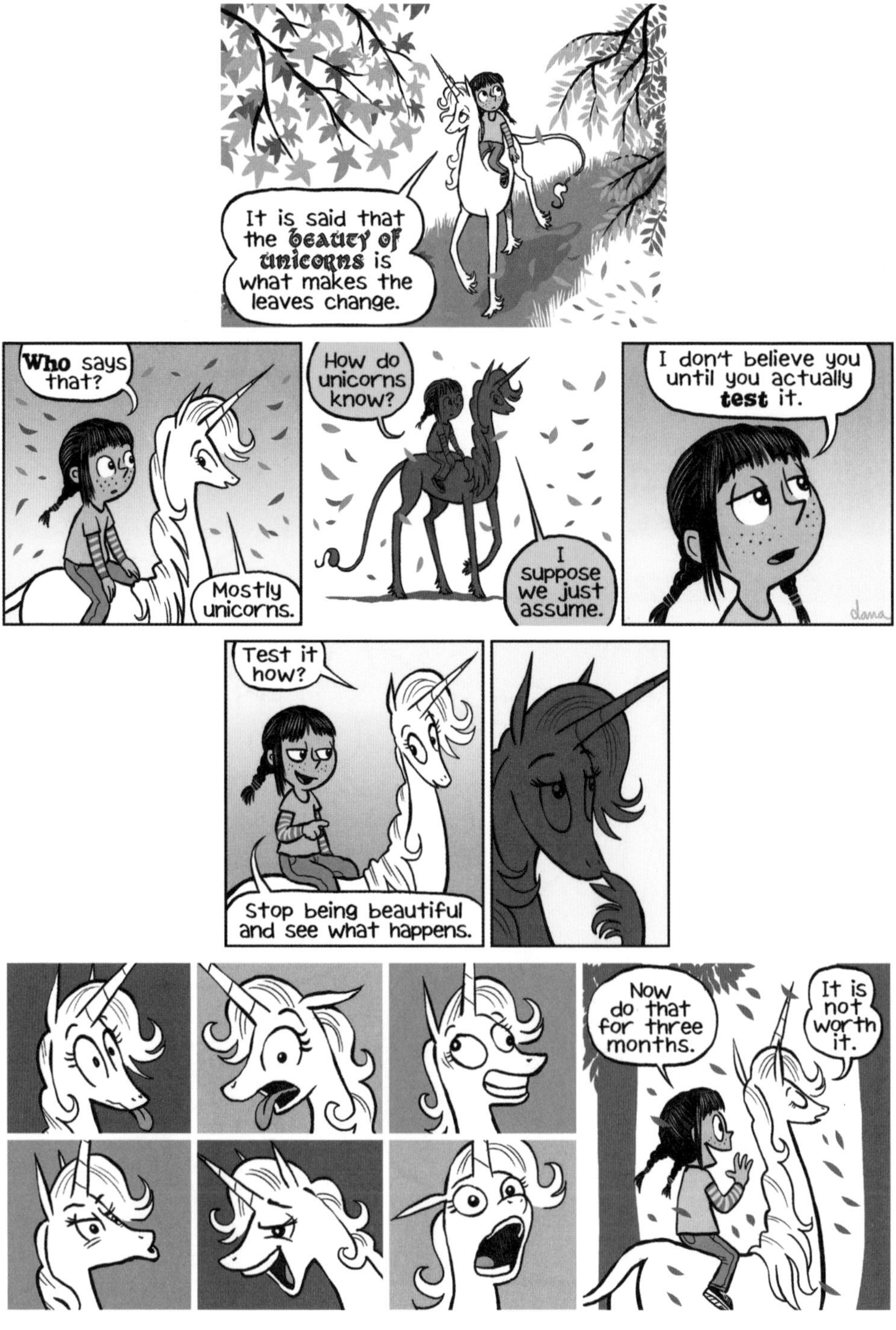
It is said that the beauty of unicorns is what makes the leaves change.
Who says that?
Mostly unicorns.
How do unicorns know?
I suppose we just assume.
I don't believe you until you actually test it.
dana
Test it how?
Stop being beautiful and see what happens.
Now do that for three months.
It is not worth it.

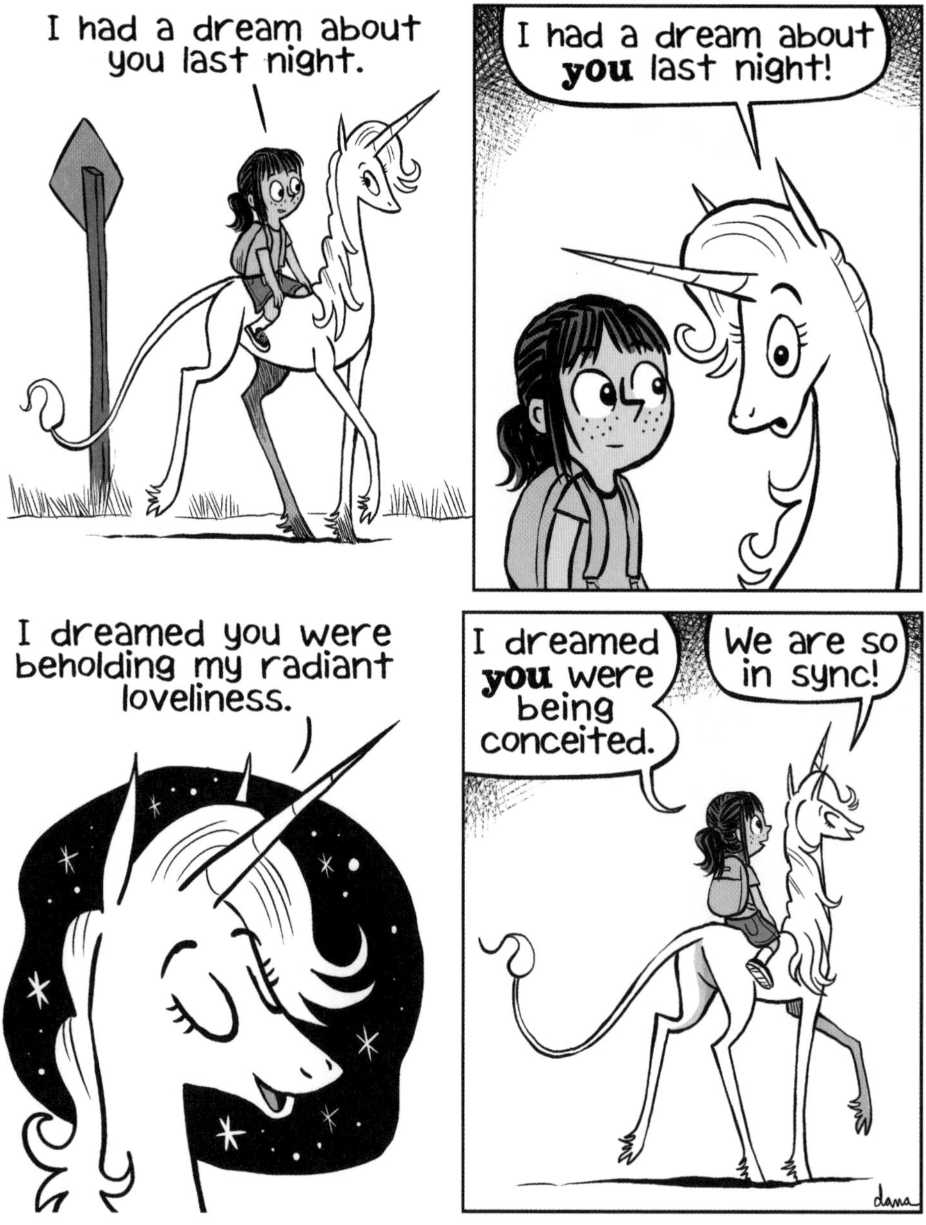
I had a dream about you last night.
I had a dream about **you** last night!
I dreamed you were beholding my radiant loveliness.
I dreamed **you** were being conceited.
We are so in sync!
dana

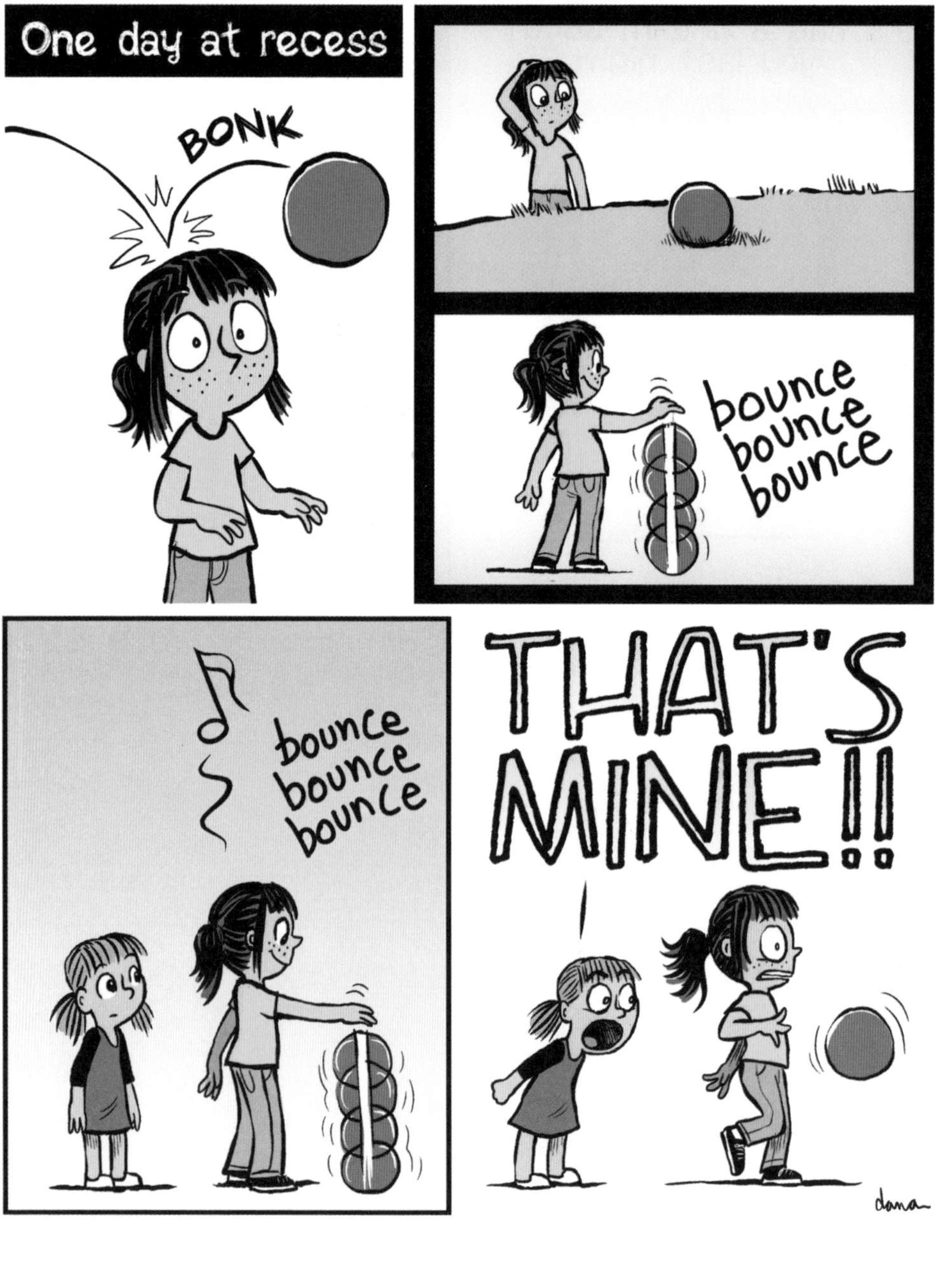
One day at recess
BONK
bounce
bounce
bounce
bounce
bounce
bounce
THAT'S MINE!!
dana

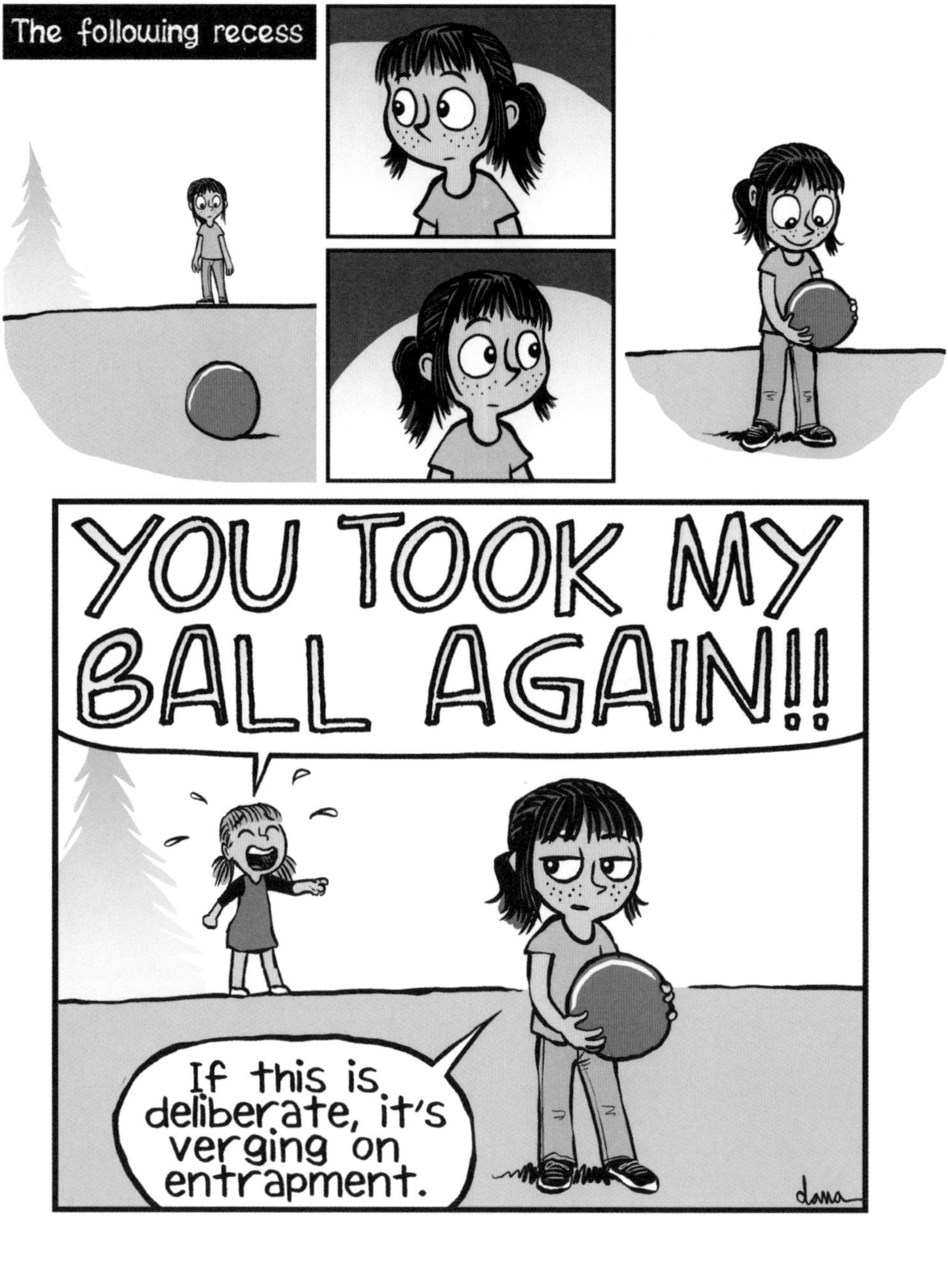
The following recess
YOU TOOK MY BALL AGAIN!!
If this is deliberate, it's verging on entrapment.
dana

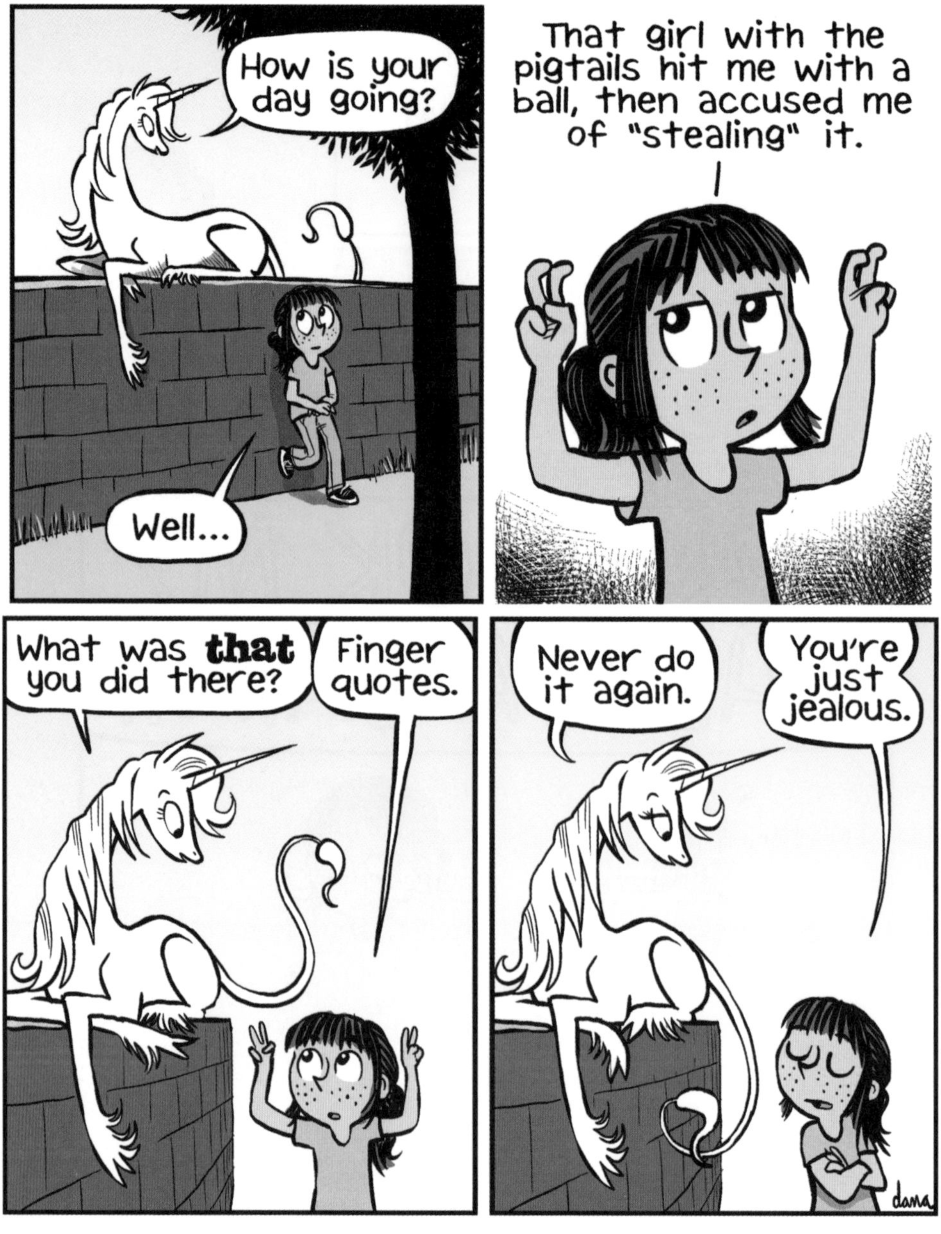
How is your day going?
Well...
That girl with the pigtails hit me with a ball, then accused me of "stealing" it.
What was **that** you did there?
Finger quotes.
Never do it again.
You're just jealous.
dana

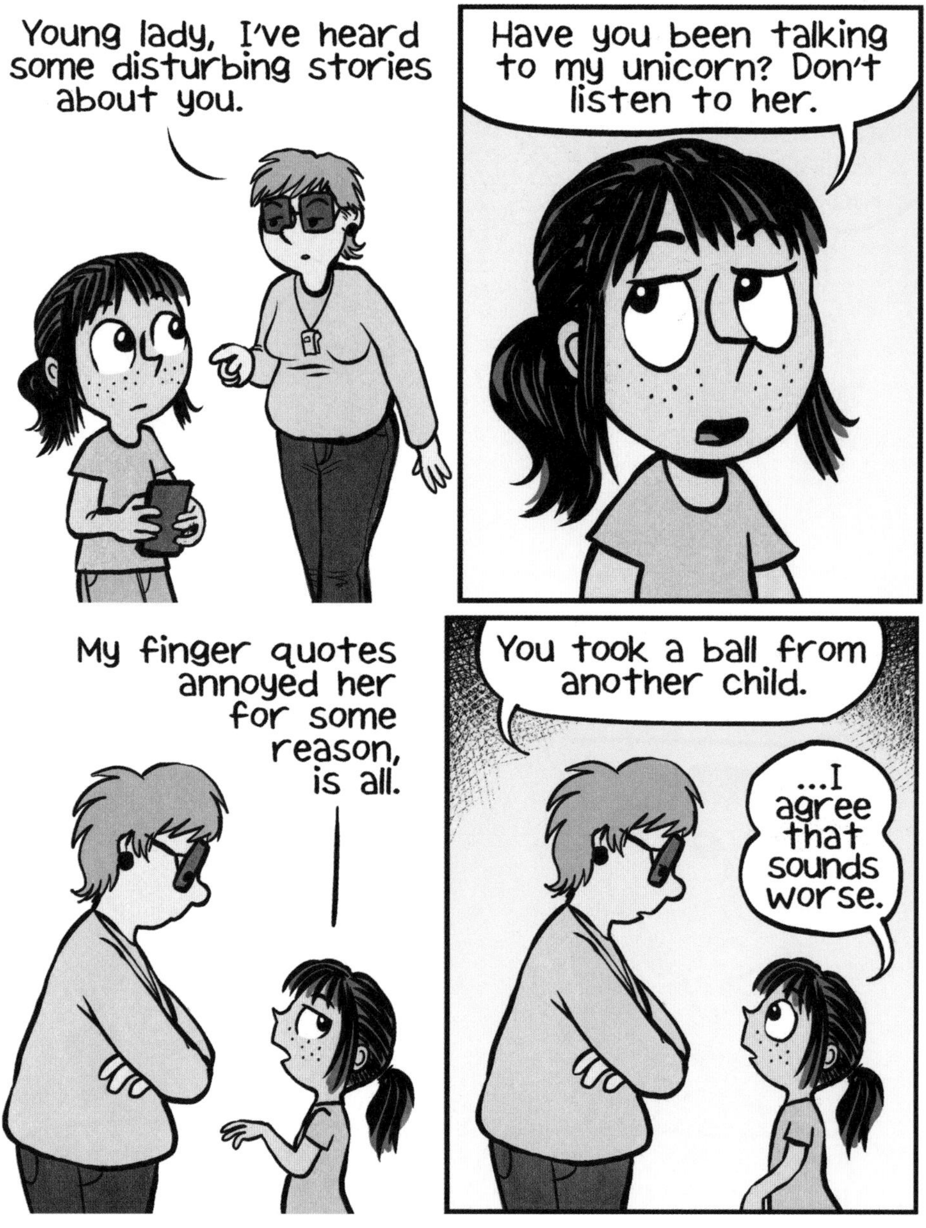
Young lady, I've heard some disturbing stories about you.
Have you been talking to my unicorn? Don't listen to her.
My finger quotes annoyed her for some reason, is all.
You took a ball from another child.
...I agree that sounds worse.

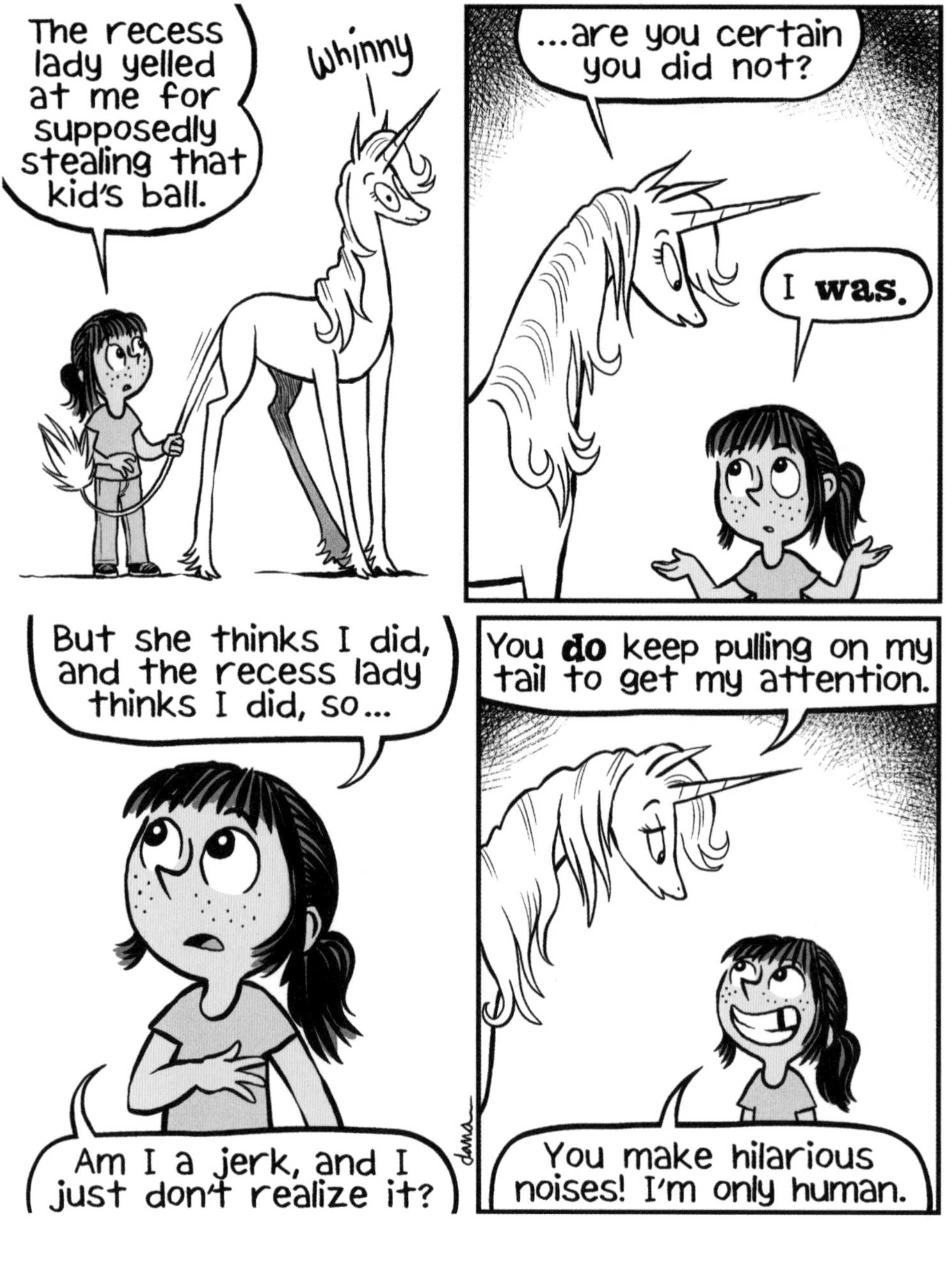
The recess lady yelled at me for supposedly stealing that kid's ball.
Whinny
...are you certain you did not?
I **was.**
But she thinks I did, and the recess lady thinks I did, so...
Am I a jerk, and I just don't realize it?
You **do** keep pulling on my tail to get my attention.
You make hilarious noises! I'm only human.

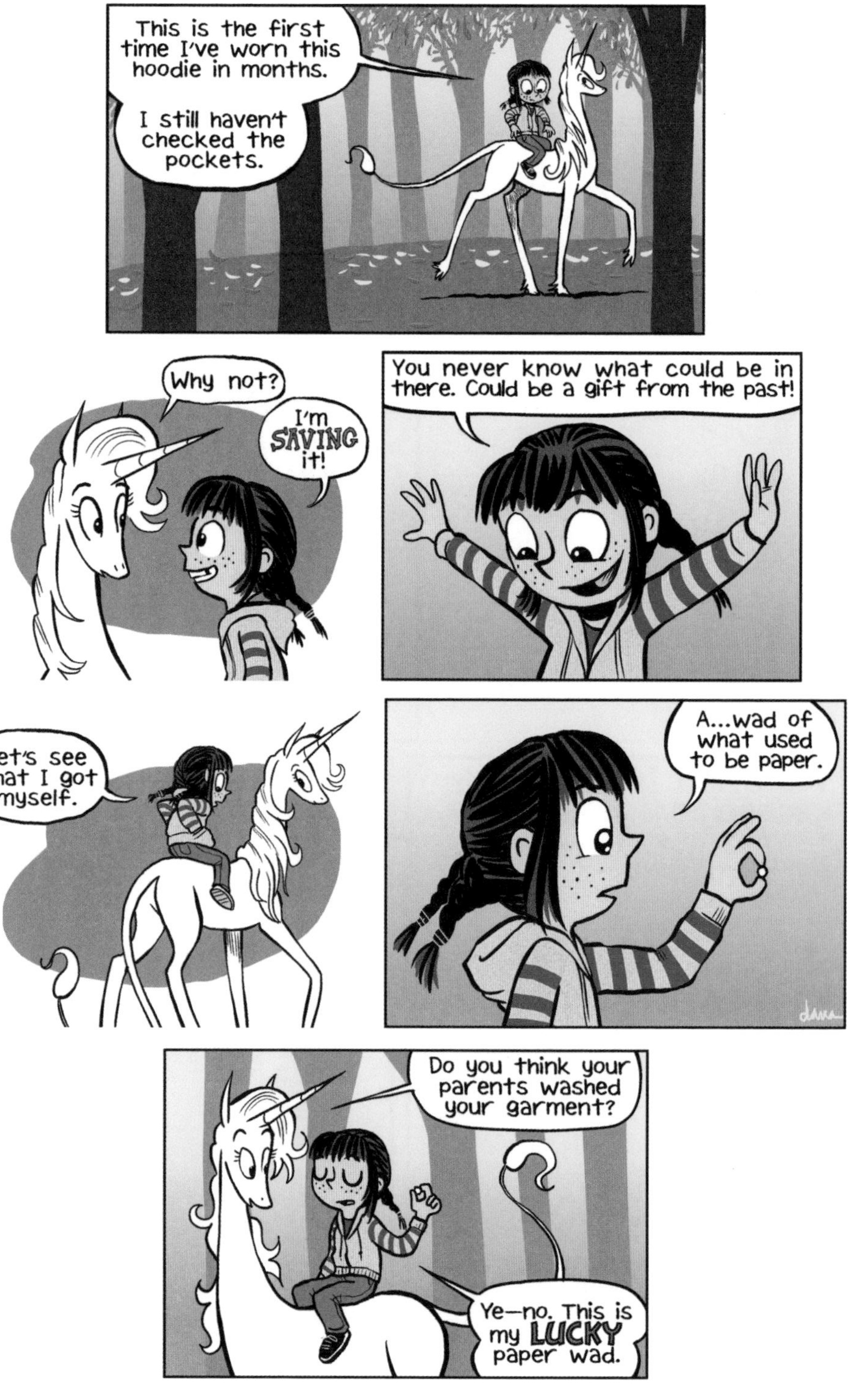
This is the first time I've worn this hoodie in months.
I still haven't checked the pockets.
Why not?
I'm SAVING it!
You never know what could be in there. Could be a gift from the past!
Let's see what I got myself.
A...wad of what used to be paper.
dana
Do you think your parents washed your garment?
Ye—no. This is my LUCKY paper wad.

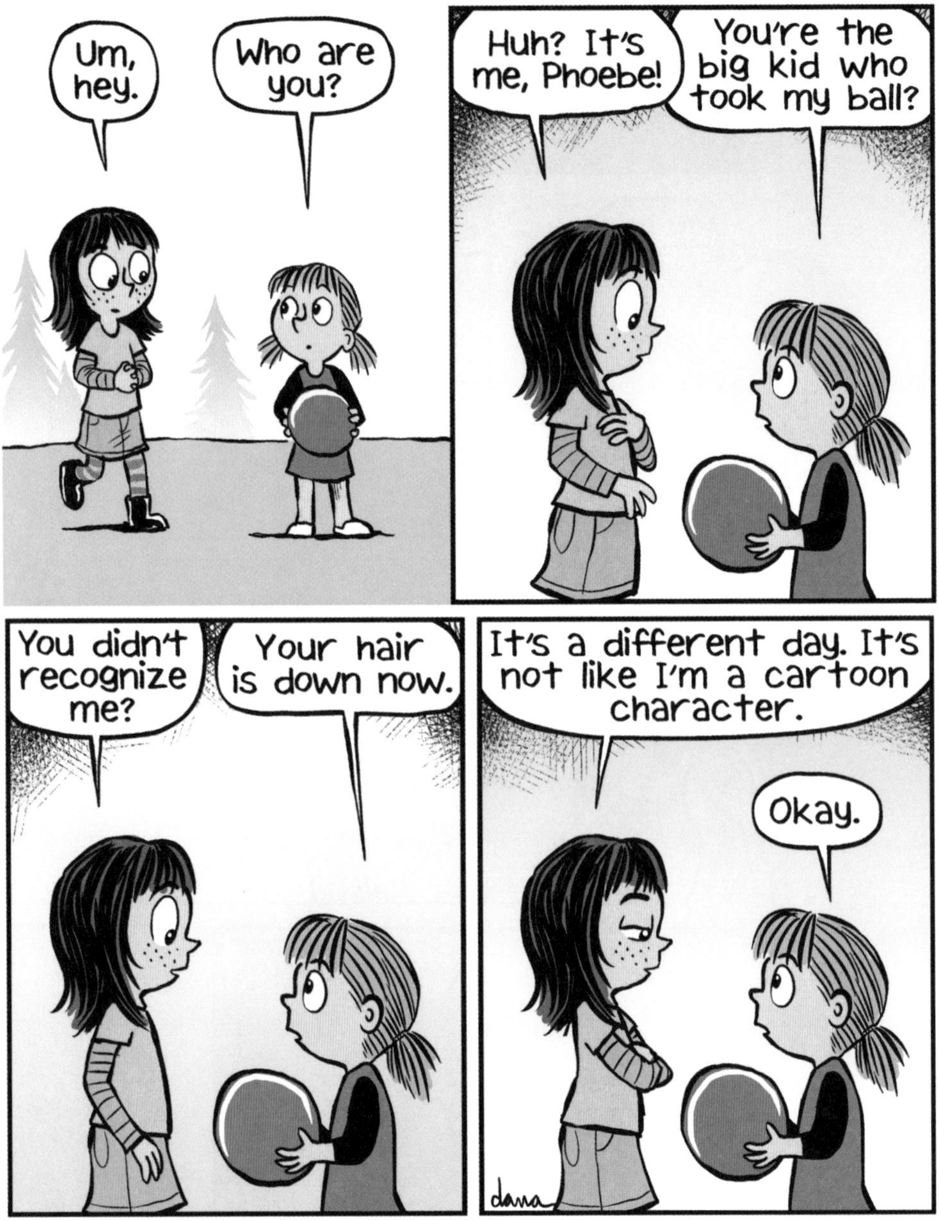
Um, hey.
Who are you?
Huh? It's me, Phoebe!
You're the big kid who took my ball?
You didn't recognize me?
Your hair is down now.
It's a different day. It's not like I'm a cartoon character.
Okay.
dana

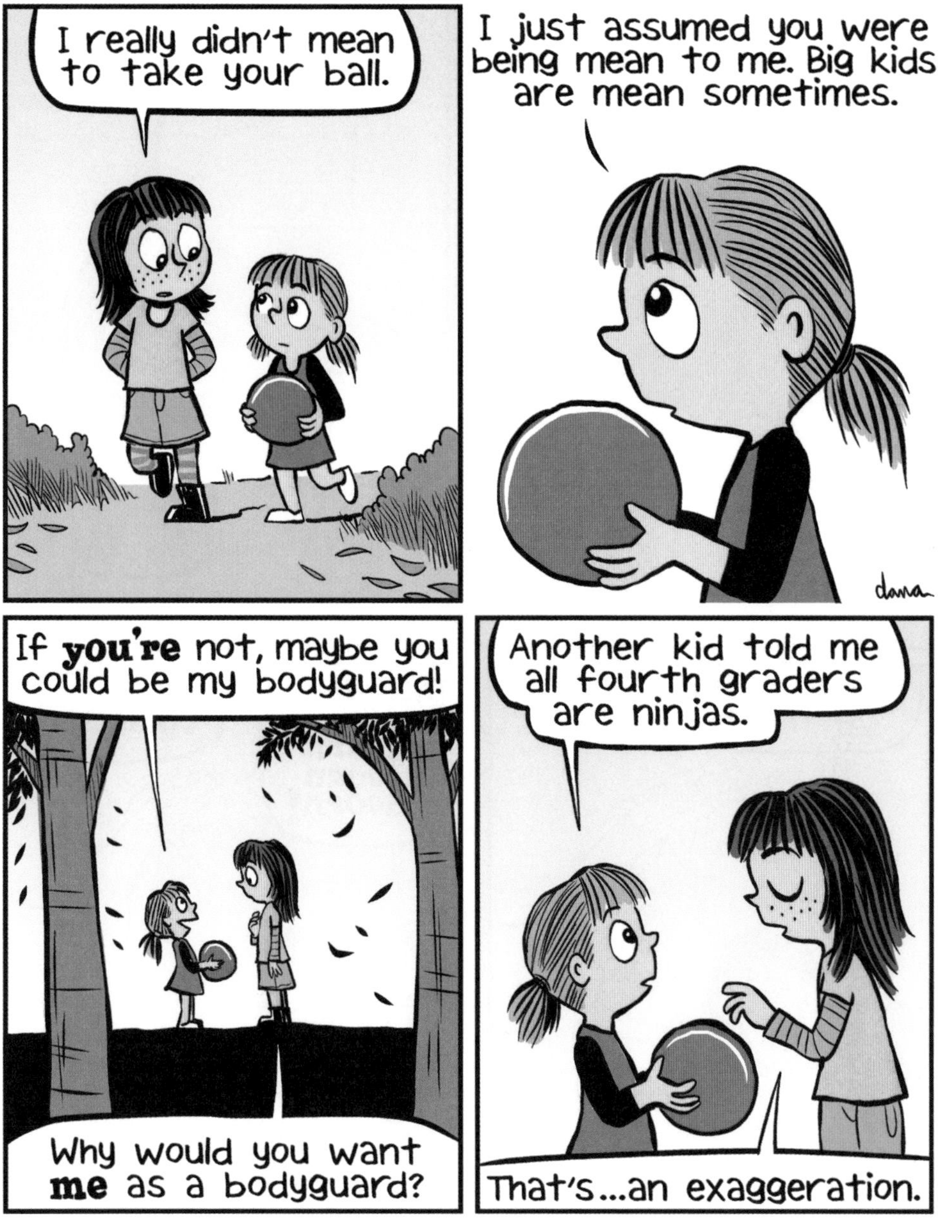
I really didn't mean to take your ball.
I just assumed you were being mean to me. Big kids are mean sometimes.
dana
If **you're** not, maybe you could be my bodyguard!
Why would you want **me** as a bodyguard?
Another kid told me all fourth graders are ninjas.
That's...an exaggeration.

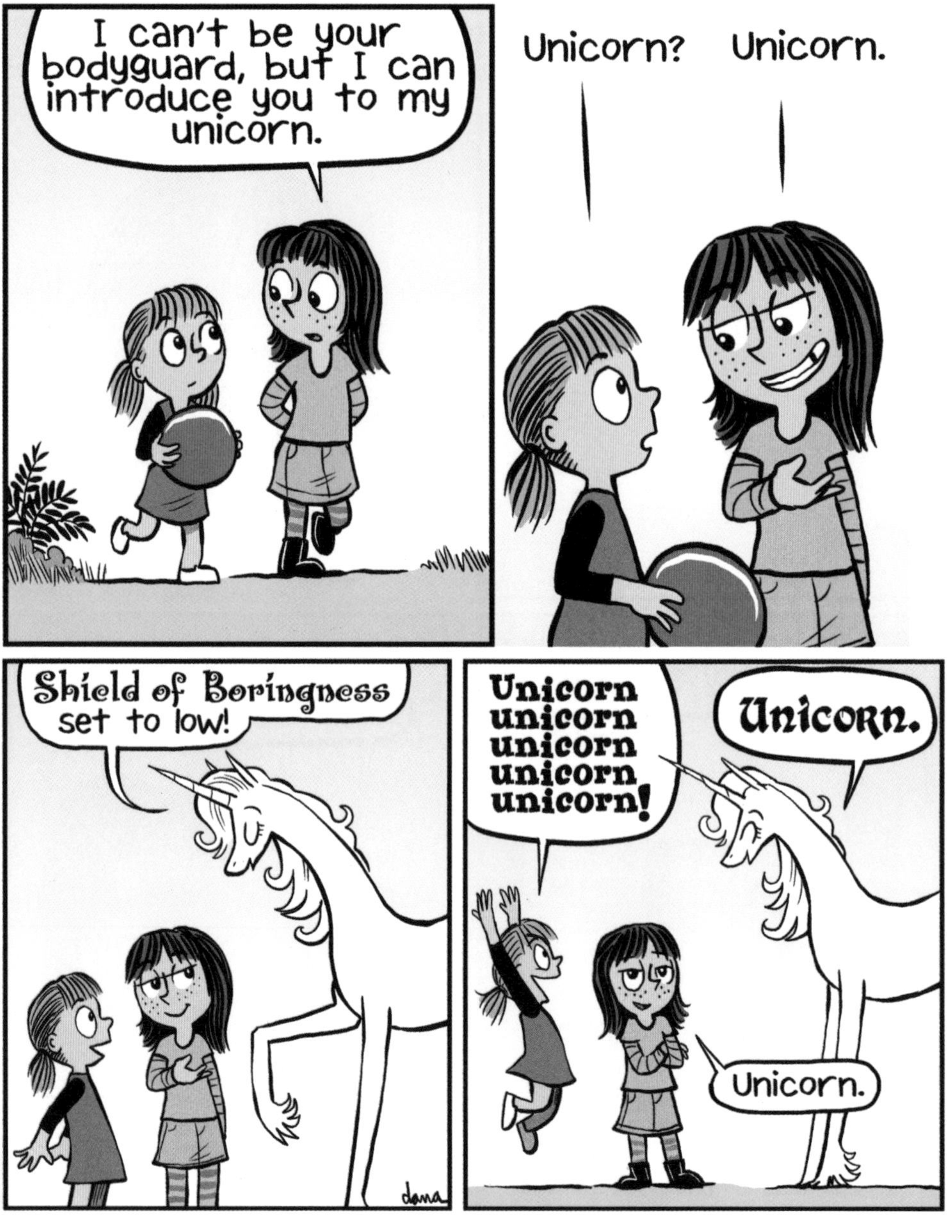
I can't be your bodyguard, but I can introduce you to my unicorn.
Unicorn?
Unicorn.
Shield of Boringness set to low!
Unicorn unicorn unicorn unicorn unicorn!
Unicorn.
Unicorn.

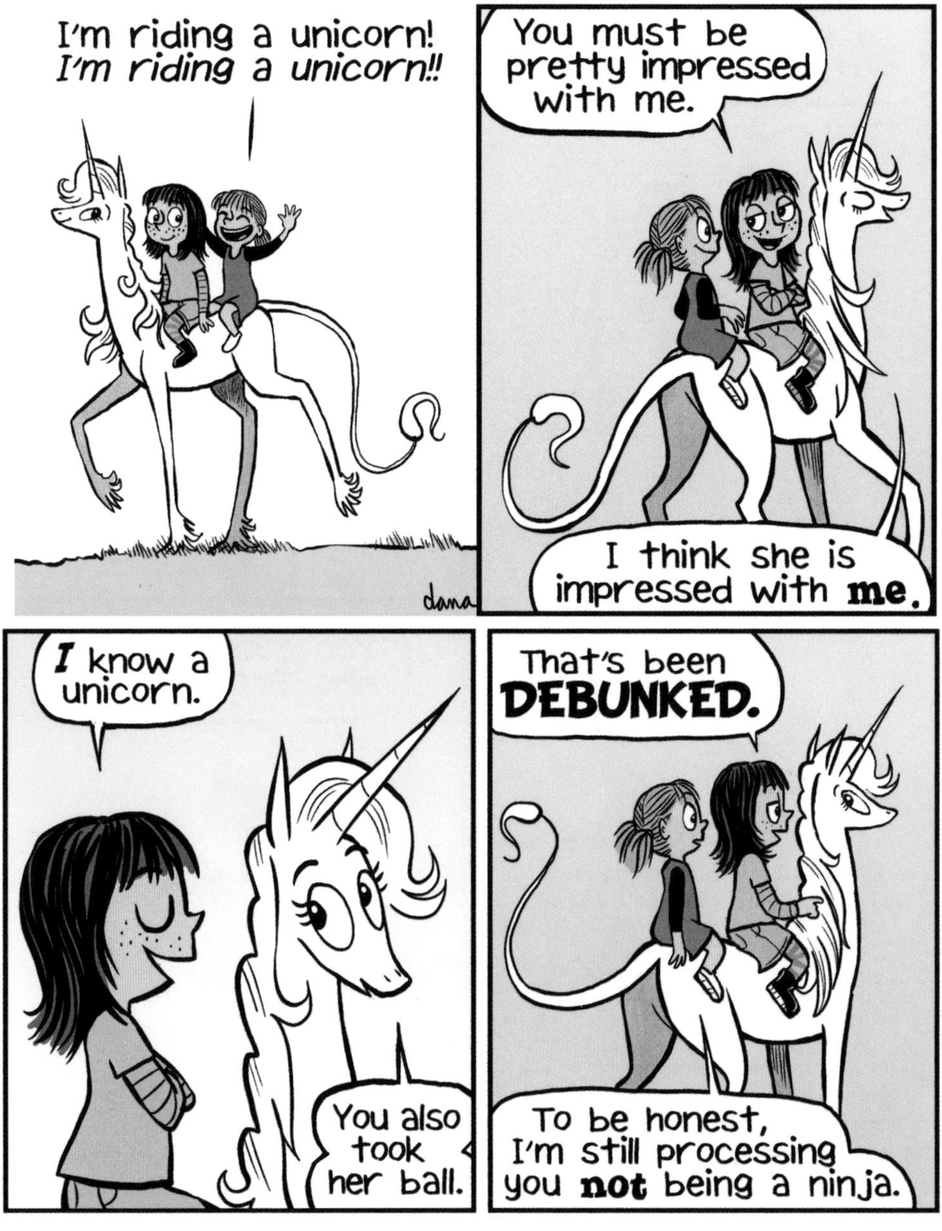
I'm riding a unicorn!
I'm riding a unicorn!!
dana
You must be pretty impressed with me.
I think she is impressed with **me**.
I know a unicorn.
You also took her ball.
That's been **DEBUNKED.**
To be honest, I'm still processing you **not** being a ninja.

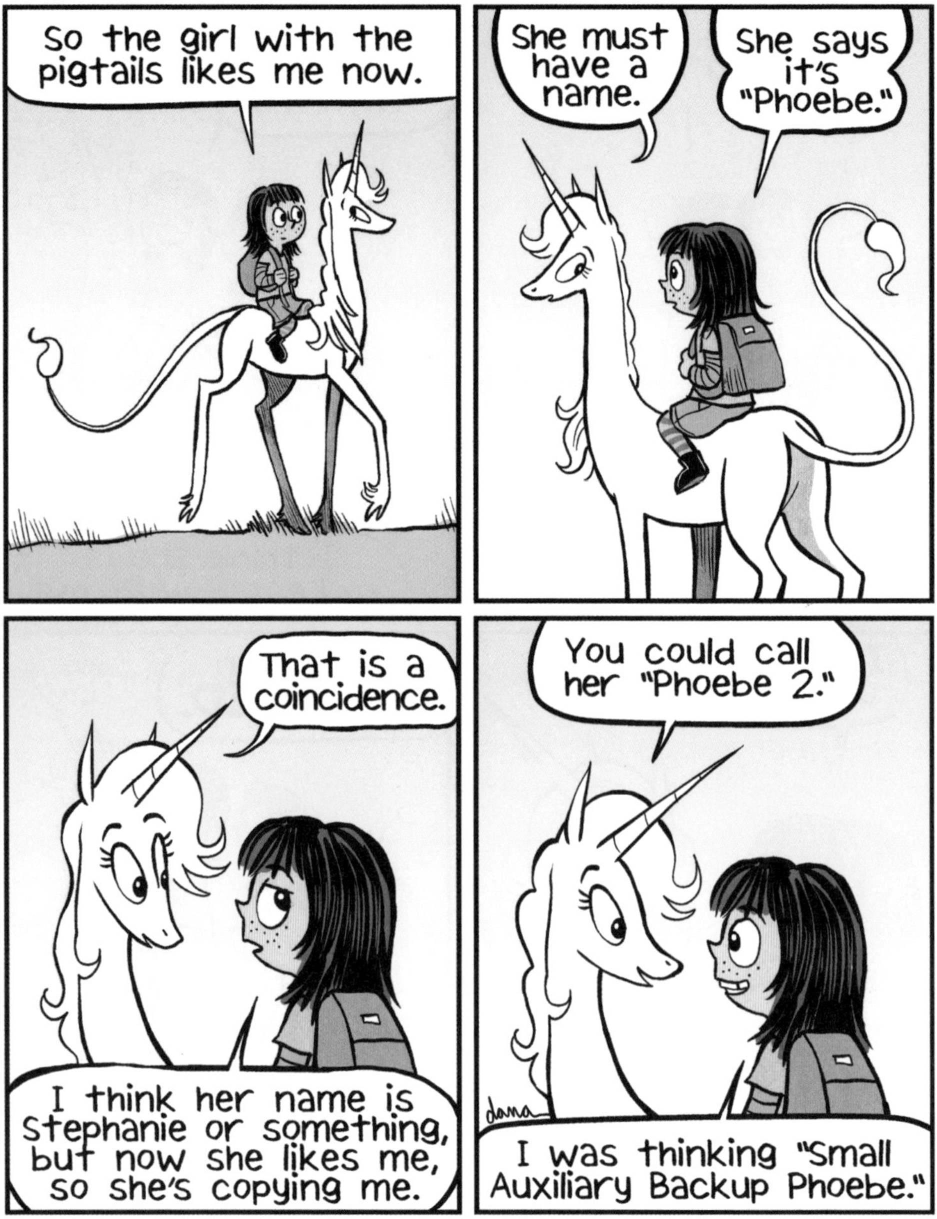
So the girl with the pigtails likes me now.
She must have a name.
She says it's "Phoebe."
That is a coincidence.
I think her name is Stephanie or something, but now she likes me, so she's copying me.
You could call her "Phoebe 2."
I was thinking "Small Auxiliary Backup Phoebe."
dana

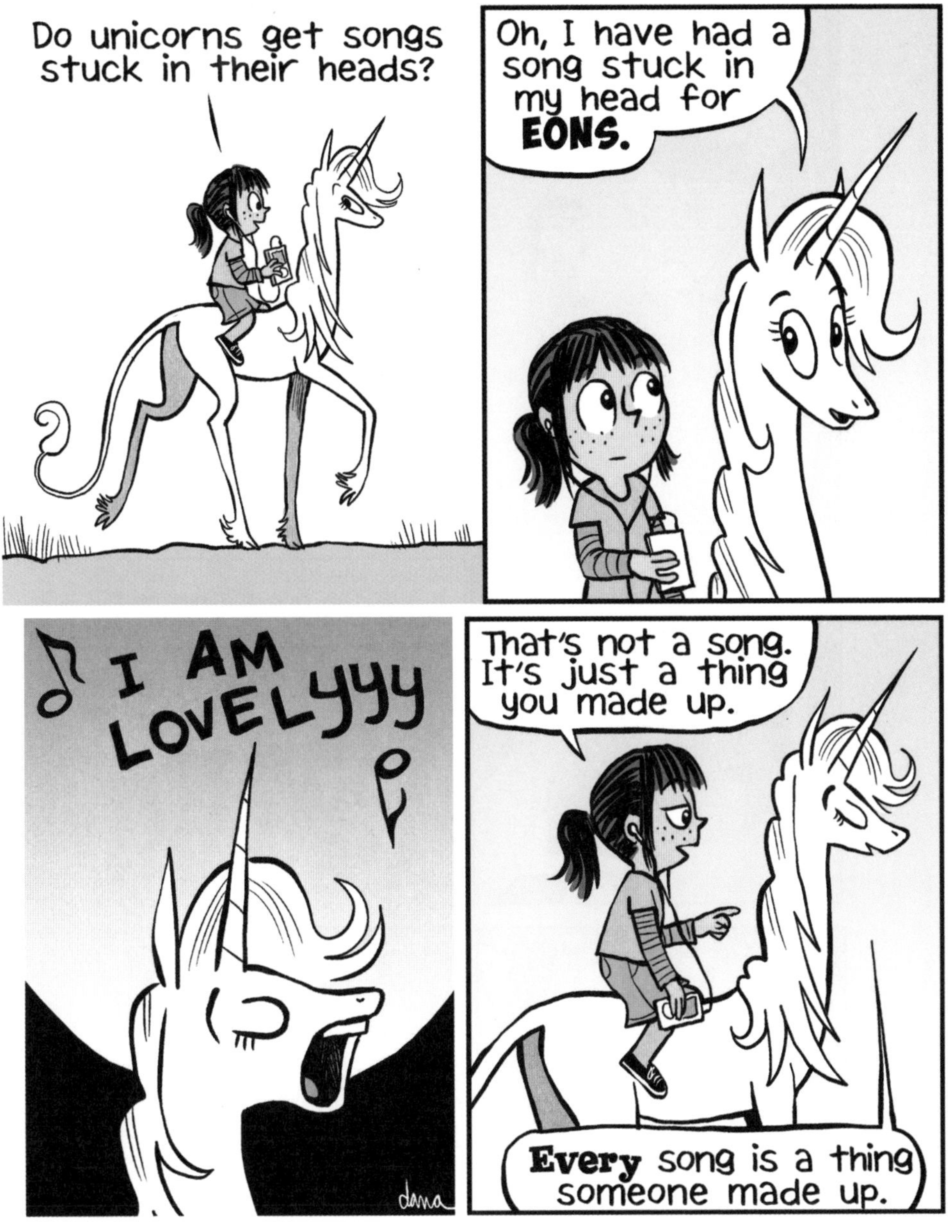
Do unicorns get songs stuck in their heads?
Oh, I have had a song stuck in my head for EONS.
I AM LOVELYYY
That's not a song. It's just a thing you made up.
Every song is a thing someone made up.
dana

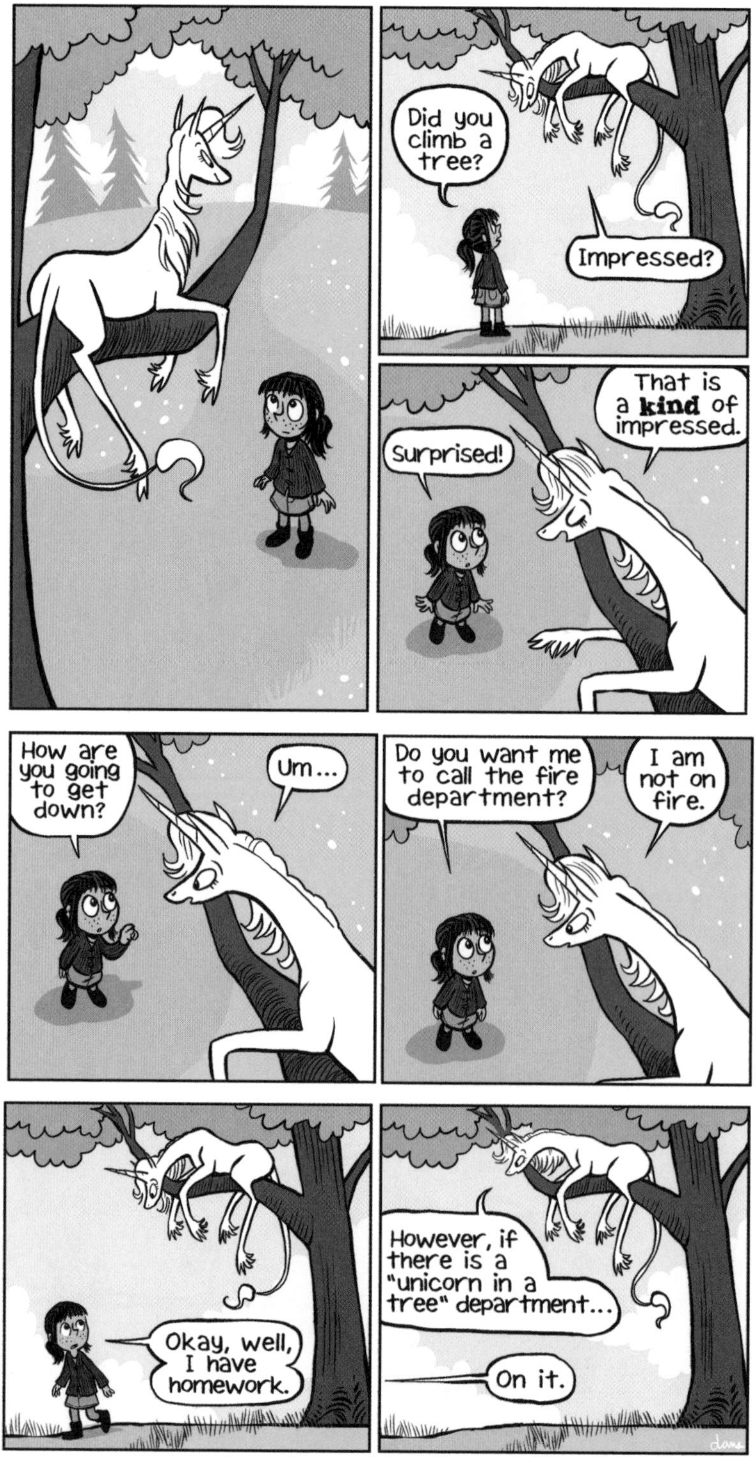

Did you climb a tree?
Impressed?
Surprised!
That is a **kind** of impressed.
How are you going to get down?
Um...
Do you want me to call the fire department?
I am not on fire.
Okay, well, I have homework.
However, if there is a "unicorn in a tree" department...
On it.

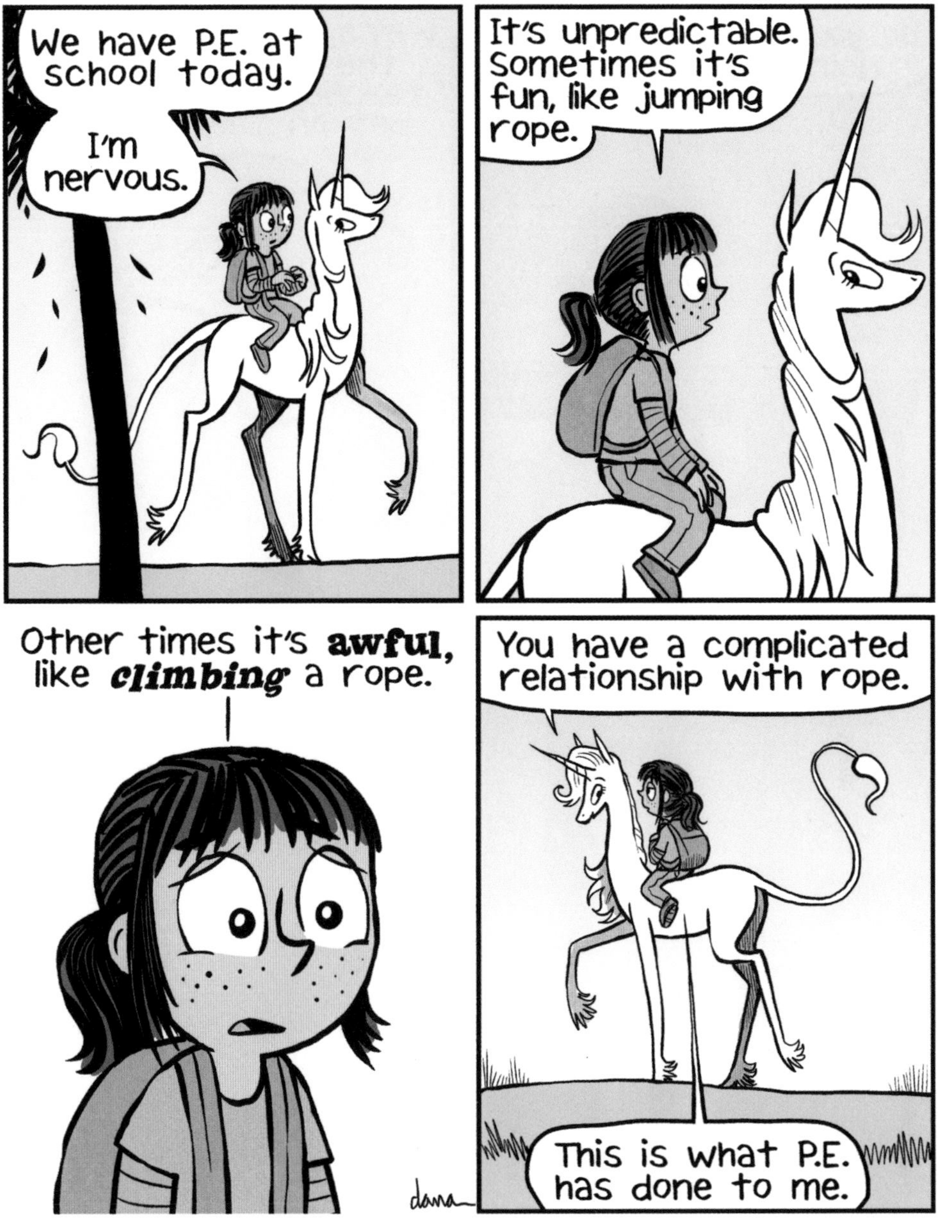
We have P.E. at school today.
I'm nervous.
It's unpredictable. Sometimes it's fun, like jumping rope.
Other times it's **awful**, like ***climbing*** a rope.
You have a complicated relationship with rope.
This is what P.E. has done to me.
dana

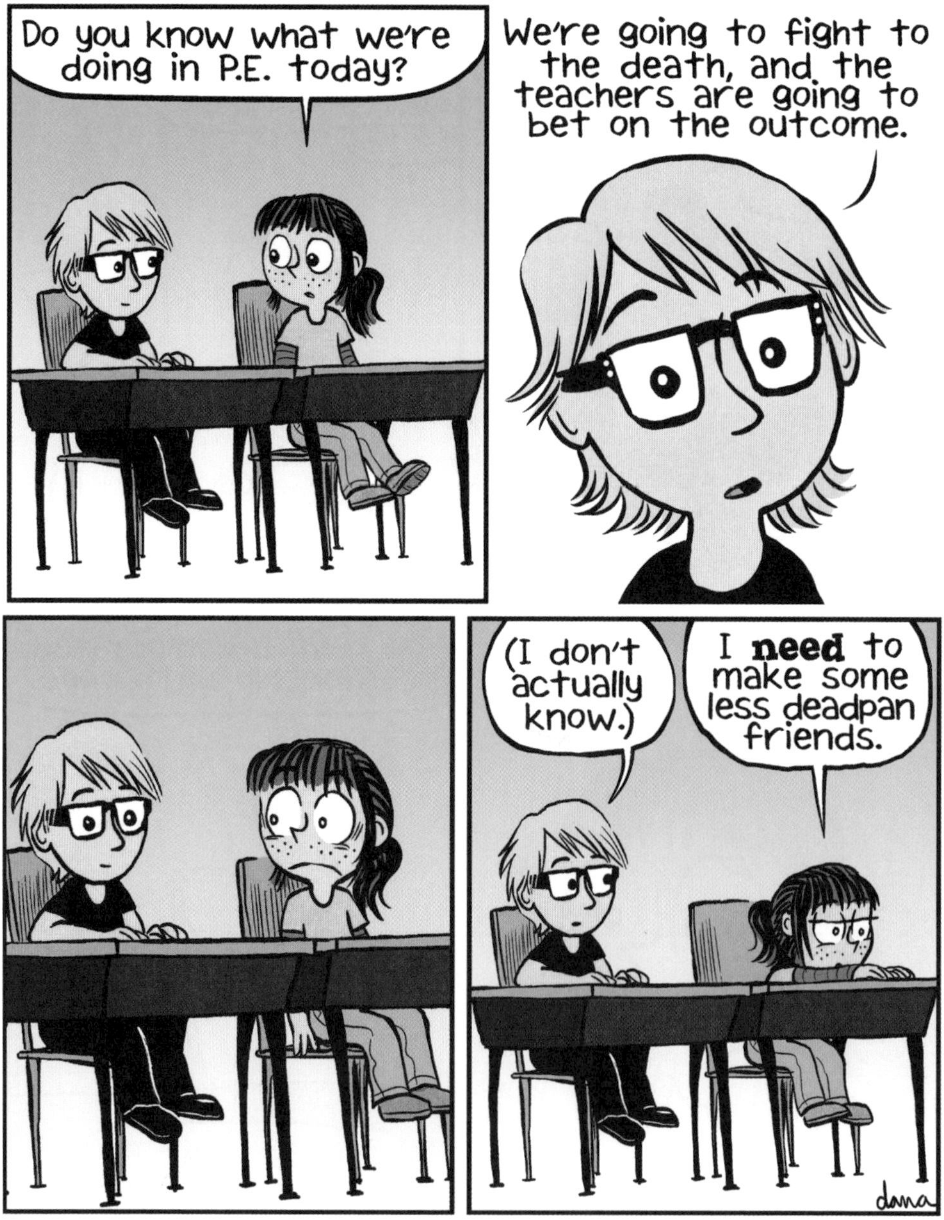
Do you know what we're doing in P.E. today?
We're going to fight to the death, and the teachers are going to bet on the outcome.
(I don't actually know.)
I **need** to make some less deadpan friends.
dana

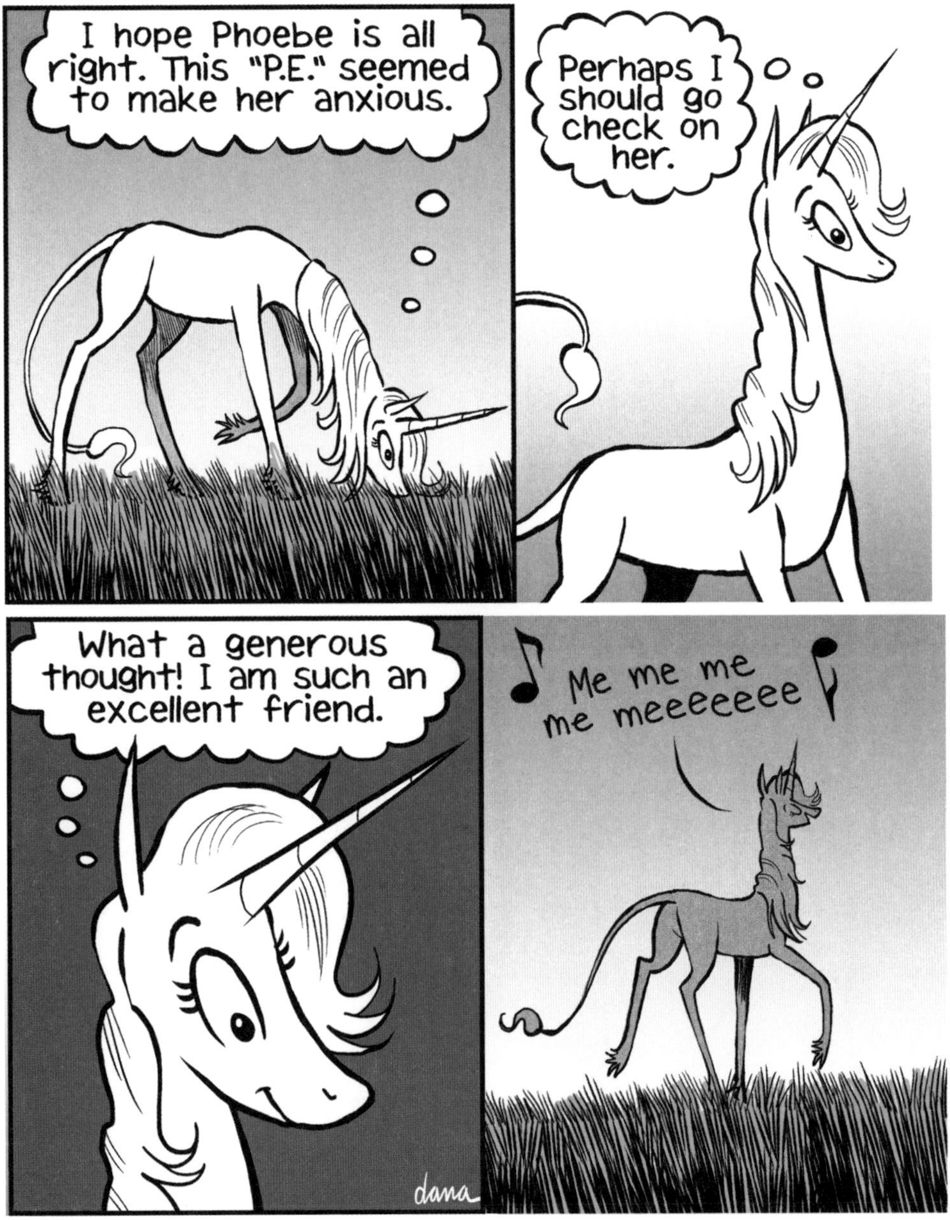
I hope Phoebe is all right. This "P.E." seemed to make her anxious.
Perhaps I should go check on her.
What a generous thought! I am such an excellent friend.
Me me me me meeeeeee
dana

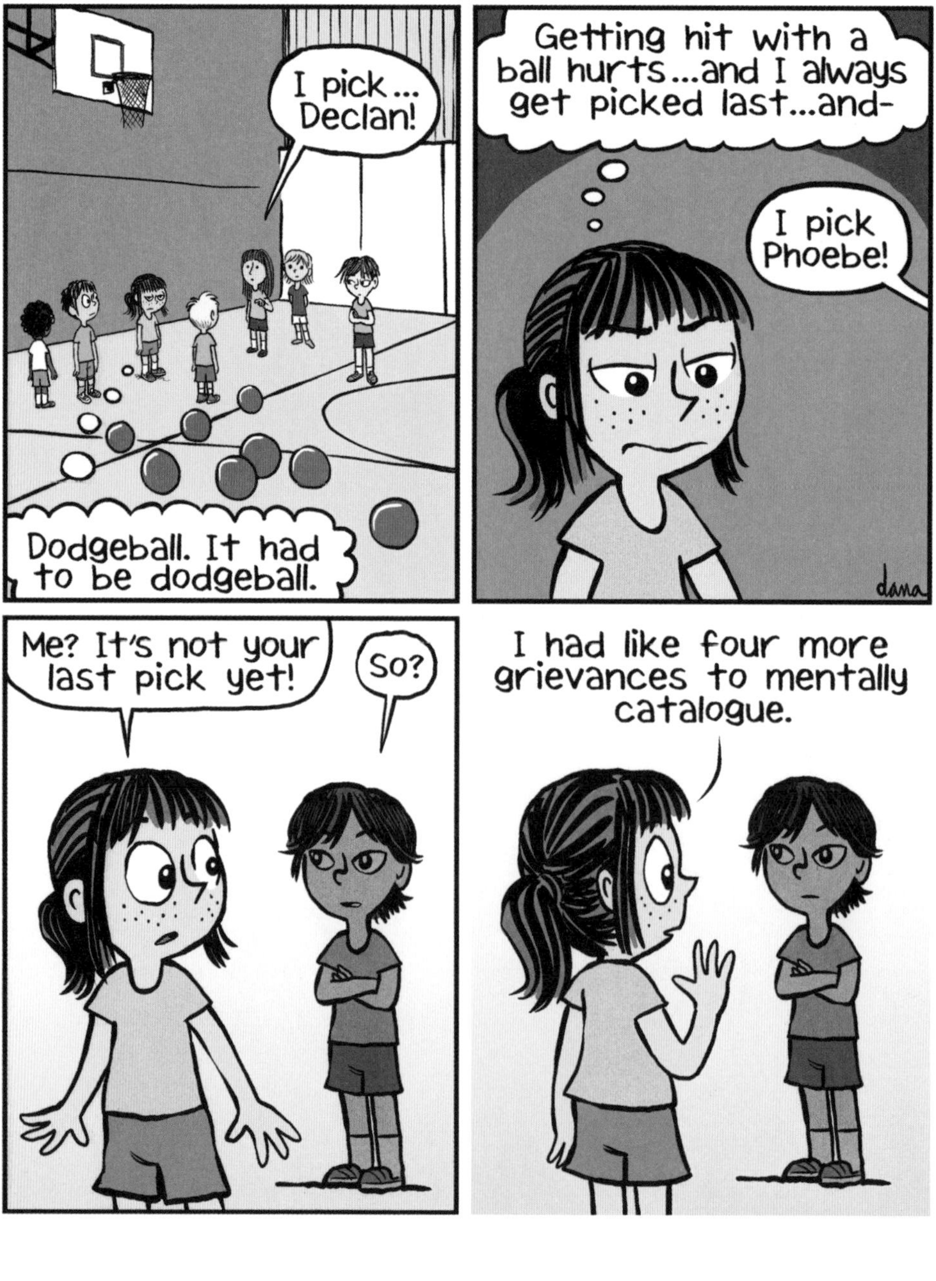
I pick... Declan!
Dodgeball. It had to be dodgeball.
Getting hit with a ball hurts...and I always get picked last...and-
I pick Phoebe!
dana
Me? It's not your last pick yet!
So?
I had like four more grievances to mentally catalogue.

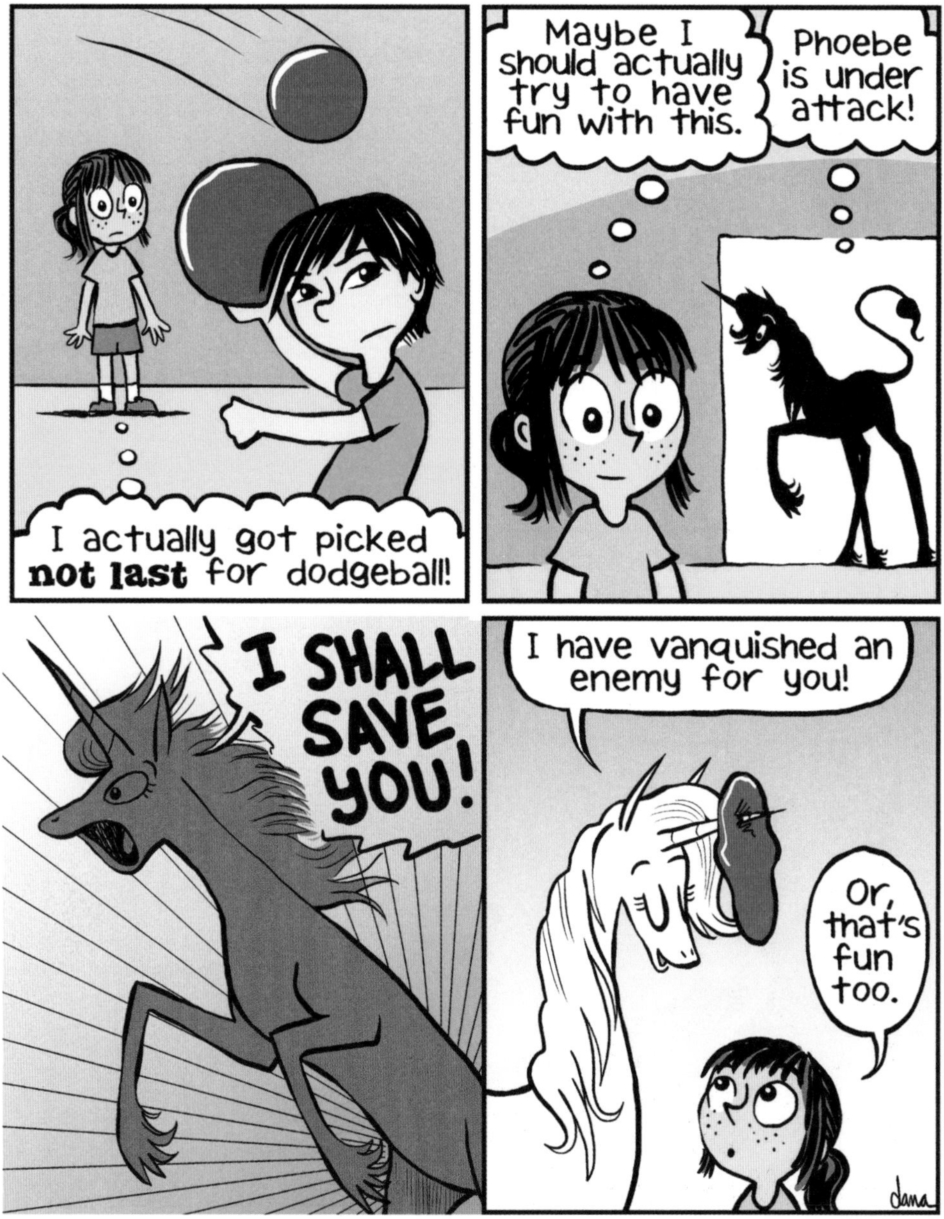
I actually got picked **not last** for dodgeball!
Maybe I should actually try to have fun with this.
Phoebe is under attack!
I SHALL SAVE YOU!
I have vanquished an enemy for you!
Or, that's fun too.
dana

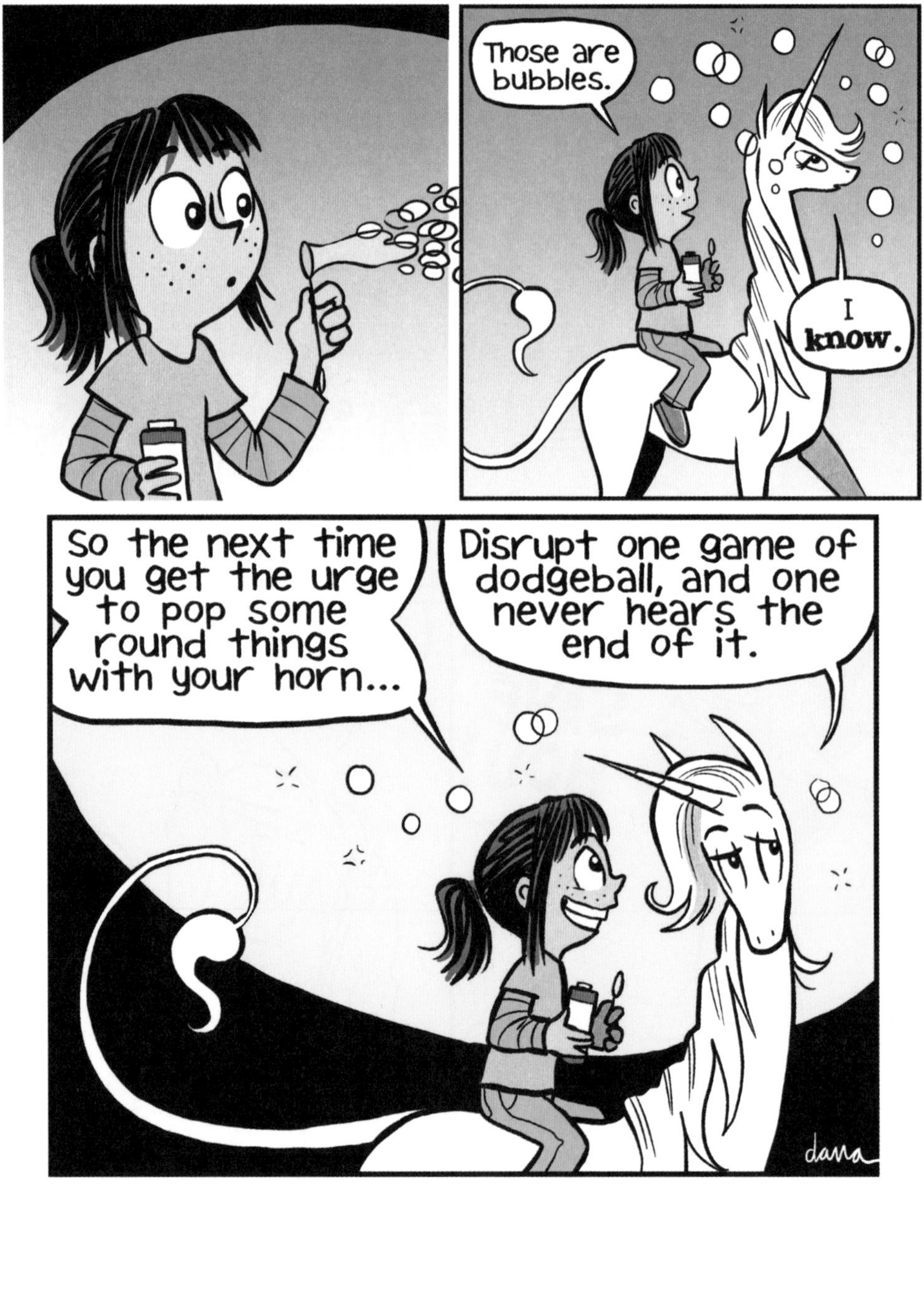
Those are bubbles.
I **know.**
So the next time you get the urge to pop some round things with your horn...
Disrupt one game of dodgeball, and one never hears the end of it.
dana

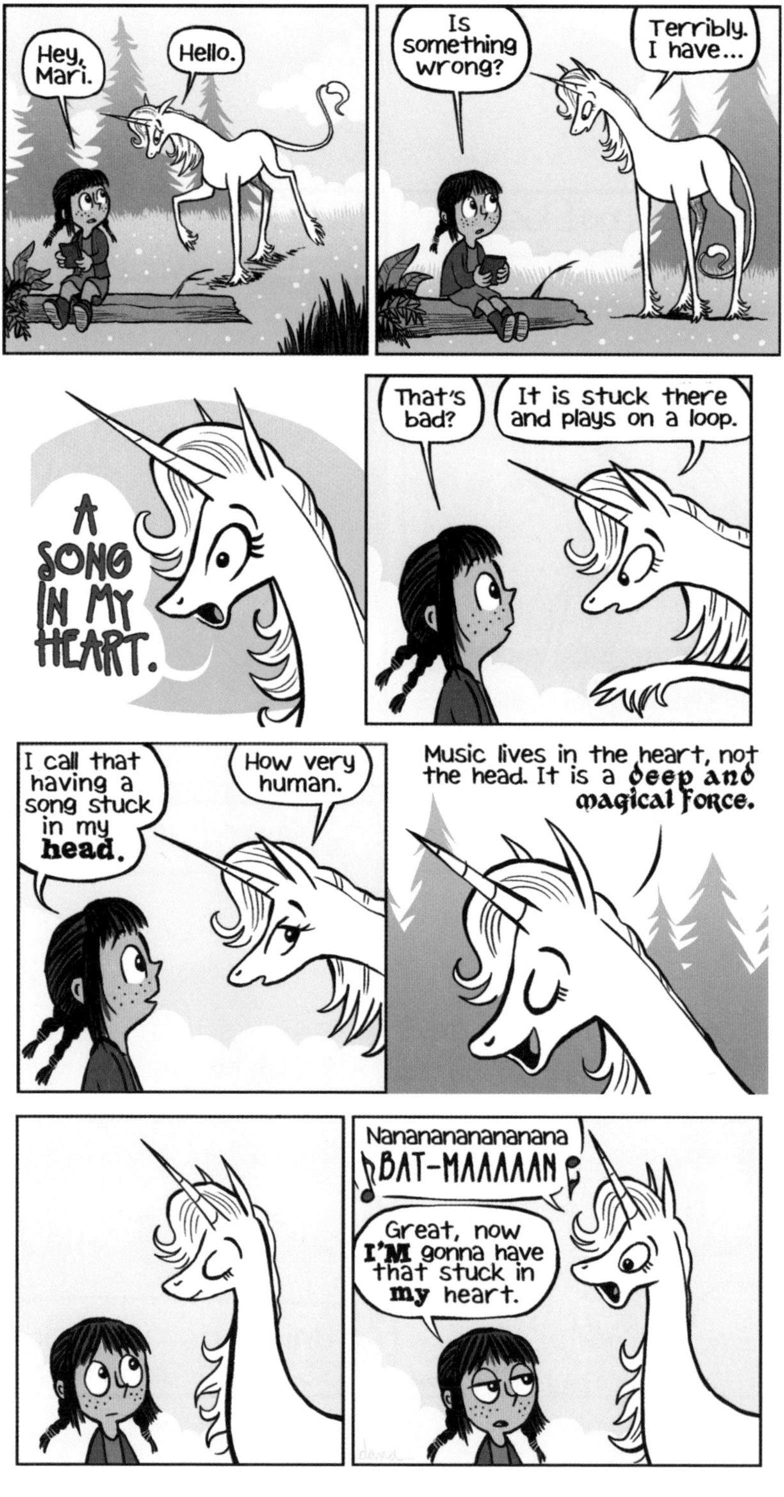
Hey, Mari.
Hello.
Is something wrong?
Terribly. I have...
A SONG IN MY HEART.
That's bad?
It is stuck there and plays on a loop.
I call that having a song stuck in my **head**.
How very human.
Music lives in the heart, not the head. It is a deep and magical force.
Nanananananananana BAT-MAAAAAN
Great, now **I'M** gonna have that stuck in **my** heart.

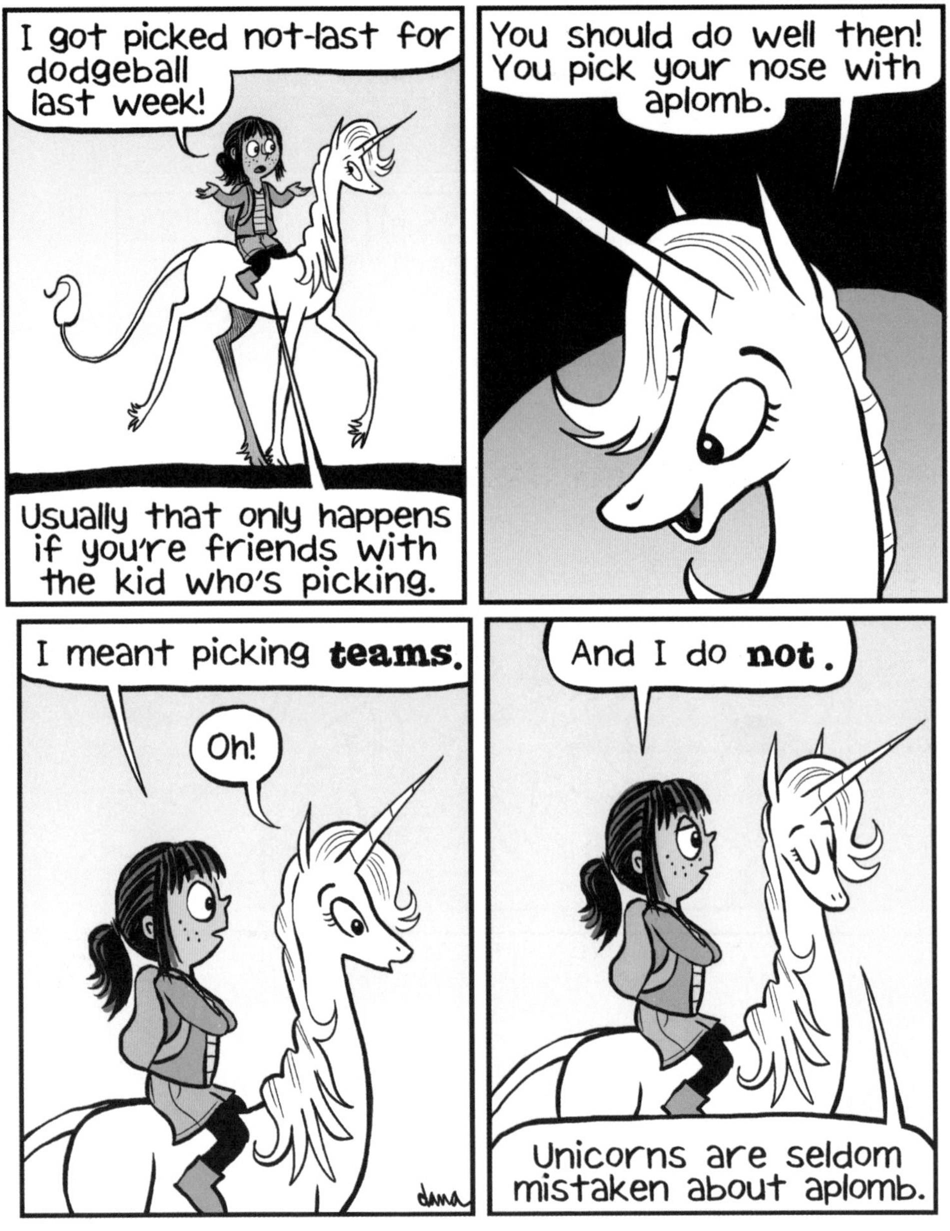

I got picked not-last for dodgeball last week!
Usually that only happens if you're friends with the kid who's picking.
You should do well then! You pick your nose with aplomb.
I meant picking teams.
Oh!
And I do not.
Unicorns are seldom mistaken about aplomb.
dana

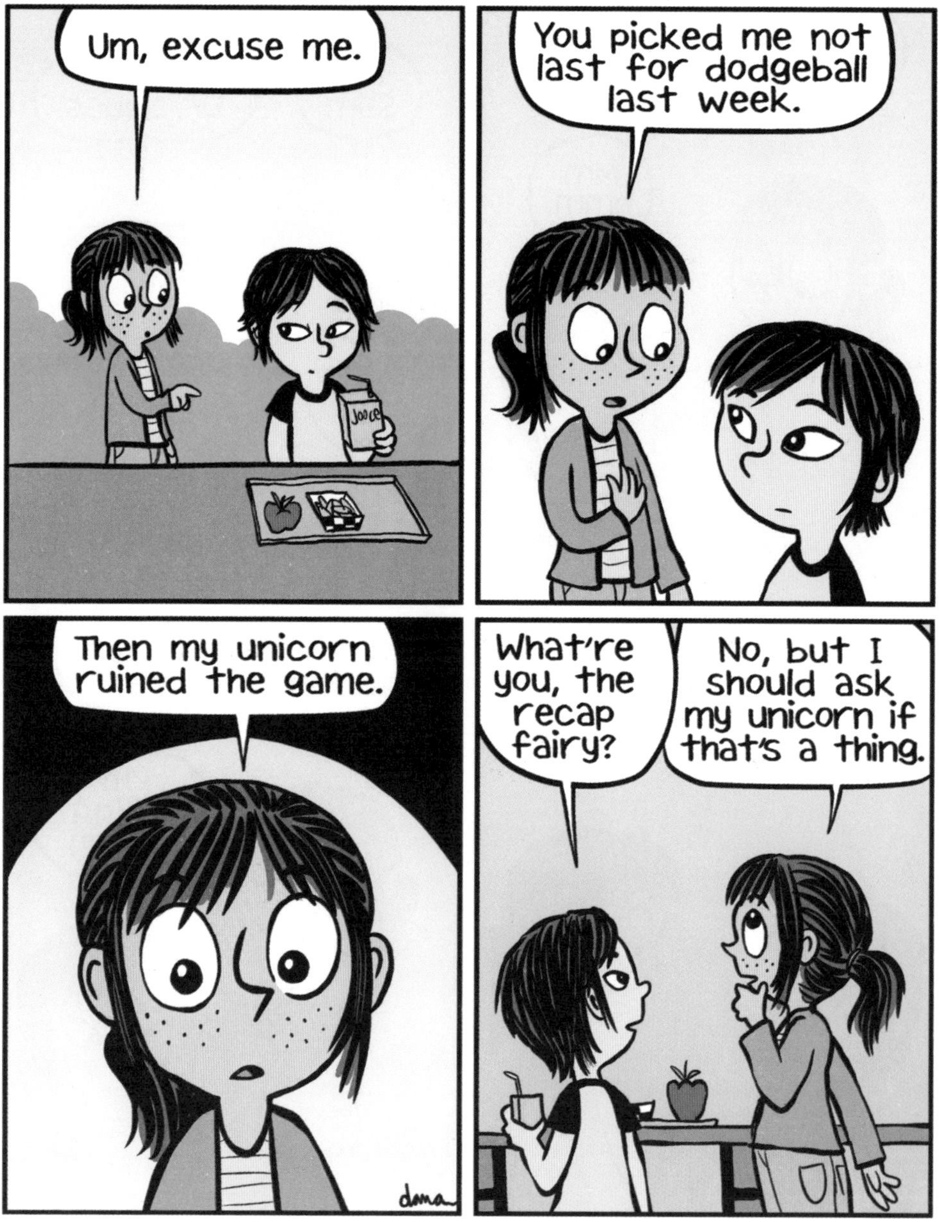

Um, excuse me.
You picked me not last for dodgeball last week.
Then my unicorn ruined the game.
What're you, the recap fairy?
No, but I should ask my unicorn if that's a thing.

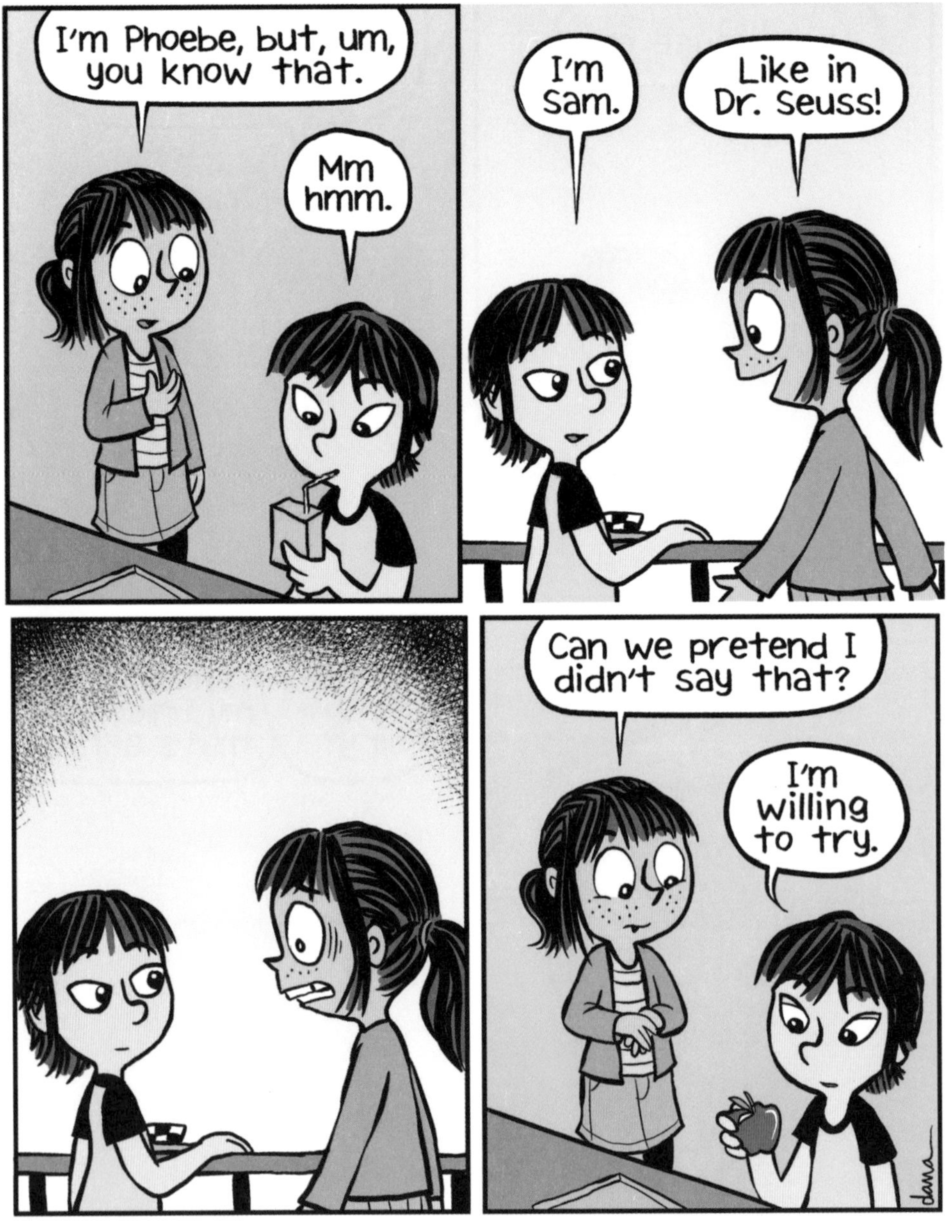
I'm Phoebe, but, um, you know that.
Mm hmm.
I'm Sam.
Like in Dr. Seuss!
Can we pretend I didn't say that?
I'm willing to try.
dana

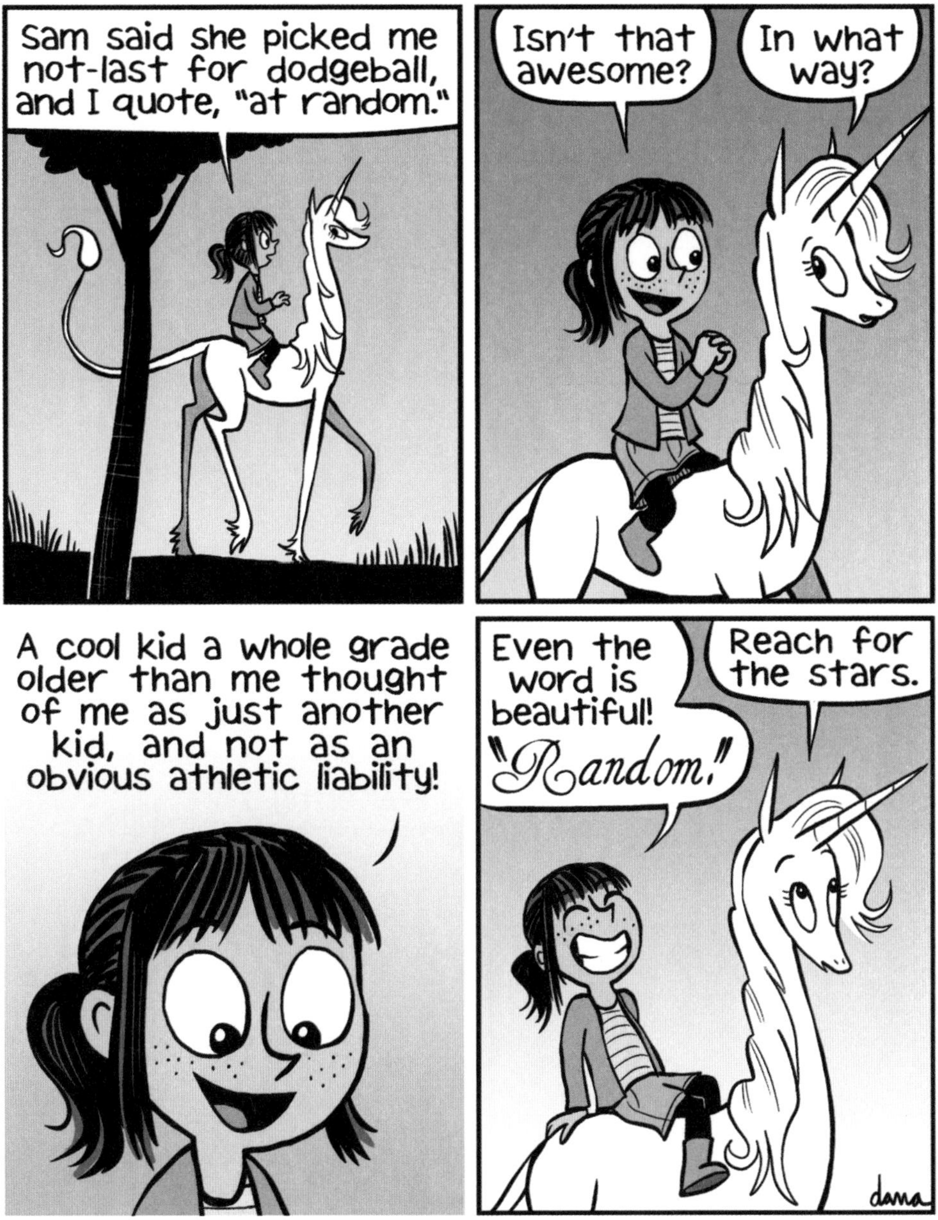
Sam said she picked me not-last for dodgeball, and I quote, "at random."
Isn't that awesome?
In what way?
A cool kid a whole grade older than me thought of me as just another kid, and not as an obvious athletic liability!
Even the word is beautiful! "Random."
Reach for the stars.
dana

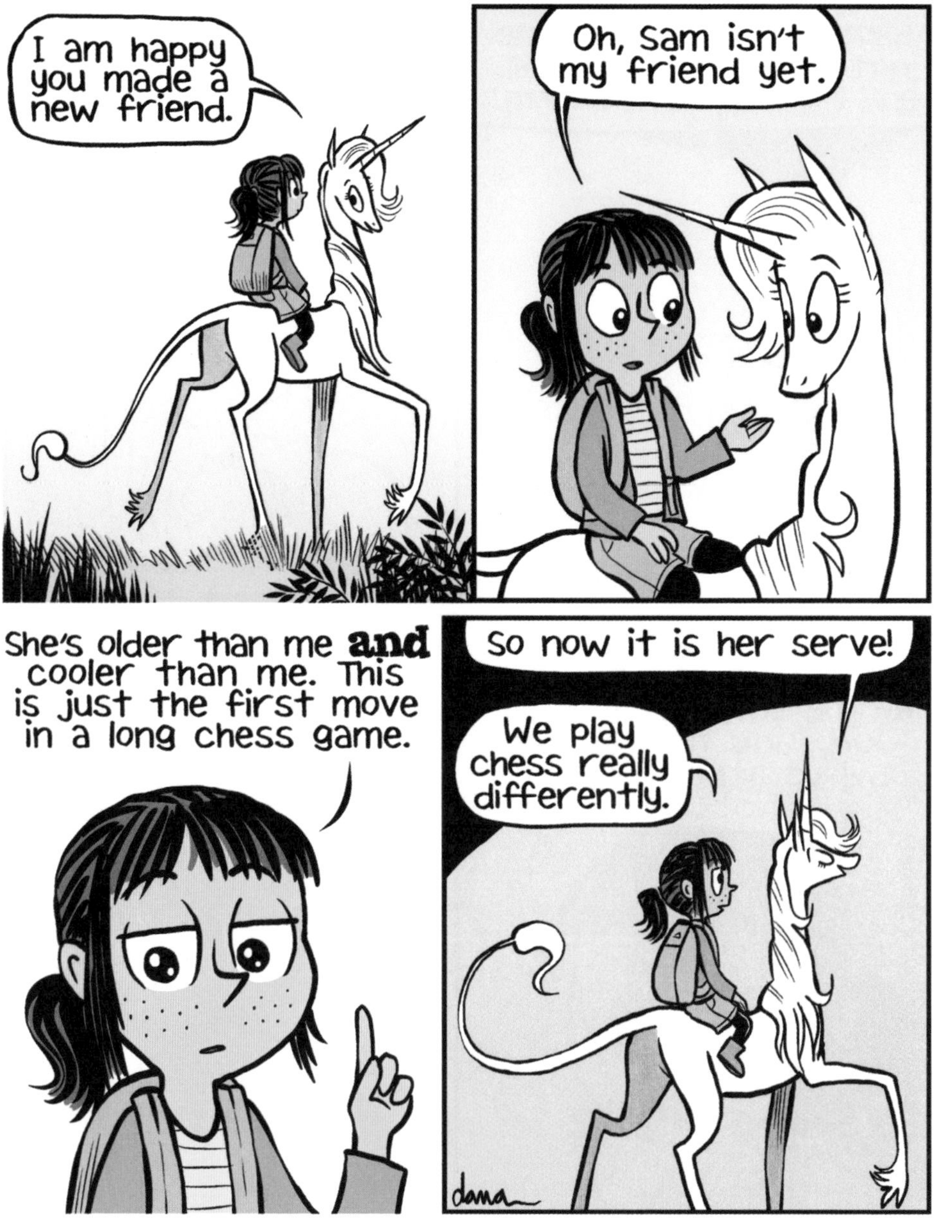
I am happy you made a new friend.
Oh, Sam isn't my friend yet.
She's older than me **and** cooler than me. This is just the first move in a long chess game.
So now it is her serve!
We play chess really differently.
dana

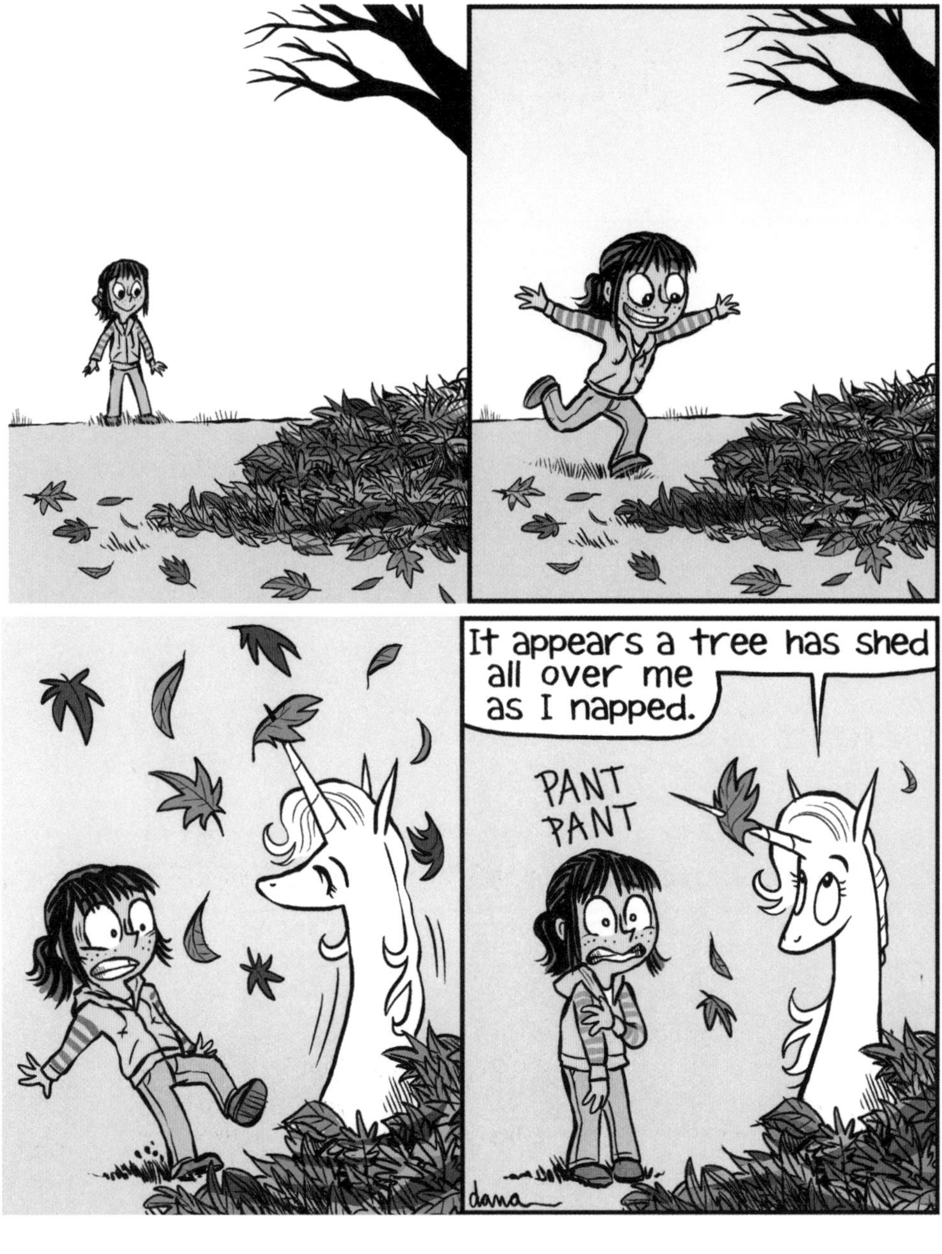
It appears a tree has shed all over me as I napped.
PANT PANT
dana

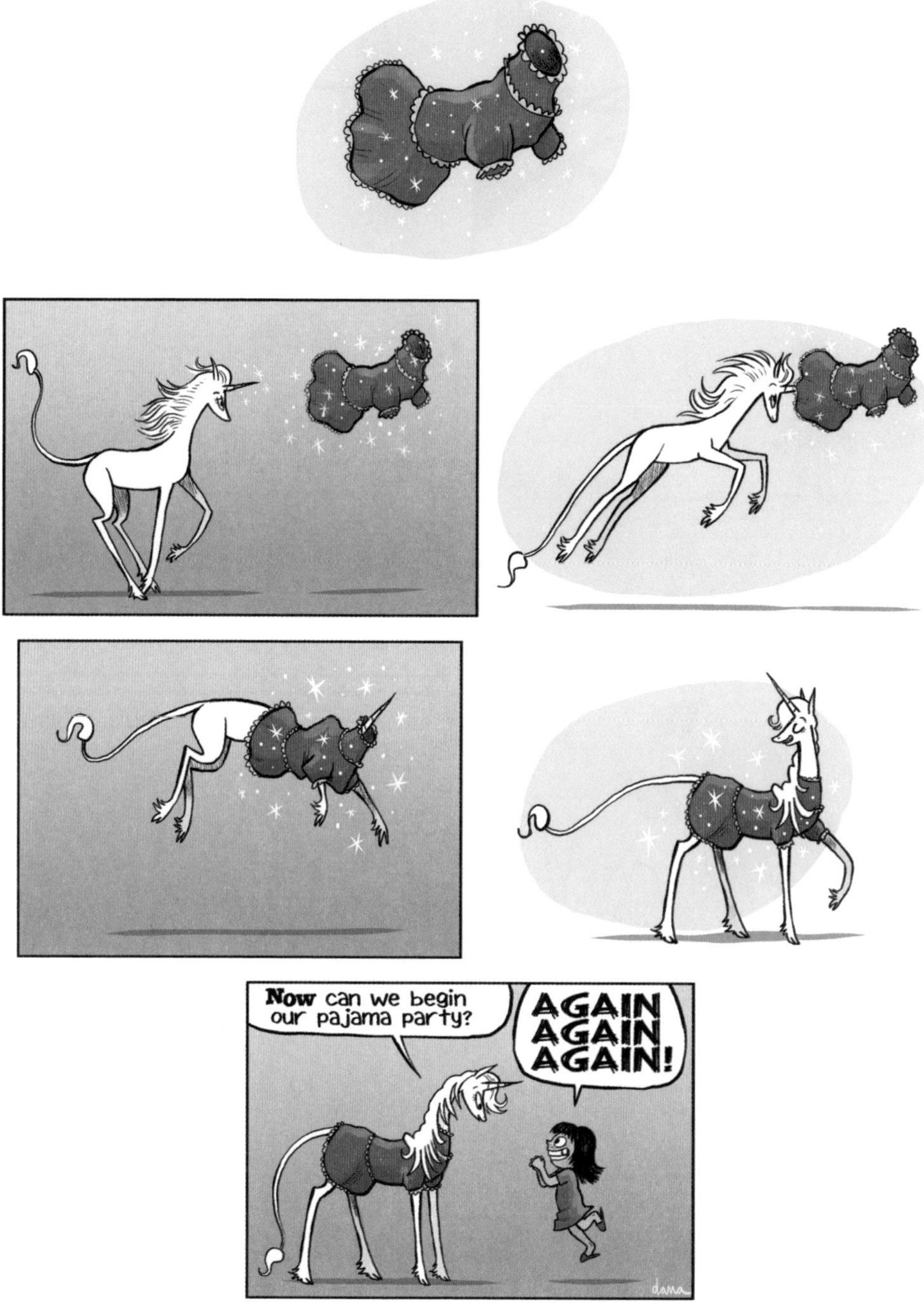
Now can we begin our pajama party?
AGAIN AGAIN AGAIN!

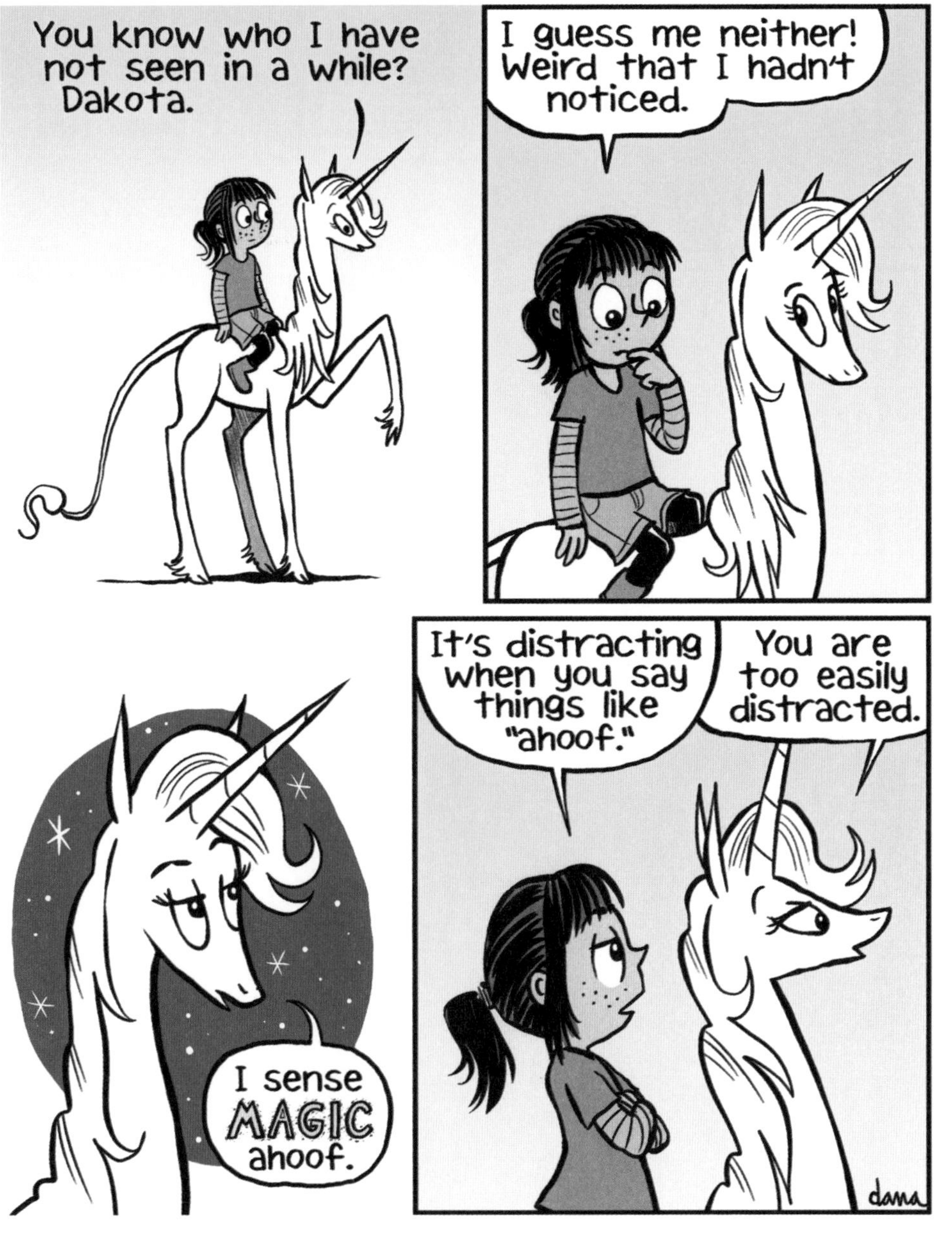
You know who I have not seen in a while? Dakota.
I guess me neither! Weird that I hadn't noticed.
I sense MAGIC ahoof.
It's distracting when you say things like "ahoof."
You are too easily distracted.
dana

I will check the area for enchantments.
beep beep
beep beep
I wanna go "beep beep" too!
That is sort of **my** thing.
dana

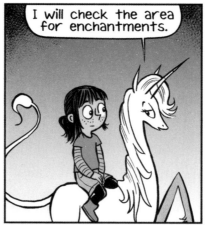

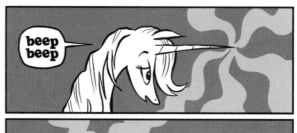

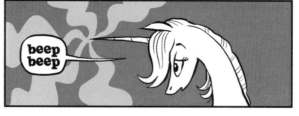

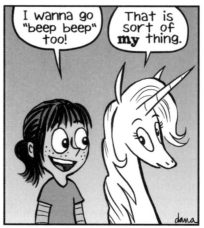

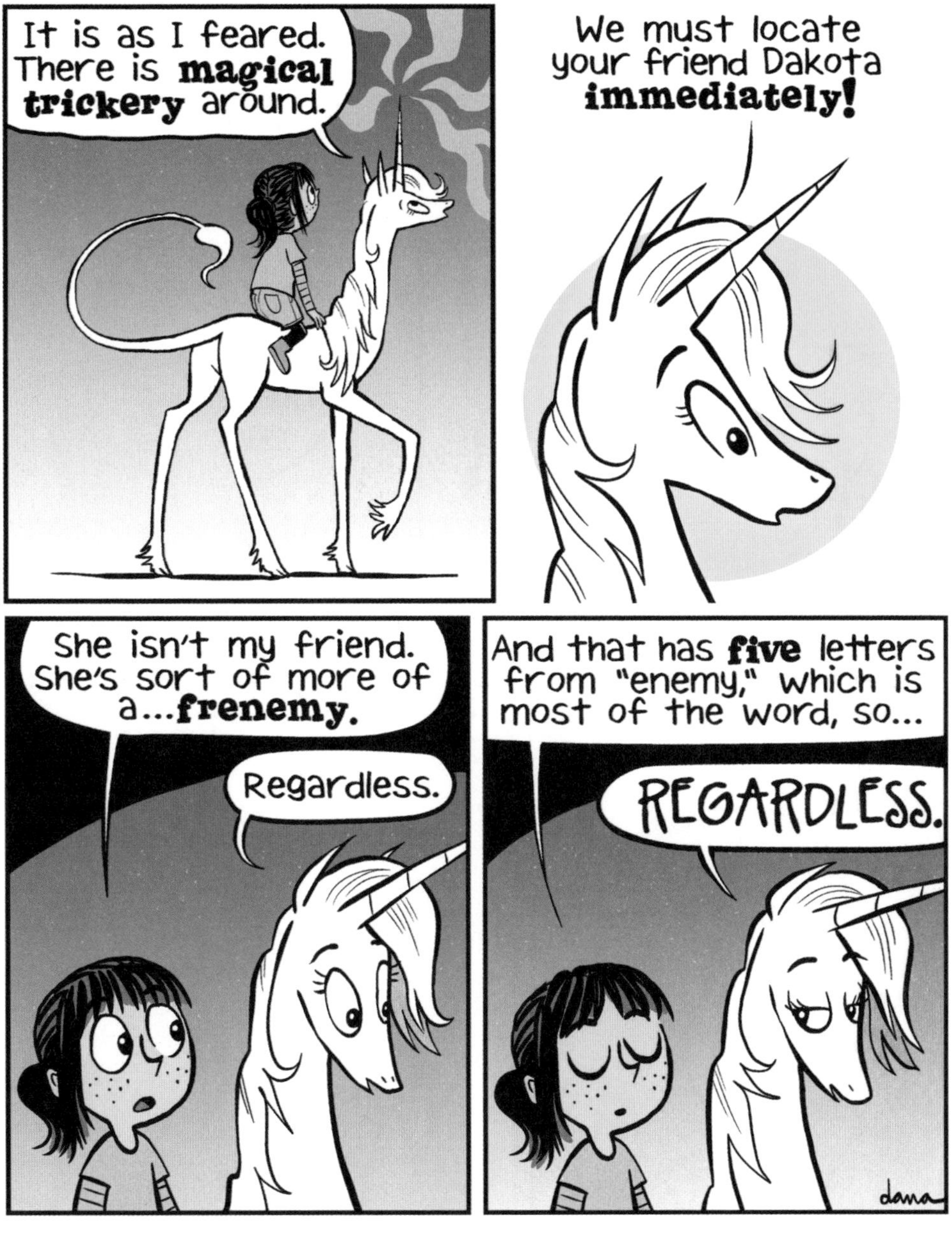
It is as I feared. There is **magical trickery** around.
We must locate your friend Dakota **immediately!**
She isn't my friend. She's sort of more of a...**frenemy.**
Regardless.
And that has **five** letters from "enemy," which is most of the word, so...
REGARDLESS.
dana

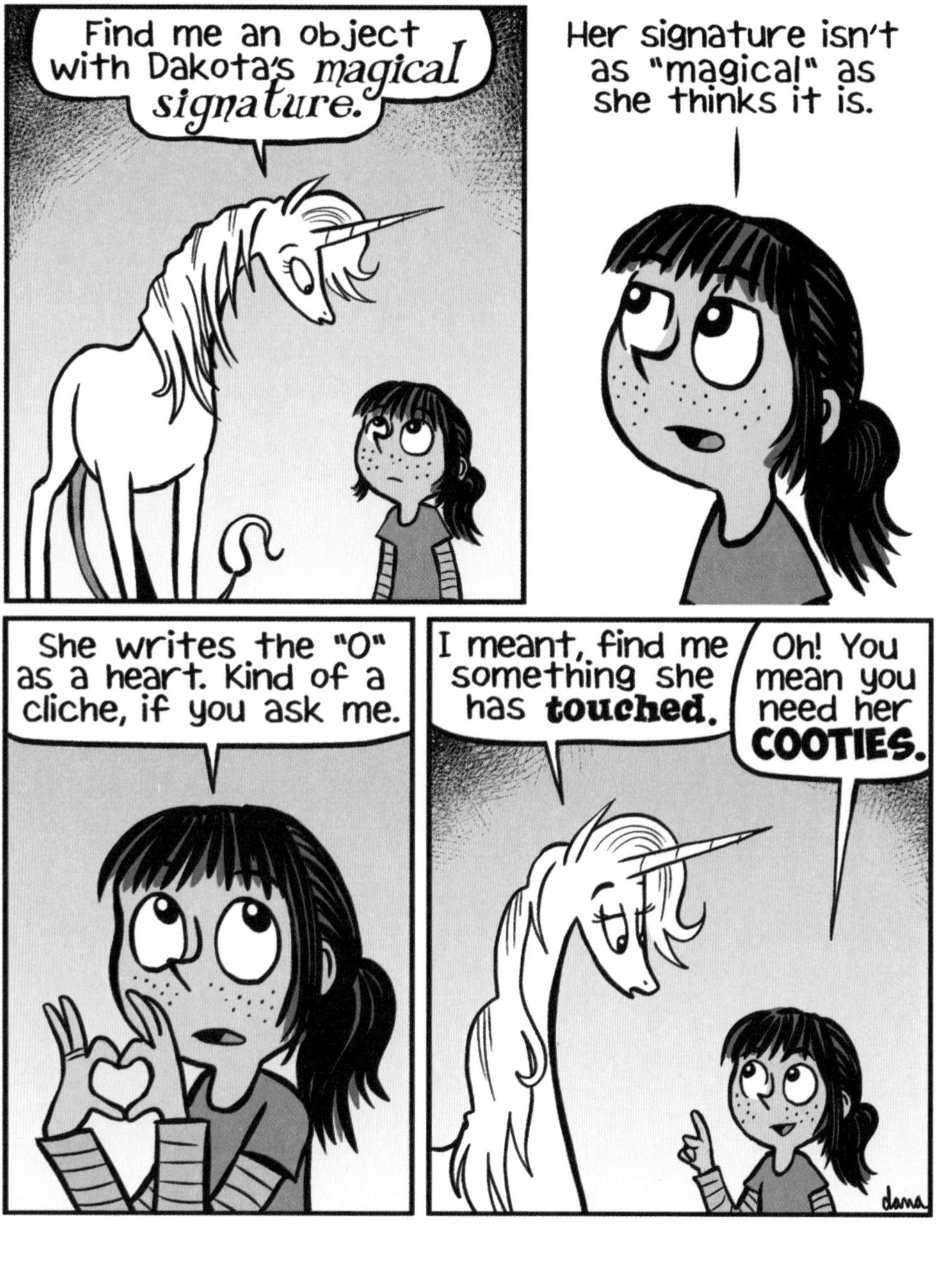
Find me an object with Dakota's *magical signature.*
Her signature isn't as "magical" as she thinks it is.
She writes the "O" as a heart. Kind of a cliche, if you ask me.
I meant, find me something she has **touched.**
Oh! You mean you need her **COOTIES.**
dana

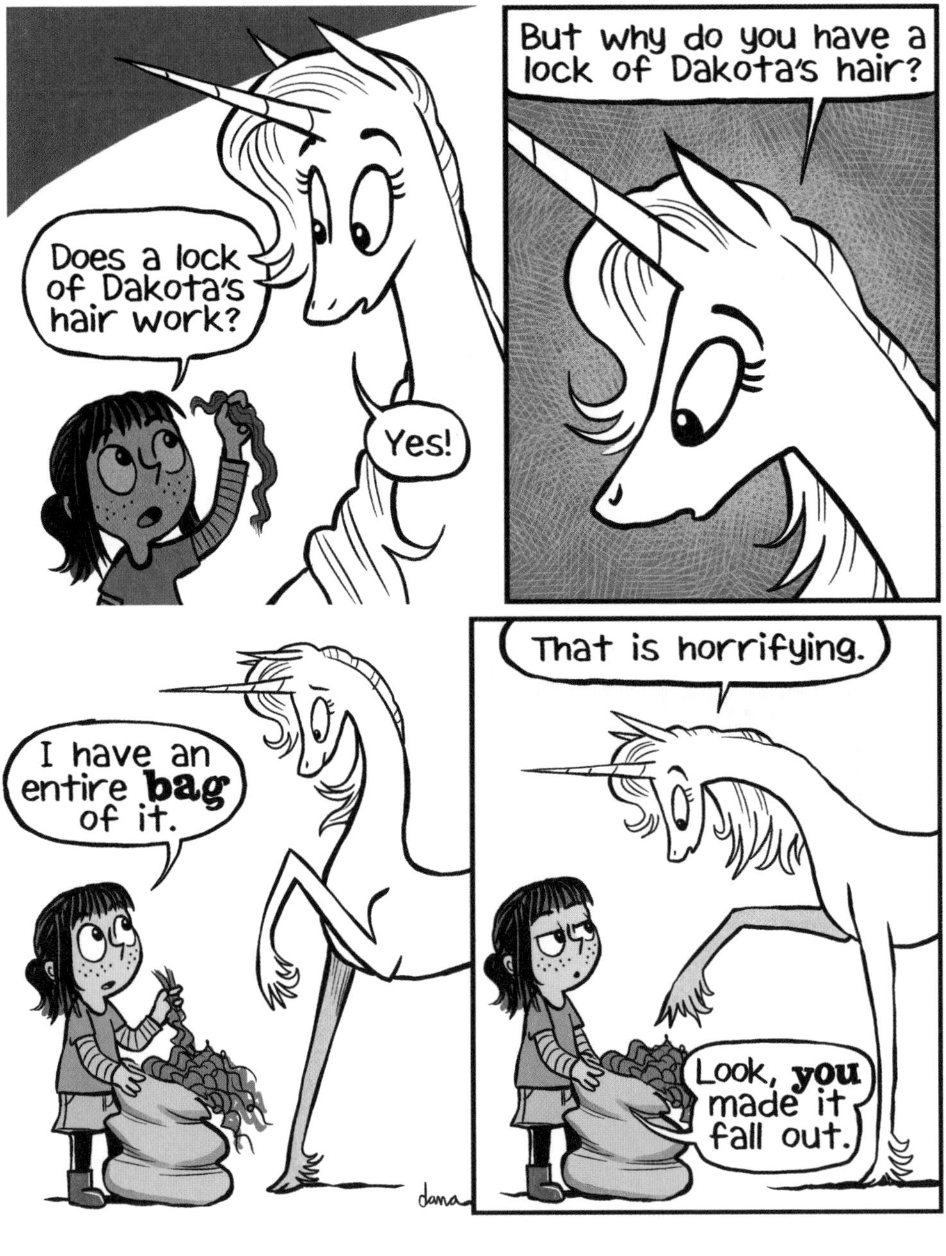
Does a lock of Dakota's hair work?
Yes!
But why do you have a lock of Dakota's hair?
I have an entire **bag** of it.
dana
That is horrifying.
Look, **you** made it fall out.

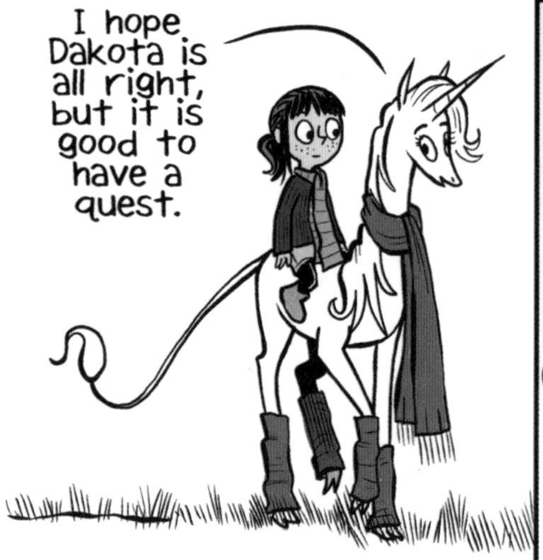
I hope Dakota is all right, but it is good to have a quest.

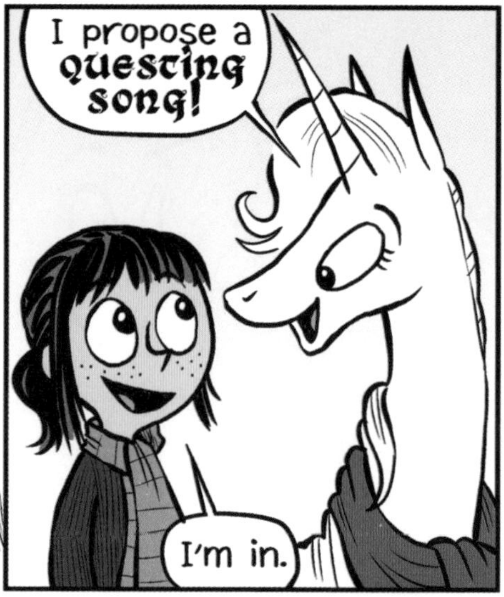
I propose a QUESTING SONG!
I'm in.

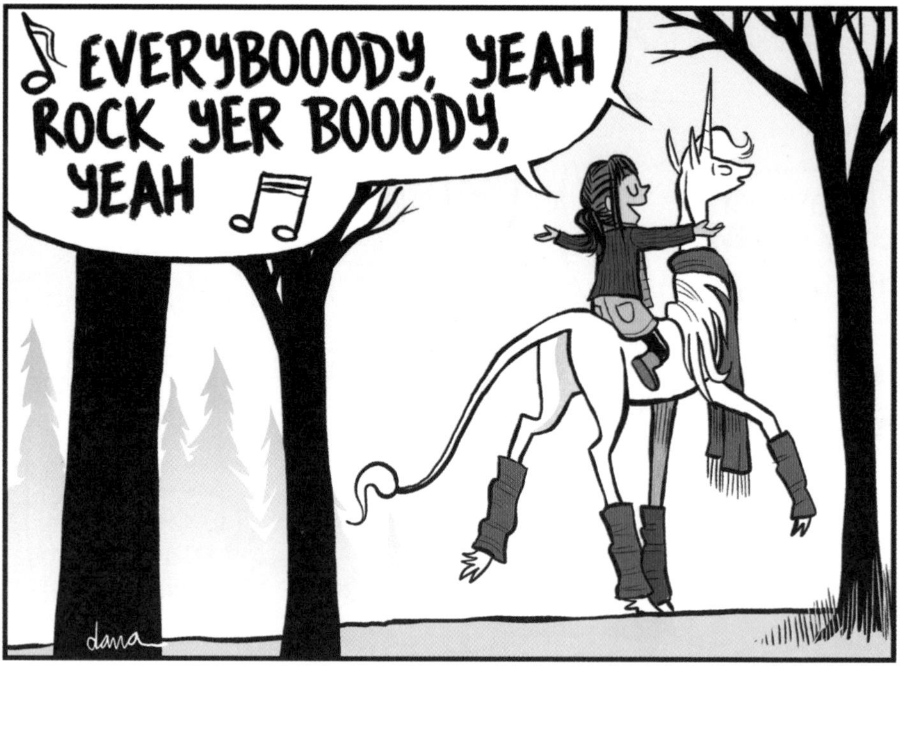
EVERYBOOODY, YEAH ROCK YER BOOODY, YEAH
dana

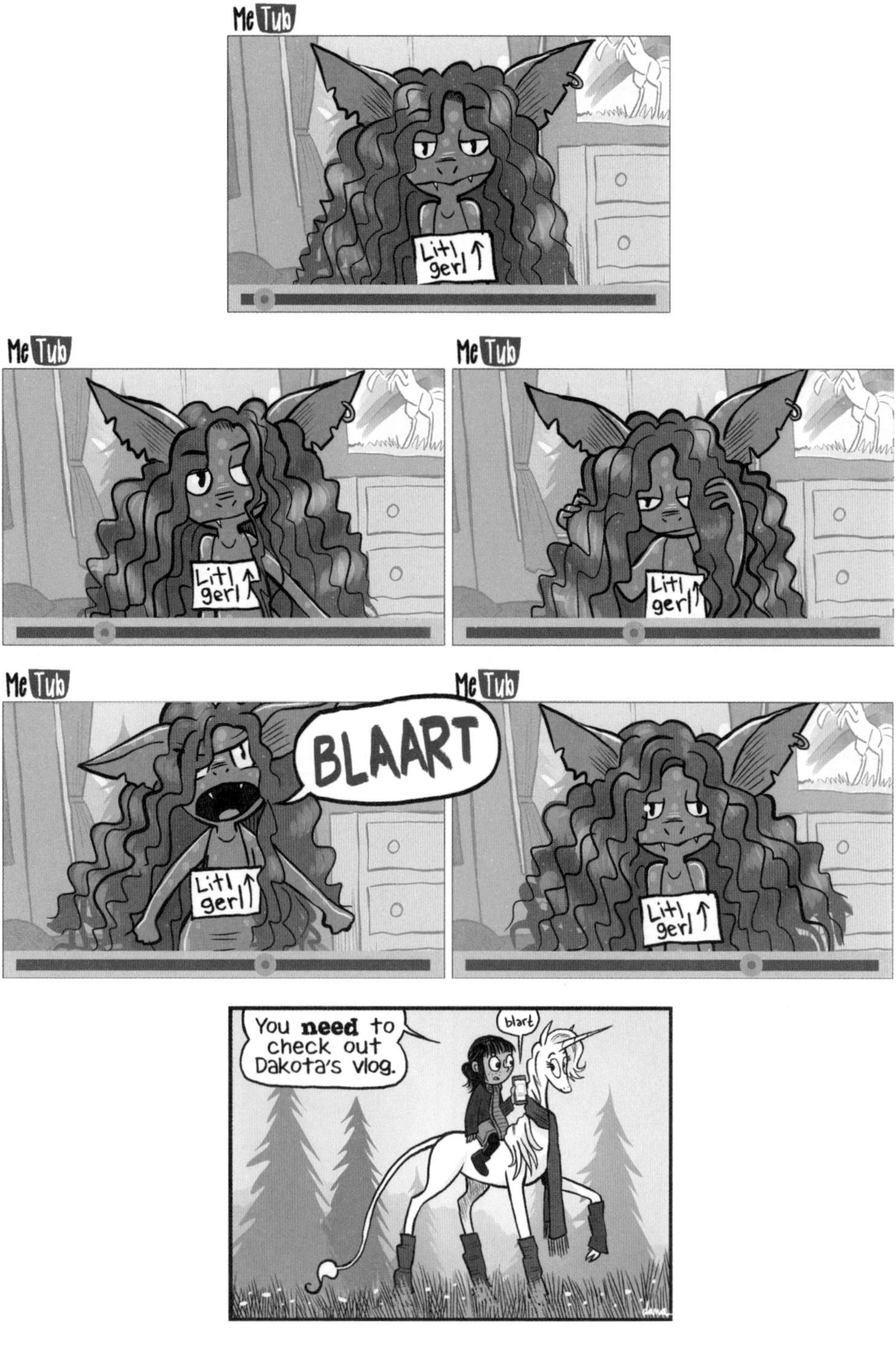
MeTub
Litl gerl ↑
MeTub
Litl gerl ↑
MeTub
Litl gerl ↑
MeTub
BLAART
Litl gerl ↑
MeTub
Litl gerl ↑
You **need** to check out Dakota's vlog.
blart

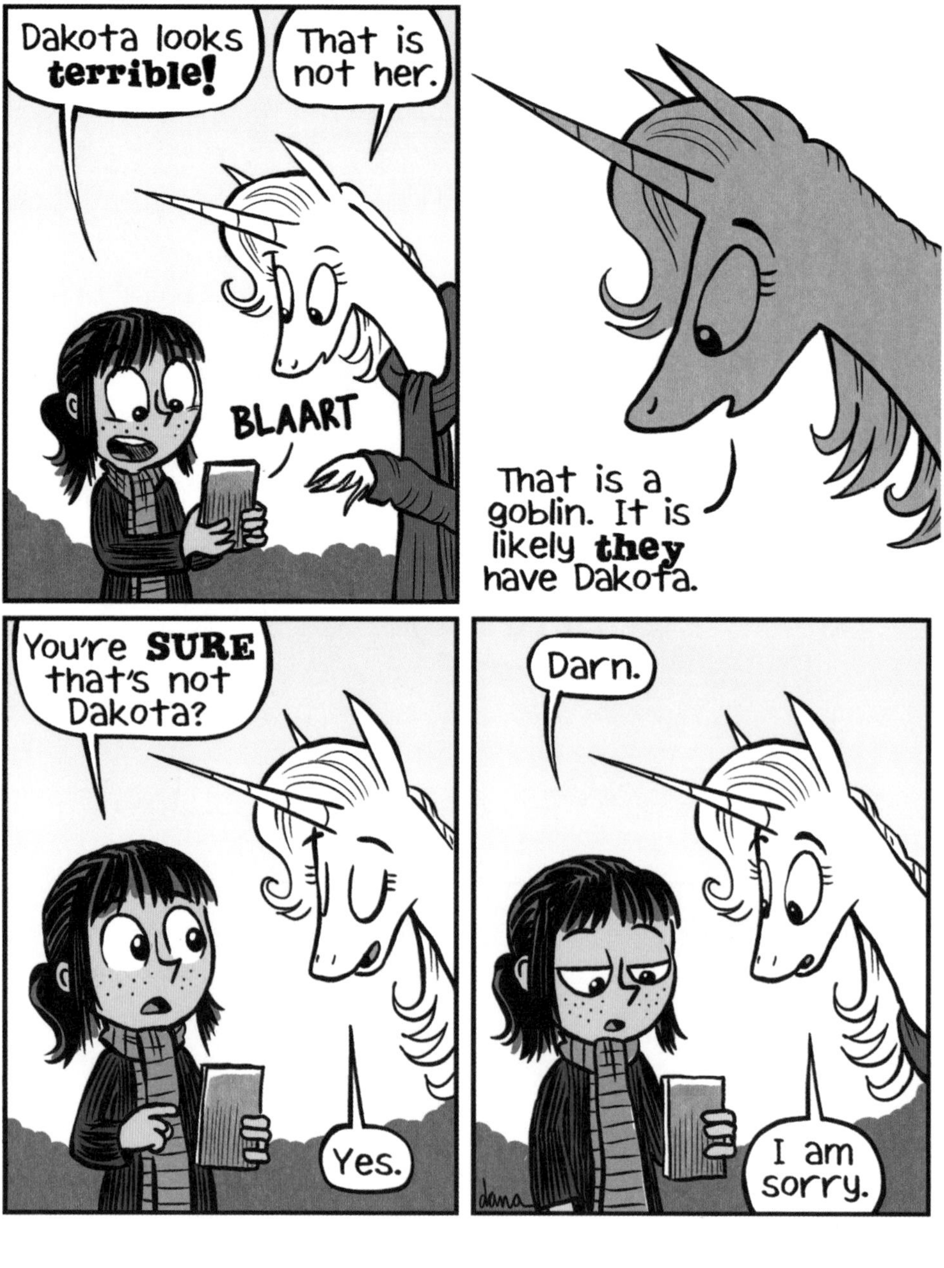

Dakota looks **terrible!**
That is not her.
BLAART
That is a goblin. It is likely **they** have Dakota.
You're **SURE** that's not Dakota?
Yes.
Darn.
I am sorry.
dana

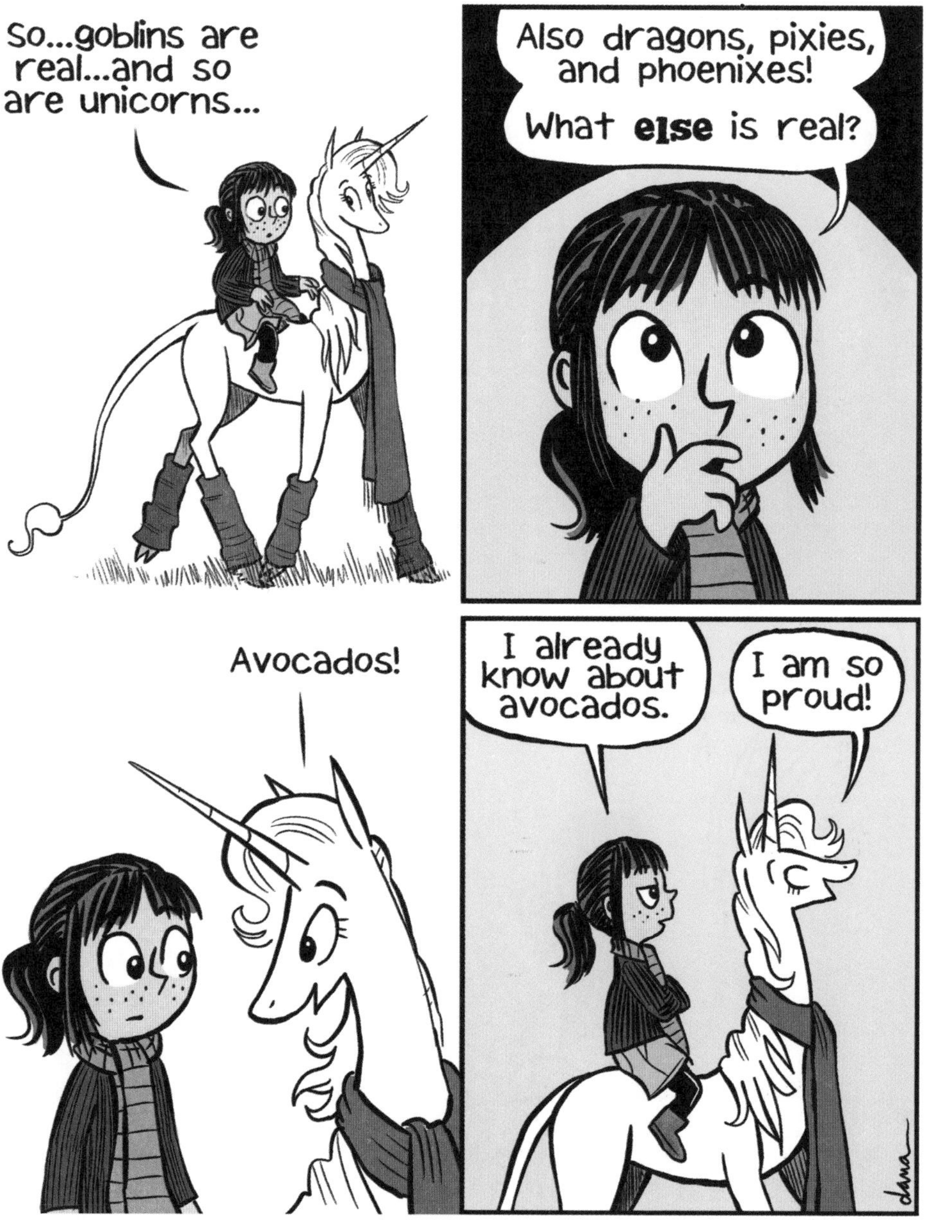
So...goblins are real...and so are unicorns...
Also dragons, pixies, and phoenixes!
What **else** is real?
Avocados!
I already know about avocados.
I am so proud!
dana

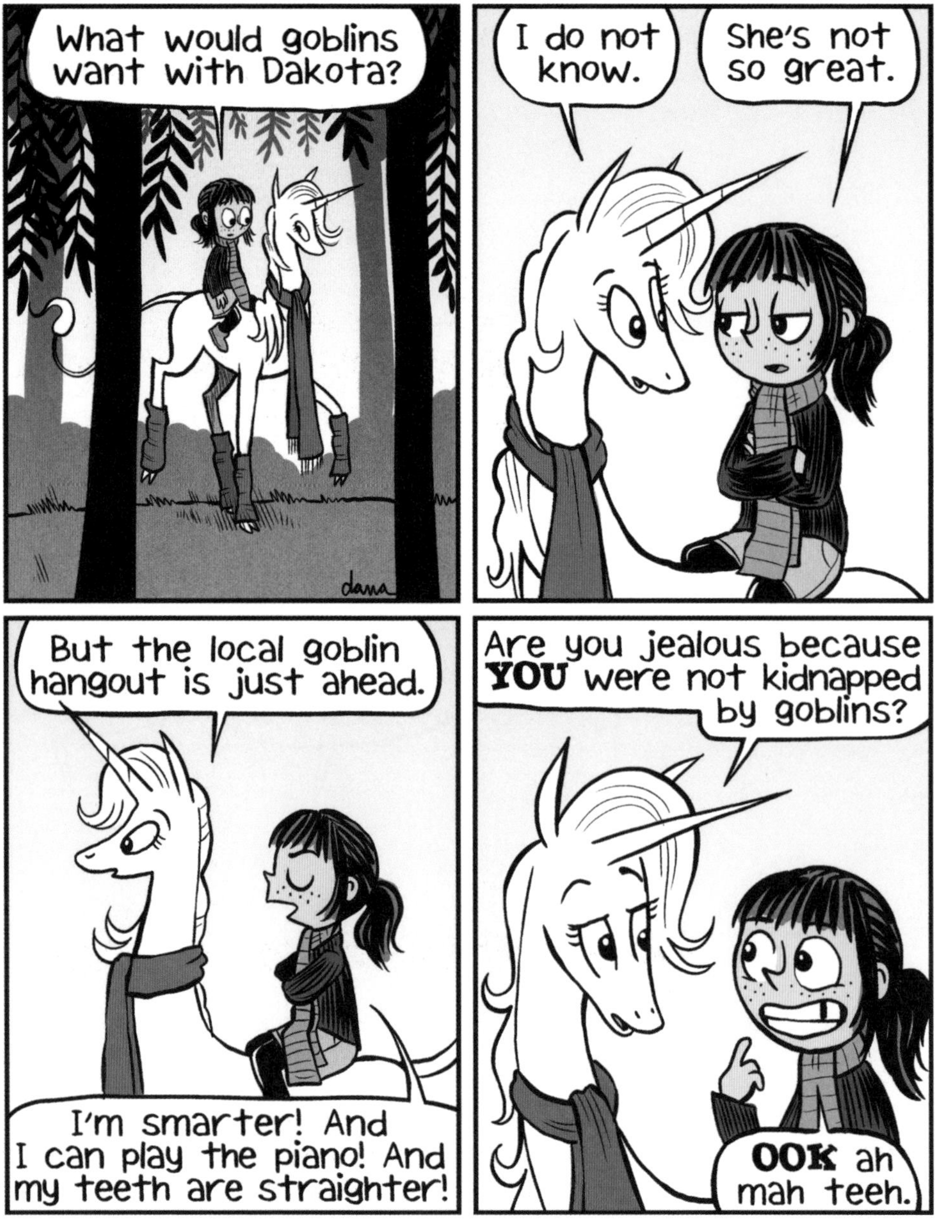
What would goblins want with Dakota?
dana
I do not know.
She's not so great.
But the local goblin hangout is just ahead.
I'm smarter! And I can play the piano! And my teeth are straighter!
Are you jealous because YOU were not kidnapped by goblins?
OOK ah mah teeh.

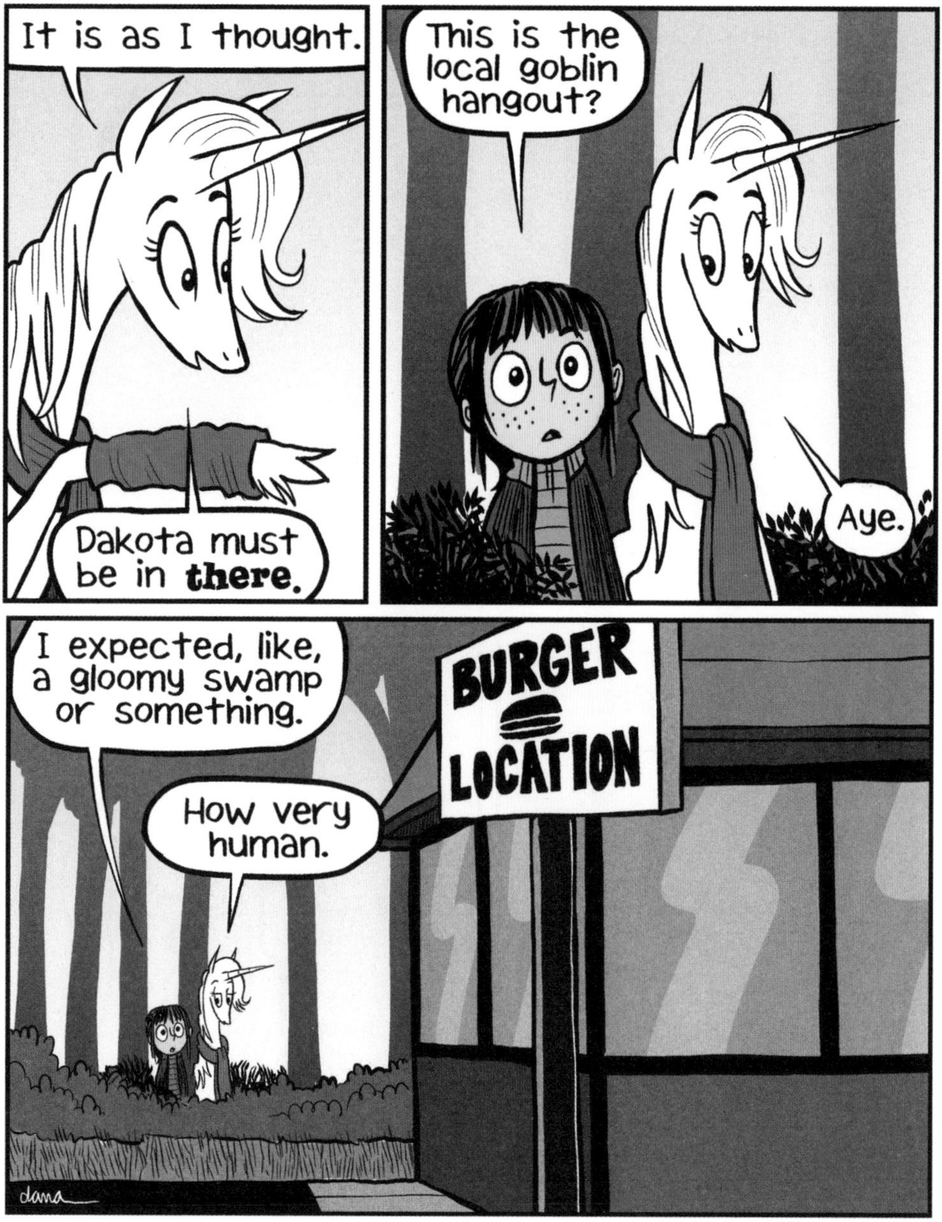
It is as I thought.
Dakota must be in **there**.
This is the local goblin hangout?
Aye.
I expected, like, a gloomy swamp or something.
How very human.
BURGER LOCATION
dana

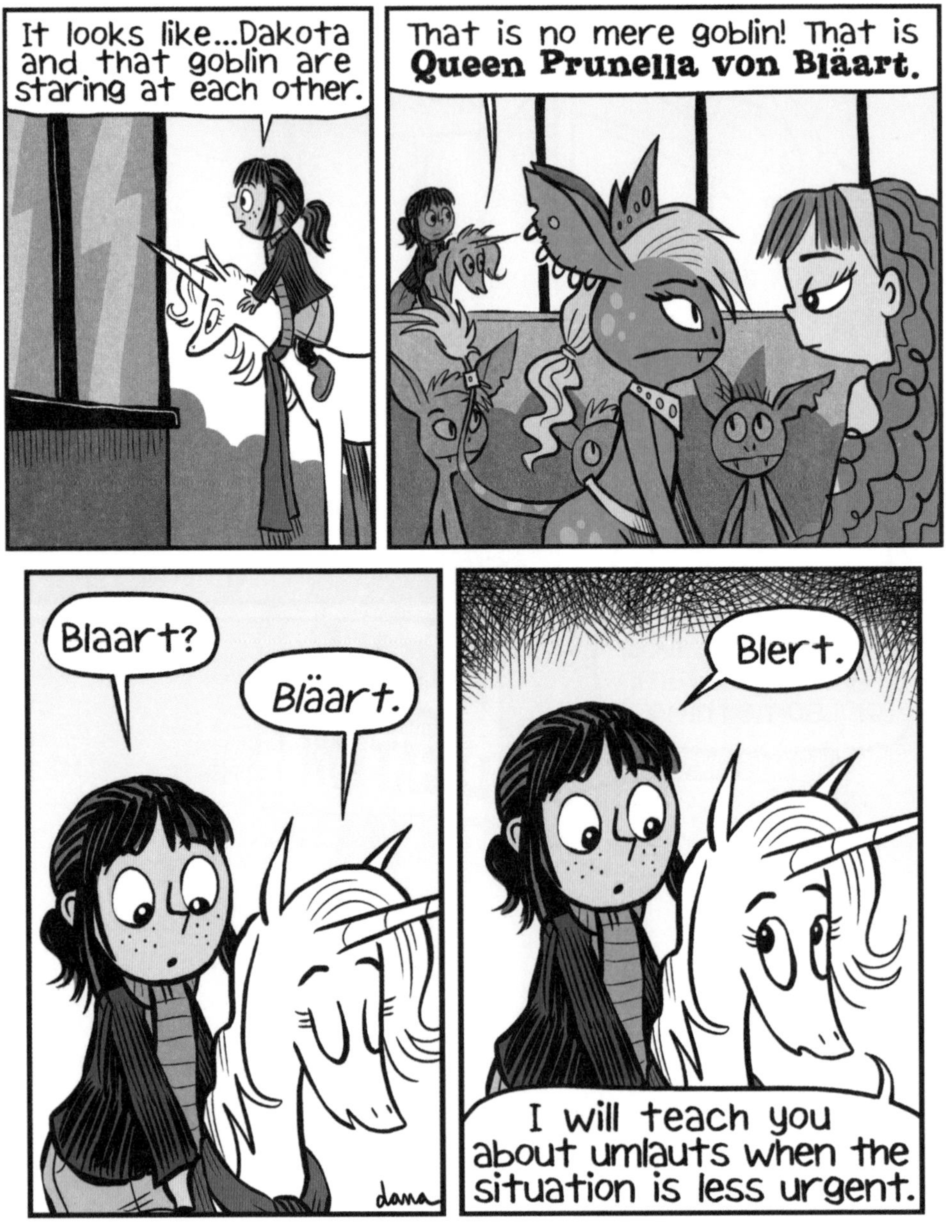
It looks like...Dakota and that goblin are staring at each other.
That is no mere goblin! That is **Queen Prunella von Bläart.**
Blaart?
Bläart.
Blert.
I will teach you about umlauts when the situation is less urgent.
dana

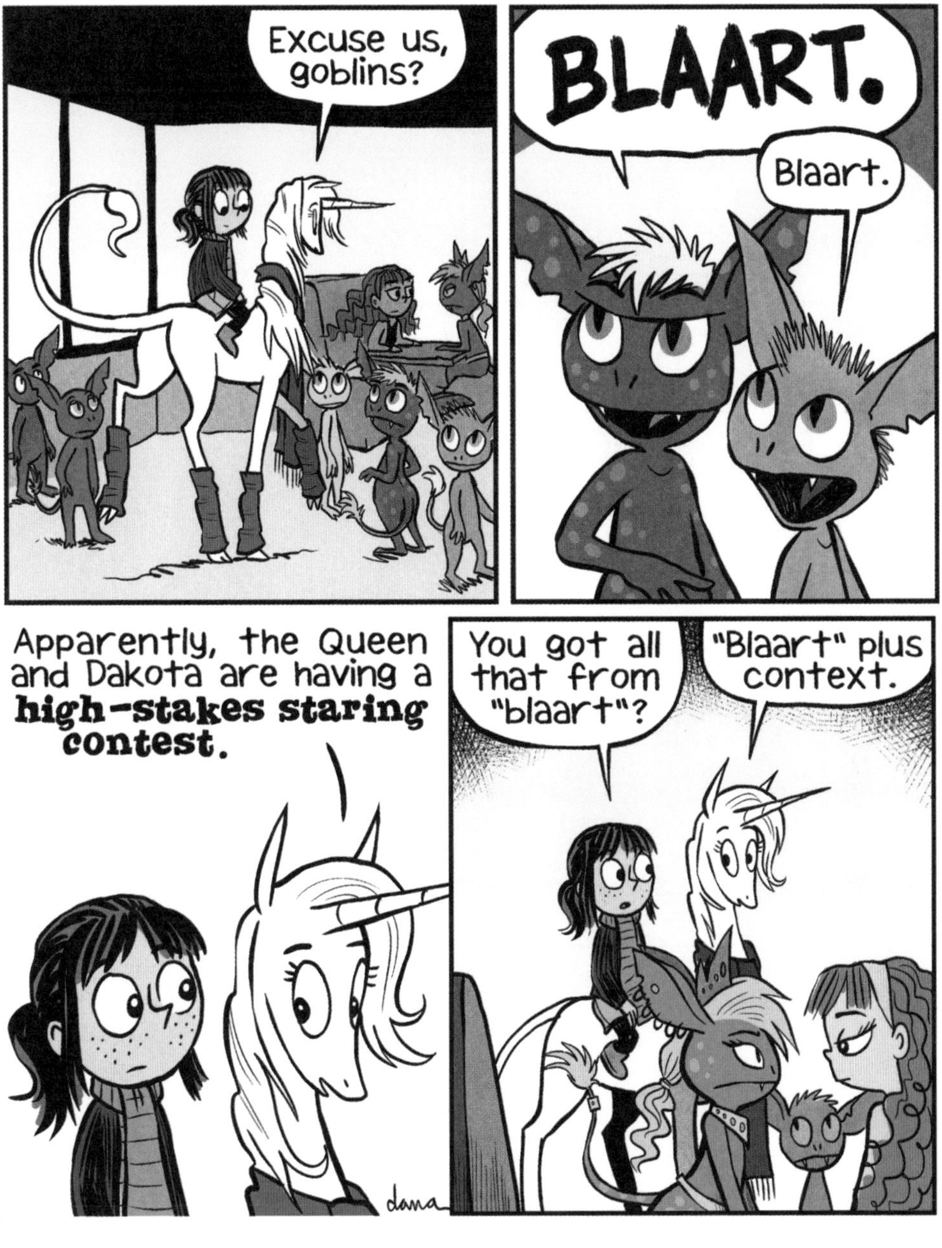
Excuse us, goblins?
BLAART.
Blaart.
Apparently, the Queen and Dakota are having a **high-stakes staring contest**.
You got all that from "blaart"?
"Blaart" plus context.
dana

A DAY IN THE LIFE OF A GOBLIN POSING AS A KID

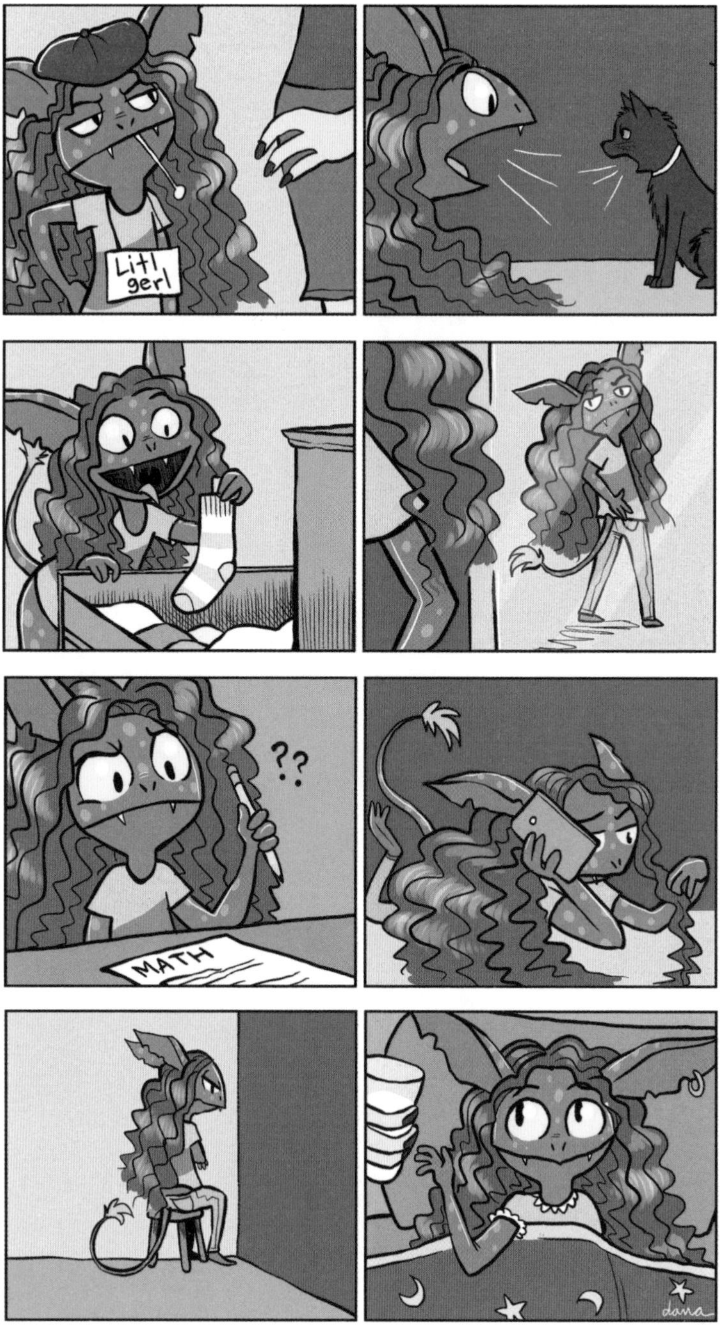
Litl gerl
??
MATH
dana

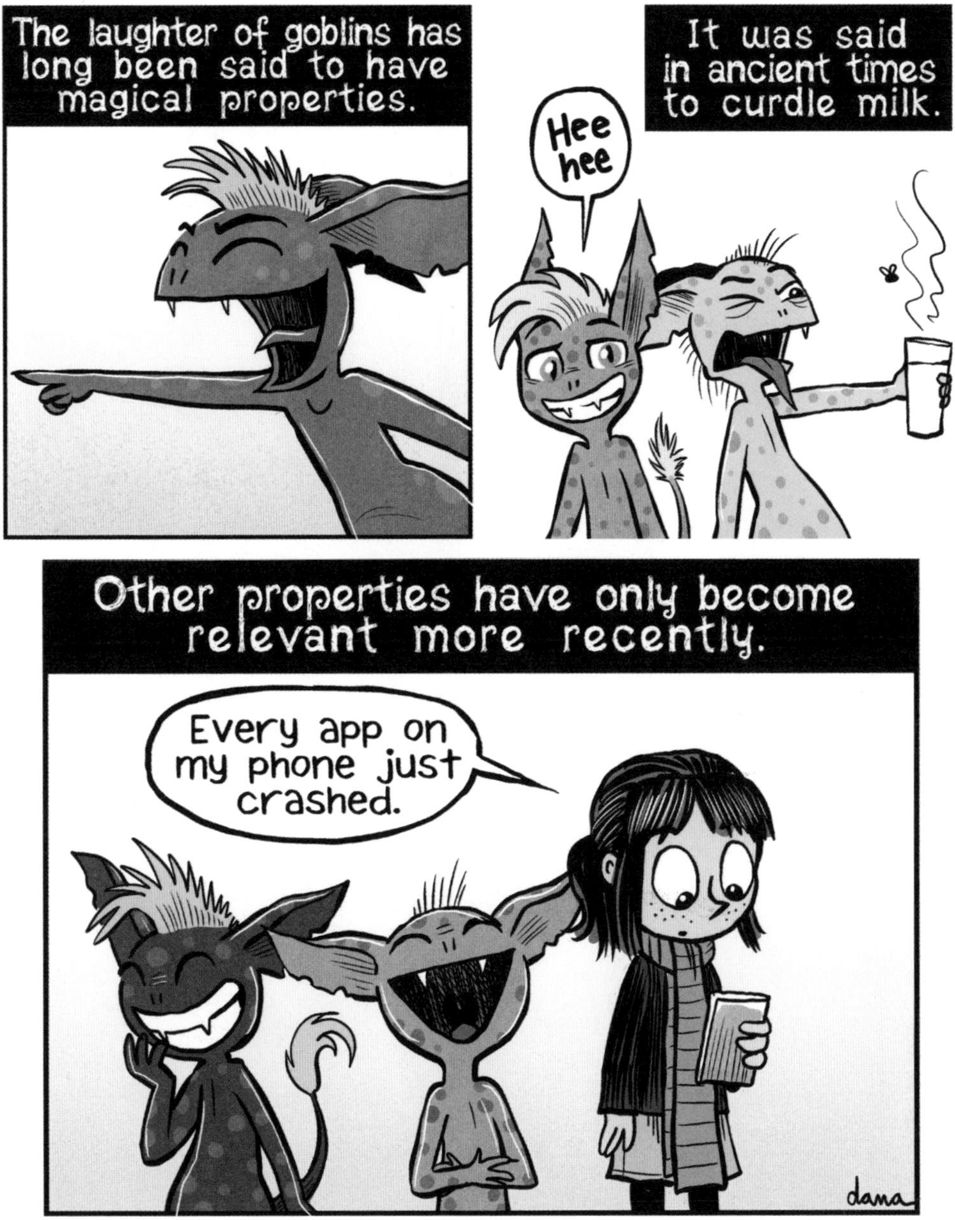
The laughter of goblins has long been said to have magical properties.
It was said in ancient times to curdle milk.
Hee hee
Other properties have only become relevant more recently.
Every app on my phone just crashed.
dana

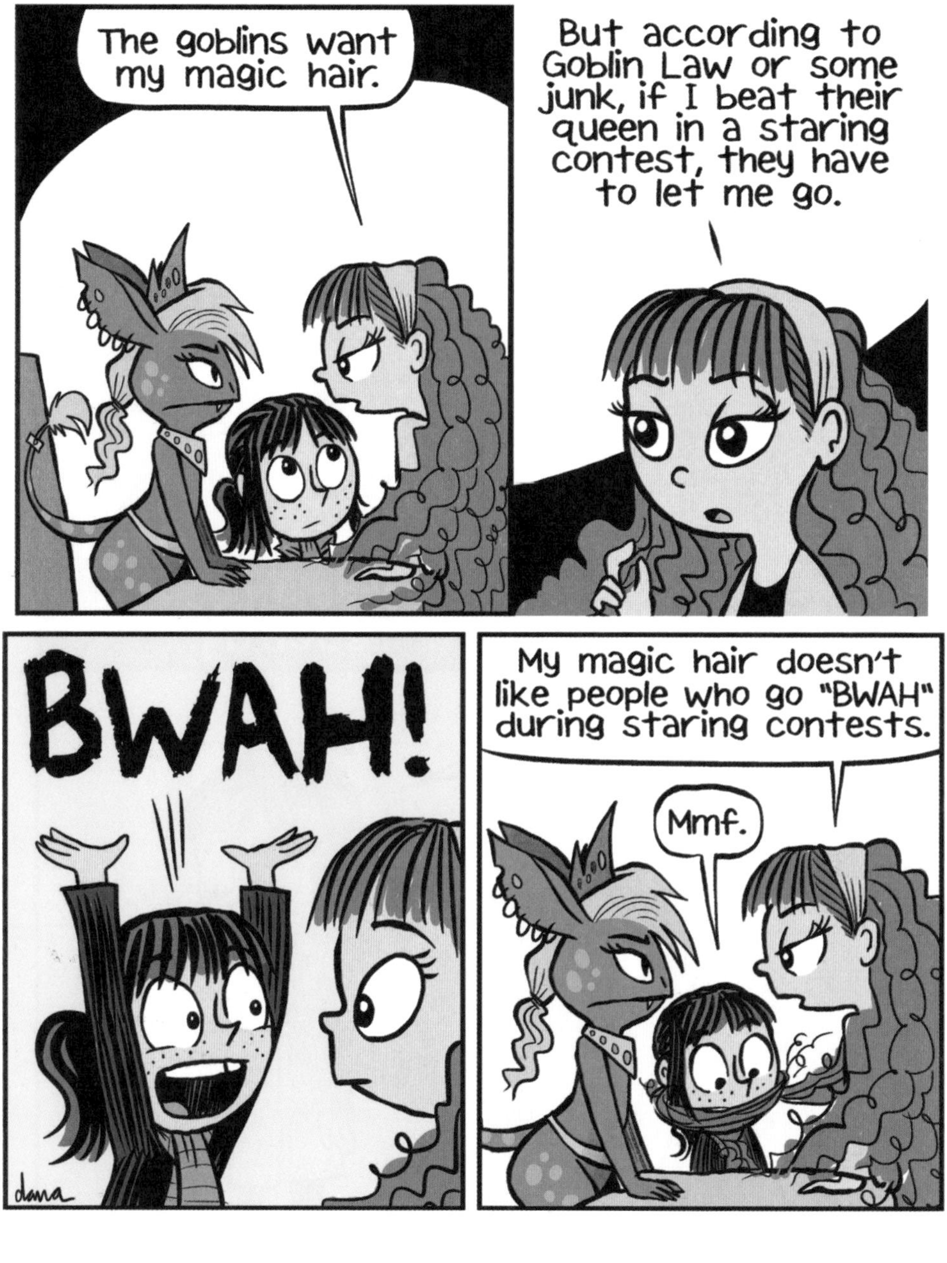
The goblins want my magic hair.
But according to Goblin Law or some junk, if I beat their queen in a staring contest, they have to let me go.
BWAH!
My magic hair doesn't like people who go "BWAH" during staring contests.
Mmf.
dana

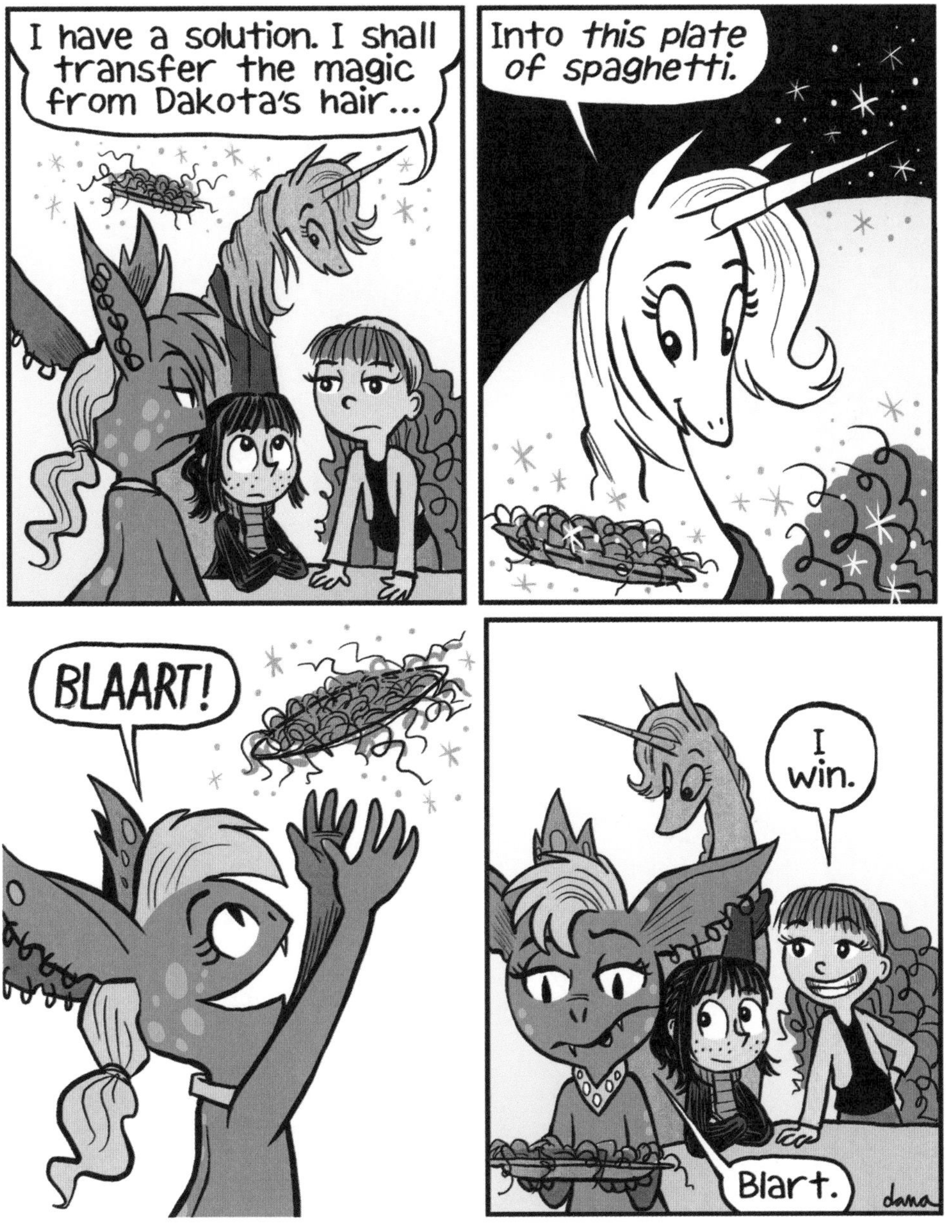
I have a solution. I shall transfer the magic from Dakota's hair...
Into this plate of spaghetti.
BLAART!
I win.
Blart.
dana

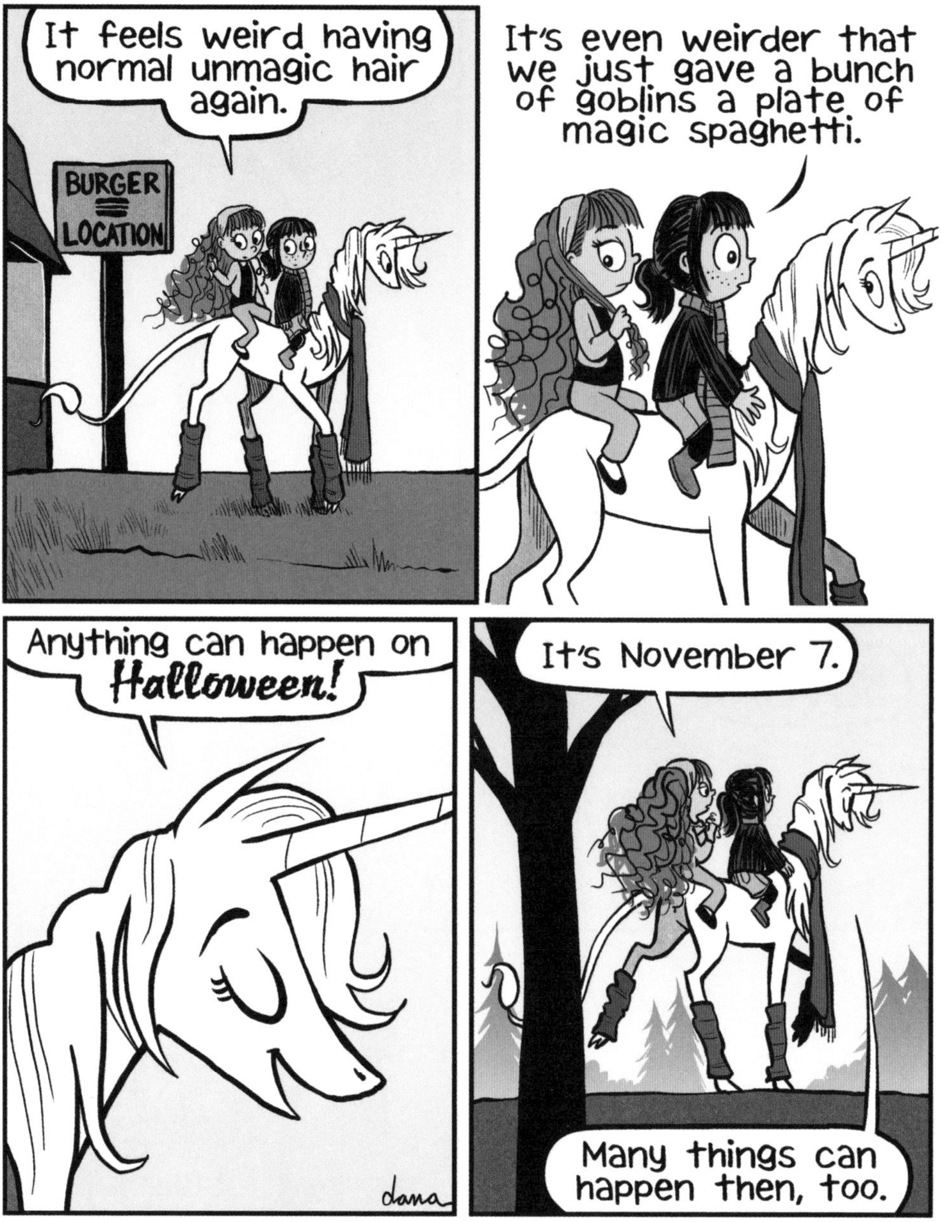
It feels weird having normal unmagic hair again.
BURGER LOCATION
It's even weirder that we just gave a bunch of goblins a plate of magic spaghetti.
Anything can happen on Halloween!
dana
It's November 7.
Many things can happen then, too.

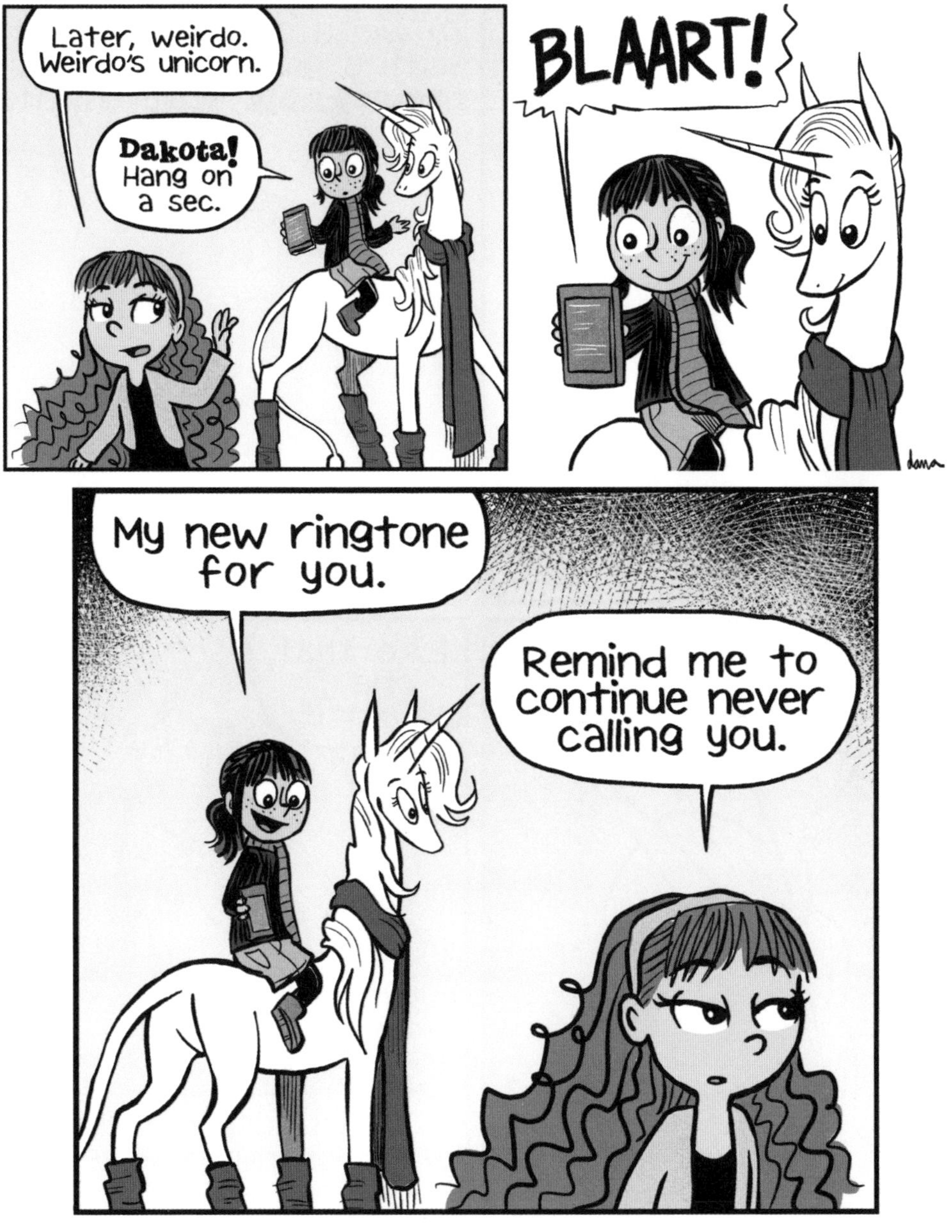
Later, weirdo. Weirdo's unicorn.
Dakota! Hang on a sec.
BLAART!
My new ringtone for you.
Remind me to continue never calling you.

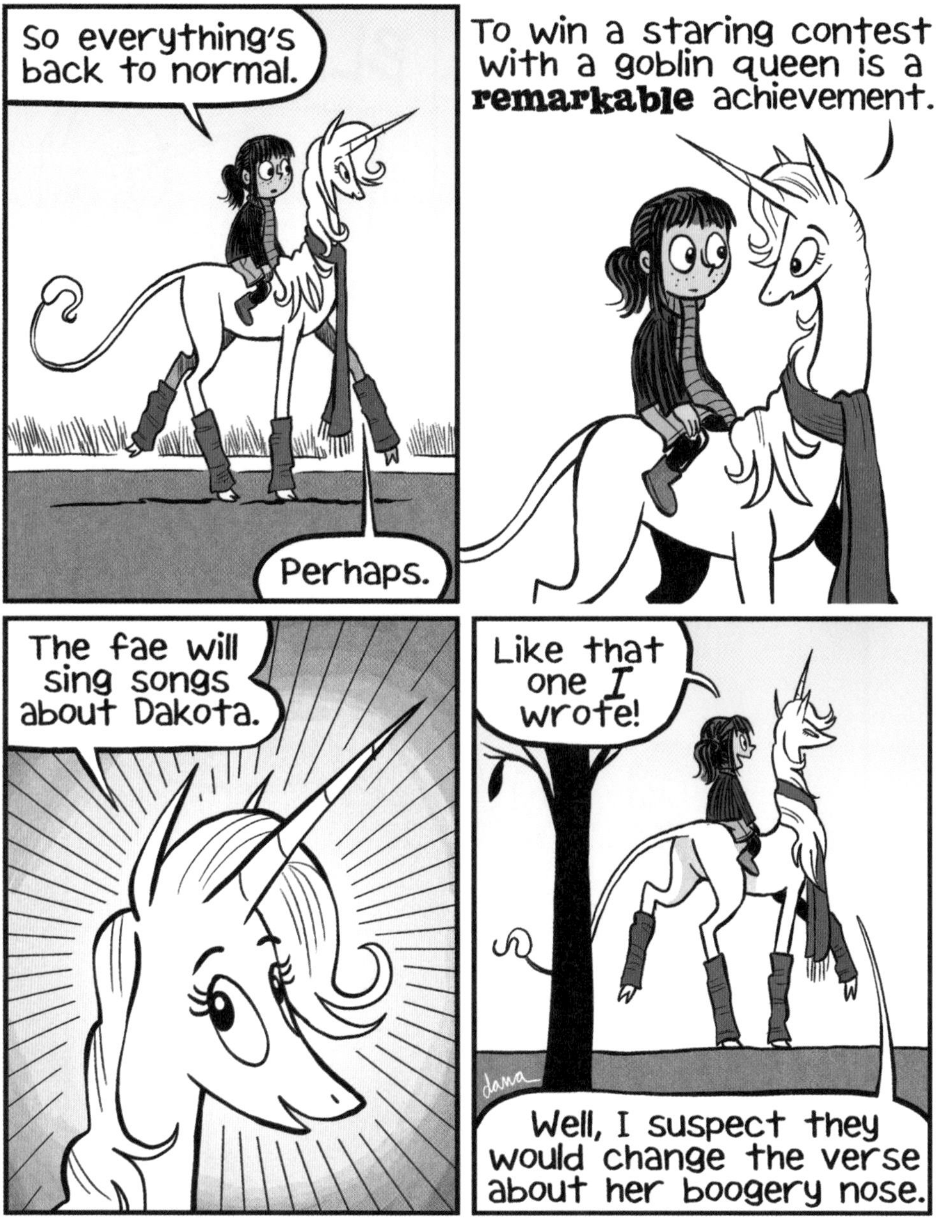
So everything's back to normal.
Perhaps.
To win a staring contest with a goblin queen is a **remarkable** achievement.
The fae will sing songs about Dakota.
Like that one *I* wrote!
Well, I suspect they would change the verse about her boogery nose.
dana

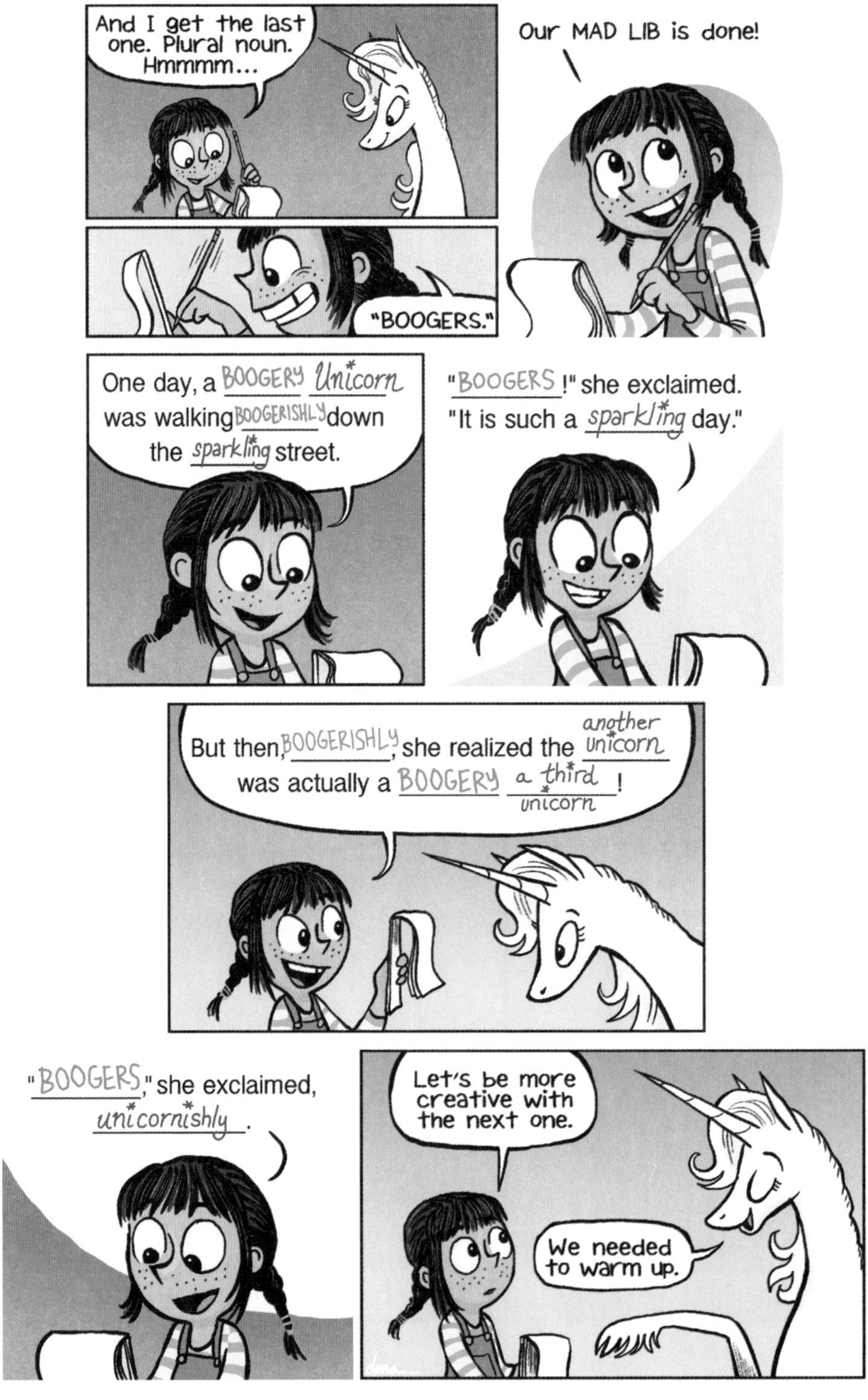
And I get the last one. Plural noun. Hmmmm...
Our MAD LIB is done!
"BOOGERS."
One day, a BOOGERY Unicorn was walking BOOGERISHLY down the sparkling street.
"BOOGERS!" she exclaimed. "It is such a sparkling day."
But then, BOOGERISHLY, she realized the another unicorn was actually a BOOGERY a third unicorn!
"BOOGERS," she exclaimed, unicornishly.
Let's be more creative with the next one.
We needed to warm up.

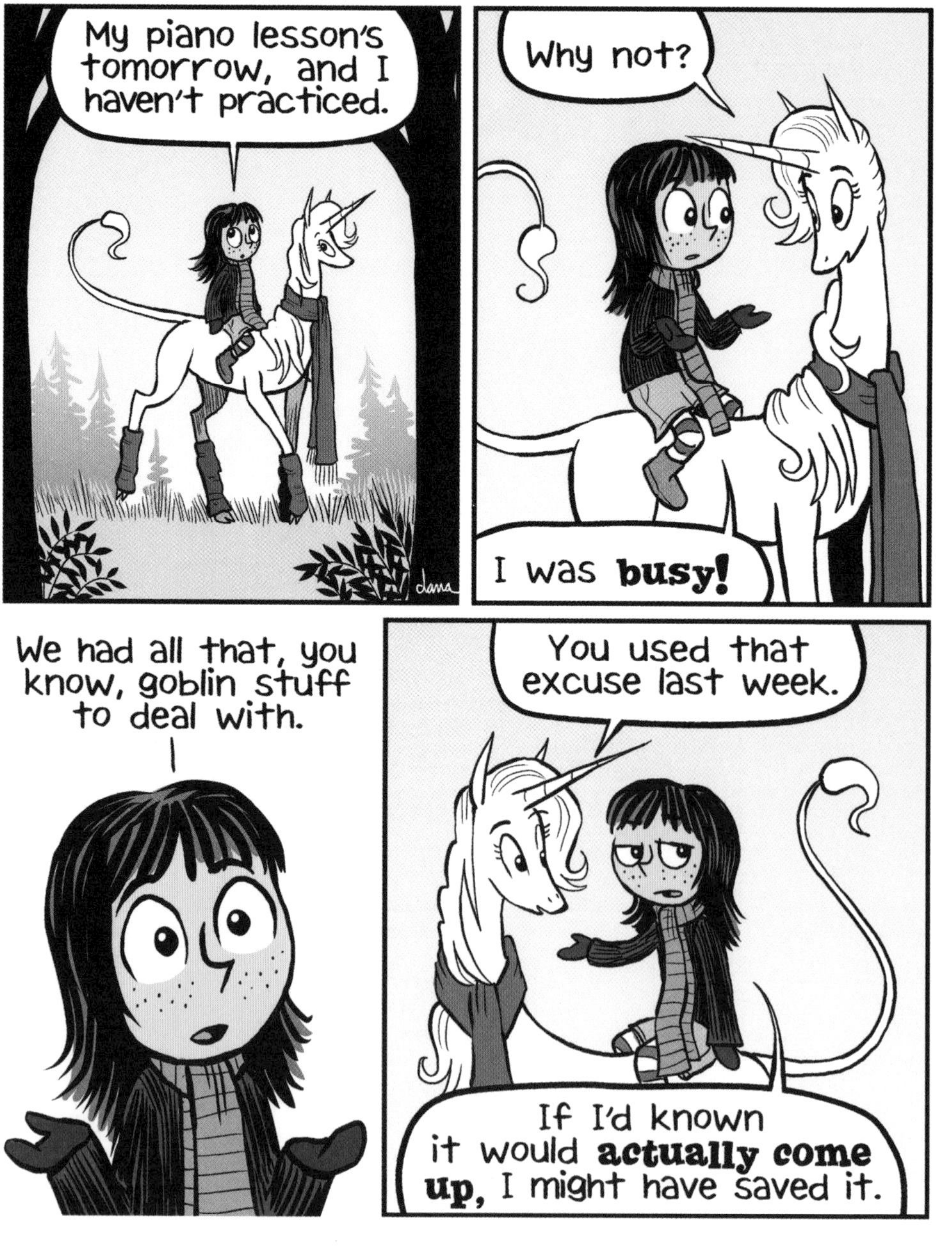
My piano lesson's tomorrow, and I haven't practiced.
dana
Why not?
I was **busy!**
We had all that, you know, goblin stuff to deal with.
You used that excuse last week.
If I'd known it would **actually come up,** I might have saved it.

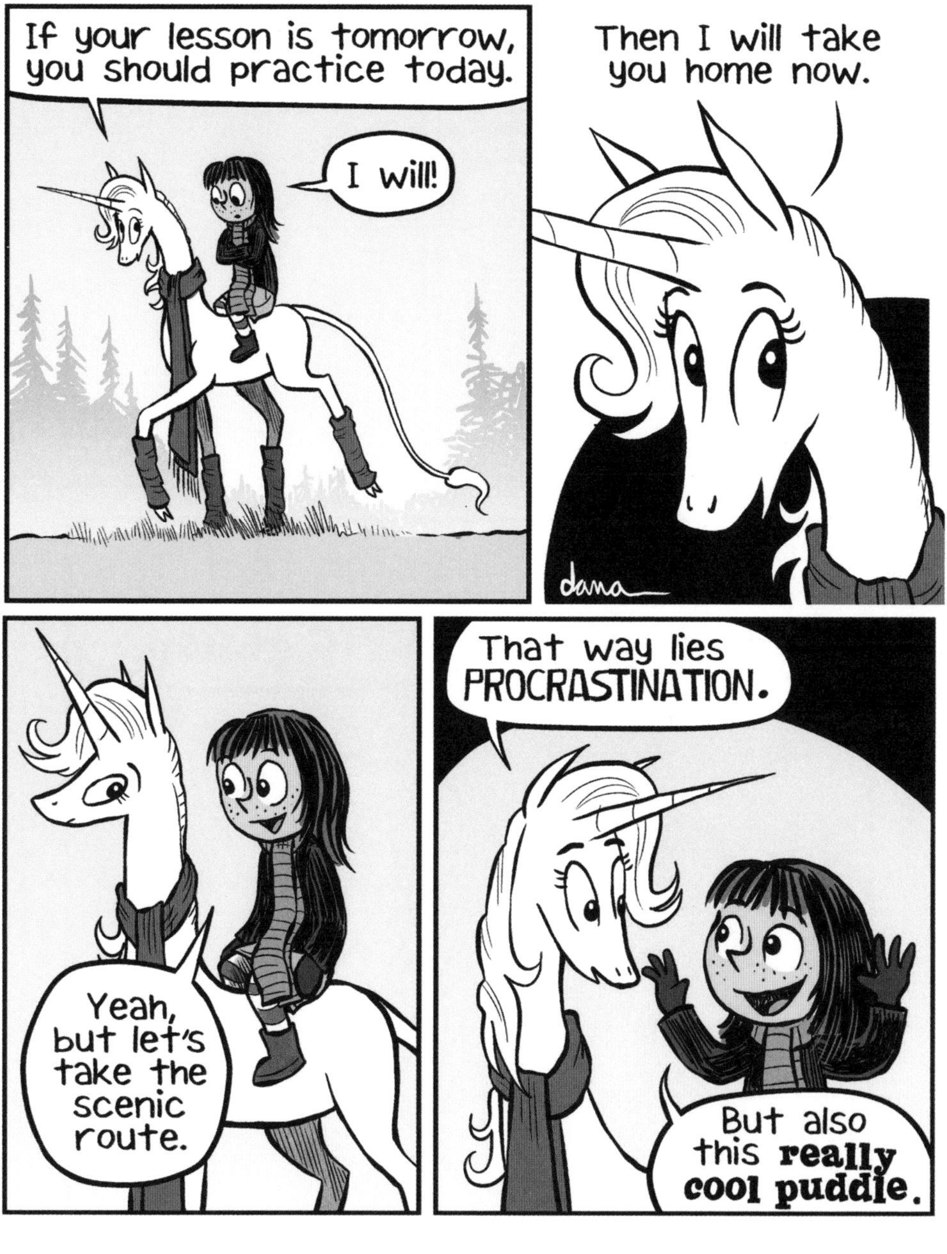
If your lesson is tomorrow, you should practice today.
I will!
Then I will take you home now.
dana
Yeah, but let's take the scenic route.
That way lies PROCRASTINATION.
But also this **really cool puddle**.

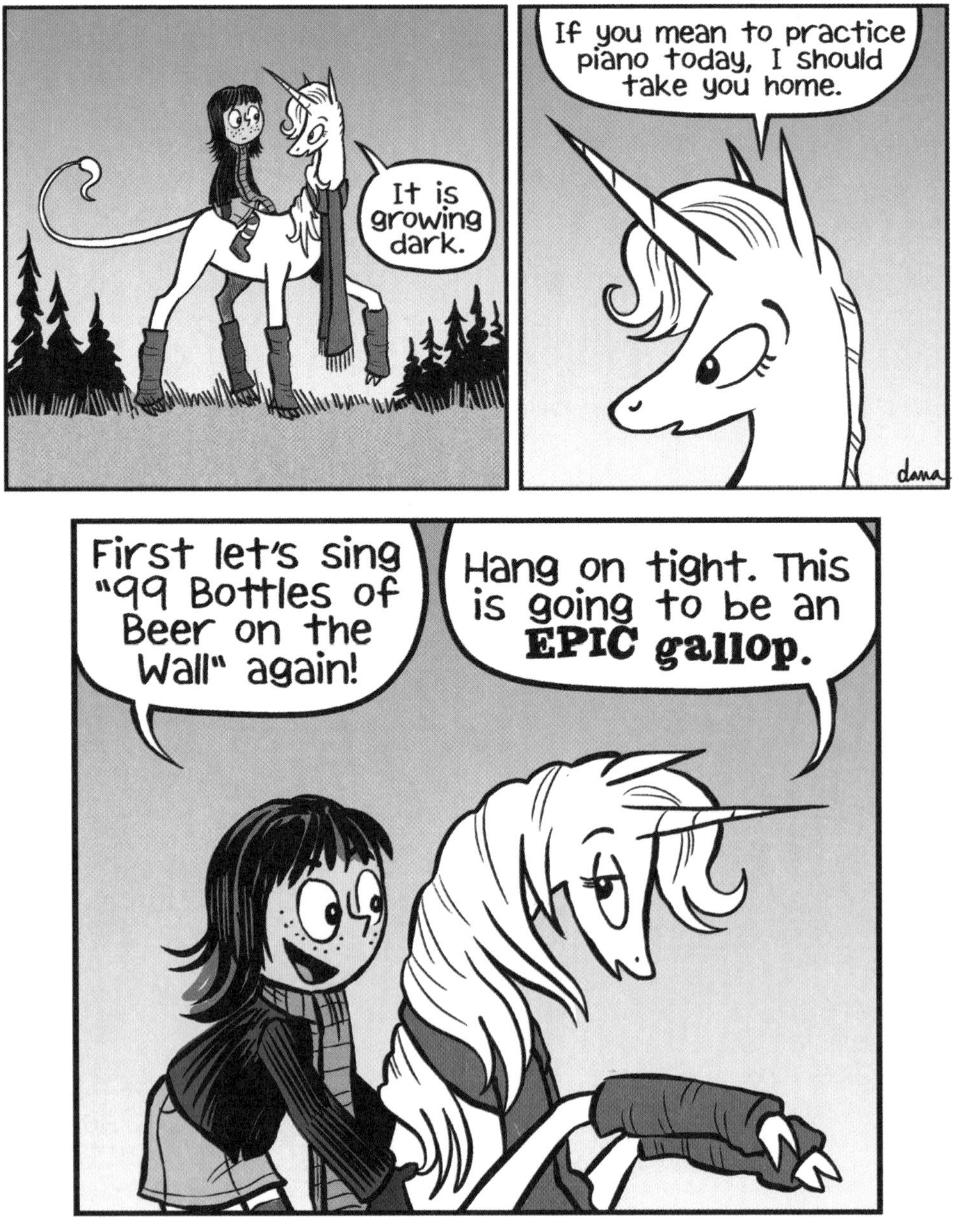
It is growing dark.
If you mean to practice piano today, I should take you home.
dana
First let's sing "99 Bottles of Beer on the Wall" again!
Hang on tight. This is going to be an **EPIC gallop.**

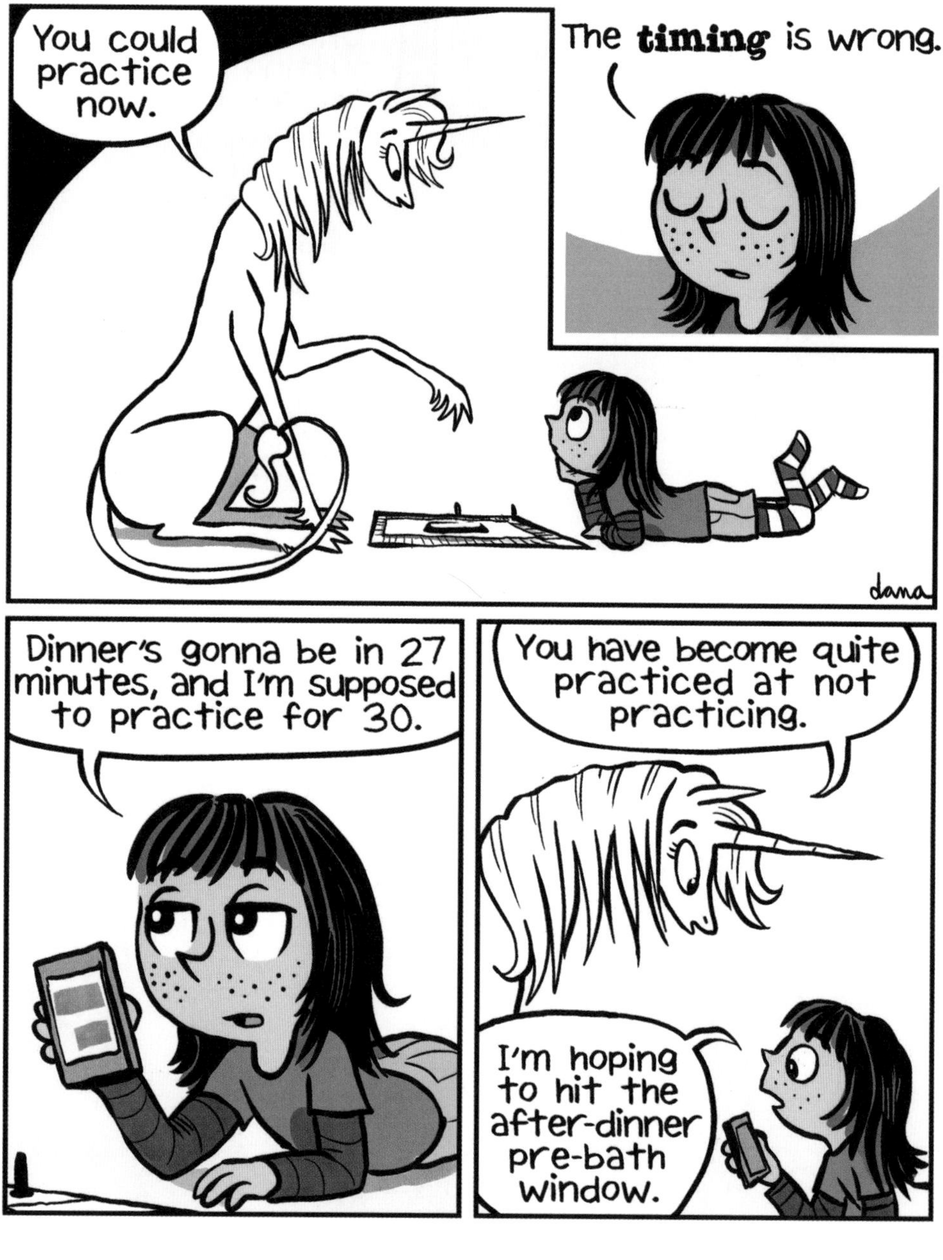
You could practice now.
The **timing** is wrong.
dana
Dinner's gonna be in 27 minutes, and I'm supposed to practice for 30.
You have become quite practiced at not practicing.
I'm hoping to hit the after-dinner pre-bath window.

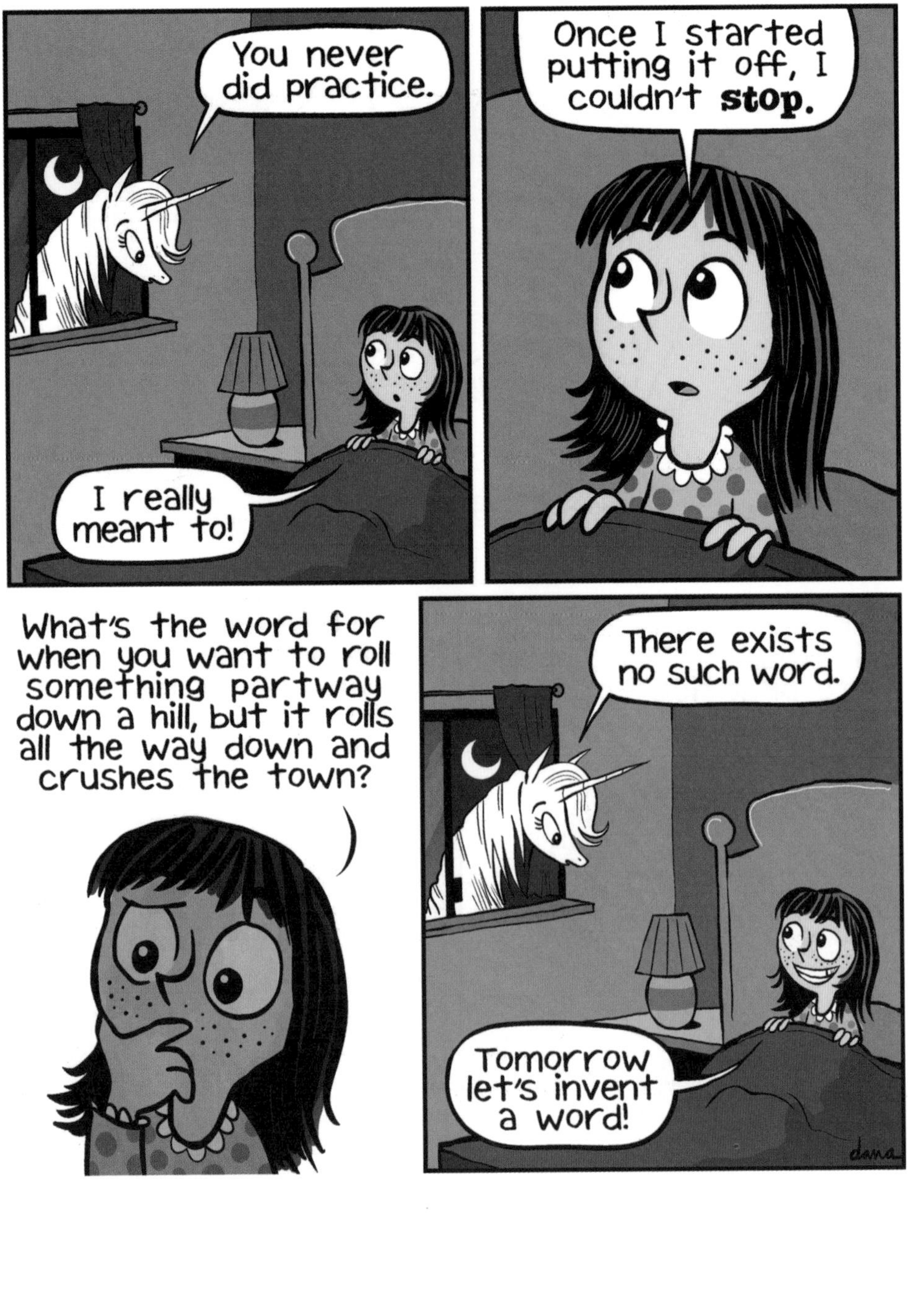
You never did practice.
I really meant to!
Once I started putting it off, I couldn't **stop.**
What's the word for when you want to roll something partway down a hill, but it rolls all the way down and crushes the town?
There exists no such word.
Tomorrow let's invent a word!
dana

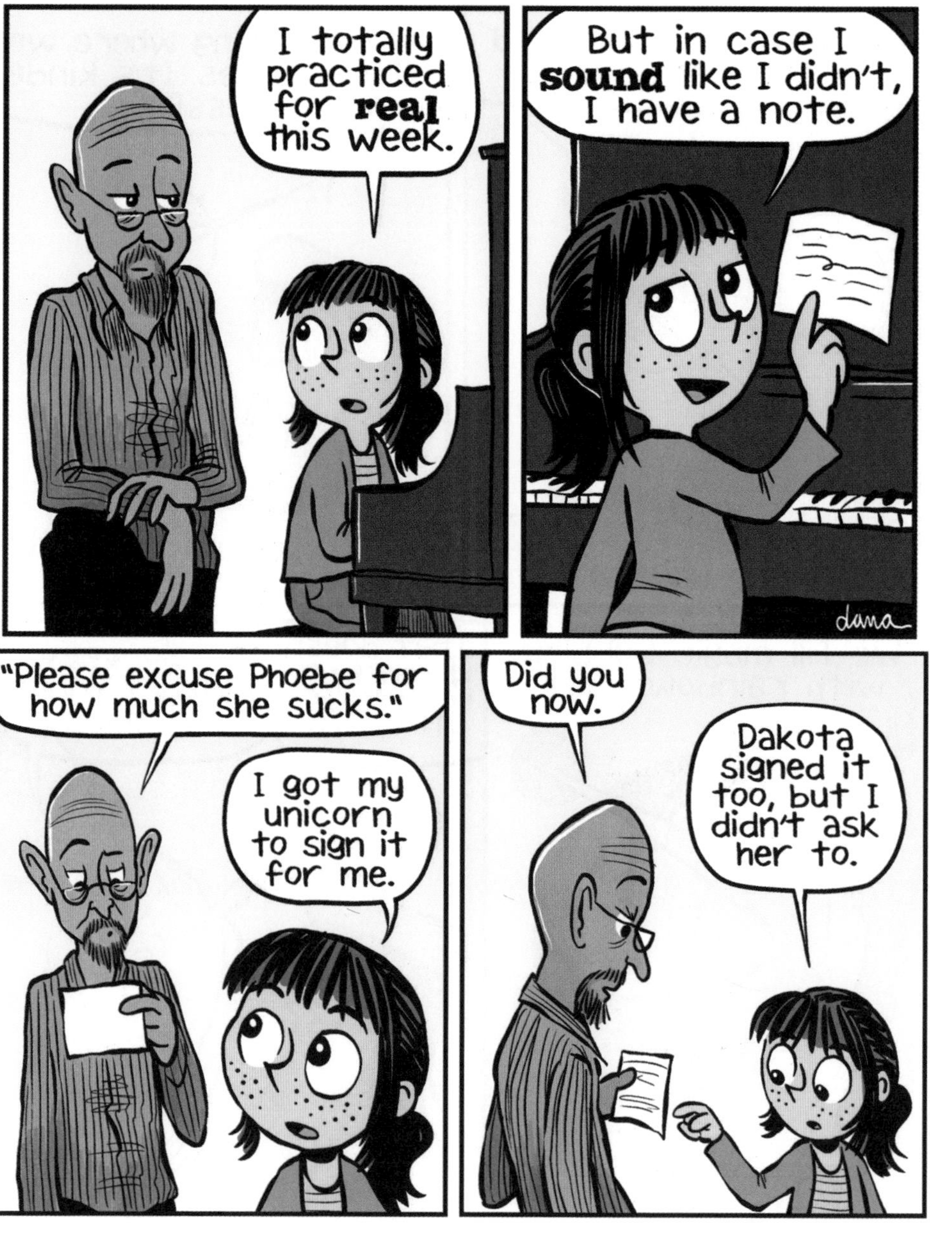
I totally practiced for **real** this week.
But in case I **sound** like I didn't, I have a note.
dana
"Please excuse Phoebe for how much she sucks."
I got my unicorn to sign it for me.
Did you now.
Dakota signed it too, but I didn't ask her to.

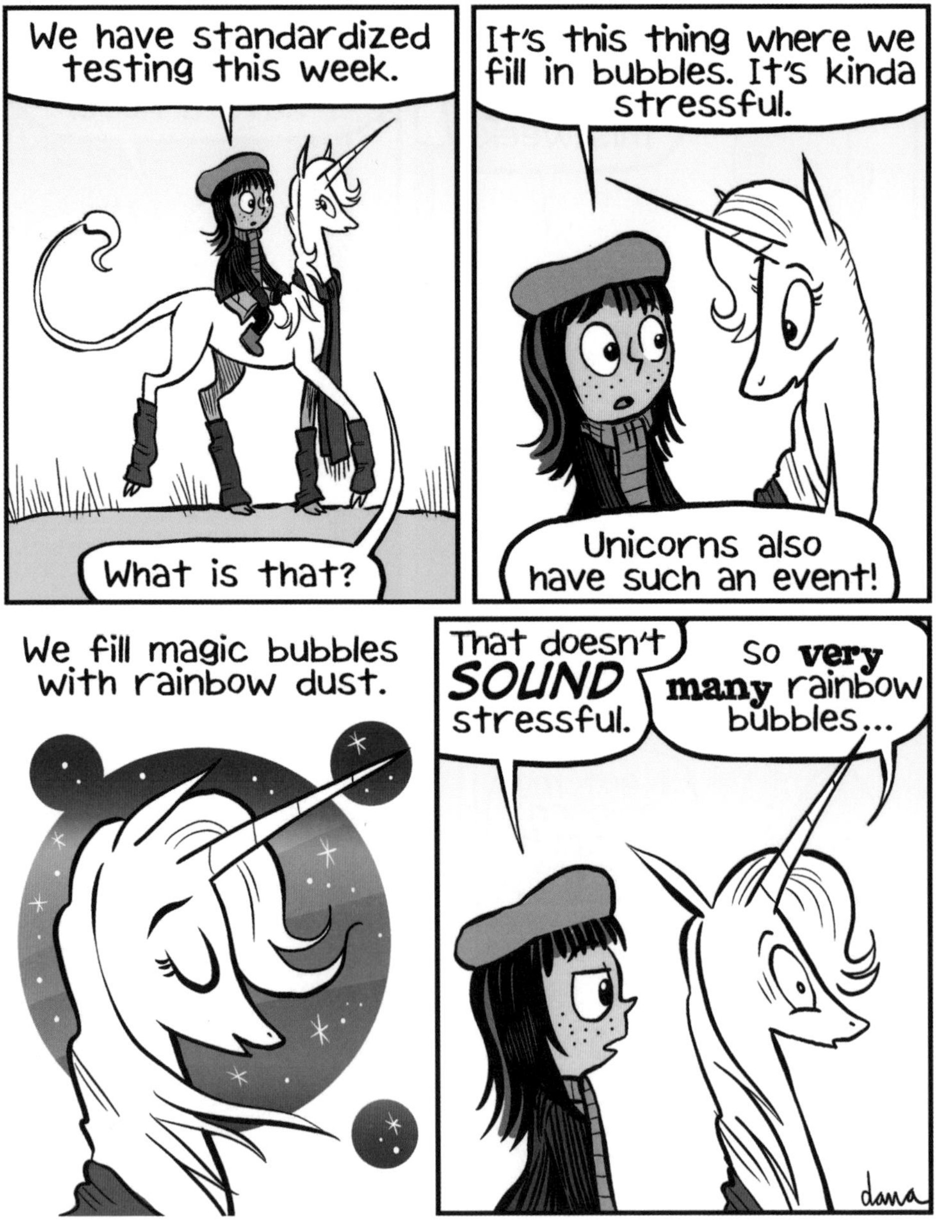
We have standardized testing this week.
What is that?
It's this thing where we fill in bubbles. It's kinda stressful.
Unicorns also have such an event!
We fill magic bubbles with rainbow dust.
That doesn't SOUND stressful.
So very many rainbow bubbles...
dana

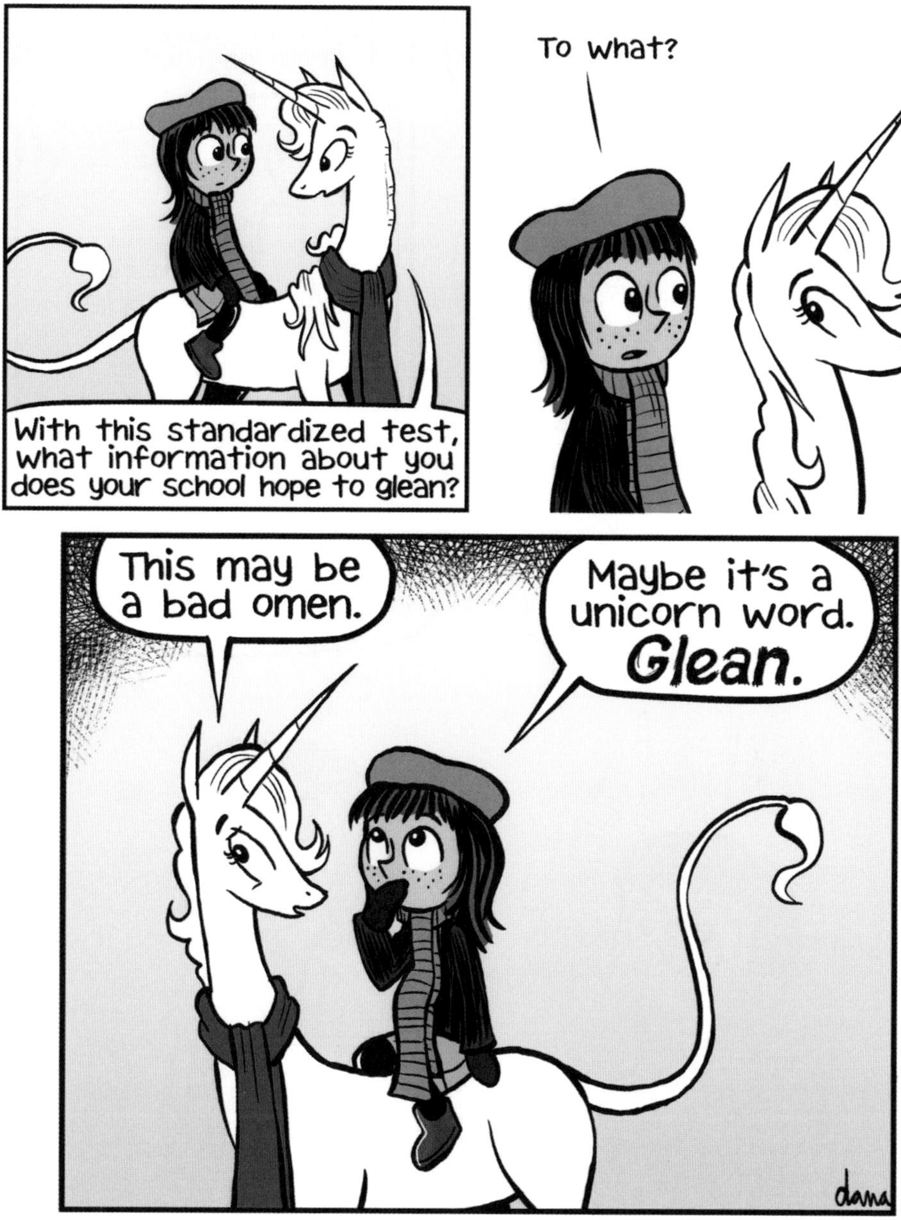
With this standardized test, what information about you does your school hope to glean?
To what?
This may be a bad omen.
Maybe it's a unicorn word. Glean.
dana

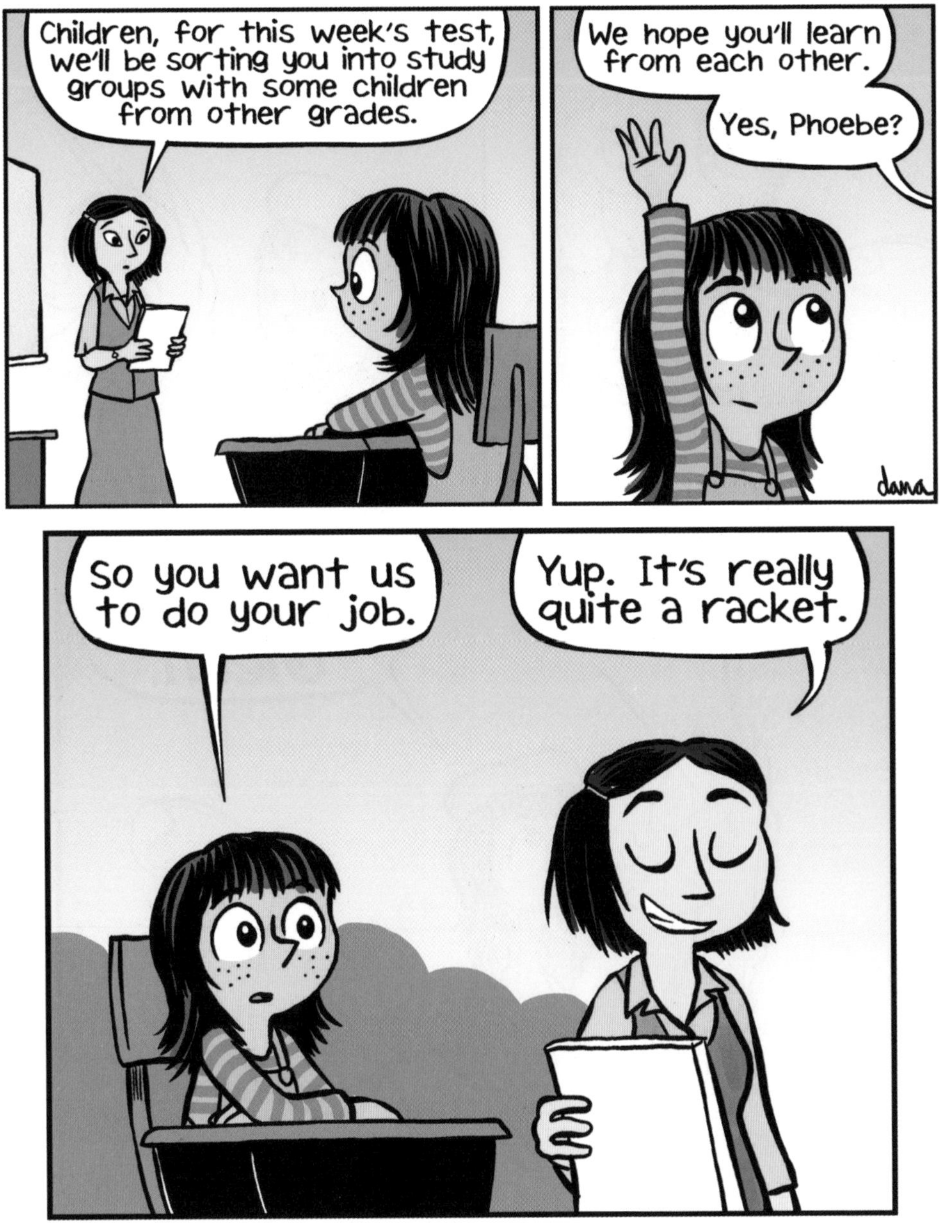
Children, for this week's test, we'll be sorting you into study groups with some children from other grades.
We hope you'll learn from each other.
Yes, Phoebe?
dana
So you want us to do your job.
Yup. It's really quite a racket.

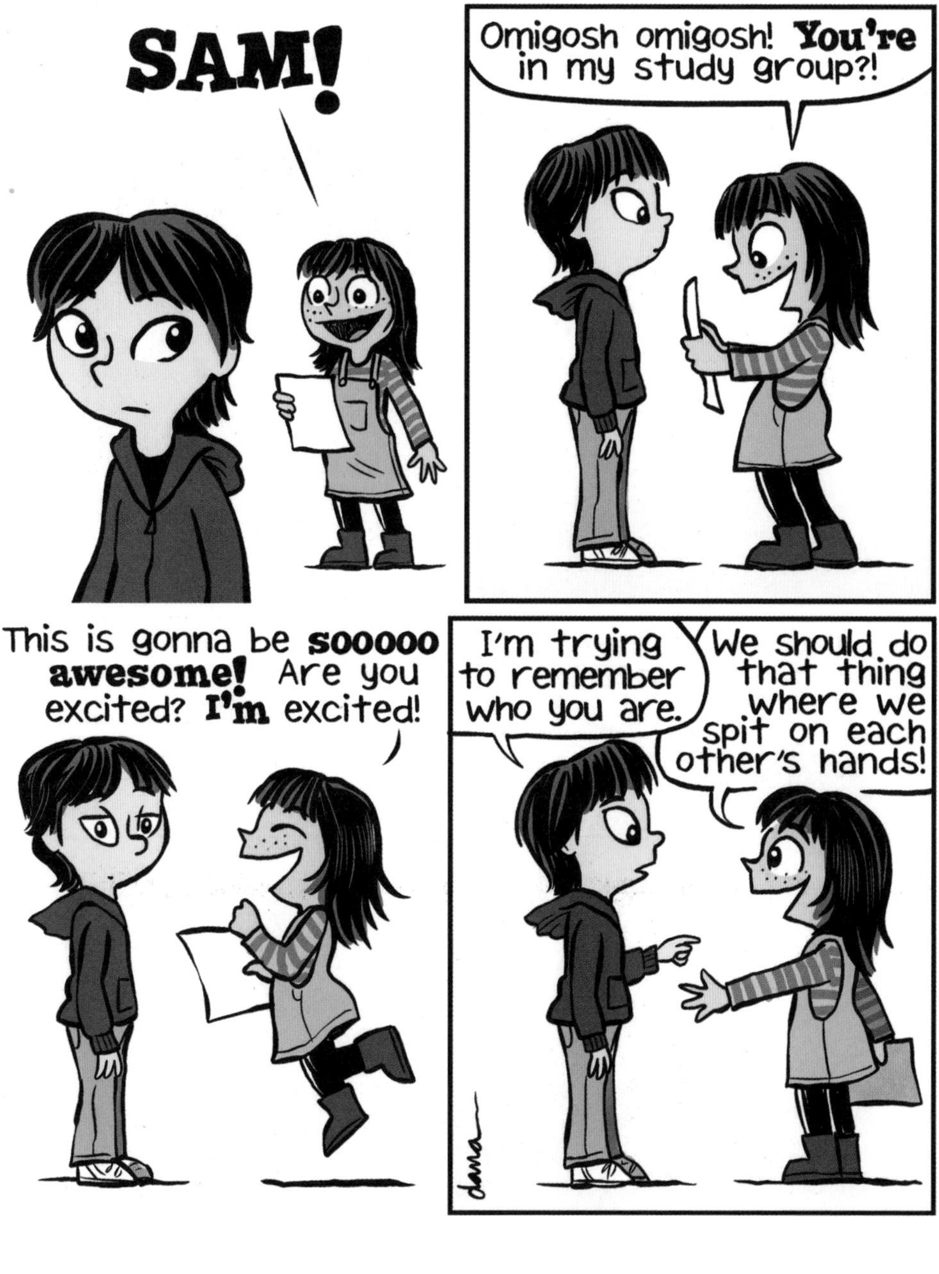
SAM!
Omigosh omigosh! **You're** in my study group?!
This is gonna be **sooooo awesome!** Are you excited? **I'm** excited!
I'm trying to remember who you are.
We should do that thing where we spit on each other's hands!
dana

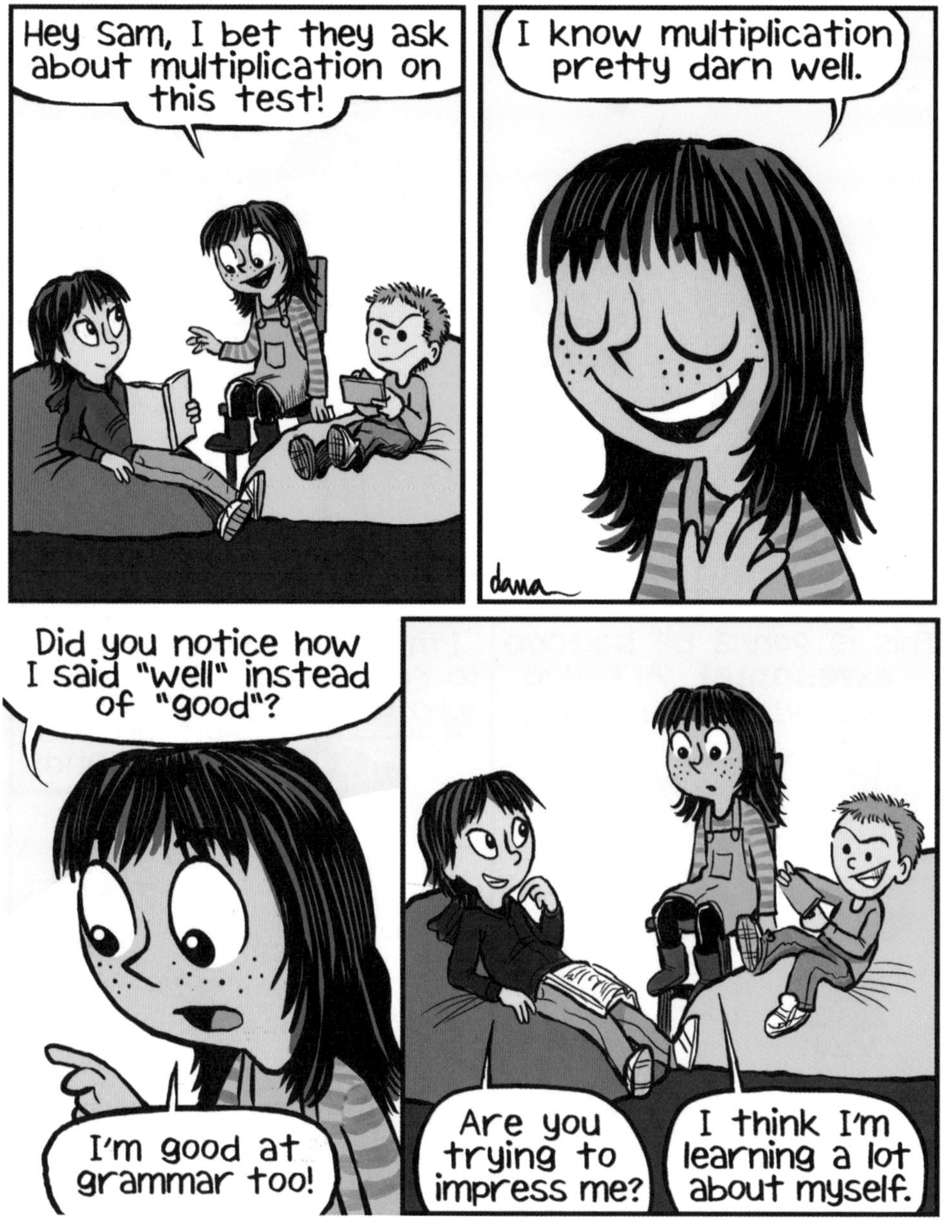
Hey Sam, I bet they ask about multiplication on this test!
I know multiplication pretty darn well.
dana
Did you notice how I said "well" instead of "good"?
I'm good at grammar too!
Are you trying to impress me?
I think I'm learning a lot about myself.

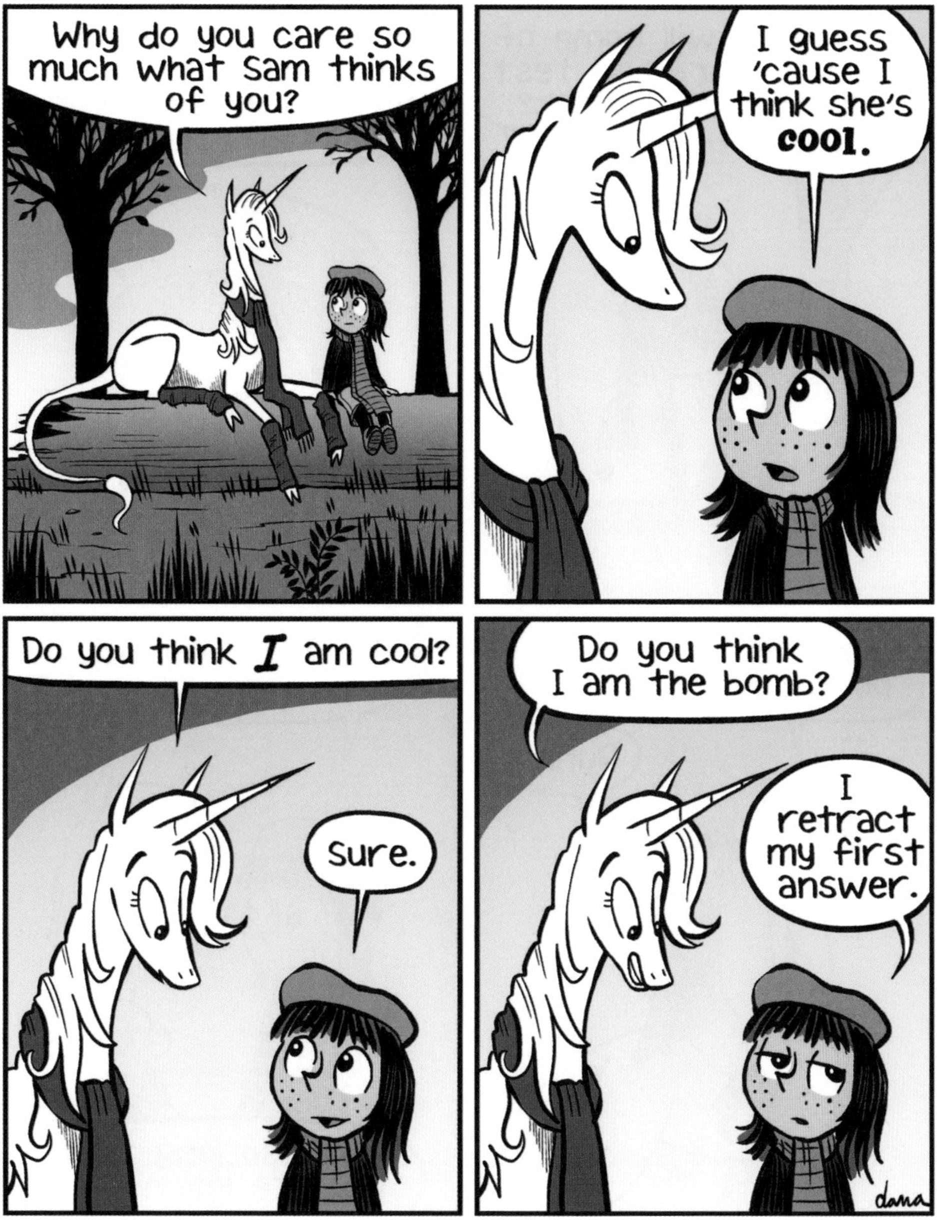
Why do you care so much what Sam thinks of you?
I guess 'cause I think she's **cool.**
Do you think *I* am cool?
Sure.
Do you think I am the bomb?
I retract my first answer.
dana

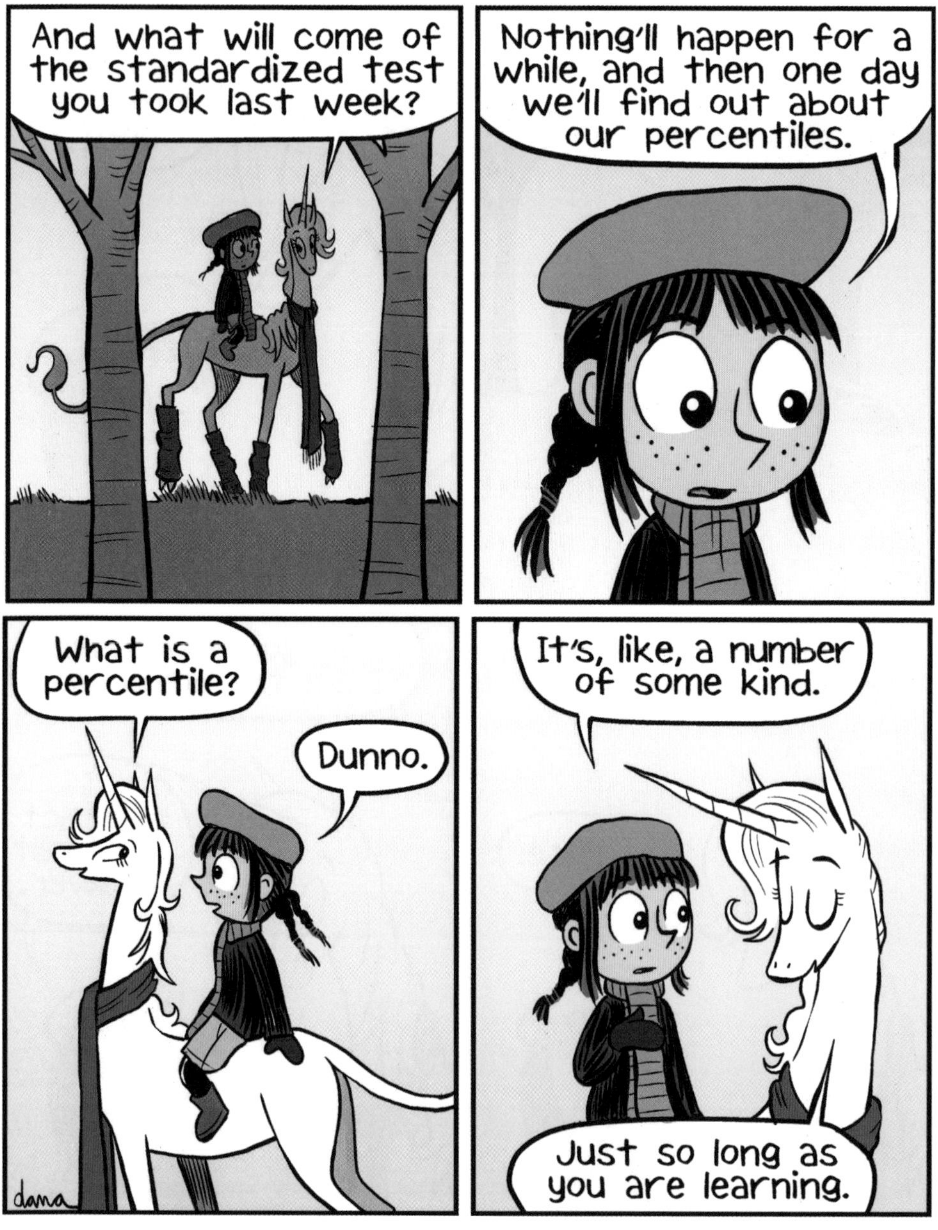
And what will come of the standardized test you took last week?
Nothing'll happen for a while, and then one day we'll find out about our percentiles.
What is a percentile?
Dunno.
It's, like, a number of some kind.
Just so long as you are learning.
dana

Let's Draw Some Supporting Characters

There are more characters than just Phoebe and Marigold! Here's a look at how I draw some of them.

Dakota and Max

Like Phoebe's, Dakota's head is based on a circle.

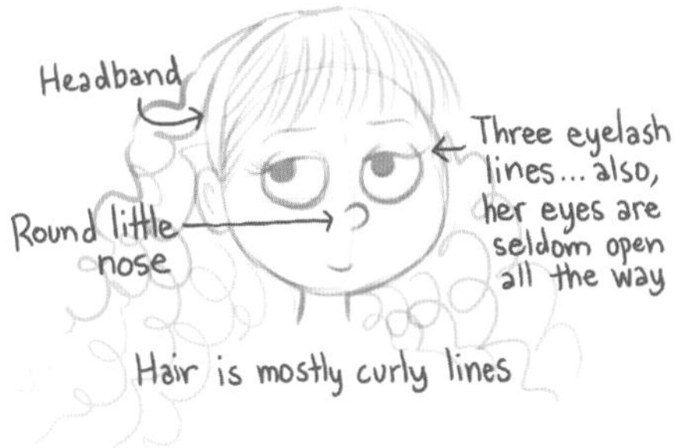
Headband
Three eyelash lines... also, her eyes are seldom open all the way
Round little nose
Hair is mostly curly lines

Max's is more of an oval.

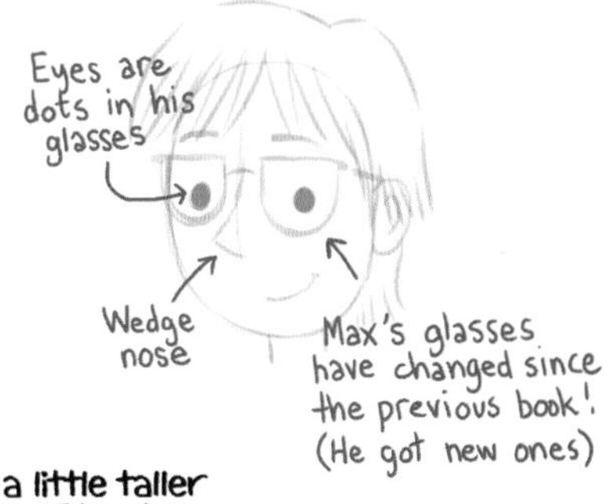
Eyes are dots in his glasses
Wedge nose
Max's glasses have changed since the previous book! (He got new ones)

Both of them are a little taller and skinnier than Phoebe.

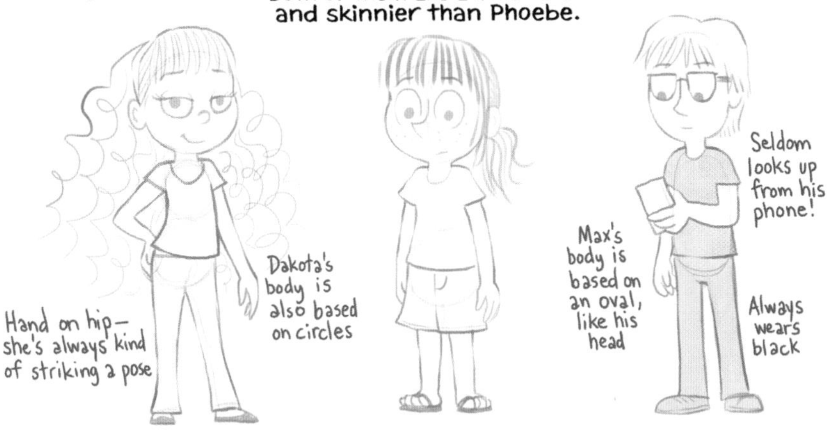
Hand on hip— she's always kind of striking a pose
Dakota's body is also based on circles
Seldom looks up from his phone!
Max's body is based on an oval, like his head
Always wears black

Todd the Candy-Breathing Dragon

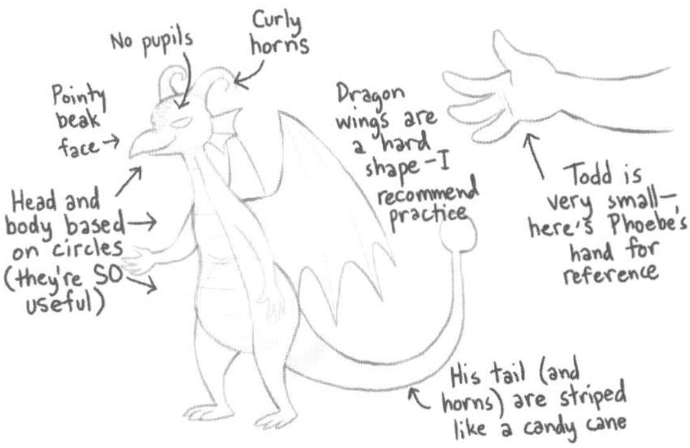
No pupils
Curly horns
Pointy beak face
Head and body based on circles (they're SO useful)
Dragon wings are a hard shape—I recommend practice
Todd is very small— here's Phoebe's hand for reference
His tail (and horns) are striped like a candy cane

Florence Unfortunate Nostrils

Florence looks a lot like her sister Marigold Heavenly Nostrils in some ways, but there are also some big differences.

Her mane (and some of her tail) are wavy lines

Always spiders, with Florence

Her glasses hook behind her ears

Her nose is less pointy than Marigold's, and her nostrils are bigger

Florence is shorter than her sister, and the difference is mostly legs

Goblins

Your typical goblin

Queen Prunella Von Bläart

mohawk

Goblin heads are possibly the roundest

ragged-edged ears

slit pupils, like a cat

nostrils, but no real nose

fangs

their bodies are sort of pear-shaped, which is really two different-sized circles

Short, kind of bent legs

floppy hair

she has a unique eye shape, (but they all have big mouths)

The queen gets to have ornamentation

Goblins come in different heights, shapes, spot patterns...they probably vary as much as humans.

Questing Mix

Marigold might be able to survive on grass when she and Phoebe go on their quest to save Dakota from the goblins, but Phoebe will need something to snack on, and you will too! This special trail mix is easy to take along or to share with friends.

INGREDIENTS:

½ cup peanuts or other nuts

½ cup mini pretzels or 1-inch pieces small pretzels

½ cup semisweet chocolate chips

½ cup dried cranberries or cherries

¼ cup Goldfish crackers

¼ cup raisins

¼ cup sunflower seeds

INSTRUCTIONS:

In a large bowl, combine all the ingredients and toss to mix well.

The trail mix will keep in an airtight container at room temperature for at least 2 weeks.

Makes about 8 servings, about 3 cups.

Alice and the Unicorn

Not surprisingly, the unicorn makes an appearance in the works of Lewis Carroll, creator of the most delightful whimsy of the Victorian age. In *Through the Looking Glass and What Alice Found There*, Alice encounters a unicorn in a passage that captures the essential paradox of the legendary beast:

> ". . . He was going on, when his eye happened to fall upon Alice: he turned round instantly, and stood for some time looking at her with an air of the deepest disgust.
>
> 'What—is—this?' he said at last.
>
> 'This is a child!' Haigha replied eagerly . . . 'We only found it today. It's as large as life, and twice as natural!'
>
> 'I always thought they were fabulous monsters!' said the Unicorn. 'Is it alive?'
>
> 'It can talk,' said Haigha solemnly.
>
> The Unicorn looked dreamily to Alice, and said, 'Talk, child.'
>
> Alice could not help her lips curling into a smile as she began: 'Do you know, I always thought Unicorns were fabulous monsters, too? I never saw one alive before!'
>
> 'Well, now we *have* seen each other,' said the Unicorn, 'if you'll believe in me, I'll believe in you. Is that a bargain?'"

Andrews McMeel Publishing
a division of Andrews McMeel Universal
1130 Walnut Street, Kansas City, Missouri 64106

www.andrewsmcmeel.com

20 21 22 23 24 SDB 13 12 11 10 9

ISBN: 978-1-4494-7628-1

Library of Congress Control Number: 2015954011

Made by:
King Yip (Dongguan) Printing & Packaging Factory Ltd.
Address and location of manufacturer:
Daning Administrative District, Humen Town
Dongguan Guangdong, China 523930
9th Printing—3/30/20

ATTENTION: SCHOOLS AND BUSINESSES

Andrews McMeel books are available at quantity discounts with bulk purchase for educational, business, or sales promotional use. For information, please e-mail the Andrews McMeel Publishing Special Sales Department: specialsales@amuniversal.com.

Look for these books!

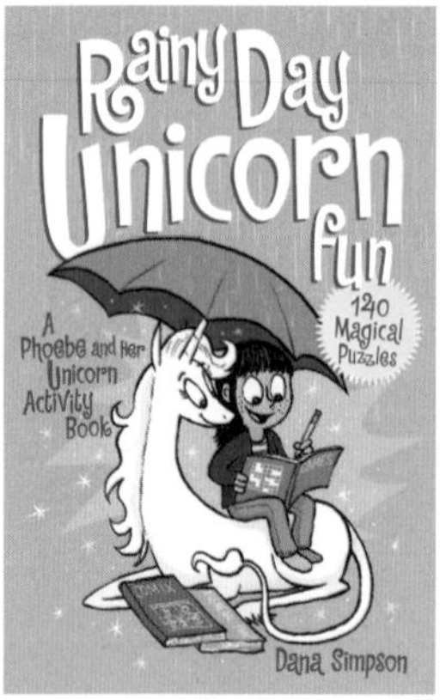
Rainy Day Unicorn Fun
140 Magical Puzzles
A Phoebe and Her Unicorn Activity Book
Dana Simpson

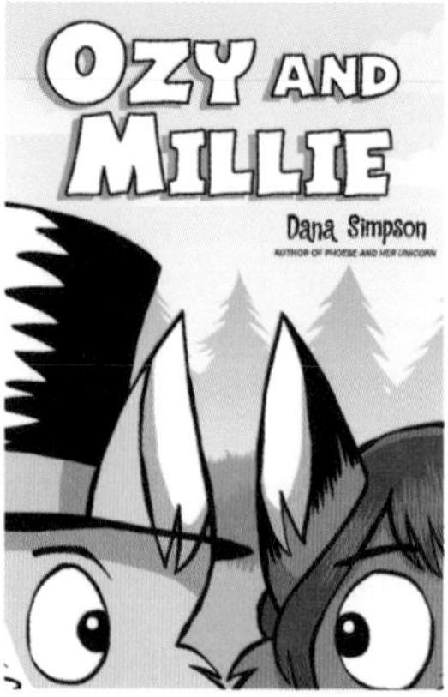
OZY AND MILLIE
Dana Simpson

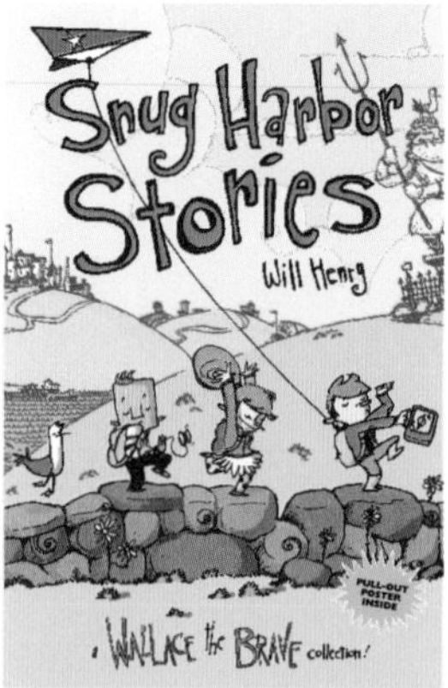
Snug Harbor Stories
Will Henry
PULL-OUT POSTER INSIDE
WALLACE the BRAVE collection!

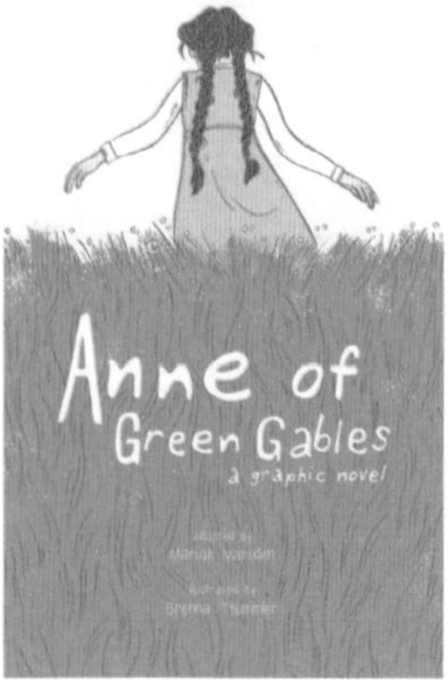
Anne of Green Gables
a graphic novel

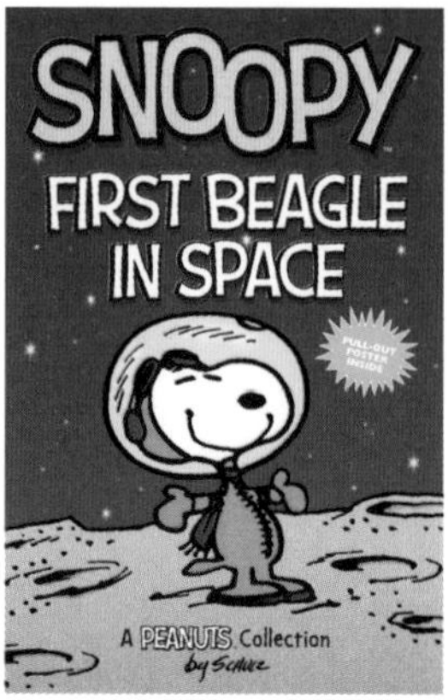
SNOOPY
FIRST BEAGLE IN SPACE
PULL-OUT POSTER INSIDE
A PEANUTS Collection
by Schulz

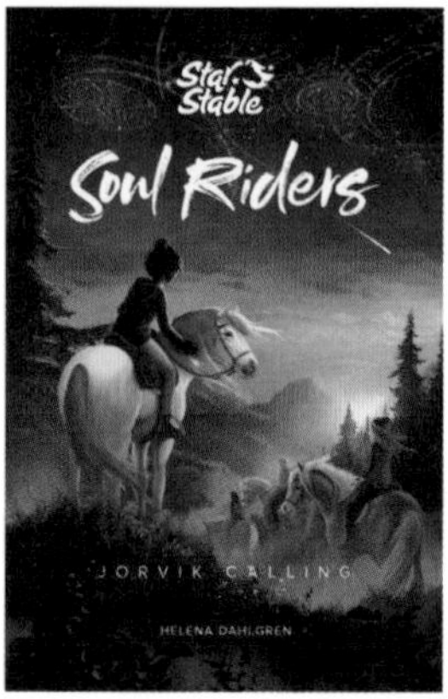
Star Stable
Soul Riders
JORVIK CALLING
HELENA DAHLGREN

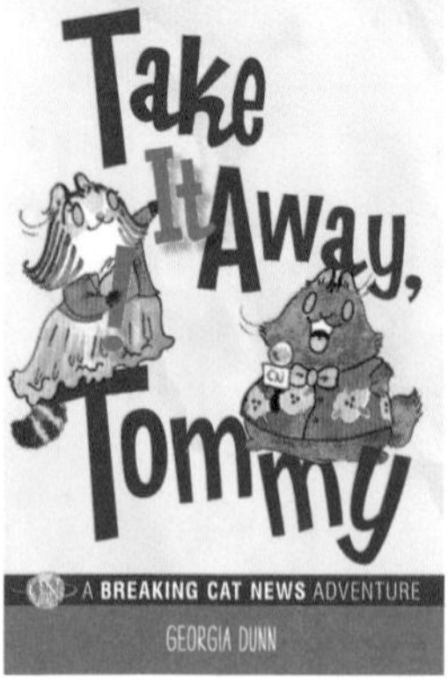
Take It Away, Tommy
A BREAKING CAT NEWS ADVENTURE
GEORGIA DUNN

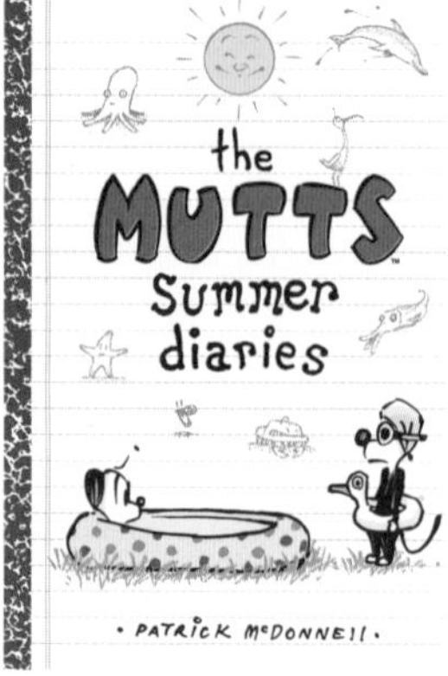
the MUTTS Summer diaries
PATRICK McDONNELL

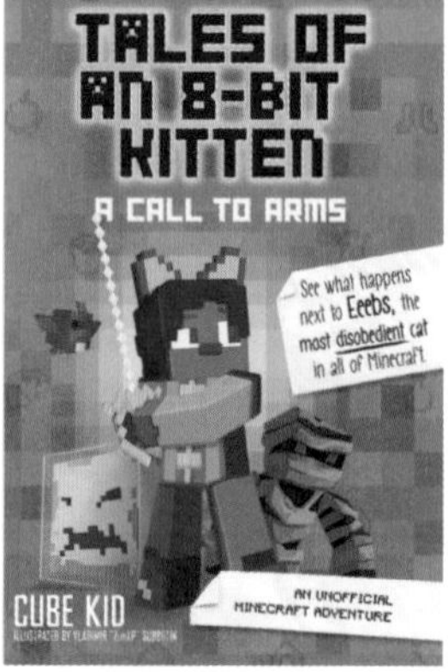
TALES OF AN 8-BIT KITTEN
A CALL TO ARMS
See what happens next to Eeebs, the most disobedient cat in all of Minecraft
CUBE KID
AN UNOFFICIAL MINECRAFT ADVENTURE